The DIRTY STREETS *of* HEAVEN

The finest in imaginative fiction
by Tad Williams

BOBBY DOLLAR
The Dirty Streets Of Heaven
Happy Hour In Hell (coming 2013)
Sleeping Late On Judgment Day (coming 2014)

SHADOWMARCH
Shadowmarch
Shadowplay
Shadowrise
Shadowheart

MEMORY, SORROW AND THORN
The Dragonbone Chair
Stone Of Farewell
To Green Angel Tower

OTHERLAND
City Of Golden Shadow
River Of Blue Fire
Mountain Of Black Glass
Sea Of Silver Light

Tailchaser's Song
The War Of The Flowers

TAD WILLIAMS

The DIRTY STREETS *of* HEAVEN

First published in Great Britain in 2012 by Hodder & Stoughton
An Hachette UK company

1

A CIP catalogue record for this title is available from the British Library.

Hardback ISBN 978 1 444 73855 1
Trade Paperback ISBN 978 1 444 73856 8

Printed and bound by Clays Ltd, St Ives plc

Hodder & Stoughton policy is to use papers that are natural, renewable and recyclable products and made from wood grown in sustainable forests. The logging and manufacturing processes are expected to conform to the environmental regulations of the country of origin.

Hodder & Stoughton Ltd
338 Euston Road
London NW1 3BH

www.hodder.co.uk

This book is dedicated to my dear friend David Charles Michael Pierce.

Dave loved stuff like this and I think he would have liked this book, too.
I hope someday we'll see each other again, and he can let me know
what I got right and what I got wrong.

Thanks for being my buddy, Dave. I miss you. We all miss you.

ACKNOWLEDGMENTS

As usual, there are far too many people whose work contributed to the writing of this book than I can ever properly thank, but these are at the top of the list:

Much gratitude to my magical wife, Deborah Beale, and my first choice for backup in a firefight, my dangerous pal Josh Stallings, for reading the rough manuscript and offering sensible advice.

Huge thanks as always to our assistant Dena Chavez and her husband Scott Chavez, who helped hold reality together for us during a crazy year while I wrote it. Couldn't have done it without you guys.

My agent, Matt Bialer, was and always is a huge source of calm in a world of stress and strange contractual language. Bless you, Matt.

Lisa Tveit makes sense of my online life, including our website at tadwilliams.com, and I can't thank her enough for that.

And of course my publishers, all of them, but especially the good people at DAW Books and my editors Betsy Wollheim and Sheila Gilbert, who keep reminding me that books should make sense.

prologue

inhuman resources

I WAS JUST stepping out of the elevator on the 43rd floor of the Five Page Mill building when the alarms began going off—those nightmarish, clear-the-building kind like the screams of tortured robots—and I realized I'd pretty well lost any chance at the subtle approach.

Did I mention that when I'm under stress I tend to revert to old habits? And being chased by monsters (as well as being made the fall guy for the biggest fuck-up between Heaven and Hell in the last few thousand years) *will* produce some stress. So that was me right then—jumpy and in need of answers. And when I'm feeling that way I tend to push on things until something happens.

I didn't calm down any when a husky security guard lurched out of the stairwell a few yards away, eyes adrenaline-wide, shoving his service pistol in my face. He shouted, "Get on the floor!" but instead of keeping the gun trained on me he started waving it to show me where to go, and I knew that I had him.

"Hold on, don't . . . don't you want to see my employee badge or something?" I was doing my best to sound like a confused and innocent corporate drone. "P-p-please don't shoot me!"

"I want you down on the floor! There!" Again he jabbed the gun toward the discreetly expensive carpeting. The alarms were making it hard to hear so I went with that, screwing up my face in fear and confusion.

"What? I didn't understand you! Don't shoot . . . !"

"God damn it, get down!" He grabbed my arm with his free hand. I leaned away to get him off balance, then yanked his wrist so that he staggered toward me, waving his gun hand in a desperate attempt to keep his balance. It didn't matter much because I hit him square in the face with my forearm, jolting his head back and dropping him like a sack of laundry. Broke his nose, too, I'm pretty sure.

I didn't know whether Vald's security guards were normal people on a normal payroll or soldiers of the Opposition, and I didn't have time to search this guy for extra nipples or whatever. (To be honest, except for a few retro covens, extra nipples have pretty much fallen out of fashion as a sign of allegiance to Hell.) So I left him alive but unconscious on the floor and tossed his gun and walkie-talkie into a trash bin in case he woke up sooner than I expected.

Everything had gone ass-up now and I knew I would be better off just leaving before anyone got killed, but I do have that problem I mentioned—when I get agitated I just kind of put my head down and keep shoving. Like a rhino with an itch, as my old boss delicately put it. Anyway, I decided I might as well see where this whole thing was going to lead.

I knew I had about seven or eight minutes maximum before the building was completely overrun by people with guns who would be happy to use them on me, so I hurried up the stairs to the 44th floor where I paused for a second or two to admire the view of Stanford University's creepy Gothic towers through the picture window at the end of the hall. The master office suite clearly took up the entire floor, so I walked through the only door and found myself standing in front of the calmest woman I have ever pointed a gun at. She was good-looking, too—slender, with Eurasian features, short, dark hair, and extremely cold eyes. I was pretty certain she'd already pushed the silent alarm.

"Who are you?" she asked in the tone of a bored DMV clerk. She didn't even look down at the barrel of the .38, although it was only inches from her nose. "And what do you want?"

"I'm here to see your boss," I explained. "Shall I just go in?"

To her credit she didn't bother to argue with me or even threaten me, just came over the desk hissing and clawing like a methedrined ocelot, doing her best to tear off my face with her long Big Apple Red fingernails. Within a few seconds of rolling around on the carpet with her I had determined that she was just as strong as I was, quite possibly a better fighter than I was, and—at least based on the weird things her eyes were doing as we rolled around on the floor and I struggled to keep her teeth away from my neck—almost certainly not a human being. I mean, the bitch was scary.

Demons don't like silver. It's one of the few old standbys that work, at least a bit. (Holy water, for instance, is about as much use against Hell's servants as Diet Pepsi.) Silver doesn't always kill them, but it almost always hurts them. Unfortunately, what with one thing and another that week I didn't have any silver bullets on me, so when I got my hand free for a moment, I just shoved the gun against her face and fired three of the ordinary kind. I had my silencer on so the .38 didn't make too much noise, but she sure as hell did. She reeled back, screeching like a power drill and clawing at the remains of her features like someone trying to get soapy water out of their eyes, then came after me again. Any normal demon in a real-world body would have gone down just from being shot in the face, but she was one of those stubbornly murderous ones—even if you cut off her arms and legs she'd be crawling across the floor like a snake, snapping at your ankles with her teeth.

I *hate* the stubborn ones.

As soon as she had rubbed the blood out of her remaining eye she leaped forward and did her best to wrap her arms around me, dragging me back down to the floor. I didn't want to use my last couple of bullets, so I did my best to beat her unconscious with the butt of my Smith & Wesson, but all I managed to do was push her jaw unnaturally far to the side of her face, which made her look like an extremely disturbing Popeye cosplay girl but didn't slow her down at all. She was on top of me again, slapping and slashing with her nails at my eyes so that all I could do was cover up. Meanwhile she was also doing her best to drive her knee up through my groin and into my chest, introducing my balls to my heart, a meeting that should never take place. This gal was serious bad news and any moment now the guards were going to come busting in and it would be all over for your new friend, Bobby Dollar.

It wasn't the first time I ever found myself with a howling, angry she-creature on top of me—and God knows it probably wasn't going to be the last, either—but as the crooked, fanged mouth of Kenneth Vald's secretary snapped at my face, showering me with bloody froth, I couldn't help reflecting on how I had yet again wound up in such an extremely unpleasant situation.

And as usual, it had been my own stupid fault.

one

an old testament cinch

LET ME go back to the beginning. It'll make more sense then. Not a *lot* of sense, but more than it probably does right now.

Pretty much everybody was already in the bar the night it all started—Monica Naber, big old Sweetheart, Young Elvis, and all the rest of the Whole Sick Choir. Oh, except that because of recent changes in the local ordinances Kool Filter was stuck downstairs, smoking out on the sidewalk. Yes, some of us angels smoke. (I used to do it, but I don't anymore.) Our bodies are loaners, after all, and it's not like we're too worried about dying. Anyway, it was a pretty normal late February night in The Compasses until my friend Sam came in towing an overcoat full of new meat.

"Fuck the poor and all their excuses," he shouted to the room. "Somebody get me a drink!" He dragged over this young guy I've never seen before and shoved him into a chair beside me. "Here's someone you need to know, kid," he said. "Meet Bobby Dollar, king of the assholes." Sam dropped into a seat on the other side of him. The youngster was trapped, but he wasn't panicking yet. He grinned at me like he was glad to see me—big, stupid, slightly sickly grin. The rest of him was thin, white, and kind of bookish, with a haircut that on anyone but an angel would have screamed, "Mom did this!" A beginner with lots of theories, I guessed, but if he was hanging out with my pal Sam he'd be getting some rude lessons in Practical Theology.

"Who's your little chum, Sammy?" I knew the kid was one of us—we can recognize each other—but he sure looked uncomfortable wearing a body. "Amateur or visiting pro?"

Junior immediately put on what I think of as the Intelligent Dog look: *I don't know what you're saying, but I'm sure as hell trying to seem like I do.* It didn't impress me a whole lot more than his nervous smile.

"Go ahead, guess." Sam craned around. "Hey, Slowpoke Rodriguez," he yelled at Chico the bartender, "how come you'll gobble my knob for free, but you won't pour me a drink for money?"

"Shut up, Riley, you're boring me," Chico said, but he dropped his bar rag and turned to the glasses cabinet.

"Sammy boy, you're even more charming than usual," I observed. "So who's this? I'm guessing trainee."

"Of course he fuckin' is, B. Can't you just smell the House on him?" That's how Sam talks about what most people refer to as "Heaven"—"up at the House." As in, the rest of us work on the Plantation.

"Really?" Monica Naber stood up in the next booth so gracefully you probably wouldn't guess she'd been drinking tequila slams since sundown. "Did you hear that, folks? We've got a rookie!"

"Oh, yeah!" That from Young Elvis. He'd been the designated New Guy for two years now and he was obviously thrilled. "Kick his newbie ass!"

"Shut your talk-hole," said Walter Sanders without looking up from his glass. "Just because you were a stupid rookie doesn't mean they all are."

Sam's new kid squirmed in the chair beside me. "I'm not really a *total* rookie. . . ."

"Yeah?" Sanders looked up this time. He's kind of an intense guy, and he stared at the kid like he was going to dissect him. "Where did you guardian? How long?"

"Guardian? But . . . I didn't . . ." The kid blinked. "I was in the Records Halls . . ."

"Records?" Sanders scowled like he'd drunk curdled milk. "You were a file clerk? And now you're an advocate? Congratulations—that's quite a jump."

Right on cue, Chico banged the register closed—it went *"ting!" "Look, Daddy,"* said Sam in a squeaky little child voice. *"Teacher says every time a bell rings an angel gets his wings."*

"Don't be mean," Monica Naber said. "It's not the kid's fault."

Junior looked grateful for her support, but there were things he didn't know. With Monica, you live by her logic but you die by her logic, too. Women, even female angels, can be colder than men in some really scary ways.

The uproar died away after a bit and most of the drinkers went back to their private conversations or solitary musings. Sam went off to pick up his drink order. I looked at the new kid, who was no longer grinning like everything was great. "So how *did* you wind up here?" I asked. "Who pulled strings for you?"

"I don't understand. What do you mean?"

"Look, you know what we do, right?"

"Advocates? Sure." He nodded vigorously. "I'm really looking forward to—"

"Shut up and try to follow me. How did you get jumped into a position that takes most of us years to get into?"

Headlights, comma, deer in. "I . . . I don't know. They just told me . . ."

"Uh huh. So who's watching out for your career? *Somebody* must be. Think hard."

"I don't know what you're talking about!"

Sam returned with his drinks, a shot glass full of bitters liberally dosed with Tabasco and a root beer to chase it with. Sam's been sober for a few years now. Doesn't keep him out of The Compasses. "Is he cryin' yet, B?"

"No, but I'm working on it. How did you pick up this wet sock, Sammy?"

"I was just up at the House. They dropped him on me." His pocket started to buzz. "Shit. A client already?" He scowled at his phone, then downed the bitters and sucked in air like someone had poured kerosene on his crotch. "Want to tag along?" he asked me. "A favor to me. You can explain things to little Clarence the Trainee Angel here."

"Clarence?" I drew back. "He's not really called that, is he?"

"That's not my name!" For the first time the youngster was showing a little back-the-fuck-up in his own defense. I liked him better, but that still didn't make for a whole lot.

"Yeah, but I don't remember the name they told me, so I'm calling you Clarence," Sam declared, finishing off his root beer and then wiping his mouth hard with the back of his hand, just like in the old days before he drank his previous body to death. "Let's go."

"Stop that. My name isn't Clarence, it's Haraheliel." The new kid was being Very Brave—a regular little soldier. "My working name is Harrison Ely."

"Okay. Clarence it is, then," I said. "Sam, my chariot or yours?"

"I'm kind of parked halfway onto the sidewalk and no one's noticed it yet, so I guess we should take mine."

It wasn't easy getting Sam's boring, company-issue sedan off the sidewalk—some truck had come along and parked to unload, and by the time we squeezed out we had left more than a little of Sam's paint on the truck's bumper. If it had been my ride I would have been screaming, but Sam doesn't care about cars.

"Where is it?" I asked him as we turned onto Main, one of downtown Jude's busiest streets, meeting place of commerce, inept street performance, and world-class panhandling. The kid was struggling to pull the long-unused seatbelt out from between the back seats. Most of the well-known skyline was behind us, but the sparkling towers of the Shores stood a short distance to the north and the weird silhouettes of the harbor cranes loomed before us, lit from below, angular as a fleet of alien landing craft.

"The water," Sam said. "Pier 16, to be exact."

"Floater?"

"Floater, sorta. Only hit the water a few minutes ago. Probably just crossed over."

"Anyone I know?"

"Some old broad named Martino. Ring any bells?"

As I shook my head, the kid piped up from the back seat. "That's a terrible way to talk about a unique human soul."

Angels, I reminded myself. *We're angels. And angels are patient.*

The Port of San Judas covers about ten square miles along the southwestern shore of San Francisco Bay. The car was in the water at the public end, a broken wooden barrier marking where it had gone over into the empty slipway. Spotlights cut through the darkness, splashing the high port office walls and turning the bay water bright as jade.

Down on the ground the harbor police and the regular cops looked like they had arrived in a hurry; a couple of tow trucks and a fire engine were also parked along the pier at odd angles. Below them a harbor diver had just surfaced after attaching cables to something; at his thumbs-up the winches on the tow trucks started turning. The cables went rigid, the motors whined, and after a long moment the back end of a large white vehicle broke the surface, but almost immediately one of the motors stuttered and died. The other strained and coughed for a few more seconds, then it gave up too. The tow truck drivers and several harbor police began to shout back and forth at each other as we climbed out of Sam's car.

"Why don't they pull it the rest of the way out?" Clarence asked, eyes wide. "That poor woman!"

"Because it's probably too heavy—full of water," I told him. "But the driver's already dead, or we wouldn't have got the call, so it doesn't matter how long she sits there. Do you know about going Outside?"

"Of course!" He was offended.

"Oh, he's a pistol, this one." Sam was already walking toward the shimmer in the air, like a vertical mirage, that announced a way out. The official term for them is "egress," but down here we call them Zippers. We make them when we need them, and we simple Earthbound angels don't really know how they work, just that they do.

As the kid and I fell in behind Sam, a couple of bystanders looked briefly in our direction but then sort of lost interest. We're not easy to notice when we're working, I've learned over the years. We're still *there,* if you know what I mean—we have real bodies—but if we don't want you to see us then you probably won't, or at least you won't remember it afterward.

Sam and the kid vanished into the shimmering line down the middle of the air and I stepped through after them.

As always, it was the quiet of Outside that struck me first, a great, heavy hush as if we had suddenly dropped into the biggest, most silent library in the universe. But in most ways we were still where we had begun—the docks, with the cop cars and safety vehicles burning the darkness with red and blue lights and the downtown skyline stretching skyward behind them like a mountain range. But the police spotlights weren't moving, nor were the cops' mouths, a helicopter over the Intel Tower, a diver floating on green jelly swells, or even the few seagulls who had been startled off the pilings by all the activity and were now frozen in mid air like stuffed displays hung from a museum ceiling. Only one thing was different Outside: a woman with short gray hair and a dark raincoat stood in the midst of the petrified policemen, though none of them could see her.

"That's her," Sam said. "You want to walk the kid through meeting the client while I'm waiting for the guardian, B? That way he can learn from the best."

"Lying bastard," I said, but I got the facts I needed from him and then led the kid down to the puddle-glazed dock.

"We look the same here," the kid said, staring at his hands. "I mean, we do, don't we? Like our earth-bodies?"

"Pretty much."

"I thought we'd look more . . . angelic." He looked embarrassed. "Like in Heaven."

"This isn't Heaven—we're still on the plane of earthly existence, more or less. We just stepped out of Time. But we don't *have* to look the same here, it's just sort of a tradition. The Other Side folk prefer to make themselves more intimidating. You'll see."

As we approached our new client, she stared at us with an expression I had seen on a lot of faces in a lot of similar situations—total, utter confusion.

"Silvia Martino," I said. "God loves you."

"What's going on?" she asked. "Who are you?" She flapped her hands at the motionless cops and firefighters. "What's wrong with these people?"

"They're alive, Mrs. Martino. I'm afraid you're not." I've dumbed down my explanations over the years. I used to think breaking it to them slowly was the kindest way, but I learned differently. "You apparently drove your car into the bay. Any reason?"

She was more than a bit beyond sixty but no old lady. In fact, she looked like someone who might get old but would never really get old, if you know what I mean. Then I remembered that she would never get any older than this moment.

"Drove my car . . . ?" She looked at the white bulk of her SUV hanging at the end of the straining tow truck cables like Moby Dick, decorated with fantails of glassy, motionless water. "Oh, dear. That's *my* car, isn't it?" Her eyes widened. She was beginning to do the math. "I was trying to turn around, and I guess I got . . . confused." She blinked. "Am I . . . am I really . . . ?"

"I'm afraid so."

Then the tears came. This is the part I hate most about my job. Sometimes your clients are so happy to be out of their sick, dying bodies that they practically dance. But those who get caught by surprise, who suddenly come to understand that there's no more, that's it, game over . . . well, those are tough. There's not much to say while they work it out, but if they need it you can put your arms around them and hold them when you're Outside, and that's just what I did. You would have, too.

After a while she was through the worst of it. She was a tough lady—I liked her. She pulled away from me and dried her eyes, then asked, "And who are you?" She looked at me more carefully now, as though I might be about to try some after-death marketing scam on her.

"My name is Doloriel. I'm an advocate angel of the Third House." I didn't bother to introduce Clarence because he would have only done something stupid like promised her that everything was going to turn out all right. (I could tell by his disappointed expression that was exactly what he'd planned to do.) Instead I pointed back at Sam, who was now talking to the lady's guardian, a wispy, half-transparent thing that gleamed in its folds like foxfire. "That fellow is Sammariel, another advocate angel. He'll speak for you."

"Speak for me? How? When?"

"At judgement," I said. "Very soon."

"Judgement . . . ?" Eyes suddenly wide and fearful.

"Just wait here, please." I pulled the kid aside and gave him some fairly harsh warnings about what he was allowed to do and say, then left him with the recently departed. He and the dead woman stared at the half-submerged car as though wishing someone would leap out of it and help the conversation along. I was glad he was keeping his mouth shut. People deal faster (and better, I think) with that terrible, ultimate realization when you let them work it out for themselves. Besides, what are you going to tell them? "Just fooling, you're not really dead! This is just a wake-up call for you to fix your life!" Because it's not. It's the end, at least of their time on Earth, and no cheerful chitchat is going to change that.

The guardian angel had just finished briefing Sam when I joined the party. "Briefing" isn't as much like the real world as it sounds: The guardians kind of make their knowledge available to us, and for the entirety of the proceedings it's just *there,* at our mental fingertips, as though the memories were our own. Thank goodness that ends again after the sentence—it would be overwhelming to carry the details of every life you've argued for, all the time. It's tough enough sometimes just dealing with the stuff that sticks.

Anyway, the guardian gave me what I guess was an interested look, although it's hard to tell with them because they're far less human in appearance than we are—a lot less corporeal, too. They don't use actual meat bodies, of course, otherwise people would be wondering why some kind of shiny human jellyfish was always floating along next to them. "You're Doloriel," it said. "I've heard of you."

"Can't say the same about you until I know your name."

"Iphaeus." It stared at me, twinkling a little. "Heard you like to piss people off."

"Wouldn't go so far as to say I like it."

"Look," interrupted Sam, "if the two of you want to get to know each other better you can always arrange a romantic dinner. Right now . . ."

The guardian gave a sort of shiver and its glow dwindled. "He's here."

Something had just stepped through a red-lit portal from the Other Place (their equivalent of the Zipper was less like a shimmering white line and more like a fiery wound) and now stood brushing imaginary lint from its immaculate, blood-colored suit.

"Grasswax," said Sam. "Shit. They're going to make me work for this one."

I heard Mrs. Martino gasp when she saw the demon, and I was sorry I'd left her with the kid. It's pretty nasty when a client realizes Hell is real. I hoped she'd make it through the actual trial without breaking down—some judges are real assholes about that. The quality of mercy may droppeth as a gentle rain from Heaven, but sometimes you'd swear there was a drought.

Another shape stepped out of the wound a few moments after Prosecutor Grasswax, a muscular, hairy demon in a cheap suit with a wolfish snout and an attitude to match. I'd seen him before, though I couldn't remember where—a nasty piece of work named Howlingfell. Bodyguards didn't usually show up for this kind of routine work on neutral turf. I wondered why the prosecutor felt he needed protection. From the way Howlingfell sniffed the air, he looked like he was working. Didn't really make much sense. His boss was ignoring him.

From a distance Grasswax the prosecutor looked pretty much like a man, but as he drew closer you could see that the shadows under his cheekbones were actually gaps in the skin like gills that showed the muscle working beneath, and his close-cropped hair was something more like bristles or even scales. Also, nobody would have mistaken those serpentine eyes for human. Like I told the kid, our opponents like to intimidate.

"Good evening, gentlemen," said Grasswax, showing his extremely long, extremely even teeth. "Who is against me? Doloriel?" The smile twisted up just a little at one corner. "That will be a treat."

"It's me," Sam said.

"Ah, Sammariel." He nodded. "Haven't seen you since Thanksgiving. That was you, wasn't it? The man with the knife?"

"Electric carving knife," Sam explained to me and the kid, who had wandered over to see his first real demons, or at least that's what his wide-eyed stare suggested. "Did his whole family."

"Very thorough." Grasswax rubbed his hands together. "Shall we get on with it?"

"Have you been advised yet?" I asked.

"Oh, quite." The prosecutor reached into his pocket and pulled out something the size of a fat little spider, but much less attractive, which he dangled in the air by one scaly leg—Hell's version of a guardian angel. "Mrs. Martino's account executive has filled me in on all the particulars."

I pulled Clarence to one side while Sam and the prosecutor called for a judge so I could review the rules of engagement for him (mostly to make sure he didn't do anything stupid.) "Okay, stand over here and listen close. This is for this lady's soul, and that's our most important job, you understand? If you do anything to compromise that I'm going to tear your halo off and beat you bloody with it. Got it?"

Clarence nodded, still wide-eyed.

"Because this is Hell we're up against, and they're going to lie and cheat and stretch every truth to the screaming point. That's why we have procedures. We can't afford to get angry, because then we don't do a good job. Got it?"

Another nod and a hint of impatience. I hate rookies.

"But most importantly, kid, *never* trust the Opposition."

"Trust them? Are you kidding . . . ?"

"It's not always this obvious. Just remember what Uncle Bobby tells you and you'll be fine." Because Uncle B. had already made all those rookie mistakes and had been lucky to survive some painful lessons. "When a demon opens his mouth, he's lying. Period. Assume anything else and your final paycheck will have to be printed on asbestos, because you'll be somewhere *very* hot."

Then Xathanatron the judge appeared like silent lightning.

It's a bit intense the first time you see a Principality manifest, which is one reason I had moved the kid out of the way. My ears rang for a week after I met my first judge up close, not to mention those floating spots of light. The important angels are . . . bright. Overwhelming. Beautiful, but with a lot of scary in it. Enough to give even the most devout second thoughts about wanting to see the Highest someday.

You couldn't really make out a face in that fierce glare or even much of a shape, as if someone had constructed a Christmas tree angel out of burning magnesium wire, but I knew it was Xathanatron because . . . well, I just knew. When you're in their presences you perceive whatever the Principalities want you to perceive about them—and nothing more. From my own experience I knew Xathanatron was severe in an old-school kind of way but rigorously fair. Sam wouldn't get cheated, but he wasn't going to get any surprise breaks either.

I put myself between Clarence and Howlingfell—the kid looked as if he was going to wet himself if he had to stand next to the demon. Mrs. Martino joined us, eyes dry now and face solemn, making an audience of four for the proceedings, but I could tell she was fighting hard for composure. I couldn't help admiring her again. I hoped we could help her.

"How come there's so many of you holy-rollers here?" Howlingfell snarled in my ear. "That ain't right."

"We heard a rumor you were going to sing 'Ave Maria.'"

"A rumor I was gonna eat your face, you mean." Usually Hell has the best writers—but not always, obviously.

"What's going to happen now?" our rookie whispered in my other ear.

"What do you think? Prosecutor Grasswax is going to try to convince the judge that Mrs. Martino here should go straight to Hell, do not pass Go, do not collect two hundred dollars. Our boy Sam is going to argue that she should be gathered unto the bosom of the Highest instead." I glanced toward the frightened, quiet soul in question. "That's how it works. Didn't they give you any prep at all?"

"I didn't get much warning." Clarence stared with the kind of sickened fascination secret Christians must have felt watching their exposed fellows being gobbled by Roman lions. "They just . . . sent me."

Sent him to fill what was supposedly Heaven's most important job—protecting human souls from the Opposition—without much of any training. Odd, you say? No kidding. I filed this bit of weirdness away for later.

Grasswax was already in full swing, pacing along the dock before the coruscating judge like a goblin dancing in front of a fireplace, jabbing his long, pointy fingers as he described in lurid detail what seemed like every petty thought, unkind word, or social misdemeanor poor old Mrs. Martino had ever made. The prosecutor didn't seem to have much in the way of ammunition, but he did mention that she had been arrested for driving while intoxicated.

"Her husband left her at a party and took off somewhere," Sam said. "Probably with a broad, Your Honor. Come on, that's clearly just a mistake in judgement on her part."

"Ah, yes. Mistakes in judgement." Grasswax offered a significant glance to the nearly featureless gleam of Xathanatron. "We'll talk more about such things."

"This could go on for hours," I said quietly to Clarence. "Are you sure you want to be here? We could go get a cup of coffee." I saw him looking at Mrs. Martino. "Not her, stupid. She's dead. She's not getting coffee with us."

He shook his head stubbornly. "I want to see."

I shrugged. "Suit yourself."

It did in fact go on for hours. You'd want it to if it was *your* judgement, wouldn't you? Your entire life being summed up, your eternal fate settled on the coin-flip of guilty or not guilty?

"It seems like a pretty basic system . . ." the kid said as he watched Sam work. Grasswax had begun to pull out his bigger ammunition, things like cruel words, religious hypocrisy, even petty theft. (She'd stolen twenty dollars from her church fundraiser once, because she didn't have the cash to get home otherwise.) Grasswax then added a string of petty sins going back to her childhood. Sam took each allegation as it came and made it clear with a shake of the head or a snort of disgust that he didn't think much of such small beer. My pal's always been a bit of a country lawyer, unhurried and deliberate. I honestly think it's the best approach with a prosecutor like Grasswax, who has been known to overplay his hand.

"Yeah, it's basic," I agreed. "Because the problem is pretty basic." I tugged him a couple of paces away from the deceased. "Only two choices, see? You're going one way or the other—even Purgatory is a win for our side, because it means you can work your way to Heaven eventually. So each time somebody wins and somebody loses, and it happens thousands and thousands of times a day. The best systems are simple ones—and after all, this one worked for us, right? You, me, Sam—we all wound up on Team Heaven. And if this lady deserves to be there, she'll be there."

I was lying, of course. It's nowhere near that simple, and one of the reasons is because a lot of what is commonly thought of as sinful is just being human. I don't know how things used to be, but the judges don't tend to put people away for minor infractions—they seem to be more interested in intent, although they can sometimes be sticklers for some of the classic old-school stuff; killing, adultery, like that. But what they'll stick on and what they'll let slide is a gray area as big as Heaven itself, and it takes years to learn how to maximize a soul's chances at judgement. But I wasn't even sure why the kid was here—I wasn't going to try to teach him everything in one night.

Howlingfell had been eavesdropping on our conversation. He laughed and swiped a long red tongue along his lips, showing a lot of pointy teeth. "You just watch, Dollar—Grasswax has got this bitch's number. She'll be flapping in the dark wind before you know it."

The kid flinched but he still wouldn't look at the demon. "But some things are more complicated than that, aren't they, Bobby? And she really hasn't done anything wrong . . . !"

"That's not for you to decide," I said, holding up a hand to silence him. "And to be honest, I'm not certain I'd trust the judgement of someone who's never argued a case before. I had an Eagle Scout once who was run over while helping a man in a wheelchair across a busy street. Open and shut, right? Fit him for a halo. Except it turned out at judgement that when he was eight years old he smothered his baby brother with a pillow. Nice-looking kid. Youth pastor at his church. No reason we ever learned. Just didn't like his little brother." It had been another weird, complicated case that didn't sum up easily, but I wasn't going to talk strategy in front of our opponents—like I said, there's a lot of gray area, and you have to learn it the hard way. Instead I cocked a thumb toward the recently deceased Mrs. Martino. "Don't fall in love with a client, kid."

"In love . . . !" He looked horrified.

"You know what I mean. Don't make it personal." Those were the most important words I knew—words that could save your afterlife.

"Adultery," announced Grasswax. "Repeatedly, and without confession. For years."

"Oh, shit," said Sam. Actually he only mouthed the words, but I could read his lips.

"A grave, grave sin against the Law of Moses," Grasswax continued. "And no repentance, either. In fact, she had just met the lover for drinks before her accident tonight, so she died . . . unshriven, as we used to say. Am I wrong?"

Sam hastily conferred with the woman's guardian. "Mitigated!" Sam said. "Her husband has a mistress."

"Oh, but surely two wrongs don't make a right, Master Sammariel." Grasswax smiled. It looked like he had horse's teeth crammed in his mouth. Wasn't pretty. "This is not the husband's judgement. As you know, she stands before a representative of God the Highest," he said, gesturing toward the burning presence of Xathanatron. "She is not being judged by the kind receivers of the Children's Host. She sinned and kept on sinning. Only death stopped it." The prosecutor grinned even wider. The conviction was beginning to look, as my old mentor Leo used to say, like an Old Testament Cinch.

"But I didn't . . . !" Silvia Martino only got out the first few words before Grasswax turned on her and flicked his taloned fingers. The sound stopped coming. She struggled on for a moment before she realized the gift of speech had been taken from her.

"No one asked you, whore," spat the prosecutor, then turned back to Sam with a grin. "Well, Advocate? Any final words of summation?"

The new kid was twitching beside me as if something was biting him. "Stop," I told him. "Don't attract attention. You won't like it." But it was no use.

"How about Thou Shalt Not Steal?" the kid shouted. "Doesn't that count?"

"Oh, shit." This time it was me saying it. Everybody turned to look at Clarence. Even Xathanatron the Principality seemed to pause, his fires darkening just a fraction.

"He's not supposed to talk!" barked Howlingfell, the ugly, coarse hairs on his neck and shoulders bristling. He started his move—he would have been all over the rookie with talons and fangs—but I kicked him hard in the back of the knee, then when his leg buckled I helped him to lie down with a swift jerk on his suit collar. The demon hit the ground hard—Outside is a real, physical place, it's just outside Time—then I dropped to a crouch beside him to make sure he was all right. Okay, I might have kneeled on his windpipe a little.

"Down, Fido," I told him quietly, crimping his neck until he stopped struggling so hard. "Let the big boys settle this."

"Here!" Suddenly rough, clawed hands were pulling at me. I wasn't going to start a brawl in front of a heavenly judge so I let myself be tugged back onto my feet, although by the time I had my balance Grasswax had pulled my jacket most of the way off. "How dare you!" he snarled, but he didn't sound entirely convincing—I think he was playing it up for the judge.

"Easy, everybody," said Sam, getting into the middle. He helped me get my jacket back over my shoulders, then patted me back into shape with a care that was almost fatherly. We've been through a lot, Sam and me. "Just a misunderstanding," he said, glaring at the kid.

Howlingfell was getting up now, too. He looked like he thought he understood everything *just fine*: his murderous scowl could have bubbled paint.

"Misunderstanding?" Grasswax surveyed us all, a look of calculated outrage twisting his unpleasant features into something even less charming. "Did I *misunderstand* when I thought I heard an *apprentice*, unsworn and unnamed before this judge, interrupting an officer of prosecution? Or did it really happen . . .?"

What Did He Mean? This from the judge, each word like a silver bell in a church tower, loud and vibrant, silencing Grasswax just as he was getting worked up to a grand, oratorical flourish. Xathanatron turned his faceless gaze toward Clarence. *Speak, Child. I Give You Leave.*

"Her husband—he . . . he s-stole from her!" To his credit, the kid at least looked properly terrified at what he'd got himself into. "He stole her youth."

"What rubbish." Grasswax wore the expression of a man forced to watch a long elementary school performance while standing outside in foul weather.

Clarence turned to face the judge. "From the day they were married, her husband only made love to her one night a month, like . . . like it was a job. Without . . . foreplay, without kissing. Rolled off and went to watch television." The youngster was scarlet, embarrassed. "Then, after their fourth child, he just stopped. Told her she'd let herself go. That she sickened him." He looked over to the deceased, but Silvia Martino seemed lost in a memory or even a dream, her eyes unfocused. "That's stealing, right?" he said at last.

I knew I shouldn't have let the kid talk to her. I felt like punching myself in the nuts for letting it happen. When did he get all that out of her? Even Sam looked as if it had caught him by surprise, and he'd talked to the guardian angel.

When Clarence was not immediately changed into hot steam it seemed pretty clear the judge was going to allow his evidence. Sam knew better than to look this gift horse in the mouth any longer than he needed to. He quickly added a strong theme of tragic suffering to his summation and rode that nag all the way home.

I still wouldn't have wanted to put money on which way Xathanatron was going to go, but when a column of lavender light surrounded the late Mrs. Silvia Martino, and a look crept over Grasswax's face that suggested some paralegal in Hell was going to get a horrible bollocking, I knew it was over and Sam had won.

Suddenly the deceased was gone. Grasswax took off a moment later, silent and very unpleasantly angry. Howlingfell pointed a shaking, clawed finger at me. "You're dead, Dollar!" he growled, but his voice was still a bit weak from my knee crushing his trachea. A moment later he followed Grasswax through the shimmering wound and then, except for the judge, it was just angels standing around in the frozen moment.

"Congrats," I told Clarence. "You've made your first batch of enemies today."

"What?"

"And not just on the other team," Sam said. "If you ever do that to me again, kid, they'll never find all the different pieces."

"Pieces . . . ?"

"Of you." He shook his head in disgust. "You get any more bright ideas, try 'em out on me or Bobby first."

I was watching Xathanatron, who to my discomfort seemed to be staring in my direction. I'd kind of hoped that scuffle with Howlingfell would have been beneath the high angel's notice.

You Are Wanted In The Celestial City, Angel Doloriel, the pillar of light told me. Sam and the kid didn't hear it, but for me it came loud enough to make my cheekbones ache. *Your Archangel Wishes To Speak With You.* Then the big glow was gone.

"C'mon," Sam said to me. "Time to go back. I'm going to buy Clarence an ice cream. I mean, we did win the case."

Me, I was feeling thirsty—that's just how I react to happy endings. But then I react to unhappy ones pretty much the same way.

two

my lucky week

I ALREADY KNOW some of the questions you want to ask. The answers are:

1) Yes, it's pretty darn interesting being an angel.

2) No, I haven't met God. Yet.

3) I can't tell you which religion was right after all, because it's not exactly clear.

4) As to what Heaven's like . . . well, bear with me and I'll try to explain.

First off, Heaven is . . . complicated. It's not just a castle on a cloud or some paradise garden. It's big, even though there's only one city—the Celestial City itself. But that city is surrounded by what they call the Fields, which are lands that stretch on and on in all directions, seemingly forever, rolling hills and meadows and even forests full of souls that I've always assumed are the departed of Earth living the good life of Eternity. If you ask them, though, they don't know any more about it than I do about my own pre-angelic life—they're just *happy*.

Usually when you're summoned you go straight to the Celestial City. You don't walk when you're there, or even fly. Nothing that simple. Even calling it a city is a bit misleading, although there are times when it seems to be exactly that, when you catch glimpses of the enormity that is around you, towers and heights and shining walkways impossibly far above your head. Wherever you go shining presences surround you like the lights of a million happy cars on a busy but absolutely safe freeway, and each of those presences is an angel. And somewhere at the heart of it, a place you can never quite see but that you always know is there, a constant glow in the edge of your sight and sense and imagination, is the Empyrean, the innermost district of Heaven where they say the Highest dwells.

Invitation only, needless to say.

But all that doesn't begin to describe Heaven, how it looks, feels, tastes. Do you remember the Electrical Parade they used to do at the Disney parks in the evenings, with all the gleaming lights and dancing characters? Well, it's a bit like that, but only if you had a strong fever that also somehow made you feel secure and comfortable and like you never wanted to ask another question because it was just too much trouble.

I got over the last part—a few of us do. Now I ask lots of questions, but mostly to myself.

Another problem: the sights you see in Heaven, the look of the citizens, even the conversations you have there tend to be slippery in the mind afterward. I'm sure I'm frustrating you, but there really is no good way to explain quite what it's like, because by the time you get back it doesn't even feel the same to you, even though you're the one it happened to. Like trying to remember exactly how everything worked in a dream. When you're up at the House, as Sam calls it, you know how to get where you need to go, you know where you are, you see things and they make sense. But just try to draw a map afterward. Doesn't work.

I don't think most of the angels in Heaven worry about things like this—certainly not the way I do. In fact, other than a few of my earthbound friends, everybody else in the angelic throng seems to believe that even wondering about how things work is a form of ingratitude. But I can't help being this way. It's just the way the Highest made me.

Don't get me wrong, though—I like Heaven okay, and I like being an angel. Beats the crap out of the alternative. Especially when you consider that the time-frame in question is eternity.

You can think of the next part as taking place in Temuel's office in the California building of the North American Continent Complex, although calling any structure in Heaven a "building" and any place in that structure an "office" is a gross oversimplification of a very strange, very shiny and floaty reality. Temuel was my special archangel—my supervisor, I guess you'd call him. Not my mentor, though, because I'd been in the department longer than he had. He was aware of that, so he shied away from the whole "boss" thing and tried to work the "older friend" angle instead, especially with me and Sam and the other veterans. We let him. It's better when everyone knows, or at least thinks they know, where they stand.

We didn't tell him his nickname, of course. There aren't too many good ways to spin "The Mule." But nobody really disliked him. He was just the boss, and an archangel to boot, and that made real affection difficult. The higher angels are just too . . . distant to get chummy with, even the more approachable ones like Temuel.

"Ah, Angel Doloriel!" he said with deliberate good cheer when I showed up. (You can't always tell by looking at them, but some angels in Heaven are "he" and some are "she," some are kind of both, and others are just "it." Nothing personal on my end.) "God loves you. How are things in Jude?"

If there's anything that makes people from San Judas wince, it's hearing people who've never been there call it "Jude," but I was already feeling the mandatory cheerfulness of Heaven bubbling through me and doing my best to go with it. "Hello, chief. Things are fine, I guess. Of course the Giants spent all last year playing like they never heard of runners in scoring position, and they could use a lefty reliever something fierce, but hey, spring training's just starting so there's always hope." Sometimes I talk about baseball just to annoy people who don't understand it. It's one of the many wonderful things about that game. "Oh, and speaking of training, Sammariel's working with this new kid."

"Ah, yes, young Haraheliel." He nodded. "How does he look so far?"

"Like a pig in a bikini. But I'm sure he'll improve." Or he'd run his mouth again at a bad time and get us all yanked out of Jude and demoted to an eternity of making pointed suggestions to minor sinners in Purgatory. "Where'd he come from, if you don't mind me asking?"

The bright visage of Temuel clouded the tiniest bit. He lifted his shining hand in a gesture of calculated vagueness. "Oh, Records, I think. He was transferred to us as a favor to one of the higher-ups."

There were so many things about that sentence that scared me that I didn't dare say a word.

"Anyway, that was really what I wanted to talk to you about," the Mule went on.

"What? You lost me."

"The new one. Sammariel's trainee. I want you to keep an eye on him."

That was even weirder. Why would anybody, let alone an archangel, be interested in a Junior Woodchuck like Clarence? "Isn't that supposed to be Sam's job, boss? Since he's training him?"

The vague, gleaming gesture again. "Yes, certainly. But Sammariel doesn't notice things the way you do, Doloriel. That's why I'm asking you. You've got the eye."

Ordinarily having a supervisor say something like that would make a guy feel good, and you'd think in Heaven it would make you feel even better, but even buoyed by pumped-in happy I was less than thrilled.

"Of course," was what I said, having not been stupid either before or after my lamented passing. I'm hoping it was lamented, anyway, although personally I can't remember it.

That really did seem to be all that the Mule had wanted, which made the whole thing even stranger—he had never been one for small talk, and even when he made some it was in an awkward sort of way, so you felt like you were keeping him from something more important. The truth is, I kind of liked the guy, or as much as you can like someone you don't understand. He'd always seemed to like me too, or at least tolerate me, and that was a difference from most of the other archangels I'd met. But a boss is a boss, and since I was up at the House anyway, he made me file a bunch of reports I'd been avoiding, stuff I should have turned over days ago to Alice, our office assistant back on Earth (another angel, as far as I know, but just based on attitude, she might be a rehabbed demon.) If the road to Hell is paved in good intentions, a friend of mine used to say, the road to Heaven is paved with bullshit and busy work.

Who was this Haraheliel kid, anyway? Who had pushed buttons to get our young Clarence out of Filing and into Operations—and why? Did he know too much about something there? Or was he supposed to be someone's spy in the Advocacy Division? Whose attention had we attracted? And why had they selected such an obvious outsider?

Wow, I can hear you saying, *spies in Heaven? Suspecting your literally angelic bosses of trying to shaft you? You sure have a bad attitude, Bobby Dollar.* Well, just stick with me a while before you make up your mind. That's all I'm asking. I've been right more often than the haters like to admit.

I had a little time to kill before going back—my earthbound body was still in my apartment in Jude getting its seven hours of sleep—so I wandered away from the North America Building, following the climbing Avenue of Contemplation past the mansions of the blessed. As I said, one of the strangest things about Heaven is that there are no maps. If you haven't been invited to where you're going or don't already have access to that particular spot, you probably won't find it, although you'll find a thousand other beautiful sights. You could stroll, or float, or whatever it is we do there (I'm still not sure after all these years—it just doesn't stick in my head when I leave) for a decade and never reach the specific place you were looking for—but as I said, I wasn't looking for anything, just wandering. I spent some time watching the Fountain of Stars and thinking big but formless thoughts. I even walked out onto Pilgrim's Bridge, although I hadn't meant to, and stopped in the middle of the span to look down on the great city and its sparkling, jostling crowds of inhabitants, thousands and thousands of souls, millions even, each one dedicated to order and love, each one happy with his or her place in the big plan. Beyond them all, at the top of the highest of Heaven's hills, lay a glow like the most gorgeous sunrise—the Empyrean, the seat of the Highest. Still, being me, I couldn't even look at that wonderful spot, the center of the Cosmos, without wondering why it was hidden away from the rest us.

Why did God make me so restless, so difficult? I've never understood it, but He must have wanted me to be that way, because He gave me enough for two.

As usual, when I woke up in my physical body once more it felt a little strange to me, as if someone had washed and ironed a favorite old pair of jeans. I put some coffee in the microwave—it's strange how much like a real body mine is in terms of its needs and crotchets—and went to the mirror while waiting for the ping.

Same face. Had it for about five or six years now. Not much different from the two or three faces before it, either. It would take an expert to know I'd changed. Same body, too—average height, average weight, maybe a little wirier and more athletic than your average guy. The man in the mirror had dark hair that needed cutting, a face (ever so slightly Mediterranean or dark European) that needed shaving, and a mouth that would have been sad and artistic if it weren't for the smile, which, although it doesn't show up often, I've been told can be slightly alarming. I wondered, as I often do, if this is how I looked in life. If so, nobody's ever mistaken me for me, if you know what I mean, but that would be quite a coincidence, I guess, to assume I'd run into anyone on Earth who might have known the old me. I might have lived in the seventeenth century for all I can guess, or wore a powdered wig and took snuff. Or I could have been a Chinese peasant. I might have been a woman, too. Could have been anybody. So why did they take that away? Why does Heaven treat souls as if they were old videotapes, erasing the priceless memories of a graduation or wedding just to record an episode of some sitcom over it? Not that I've got anything against situation comedy, but if we don't get to remember what we did with our lives—even if for most of us those lives probably sucked—why did we have to go through it in the first place?

These were my mirror thoughts. Pretty ordinary for me.

Cynical, they say. *Not trusting. Bad angel!*

But like I said, God must want me to be this way. Either that or He just doesn't give a shit. To this point, I'm staying hopeful.

They were decorating Beeger Square that afternoon for the last thrash of Carnival season, which would kick off this weekend. San Judas does love its Carnival. The light poles were strung with tinsel and hung with big, scary-looking masks, and the city workers had built a temporary stage in one corner of the square—fortunately the farthest one from the Alhambra Building, where we all hang out. The folks at The Compasses hated to be distracted by amateurs.

The bar is called The Compasses because about a hundred years ago, before they turned the Alhambra into the first skyscraper in San Judas, the site of our contemporary oasis had been a fourth-floor room in the old Alhambra Theatre that the Masons had used as a meeting lodge. A stone plaque with the Square and Compasses, the symbol of their order, still hung over the front door of the building.

"But all the squares are outside," as Sam liked to say. "So we only need the compasses." And that's how it got its name.

It was a slow day inside. The only regulars I saw were Sweetheart and Monica Naber at the bar watching CNN on the wallscreen and Chico the bartender polishing glasses, as usual looking about as warmly human as a statue of Lenin.

"Ooh," Sweetheart said when he saw me come in, "I can smell the grumpiness from here, honey." Sweetheart is built like an NFL defensive tackle but he's as camp as a Brazilian soap opera, one of the few of us earthbound who really seems to enjoy life. "Bad time at headquarters?"

News travels fast at The Compasses. "Not really. Just the usual supervisorial jerking-around." In fact, the whole Clarence thing worried me enough that I didn't want to talk about it with anyone except Sam.

Sweetheart nodded. "I hear you, sugar. I never go near the place if I can help it—all that muted splendor makes my eyes itch." He grinned. "Got any plans for Carnival? Are you coming to my party? 'Cause you can't let Carnival go by without dancing, sweetie!"

I sometimes think Sweetheart has gone a bit native.

Monica looked up when I slid onto the stool next to hers. Chico, who was always eager to avoid conversation, edged away to give us some privacy.

"Hey," she said. "You look rough. Stairway to Heaven?"

"It's not the lyrics that make it so good, it's the guitar solo. But yeah. Just got back." I was curious if she knew anything about the kid but I didn't want to give out too many particulars about what the Mule had said. "Where's Sam?"

"And his trusty sidekick Mini-Sam? Haven't seen them yet. Sanders and Elvis have some kind of bet going about how fast an armadillo can run so they took off about half an hour ago for the zoo. Kool's got a client over in Spanishtown. Things have been slow. I blame clean living." She looked at me a little funny, perhaps wondering why I was sitting next to her making friendly chat. See, Monica and I had been through a little thing together not too far back and some of the skin was still raw, if you know what I mean. Long story. But she was naturally suspicious of my intentions. Hell, *I'm* naturally suspicious of my intentions most of the time.

"Speaking of the kid," I said, "they say he comes straight out of the Halls of Records."

She laughed. "And you want to know if I've heard anything about that? Sorry, Bobby. What do you care, anyway? They didn't stick *you* with him." She stood up. "Any requests?"

For a moment I thought she was going to sing or something, then I saw she was headed for the jukebox. "Nothing that will make my head hurt." I watched her walk across the room. Nice shape. We call her Monica because she's dark-haired, cute, and a bit a bit of a bossy group-mom, like that character on *Friends*. Naber . . . well, that's because it's hard to say "Nahebaroth" properly without making your throat sore. She's a good person, except her taste in men is appalling, me being the prime example. I was told by another female friend once that when I get morose it's "like being around a grumpy cat—you'll let someone feed you, but Heaven forbid anything more." And we were doing pretty well at the time she said it.

The bar fell into an unexpected moment of silence as the antique jukebox clicked and hummed, then the record was flipped onto the turntable and the needle dropped. I used to think of The Compasses' jukebox as a metaphor for how every soul in God's Kingdom mattered, but I'm not certain any more that the conceit really works.

As Monica strolled back through the mostly empty tables, Steely Dan's "Haitian Divorce" began to honk its way through the introduction. Naber had a little sway in her walk. I suddenly realized that I hadn't been seeing Naber suspicious, I'd been seeing Naber flirtatious, but I'd forgotten what it looked like. She'd been on that stool for a while, drinking mai tais or some other godawful tropical poison, and that meant she was liable to do something dangerous. Extremely liable.

"What are you looking so miserable for, anyway?" she asked as she slid in beside me, still moving to the music. "Jeez, B, if you'd cheer up a little something nice might even happen to you tonight."

Frisky *and* nostalgic. Things were about to get really complicated. We'd had a great time together for a while, but it ended in a protracted firefight of name-calling and running-for-the-hills—the former her, the latter me—so there was no way in hell I was going to start anything up again unless I was *real* drunk and *real* stupid, and I hadn't had a drink yet that night.

Then, just that moment, as if to prove that the Highest still loved little Bobby Dollar very, very much, my phone started buzzing in my pocket.

Monica looked down at my vibrating pants. "Somehow, I don't think that's because you're happy to see me."

"Gotta take it. It's work."

"You go and get some, honey!" Sweetheart shouted. I'm not sure what he meant.

"Shit," I said, staring at the screen. "Alice says this should have been Sam's, not mine, but she's passing it on to me. Looks like I've got a date with old money."

Monica did her best to look amused, but I could tell she was disappointed, which made me more than nervous. When did she decide I was anything but another guy who'd messed her up? If Monica had decided to forgive me—to forgive me with benefits, even—it was going to make The Compasses a bit hot for me.

"Is it Woodside?" she asked. That's a place in the hills at the edge of the city where the horses have more rights than most human beings.

"Nope, down in the flats. Palo Alto district."

She sighed and sat up, pulled her drink into closer range. "Break a leg, then. No, I'm feeling generous—break both."

I left Monica nursing her drink, looking vaguely sad. I think that phone message saved us both from a lot of bad luck. Well, at least her. As you'll see, it was a different story for me.

I tease Sam about his boring company ride, but to be fair, there are a few benighted souls who remain unimpressed by my custom '71 Matador Machine, despite its handsome copper paint job and checkered interior upholstery. In fact, someone (it might have been Monica Naber) once referred to it as "a car for under-endowed teenagers." To each their own. I know what I like, and one thing I like about the Matador is that I could smash that beast into a tank at sixty and not even stall the engine. I prefer a stout piece of machinery around me. Dying is never fun, even the third or fourth time.

At that time of the day in San Judas it's a lot faster to take surface streets than the freeway. Twenty minutes later, give or take, I was cruising east down University Avenue through a genteel, greenery-shrouded district where even the palm trees had their own physicians. (I'm not lying. The Palo Alto Neighborhood Association hires specialists to climb them once a month to check them for nut-rot or whatever.)

The main drag was lined with expensive apartment buildings but behind them lay the real neighborhood—if by "real" you mean "million dollar down payment, minimum," where people such as rich Stanford alums and old-school corporate big shots lived and enjoyed their money in quiet surroundings. (The newer, younger Silicon Valley money tended to wind up in flashier parts of the city, like townhouses around one of the public squares, Atherton Park, or out at the Shores.)

The mansion in question stood on one of the winding side streets, a mock Tudor with half an acre of lawns and hedges. Two SJPD cars and an ambulance were already parked in the long driveway and the garage door was open. A couple of guys in paramedic outfits with oxygen masks were just removing the body from the car inside the garage, a late model piece of expensive overseas engineering. I got a glimpse of the deceased as they pulled him out—white haired Caucasian guy, trim, wearing a dressing gown and pajama bottoms. His skin was a lovely fuchsia pink, classic symptom of carbon monoxide poisoning.

Well, it sure *looked* like suicide.

I summoned a Zipper and stepped through. Everything seemed to change just a little—the angle of the sun, the quality of the light—and the cops and paramedics all stopped moving at the same time, as if they were playing a kids' game. I wandered over to the car to look at the deceased's face. It seemed familiar. I might have met him somewhere, or he might have been in the newspaper. I turned and found the hovering glow of the late Mr. Monoxide's guardian beside me.

"Doloriel," I said, starting introductions.

"Yurath," said the glow.

"Who is he?"

"Don't you recognize him?" Little Yurath seemed a bit anxious, bobbing like a firefly in a strong breeze. Of course, its job of several decades was just about to end. Yurath might even have liked the guy. That happens sometimes. "Edward Lynes Walker. Founded a bunch of companies, including one of the biggest in Northern California. Philanthropist. Community leader. They even named a satellite after him."

"Sadly, he's still just as dead," I pointed out. "Okay, so everyone loves him. Any reason this shouldn't be a slam dunk for our side? Besides it being a suicide, I mean?" The rules on offing yourself have loosened up a bit. If Yurath could provide me with even the slightest history of painful medical problems or serious emotional trauma I was pretty sure the way Walker went out wouldn't hurt our case too much.

"I can think of at least one reason," the guardian said. "Look behind you."

I could already feel him, but I turned and pretended to be surprised. "Prosecutor Grasswax. Goodness, this is my lucky week! Two days in a row! And Mr. Howlingfell—say, that's a nasty bruise on your throat."

Howlingfell just balled his fists and looked away but Grasswax showed me all his teeth. It took a while. "Doloriel. I'm sure you and your friends sat up late last night celebrating your victory."

"Nope. I went home early, then visited old friends. Not that it's your business."

Grasswax leaned forward. Even Outside, where there was no air in the normal sense, his breath was like standing downwind from a slaughterhouse. "You like to make jokes, don't you, Doloriel—no, Bobby Dollar, isn't that what they call you at . . . what is it? The Compasses?" He said the bar's name as if it tasted bad. "You must have found it very amusing when your little clot of an apprentice made me look bad in front of one of the Principalities."

Anybody else that disgusting and standing that close to me would have got slugged, but you just don't take a swing at one of Hell's official prosecutors. Keeping the balance between the two sides is very, very delicate and the rules of what we do make it clear that loss of control is no different than going renegade, so I did my best to breathe through my mouth. "He's not my apprentice, Grasswax, and I didn't have anything to do with that. Let's just get on with business. I've got no quarrel with you."

He gave me a long look that actually made my skin itch. "If you say so."

"But that's the problem!" It was Yurath, the guardian, still bouncing around like it had to go to the bathroom—which, believe me, is not a problem guardian angels have. Its voice was unpleasantly shrill. "How can we? We can't!"

Grasswax rubbed his fingers on the lapels of his magma-colored suit as though even talking to such a low-ranking angel left something unpleasant on him. "What are you talking about?"

"Where is he?" squeaked Yurath. "Where did he go?"

"What?" Grasswax looked around at the tableau of frozen police and unmoving paramedics. "Who?"

It suddenly hit me. It hit me hard. "The deceased," I said. "He's talking about the deceased. Walker's not here."

And it was true. The gurney containing Walker's body was frozen on its way to the ambulance, but the man's soul—the permanent, immortal portion of Edward Lynes Walker that was our particular responsibility—was nowhere to be seen.

There's not a lot of territory Outside to search when you step through a Zipper. The farther you get from the egress, the less real it becomes until eventually it's just gray nothing. Nevertheless, we all searched carefully, even Grasswax, but the timeless bubble we inhabited was unquestionably short one soul.

"Oh, for God's sake," I said with real feeling, making the guardian flutter in distress. "Oh, sweet Jesus." This had never happened before—not to me, not to anyone as far as I knew. My so-called lucky week had just gone fully thermonuclear.

Grasswax swore too. I don't remember exactly what he said, but I remember being impressed—they can really curse in Hell. In fact, if I hadn't been so damn terrified at that moment I would have written some of it down.

three

different than sunday school

"WHAT KIND of crude, stupid trick . . . ?" Grasswax happy would have been unpleasant; Grasswax angry was a lot worse. For one thing, he was bubbling out the slits in his cheek. "You think you can humiliate me twice in two days? I don't care how far up I have to go or how many ladders I have to shake, Doloriel, I'll see you skinned and screaming for this!"

Do not strike even the most deserving members of the opposition, I reminded myself, *especially prosecutors, who will purposefully incite you—that is the stuff of which interhierarchical incidents are made.* Right out of the advocate's manual. "I didn't have anything to do with this, Grasswax. I got here when you did!"

"Souls do not simply disappear."

"I didn't say this one did. I just said it wasn't here. Probably just some minor screw-up."

"Minor screw-up?" The prosecutor was practically shrieking. Red froth flew through the air. "Pearl Harbor was a minor screw-up—this is a *problem!*"

He was right, of course. Things like this didn't happen. Ever. "Okay, okay, you call your supervisor, I'll call mine. We'll get it all straightened out."

But even before the words were out of my mouth angels and demons started popping out of the air on all sides, more Zippers opening than half-price night at the Nevada Cottontail Ranch. Security had been breached bigtime, and now the emergency troops were showing up. This wasn't just a problem, I realized, it was an actual, honest-to-front-office *crisis*, and yours truly was stuck right in the middle of it.

I suppose I'd better take a few moments to explain how some of this angel stuff works. It's a little different than what you learned in Sunday school, and it definitely comes up short on harps and clouds.

First of all, don't bother asking me about what my life used to be like when I was alive or how I died, because I don't know. None of the folks I work with do. We might always have been angels but we tend not to think so, since our memories only go back a few decades at most, and we all feel pretty comfortable inhabiting living bodies and hanging around in the actual world. The oldest angel I ever met in terms of service time was my first boss, Leo, who could remember working all the way back in the 1940s. That doesn't prove anything, of course. They might recycle us like glass bottles for all I know, steam us out each time and then fill us up again, century after century. When you're an angel of the Lord you just have to get used to certain ambiguities.

There are tons of angels, and not just in Heaven. For one thing, every single man, woman, and child on this planet has a guardian angel. You can't see 'em, feel 'em, or usually even sense 'em, but they're right there with you from your first slap on the backside until the moment you take your last breath . . . and a little bit beyond. Some people think they also work to keep you safe from physical danger and from the snares of the Opposition, which could be true, but I haven't heard anything for certain about that. Anyway, it's not my jurisdiction. As you may have gathered, I'm an advocate.

Okay, so at one per living soul that means there's got to be seven billion guardians at any one time. I'm assuming when they finish with one person's life they start on another's, but again, this is all guesswork. We advocates are a bit more rare. Me and Sam and Monica and the others each seem to work about five deaths a week, so let's call it 250 or so per year per angel. At a rate of 50 million or so deaths worldwide every year that makes work for about 200,000 advocates (assuming everyone in Timbuktu and Katmandu is on the same afterlife system as us, which is far from certain). For every ten or so there's also one or two working field support for the others, but other than Chico the bartender (and did I mention Alice?) you haven't met any of those yet.

I know, I know, numbers are not what you're interested in, except those of you who are engineers. No, you want to learn how it all *works*, don't you?

All of us Earth-based angels, guardians and advocates and even special ops (don't ask because I'm not telling), report to archangels. The archangels report to Principalities, who also judge individual souls, as you've seen. Together we're called the Angels of the Third House, which is Earth inside Time.

There are at least two other Houses, or spheres, each with three more types of angels, but this isn't Sunday school so I'll save that for another time. Above it all is the Highest. I haven't met Him yet. I understand He's pretty busy, what with making the universe work like perfect clockwork and yet keeping His eye on the sparrow and all that. And as I think I said, I've never known anyone else who's met Him either (or else none of them bothered to mention it to me).

We advocates are expected to live among the folks we're going to be defending, to know them and understand their ways, which is why we have bodies. They're not our real bodies, I'm told—not that anyone knows that for certain, but as I said, I've never been recognized by a relative or an acquaintance and I don't know anyone else who has either. Anyway, between being part of a small group (by comparison to the guardians or the Holy Host or whatever) and living and working on Earth, being an advocate is a bit like getting sent to one of those backwater colonial outposts: after a while, you couldn't move back to the old country if you tried. I sure as heck couldn't live in the Celestial City for very long. Too bright. Too many people singing. And a distinct lack of distilled spirits, the only kind I really like.

On the negative side, we're among the few angels who actually have to deal with the Opposition on a day to day basis, really get to know them, and it's pretty much as unpleasant as you'd think. For one thing, most of the Hell-folk take the struggle really, *really* seriously. They're kind of like student government nerds with fangs. They've been at war with Heaven for millennia and they intend to beat us someday. They're not stupid enough to provoke something big—that might bring down both sides—but they're always scraping away at the foundations like cartoon tooth decay. As far as they're concerned Milton and the others who say they can't ever beat us are just propaganda artists shilling for Heaven in hope of a cushy spot up at the House. Like I said, they're playing the long game, and they're always playing to *win*. It just tires you out sometimes.

Why don't haters get tired as fast as the rest of us? There's a question you'd think the afterlife would have answered for me, but no.

Meanwhile, there are also a few odd souls from both sides who've dropped out of the game altogether: tweeners and renegades. Most of them sell information to survive and so most of them have some kind of price on their heads. We advocates deal with them, from time to time. I even like some of them in a guarded sort of way.

Put it all together and it's more than a bit like the Cold War used to be—deadly dangerous but invisible to most of the living, and we're all expected to play our part in the struggle. My job is to make certain that as many souls as possible make it into Heaven, and like my friend Sam I'm pretty good at what I do, which is one reason why, even though my attitude sucks, my bosses mostly leave me alone.

Another reason, as I was about to discover, was that even the big boys up at the House don't know everything. That was a lesson I would rather not have learned.

So there I was, standing in the Outside version of Edward L. Walker's driveway while various heavenly and infernal minions fresh in from headquarters made themselves useful (or at least busy). Some were drawing glittering golden lines in the air or scrying with instruments of black glass. Grasswax gave me a look of quite impressive hatred from his place at the center of it all, then snatched a small, sticky-looking thing out of the air, which I assumed was Hell's version of Walker's guardian angel, and carried it to one side where the two of them proceeded to enjoy a spirited conversation—"spirited" meaning that Grasswax shook the Hell-minion around like someone trying to flick snot off his finger as the minion squealed out its innocence.

"He was here, Master, he was here! We was with him when he died!"

"Then where *is* he?" Grasswax stared at the underling until it started to steam like an abalone on a hot stone.

"We doesn't know! We is confused!"

"Curse you. I'll have to call Scorchscar." The prosecutor produced a handful of fire and held it up before his face and said, "Prosecutor to Prosecutor's Office, put me through to the inquisitor immediately." He scowled at me, his cheek-holes pulsing wetly. The weird thing was,

Grasswax was more scared than he was acting, or at least that's how it seemed to me. Not that I'm an expert on infernal psychology. "By the Master's hot, pimpled arse—I'll be stuck here for hours!" he snarled at me. "This is all your fault somehow, you fucking little cloud-jockey, and I'll make you pay for it. Don't you try to sneak off!"

I turned away with the prosecutor's charming voice still ringing in my ears: I had my own call to make. Just because the house in old Palo Alto was now so full of shining angelic presences that it looked like a Christmas display didn't mean I could assume everybody knew who needed to. I took out my phone, which in its Outside form appeared as a rod of silvery light. A moment later Temuel was in front of me, although nobody else could see him or hear him.

"You're joking, right?" he said when I told him the situation, but the Mule didn't sound quite as dumbfounded as I would have expected. "No? Then I'll get a fixer out there right away." Then the magnitude of it apparently began to set in. "This is bad, you know. This is very, very bad, Doloriel. Hang tight and don't say anything to the Opposition."

"Not even, 'Let go of my balls?' Because I can promise you, Grasswax is squeezing pretty hard at the moment."

"Just do your job." And that was all. He was gone. But if Temuel hadn't known about the missing soul then where had all these heavenly functionaries come from? Not to mention all the nasty little things from the Opposition side? I put the question away for later, because just then a new, extra-shiny Zipper flared beside me and the Mule's fixer appeared.

Another quick note: "Fixer" is actually a sort of job description. They're really called "ministers"—not the priest kind but more like a government minister. You hardly ever see one. You hardly ever *want* to see one. Their job is to quickly remove the "fuck" from "fuck-up", and nobody wants to be involved in one of those situations.

I already was, of course. A really big one, from the looks of it. I had a feeling it was going to be a long time until I saw my apartment again.

The fixer/minister looked a bit like a plague doctor from the seventeenth century, in long white robes and a strange white mask that might have represented a novelty drinking bird or a Winnie-the-Pooh Heffalump. He also may not have had any feet under those robes, but it was hard to see because he kind of glowed down at the bottom. He also moved like someone who knew no hurry.

He spent a long time staring at the car and the corpse, then at last turned to me. *"You Are the Advocate?"* He even talked with audible capitals.

"Yes, Minister."

"Tell Us What You Know."

I did, as concisely as I could, without guesses or assumptions. I had met one of these guys before (that's another story) and knew that the last thing you wanted to do was waste their time. The one I met before had been half a whim away from demoting me all the way to the Bless the Beasts Division, where I'd be watching over depressed field mice, and that case hadn't been anywhere near this serious.

I had just finished my story when another light glimmered in the air, this one dull and smoky-red, and someone else stepped through—or some several, to be precise: a woman and two men, although all those terms fall very far short, descriptively speaking. My friend Sweetheart is about the size of an Alaskan bear but these two guys could have been his bigger brothers. Both had necks wider than my chest and sported the dead gray skin common among the less pain-sensitive minions of Hell, as well as facial expressions that suggested a hammer-blow on the head would barely get their attention. In short, they had the look of argument-winners—the "you and what army?" kind of arguments.

The female demon, though, was something else. I don't think I'd ever seen anything like her outside of a few fetish magazines (professional research only, of course). She was tiny, for one thing, especially standing between those two bonebreakers, and she was also astonishingly lovely by any normal standard, with straight white-blonde hair, skin as pale as milk, and long, stockinged legs prominently displayed by a schoolgirl miniskirt. She looked like Wonderland's Alice as dressed for success by a committee of manga-reading Japanese businessmen. I didn't expect to see one of the Opposition's heavy hitters looking so mainstream. Usually they're big on horns and fangs and weird, crusty skin.

As she got closer she only got more gorgeous, although now it was plain that the irises of her eyes were the color of . . . well, of something really red. (I was going to say "blood" but that's a bit of a cliché already, isn't it? But that's certainly what color they were—like big shiny drops of the stuff.)

"What piece of shit are you handing me this time, Grasswax?" she asked as she reached us. She might have had the trace of an older accent, but mostly she sounded like Hayley Mills, one of those sweet, super-plummy upper class English voices—"Oh, Mummy, I've lost my pony and I'm ever so weepy about it!" But Grasswax positively flinched when he saw her. Oh, my goodness yes, she was cute, but she was also the scariest thing I'd run into lately, that was for sure. This she-thing was one of the nobility of Hell, after all, so she had to be quite a few notches above me on even the most generous comparative organization chart.

The fixer from our side gave her a little nod of respect. "Countess."

She barely glanced back at him. "Minister."

She walked past me as if I wasn't there and pulled Grasswax aside. From the look on his face I guessed she wasn't going to be asking him the whereabouts of a good coffee bar. I was still staring as she led him away, so much so that the fixer had to make a throat-clearing noise.

"Angel Doloriel?"

It was hard to turn away from her, even when the competition was an impatient, high-ranking angel. The other side's fixer was a small, slender woman, but something about the way she walked was mesmerizing. You know the chesty way some small dogs have that shows they think they're really big dogs? The Countess, whoever and whatever she was, might dress like a schoolgirl but she walked like a very confident stripper.

No, classier. Like a prima ballerina. Yeah, a ballerina from Hell.

"Sorry, Minister. I was . . . thinking."

"I Hope I'm Not Taking Too Much Of Your Valuable Time, Doloriel." Now that I could see him closer up it became clear that the minister wasn't exactly normal himself. For one thing, unlike most higher angels, the fixer had eyes, but they were almost entirely white except for a pinprick of black at the center, which, with the mask, made it a little hard to tell where he was looking. The other thing was that he had at least six or seven fingers on each white-gloved hand. I couldn't help wondering what *that* was about.

"Not at all. Sorry." I turned my back on the prosecutor and his boss so I could concentrate on my superior. The beautiful little Countess was a demon, I reminded myself—a powerful one. Infernal nobility can appear in any form they choose to, but what was inside that yummy exterior was certain to be extremely ugly. More important, personal experience told me that each and every one of Hell's residents would tear me into little pieces if I let my guard down. No matter what they looked like, they were all monsters of corruption. "What can I tell you, Minister?"

"Repeat Once More All That Happened From The Moment You Received The Call," he demanded.

Under his strangely unemotional gaze I went back over everything I could remember. I didn't say anything about Sam and his trainee, but I did mention I had seen Grasswax just the day before on another case.

"And You Are Certain You Arrived Here Before The Prosecutor Did?" The beak of his mask swung toward me as if sniffing for truthfulness. *"Quite Certain?"*

"You don't think Grasswax would actually do something that crazy, do you?" I wondered whether I should mention again how angry the prosecutor had seemed to be about the missing soul. Did Grasswax have a guilty conscience? "How? How would he even have pulled it off?"

"We Couldn't Say." The minister made a sniffing, offended noise. *"But If You Are Saying He Couldn't Possibly Have Managed It, Then Your Role In The Matter Becomes Even More Significant."*

Oh, no. No way I was going to get rolled up for something I didn't do. "I'm not saying any such thing, Minister. I had nothing to do with any of it. I was as surprised as you are."

"Really? Then You Might Be Aware We Are Not Particularly Surprised." He shook his snouted head, looking more than ever like a very creepy child's imaginary friend. *"We Feared It Might Come To This."*

I had no idea what he meant and told him so.

"We Have Heard Enough From You To Make Our Report, Angel Doloriel," was all he said. *"You May Go. God Loves You."*

Most of the regulars had drifted into The Compasses by the time I made it back, although there was still no sign of Sam or his sidekick. I had stopped at Morton's Café to eat an early dinner and watch the shadows lengthen across downtown as the sun stopped trying to light the darker bits of San Judas and eventually gave up and went to bed. Now the lights of downtown and the big black empty of the harbor filled the windows.

"Are you all right?" Monica asked when she saw me. "I was worried about you." She had sobered up a bit, so maybe she was telling the truth. "Was that guy's soul really *missing*?"

"You heard about it already?"

"Of course we did. Somebody called in a minister and *that* never stays secret long. Alice at the office said everybody in the city's talking about it!" Which meant everybody in the city with wings and horns, anyway, although the Walker suicide was probably going to draw quite a bit of earthly attention as well. "What was it like?"

I shrugged. "What was it like? Like nothing. They pulled out the corpse but the important part of the guy just wasn't there."

"Oooh." Monica made a face of sympathetic worry. "How freaky!"

Jimmy the Table and Sweetheart and some of the others made their way over. The one good side of the whole nasty mess was that for at least one night I didn't have to pay for my own drinks.

"Do you think the Other Side did it?" Monica asked. "Are they trying to provoke something?"

"Jeez, how should I know? They sent in one of their own fixers quick enough. Female, called the Countess?"

Jimmy the Table let out a shrill laugh. "I heard about that bitch! They said she wore a necklace of human balls to the company Christmas party!"

"I don't think the Opposition celebrates Christmas, darling," Sweetheart gently told him.

"Some party, then—don't matter." Jimmy was very pleased to be the one with information. "Anyway, if they put *her* in charge, that's some serious shit. You ask anyone who knows—the Countess is a definite bad ass. You remember Zippy? Zippoo-whatever?"

"Zepuriel," said Sweetheart. "The one with the cute bottom?"

"Whatever," said Jimmy, refusing for once to be baited. "Why do you think he transferred out of the advocates back to Painting Rainbows Division or wherever he wound up? He met up with her on a job, and she ripped him up so bad he never got over it."

"You are entirely full of shit," said Walter Sanders from behind his beer in the corner. "Never happened."

"Screw you, I was there!" said Jimmy, and half a minute later they had forgotten all about the rest of us and were happily insulting each other in a way that an outsider would think was deadly serious. Some combination of the Table, Walter Sanders, and young Elvis were always arguing about some stupid thing, but I didn't mind. You spend a lot of time passing time when you've got Eternity on the clock.

"I've heard of her," Monica told me when the rest of the Whole Sick Choir had finally eddied away. "Jimmy's right about one thing—everything I've heard about that bitch is bad news."

"Doesn't matter to me," I said. Actually, I couldn't stop thinking about Hell's fixer and her slender pale legs and fairy-tale face. Even for the most confirmed Hell-haters among us heavenly sorts, it's hard to remember sometimes what's underneath the exterior if the bodywork is good enough. Of course, I wasn't stupid enough to admit that to Monica. "I'm done with it. Filed my report with the minister and another one with the Mule. And if this missing-soul thing is real, it's way out of our league, anyway. I doubt any of us will ever hear about it again."

It's amazing the stupid things I say sometimes. I mean, you could start an entire branch of scientific research about the stuff I say that gets proved wrong while I'm still busy saying it. Because less than an hour later, Sam and young Clarence walked in, which at the time I thought was a very good thing, because Monica and I were sharing a table and I was having trouble remembering why we stopped doing those things we used to do together. Yes, I'd had a few. Anyway, Sam and his pup angel walked in, and I took one look at young Clarence and knew I didn't want to hear it. He had that excited-rookie look on his face—the kind of thing that never brings anyone any good. At the cheap end it only steals a few priceless hours of your immortal life, but the cost can and often does go much higher.

"You remember Grasswax the prosecutor?" Clarence asked.

"Just saw him a few hours ago. In fact, I see more of him these days than I do you guys. What of it?"

Clarence's eyes were big. "He's dead."

I stared at him and wondered if I had ever been that new. "Nobody dies, kid. At least nobody like us. You mean his body got killed?"

The rookie blushed. "I guess so."

Like our side, the bad guys hand out mortal forms to those who do their earthly work; if lost to accident or actual malice those bodies can be replaced. But trust me—getting killed can still be extremely unpleasant, even when you don't permanently die from it. I turned back to Sam, who seemed unusually grim. "I just saw the red bastard an hour or two ago. Is this real?"

"Real and real bad," Sam said, nodding. "And real messy, apparently—they found him at the scene of that last death, the weird one with the vanishing soul everyone's losing their shit about. We just got interrogated by a minister because we won that Martino case against him yesterday."

Which explained where Sam and the rookie had been, at least for the later part of the day. I realized I still hadn't told Sam what Temuel had said about the kid, but I didn't want to get distracted now. "Oh, man," I said, "Grasswax got killed at the Walker house? It must have happened right after I left."

"Then I'm surprised you haven't been questioned about it yet, actually." Sam's tone was a little odd, but I put it down to the circumstances. Not that one of the Opposition getting rubbed out was unheard of, but it wasn't common, and on top of the inexplicable case of Edward Lynes Walker, it had clearly been a day for strange stuff.

"I already got put through the mill on the suicide guy, so maybe they don't need . . ." was all I had time to say before I felt a presence in my head, a dazzle of power and a sounding ring like trumpets.

Angel Doloriel, You Are Summoned, it said. *Come With All Haste.*

Come where? Why, back to the Walker house in Palo Alto. Scene of the crime.

In fact, the scene of both crimes, now that I thought about it.

four
the bloody net

I LIKED MY situation less and less by the moment—in fact, the whole thing stank. Why was I being called back to the Walker house? If my bosses wanted to quiz me beyond what the fixer/minister had already done, why not just summon me to Heaven? Temuel had called me in for nothing more important than chatting about young Clarence, so something like *this* obviously rated a visit to the House.

Another question that was still itching me: Who had called in the shock troops so quickly? As soon as Edward Walker's soul turned up missing, worker bees from both sides had descended on the scene before either Grasswax or I could check in with our bosses—or at least that was how it had looked. My team and the Opposition are both very into procedure, as I had learned many times to my sorrow. What happened this time?

And to muddy the waters even further, only hours later Grasswax was dead and I was apparently wanted back on the scene for more questioning but I was the one who had questions that needed answering. Who had bothered to kill Grasswax's mortal form? It's not like it would shut him up about anything—earthbound employees of both sides wound up dead all the time. I've been there myself. We get debriefed about what happened and then decanted into another body.

Altogether, the affair had more loose ends than Swinger's Night in a bucket of worms, so I had a lot to think about as I skittered down the Bayshore through a canyon of glowing high-rise windows to the Palo

Alto district, then made my way along the tree-lined streets until I was back in front of the Walker residence.

I parked as close to the house as I could. The street was still full of police vehicles and news trucks even though the death had happened this morning and by now the streetlights had come on. I'd already heard the story on the car radio—"Scientist and Philanthropist Takes His Own Life," was the basic gist, featuring several quotes from Walker's friends and family about how they had no idea he was despondent or even worried, although there were also unsubstantiated rumors that he might have been ill with something serious.

Anyway, it wasn't the real-world version of the Walker place that I wanted (although I was beginning to have a few questions about that as well). I opened a Zipper and the few police technicians still lingering around the open garage tented with white plastic froze into immobility as I stepped Outside, but I scarcely noticed because what I stepped into on the far side of the Zipper was your basic hive of activity. Opposition minions were everywhere, dozens of types, some indistinguishable from deformed humans, others so unpleasantly different I couldn't look at them for very long.

Only one member of our team was waiting for me there, but he was enough all by himself. I think it was the same fixer as before—certainly the bizarre plague mask seemed the same— but it's hard to tell with the higher angels since they can manifest in all kinds of ways. Outward appearances only seem to be important to earthbound types like me, staggering around in meat bodies all the time, living mostly in three dimensions.

Anyway, the minister was waiting for me and he didn't stand on ceremony, either. I scarcely had time to get both my feet on the Outside ground before he started asking me questions. The first were the obvious ones, many of which I'd already answered for him—what had happened here earlier today, what had I seen, what had Grasswax said, and so on. But then he started asking me what happened after I left him, and about The Compasses crew, especially Sam and his new pup, Clarence, all of which made me a bit uncomfy. I answered everything as honestly as I could, of course: I don't even know if it's possible to lie to a minister at work, and I certainly wouldn't try it under any remotely normal circumstances.

When the fixer had grilled me for what seemed like most of an hour he suddenly clammed up, then after a pause long enough that it seemed he might be conferring with someone else I couldn't see, he said, *"Come With Us."*

He led me along the side of the house, me walking (even Outside it's hard to make a human body do anything but act like a normal body) and him sort of gliding in front of me like an upright floor polisher with no one holding the handle.

"What We Are About To Do Is Irregular, Angel Doloriel, But So Are The Circumstances," he said. *"Remember, You Will Give No Answer Until We Indicate You May Do So."* I had no idea what he was talking about since he'd already asked me dozens of questions. Then we stepped into the Outside version of the Walker back yard, and I got the shock of my afterlife. I definitely owed Clarence an apology.

See, normally what I'd told him was right—people like us don't get killed, only our earthly bodies do; the Opposition is just as good as we are at plugging the disembodied soul into a new sack of meat, then voilà! Instant resurrection! Like I said, I've been through it a few times myself, leaving a corpse behind each time. And here was Grasswax's mortal body, the earthly flesh-and-blood version of him, lying beside the pool in a puddle of chlorinated water, covered with a police blanket. And normally that would have been all—just a defunct carcass, and the real Grasswax's slimy but immortal soul off to the Opposition's Tijuana-style tuck and roll body shop. But as I stood looking through the frame of a little ivy-covered arbor in Edward Walker's backyard, I could also see the Other Side version of Grasswax—the *real* Grasswax, just like it's the real Doloriel talking to you now—and what had happened to him was a lot less pretty than just drowning in a suburban pool. In fact, it was disgusting and horrifying.

The ancient Norsemen used to have a punishment for traitors called the Blood Eagle, where they chopped through a guy's back ribs and pulled his lungs out through the holes to make bloody wings. That would have been an unpleasant way to go, but the bullyboys of Hell had an even better method they called the Bloody Net. I won't go into details, but it has to do with carefully pulling out the victim's nerve bundles and blood vessels with sharp tools—while he's still alive, of course—then hanging him up by that network of shrieking tissue and dumping nasty little things called Nerve Chewers on him to gnaw on the exposed bits until the lucky fellow finally expires. I'd heard of it, but I have to admit I never dreamed it was real. I also don't understand how you do that to someone's supposedly immortal form, but damn me if these guys hadn't managed.

The real Grasswax had been mostly reduced to fibers strung between two trees at opposite ends of the yard, a sagging, shiny red hammock. What was left of the most important bits—and remember, this was the *real* Grasswax, the Outside Grasswax—still hung there, and I will never forget the expression on the remains of his face. I had never felt sorry for a minion of Hell before, but I did then. Remember, there's no time Outside— it might have taken him days or even weeks to die.

"Shit," I said quietly. The minster was standing behind me, staring imperturbably at the ghastly mess as though he saw worse all the time. Maybe he did, and if so, I was definitely scratching "fixer" off my list of potential career moves.

"Remember What We Told You," the angelic thing with the white mask told me. *"Answer Each Question Only After We Give Permission."*

I barely registered what he was saying because at that moment something very tall and unpleasant tottered out of the Walker house. It was dull, shiny black all over, like a beetle's shell, and trailed sticky black fibers from every limb. It had quite a few limbs. Its eyes looked like clots of blood illuminated from inside. I was assuming they were eyes, because they were side by side in the lump on the top of its body. Basically, it was altogether ghastly, the more so because every now and then it moved in an almost human way. Almost.

"Thizzz izzz the advoc-c-c-cate Doloriel?" it asked. If you recorded a shrieking chain saw, and then slowed it down until it sounded like it was playing through syrup, you'd have the voice, pretty much. The buzzing got into my bones and guts; just standing next to it made my stomach try to climb up my esophagus and flee the vicinity—I mean, it felt *bad*. This was no ordinary employee of Hell.

"Yes, Chancellor." The minister said it politely, but I don't think he liked being outranked by the Opposition. *"We Are Pleased To Cooperate In Your Investigation. You May Ask Your Questions."* The minister's voice floated into my thoughts. *"This is Chancellor Urgulap of the Second Hierarchy. He is investigating the murder of Prosecutor Grasswax. We are extending him a professional courtesy."*

I don't remember much of what the buzzing thing asked me, to be honest—just standing in front of it was one of the most unpleasant things I'd ever experienced (and I've seen a lot of nasty). Most of the questions seemed fairly ordinary, though, not that different from what the minister had just asked me. I looked to the fixer each time before I answered, and each time he gave me a little mental nudge that meant, "Yes, you may." It was only after one question that he seemed reluctant to give his permission.

"And have you zzzzzpok-k-ken to any of your masterzzz or comradzzz about thizz matter?"

The heavenly minister hesitated at this one—I could feel it. He relented a moment later, but now I was a little spooked. I didn't want to drop anyone else into danger, certainly not Sam or even his rookie tagalong. "Not really. Just my supervisor, Temuel." After all, it would have been weird if I *hadn't* discussed it with the Mule, and it sure wasn't my job to protect middle management.

The chancellor stared at me with those squashed neon berries as if sensing my incomplete honesty. At last it turned and limped away. It must have opened a Zipper but I never saw it. One moment the Chancellor was there, a thing like a giant, melted bug standing upright on the patio beside the pool, then it was just gone. I can't begin to describe the physical relief that came with its absence.

"Thank You For Your Assistance, Angel Doloriel," the masked fixer said. *"As You See, We Are Cooperating With The Opposition In All Ways Possible In This Matter. If Anyone Else Contacts You About This, Or In Any Way Shows Inappropriate Interest, You Will Immediately Alert Us. God Loves You. You May Go."*

And go I did. After all, Grasswax's hideously mangled form was still hanging between the trees, the sightless eyes watching me with what seemed like disappointment.

Don't know what you were expecting from me, Brother Demon, I thought as I stepped back into the world of time. *I don't want anything to do with the heavy hitters, either my side's or yours.*

Before I got to the Walker house I had been pretty certain I would drop by The Compasses on my way back, but now I felt unsettled right down to the soles of my feet, and I just wanted to go home and bathe myself in holy water. Since I didn't have any holy water, vodka would have to serve, and the bath would have to be on the inside rather than the outside. I kept a bottle of 42 Below in the freezer for just these kinds of spiritual emergencies.

* * *

Monica had left a message on my phone wanting to know how things had gone, and I also had a reminder from Sam that we were getting together after work tomorrow for our monthly dinner (an old custom of ours I'll tell you about another time) but I didn't really want to talk to anyone. I wanted to get quickly and quietly blotto because I felt like a garage full of car alarms right after a major earthquake.

When I got through the door of my apartment I pulled out the vodka, cracked the cap, then poured myself a couple of fingers in a glass and put on some Miles as thinking music. As "So What" began to curl around my living room like cigarette smoke I took a fiercely cold swallow and tried to make sense out of everything that had happened in the last day, from the unprecedented absence of Edward Walker's soul to the sudden passing of Prosecutor Grasswax in the grisliest fashion imaginable.

My old boss Leo used to say that when you're working for any gigantic and corrupt bureaucracy, whether it's the British East India Company, the Politburo, or the NCAA, the first lesson is this: Don't wait to find out exactly how they're going to screw you before you start protecting yourself—get to work when you spot the first signs of trouble. This whole Walker thing was full of holes, and from long experience I felt sure more weird things were going to be crawling out of those holes very soon.

In fact this particular little clusterfuck, with its missing souls and dead demon-prosecutors, had all the warning signs of one of the worst snafus in recent memory, and if I wasn't smack in the middle of it I was close enough to feel the heat most unpleasantly. It was time to start the counter-offensive—if I could do so without making things worse for myself, that is.

I poured myself another glass of numbness and thought about where to start.

About an hour later I noticed I had finished my third drink but had never poured myself a fourth. I got up to rectify that, noted that Miles had gone quiet, and put on some Robert Johnson. "Me and the Devil Blues." Seemed like an appropriate night for Mr. Johnson and his crossroads bargain.

Early this mornin', when you knocked upon my door
Early this mornin', ooh, when you knocked upon my door

And I said, "Hello, Satan, I believe it's time to go."

Even in a body that wasn't one hundred percent my own, I couldn't repress a shiver. It looked like I'd be doing a lot of things I wouldn't much like in the next few days, including having a conversation with my best friend Sam about why he wasn't being entirely honest with me. Alice in the office had said when she gave me the case that Edward Walker was supposed to be Sam's client, and if our situations had been reversed I certainly would have explained to *my* old buddy by now why I missed taking a client that landed him deep in the shit.

The more I thought about it, the more I realized I needed more information about everything—about dead Mr. Walker, even about Grasswax. But information about Hell's labor force wasn't easy to come by through regular channels. I was going to have to pay a visit to Fatback.

five

pig man

ORDINARY WORK kept me busy much of the next day. Alice sent me a downtown client, a hit and run on the 84 over by Shell Mound Road. It was pretty much a slam dunk case—the victim was a twelve-year-old school kid crossing the intersection on the way home for lunch. The prosecutor, a new guy named Weepslug took one look at the scene and rolled his eye in disgust. (He only had one, more or less in the middle.) In fact it would all have been over in a very short time indeed—this wasn't the kind of kid hiding any ugly secrets—but the rules about children are very, very strict, and we had to go through every formality. By the time the judge ruled, and I could finally leave the pathetic scene behind—the whole time we were arguing the case the kid's twisted bicycle and one shoe were still lying in the middle of the road—my day was pretty much shot. Even winning the case wasn't going to wipe away the memories of that child crying when he realized he wasn't going home to his mom and dad.

Sometimes I hate what I do.

At one point, while the judge was questioning the deceased—they do that when it's a minor—Weepslug turned to me and said, "You heard about Grasswax?"

I wondered if he really didn't know. "Oh, yeah, I heard."

"He was a bastard, but trust me, nobody deserves that."

"I was under the impression you guys thought being a bastard was good."

He gave me a strange look. For a demon I kind of liked him—his single, bleary eye had a bemused expression, and although he was almost twice my height he didn't use that to intimidate. Not that I trusted him an inch, of course. "There's good bad and then there's *bad* bad," he said. "G-Wax made some enemies on both sides."

"You think somebody on *my* side of the scrimmage line might have done this?" This was a new idea. It wasn't in character for our side, but that could be exactly how someone wanted it to seem. Still, the Bloody Net . . . !

The prosecutor's forehead wrinkled in distress; it made his face look like someone had sat on a Christmas ham. "I'm not saying anything," Weepslug declared, quick and loud. "I don't know anything."

"Neither do I," I assured him. "There's no greater bliss than ignorance."

"Oh, look!" yelled Sweetheart when I walked into The Compasses just before six, "It's Heaven's Most Wanted!"

"Yeah, cute, very cute."

Sam was at the bar with a ginger ale and a *San Judas Courier* spread out across the counter. Newspapers were another way my buddy liked to cultivate his old-school act. "Check it out," he said as I approached. "His working name was Darko Grazuvac."

It took me a moment. "Grasswax? He got an obituary?"

"Obituary, hell—he got an above-the-fold story. After all, he did just turn up drowned at the scene of a headline suicide. What did you expect?"

This was making me more and more uneasy. Neither our side nor the Opposition liked publicity, especially not this kind—having reporters digging into the backgrounds of people whose pasts were largely invented is never a good thing for either of us. "So, why would anyone bump him off right there at the Walker guy's house?"

Sam shrugged and downed his ginger ale. "Sending a message? Dunno. Let's go eat."

You could get a meal of sorts at The Compasses but it wasn't the kind of thing you wanted to do if you were going to keep living in the same body afterward, so we wandered across Beeger Square to Boxer Rebellion, my favorite Chinese place. It's small and unpretentious, and for a Chinese restaurant (which tend to the businesslike over the sentimental in my experience) also quite friendly.

Normally having a pair of chopsticks in my fist and a plate of their sesame seed mutton in front of me is enough to convince me that the Highest is on His throne and all's right with the world, but tonight it wasn't working.

"So what's going on?" I asked Sam. "Where were you yesterday? Why did I get what should have been your client, and how come you didn't say anything about it when I saw you?"

He swirled his tea around in his cup before drinking it down. "You mean the Walker thing? Damned if I know, old buddy. Why you got it, I mean. Why I *didn't* get it—well, that was the kid's fault."

"Clarence? That kid?"

Sam thinks chopsticks are for poseurs. He took a big spoonful of pork and *suan cai* stew and looked at it like he wasn't certain what it was, even though he orders the same thing every time. "Yeah. He had me back and forth from Outside to Inside all day, asking me to show him how different things worked. When the call came down we had just stepped through a Zipper because he wanted to watch to see if my appearance changed Outside."

"Curious little bastard. But you're supposed to be training him, not letting him dictate your schedule." I was still pissed off. Not that I wanted all this crap landing on Sam, but I sure as hell hadn't wanted it on me, either.

"Yeah, but that wasn't the problem. When the call came, I got it, but I couldn't answer it. And when I tried to step back Inside to see if that helped, I couldn't make the Zipper work. Lasted what felt like about ten minutes and by then the call had rolled over—I didn't know it went to you, though." He shrugged. "Pretty weird, huh?"

"Damn weird. Have you mentioned that to anyone?"

"Anyone? Everyone! You forget, I had to talk to the fixer about everything that happened that day. That's all I know—it wasn't like one of the fixers from the House was going to tell me what had been going on with the Zippers. But that's not what's *really* bugging me." He shook his big head. Sam looks about twenty years older than his body's supposed to look. Part of it is just the way he moves, that kind of unhurried, good-old-boy thing. He talks the same way, and it can drive you crazy. Now he made me wait while he took two more spoonfuls of soup and all but sent them out to the forensic lab for tests, swirling the cabbage around in his mouth for what seemed like minutes. (Just because we've been friends for years doesn't mean I never think about murdering him.) "It was too convenient, the way it all happened," he finally said. "If the kid hadn't wanted me to be there, I wouldn't have been Outside when it all went down—wouldn't have been stuck. No, there's definitely something unusual going on with our young Clarence," he finally said.

"Well, shit, no kidding. I already knew that." I told him about the odd conversation I'd had with the Mule, how he'd asked me to keep an eye on the new boy.

Sam nodded slowly. "Haraheliel. That's his angel name, right? You ever heard of him before?"

"Nope. But someone might have. He claims he was in Records—Filing, he says. Maybe we should see if anyone else remembers him."

"I could do that," Sam told me, slurping up a little broth. "But you'd have to do me a favor and take him off my hands for a couple of days. I can't get anything done with him hanging around."

"Then maybe I should be the one to do the investigating."

Sam frowned. "Look, B, the kid likes you. He's been asking about you, so it'd be a natural, and I got a buddy or two working in the Records Halls that I know from the old days. They should have some ideas how the kid wound up here."

I thought about it. Sam did know a lot of people, but our fellow advocate Walter Sanders knew people in Records, too so I could just as easily ask him. But when a friend asks a favor . . . "Okay. But I can't take him off you 'til the day after tomorrow. I'm going to be too busy before that."

"Doing what?"

"Looking into some things of my own. I'll fill you in if anything interesting comes up."

Sam considered, then lifted his teacup. It took me a moment, but at last I caught on and raised my beer bottle to clink against the delicate porcelain. "Confusion to our enemies!" he said, our familiar toast.

"Amen to that," said I.

Once upon a time most of San Judas was agricultural land—numberless small farms, orchards, you name it. Then the city began to grow, and everything that wasn't city gradually got pushed farther and farther away, until nowadays you can't find much that resembles real agriculture except backyard wineries and people growing pot in their garages. But there were still a few exceptions, and after I said goodbye to Sam I retrieved my car from the handicapped parking space (yes, angels cheat sometimes, but come on, we're doing God's work!) and went back to my apartment to kill some time. A little before eleven I got back behind the wheel and headed up into the hills in search of one particular farm.

It wouldn't be easy to find Casa de Maldición in the daytime, but since I always go there at night it's usually damn near impossible. It's in the hills off the old Alpine Road, past Skyline and down a long winding rural road in a particularly empty section of unincorporated county. In general it's the kind of place that rich people and hermits live, and neither of those care much about sidewalks—they attract riffraff—or streetlights (which, presumably, draw more of the same). Casa M. itself is on a hill up a little spur road off the winding one. In the deep darkness of the evening, well beyond city lights, it would have been invisible to most people, but I'd been here before and had the windows rolled down. The stench let me know when I was close.

Ever smelled a pig farm, even a small one? Honestly, if you haven't, don't bother. There are many things in life not worth experiencing if you don't need to—amputation, crab lice—and porcine husbandry is one of them. Trust me.

I often wondered whether Fatback surrounded himself with pigs for company or protection. Certainly the presence of several dozen swine on his property meant that only the very determined (or the completely nostril-deaf) ever ventured up the wandering track to the rather nice house at the top. In the darkness I could just make out the smaller (but still good-sized) pig barn off to one side and hear the gentle grunting of its occupants.

The old man named Javier opened the door. He'd pretty much been born working for Fatback's family—his father and grandfather had served before him. He never seemed to get much older between the times I saw him, but he sure as hell wasn't getting any younger either. He looked like something you would find lying in the desert and then waste half an hour trying to decide what it used to be.

He blinked, even though I was the one standing in the dark and what little light there was came from his side of the doorway. "Hello, Mr. Dollar," he said at last. "Long time, good to see you. If you come to talk to Mr. George, he not quite ready yet."

"That's okay. I don't have much time so just take me in to him, and I'll wait."

Javier didn't really like to do it—he still hung onto some vestige of Old-World pride in his employer and didn't like to display him at less than his best—but he knew me and knew who my bosses were, so he nodded and beckoned me to follow him into the house. As we went past the kitchen I saw a half-eaten plate of rice and beans and realized I'd interrupted the caretaker's dinner. A small television on the counter was showing some Mexican game show.

We walked through the house and out the back. He pointed to the big barn, which stood by itself about ten yards away down the hill, connected to the main house by a long stairway. I nodded and thanked him. He went back to his meal.

The smell, which was eye-watering everywhere else on the property, rolled out of the barn door like a full scale chemical weapons attack, so that for a moment I couldn't even go inside, but had to stand there and try to fan a hole in it with my hand. It didn't work—it never did—but at last I was able to deal with it enough to walk inside.

Most of the barn was taken up with a central pen about twenty by thirty feet or so, with a chest-high rail and a bottom about a foot or so deep in stinking mud—and I mean stinking. At one end of the enclosure, dim and pale in the flickering overhead light, crouched a huge, naked bald man smeared with mud and worse. He looked up at me and his squinting eyes gleamed.

"Hello, George," I said. Nobody called him Fatback to his face—it wasn't polite. Not that he understood me at the moment, anyway.

He let out a squeal of rage at the sound of my voice and hurtled across the pen on his hands and knees, splashing mud and shit and pig slops everywhere, but slipped and skidded head first into the barrier with a grunt of pain and frustration. He sank back in the muck and sat looking at me sullenly, blood now trickling from a cut on his forehead. I sighed and checked my watch; 11:52. Still eight minutes to go.

I moved safely out of splashing range and watched him as the time ticked away. He watched me back. It was unpleasant, being stared at by those narrow eyes. There wasn't anything human in them as far as I could see, but there was an awful lot of murderous anger. I was glad old Javier seemed to keep the pen in good repair.

Casa de Maldición is Spanish for "House of the Curse," but what had happened to George was worse than that. The child of an old Californio family (the Spanish-speaking folks who owned everything before the gringos showed up) George Noceda had inherited not just a lot of family property in the Pulgas Ridge area but the family's major obligation as well, which happened to be a debt to the dark powers. (Nowadays we call 'em by more respectable names, like "the Opposition," but it's still the same old firm.) In return for unnatural prosperity for the family, for several hundred years, every oldest male child of the Noceda line had been were-hogs, doomed each night to become a ravening beast between the hours of midnight and sunup. All through the nineteenth and twentieth centuries the family did their best to keep the suffering male heir locked up at night. Mistakes were made (and more than a few local monster legends had been started because of those mistakes) but by and large the family had come to accept the price of the bargain some ancestor had made in return for their good fortune in all other matters.

Then along came George. A creature of the late twentieth century, he had never doubted in the power of dark magic—after all, he had started to smell powerfully of chitterlings when most boys were just growing their first scraggly mustaches, and had changed for the first time soon thereafter. But like most of the people of this modern age, he didn't think *he* should have to take the fall for something his great-great-great grandparents had done. So he made a deal with the Opposition: he would sacrifice most of the family fortune, land, wealth, and prestige, and in return Hell's minions promised they would reverse the curse.

Poor George. Like so many others before him, he underestimated what he was dealing with. He got what he wanted, to the letter of his new contract, and the curse was, in fact, reversed. So from then on, each night at twelve, the same thing happened. In fact, it was happening now.

The fat, naked man suddenly fell face down into the filthy mud, bellowing like he was on fire. He began to thrash, sending gouts of stinking slime everywhere. I stepped back to the front door to protect my coat, which wasn't all that expensive but was a favorite. The noise went on as the huddled figure in the muddy pen writhed and changed, grew darker and misshapen, until it had taken on an entirely new form, that of an immense, black, bristle-skinned boar hog.

The hog finally stopped squealing. It rolled over and sat up on its haunches, then turned its beady eyes in my direction.

"That hurts like an unholy bitch," he said. "Every time."

"Nice to see you, George."

He wrinkled his snout. "Oh, I'm sure, Bobby. A treat for all ages." He saw something floating in the muck before him and sucked it up, then began to chew. "Corn cob," he explained when he saw my horrified look. "Fiber. And oh my sweet and precious God do I need it . . . !"

I was getting more information than I wanted, and it would only get worse. George was garrulous in this form—pig's body, man's mind—and usually had no one to talk to but Javier or one of the old man's sons, the only other people who still lived on this shrunken remnant of what had once been a grand seigneurial property. Of course, when he was in his other form, his dawn-to-midnight form of a pig's mind in a man's body, he wasn't much for conversation.

They reversed the curse, you see. Just like they promised. Who do you think invented lawyers in the first place?

"So what brings you up to my neck of the woods, Mr. D?" George asked. "What can I do for you?"

"I need information on a citizen named Edward Lynes Walker and also on Grasswax, infernal prosecutor." Fatback was the only outsider I could safely approach in the current climate. The Opposition had hosed him in a completely legitimate way, but George had never forgiven them, and he made it his life's work to keep a close eye on their dealings. That was why a large portion of what remained of his family's once vast fortune went toward funding a small research agency of which George was the only client. The only other thing in the room beside George's pen was the projection monitor screen he used to view what they sent him, and to troll the net for what he could find himself.

All voice-controlled, of course. He's a pig.

"Sure, I'll see what I can find for you, Mr. D." He cleared his throat and said, "*Radiant*." At the code word the screen flicked on, bathing the room in cool light. "Hey, you want to do me a favor while I'm starting the search? Get that rake and scratch my back."

I did what he asked, holding my breath. George isn't a bad guy, and it's not his fault he smells like Death's diaper.

"Hijole!" he said as the latest gleanings scrolled past. "This Grasswax thing is some crazy shit! Does it have anything to do with the Walker death?"

"I doubt it." I didn't want to tell him anything he didn't need to know, not because I didn't trust him—his hatred of the Opposition was genuine—but because I didn't know exactly what I was dealing with. "I don't know, maybe."

"Well, there's a ton of stuff about both of them flying around. It'll take me a while to pull it together and make sense of it. How do you want it, electronic or hard copy?"

"Electronic. And use my private email address, will you?" I didn't want it going through Alice, who didn't even know what the word "private" meant. "Oh, and there's one other thing. I need to get in touch with someone from the Opposition."

Fatback turned sour little piggy eyes on me. "Forget it. I'm not doing that for you or anyone else, Mr. D. We've always got along well, you and I, but if you want a go-between, find someone else."

"I'm not asking you to set up a meeting, George, just to tell me where I can find a particular member of the other side. I'll do the rest." Now that I was about to say it, the whole thing seemed ludicrous—suicidal, even—but I plunged ahead anyway. "I need to track down a fixer called 'Countess', a big shot. I don't know the rest of her name." I gave him a quick description of her appearance, at least the time I'd seen her, and told him what little I knew, including that she'd been brought in to clean up after the Walker mess.

"So you *are* tangled up in the Grasswax thing," George said cheerfully. "Well, any dead devil is a reason to celebrate as far as I'm concerned. Go tell Javier I'm hungry, and I'll see what I can find out about her."

Javier was putting the remains of his own dinner into the kitchen garbage can. When I told him what his boss wanted he lifted out the liner bag and trundled the whole mess out to the pig barn. I decided I didn't need to watch Fatback getting fed, so I stayed in the kitchen listening idly to Spanish chatter on the television for a while, then when that got boring, I stepped out onto the back porch and was serenaded by the other pigs snorting sleepily in their own barn a short distance down the slope.

Javier finally came back. "He ready for you now, Mr. Dollar."

"I think I've got what you need," George told me when I approached his pen. He was looking up at the screen on the wall and a whole column of addresses, ears twitching. "I can't find an address or any hint of home turf for her. The bad guys move around more than you guys do. But I've got something that might work just as well. Try a place called The Water Hole on the Camino Real by the university's north gates."

"Really? The Water Hole?" I knew of the place and to be honest it seemed a little lightweight for a heavy hitter like the Countess.

"Yeah, really—at least if it's the Countess of Cold Hands you're talking about." He showed me a blurry image that looked like it had been shot from concealment without a sufficient lens, but even so it was impossible to mistake that small, pale, extremely alluring form.

"Yep. That's her. But The Water Hole? I thought it was a student place."

"Whatever. It's the only spot I've managed to find a sighting of her that you also might have a chance of getting out of."

"Don't you mean 'into'"?

"Oh, I doubt you'll have any problems getting *in*, Bobby." His snout curled in that sour little smile again.

"Cute."

"That's me. I'll send you the rest of the stuff when it's ready."

"Thanks, George. Don't forget to bill me."

"No worries there." He grunted and settled down into the mud. "On your way out will you ask Javier to bring me Meredith? I'm feeling the need of a little company."

"Meredith?" I didn't get it. "Who's Meredith?"

"A very, very nice young lady. Of the four-footed variety."

I was glad to hear he'd finally found someone. "A were-hog like you?"

He was silent for a moment, but then he laughed. There are few things odder than hearing a pig laugh in the middle of the night. "No, no, just an ordinary American Landrace sow, but she has a sweet disposition—a certain tenderness—and a lovely shape." His look became stern. "Don't judge me, sir. Don't you dare judge me."

Not judging, I thanked him, and made my way quickly back to my car. I had my windows open all the way down Alpine but didn't get rid of the smell until I reached the bottom of the hills.

six
waking up in trouble

IT WAS still dark outside when my bladder woke me. That's pretty much how it works: use a body, become slave to various unpleasant internal systems. By the way, there are no bathrooms in Heaven, although angels eat and drink there, after a fashion. Which, now that I think of it, is pretty weird.

Generally my earthly bodies are in reasonable working order, thirtyish in appearance but a good bit stronger and more durable than your average human of that age. So the fact that I was trying to find my way to the john in the dark meant one of two things: either my kidneys were failing or I'd had *far* too much to drink the previous night. The way my head felt suggested that it was the latter.

The suspicion was strengthened when I couldn't recognize the bathroom floor under my bare feet. My apartment had cheap tiles, but this was carpeted. Misadventure was confirmed when I got back and realized someone else was in the bed.

"You done crashing around like a fucking rhinoceros?" asked Monica, mush-mouthed with sleep. "Shut up already."

I wanted to ask her what I was doing at her place but I was beginning to remember just enough to guess. I'd got back to The Compasses about half an hour before closing time and had done my best to drink away the smell of pig shit and the memory of Fatback's eyes, both the sad ones in his pig face and the mindless, nasty ones in his human face. At some point Monica had been sitting in a booth drinking with me, and we had been breathing tipsily in each other's faces as we talked. Q.E.D.

That was as much thinking as I could do with a head that felt like a used sweat sock stuffed with wet cement. I crawled in beside Monica, spent a minute getting used to the unfamiliar feeling of a bed with relatively clean sheets, then tumbled back into sleep.

"Wake up, Laughing Boy." Monica was standing at the bedroom window, sipping from a glass of water and looking through the slats of the blinds. She was pretty much naked. I could see just enough of Cedar Street outside to know it was morning, the gray kind, the stay-in-bed kind, but it was more interesting looking at Monica. *If only she wasn't so damn cute,* I thought: "cute" is one of my many, many weaknesses. "The refrigerator's empty, and the only coffee's instant, B." She turned to survey me. "I think you're going to buy me breakfast."

Wasn't much I could say to that except, "Yes, Ma'am." Besides, I really needed the coffee. I swear, you don't understand what slaves humans are to these meat sacks until you've spent some time not wearing one. And like I said, it was nice to look at Monica standing there, her graceful long back and wide hips. She wasn't skinny like the woman on *Friends*, and her curves always looked good on her. Of course, the fact that she was showing me all this after the way our previous relationship had ended meant I needed to be careful. A drunken slip was one thing, but I was very far away from wanting to start all over with her.

"Your phone's been ringing and ringing for over an hour," she said. "Anything going on?"

Research coming in from Fatback, I guessed, but something about her interest didn't feel entirely natural. I wondered if that was jealousy making its way back into the Bobby-and-Monica equation or something else—paranoia on my part? Or was I being too hard on myself, when a certain amount of paranoia was sensible? After all, it had been a pretty interesting week.

"Nothing too interesting," I said as casually as I could, then groaned as I sat up and began hunting around on the floor for some pants. "My skull hurts. Hell, even my hair hurts. How much did we drink?"

She looked at me over one shoulder as she pulled on a clingy sweater. She didn't seem as badly off as I was. In fact, she seemed to be enjoying herself. "Enough to make Chico cry. Where do you want to go? That pancake place still open?"

She said it lightly but my alarms went off. Monica and I used to go to the pancake place on Sunday mornings in the midst of our most domestic phase, when one of us was sleeping at the other one's place most nights of the week. "Nah. This time of the day we'd have to wait half an hour for a table. Let's go to Oyster Bill's."

"Oyster Bill's? Their French toast tastes like cardboard." She frowned. "You're not freaking out on me already, are you, Dollar? One drunken fuck, and you're getting ready to run for the hills again? I just wanted some decent pancakes."

"No, no, that's fine," I said, although not entirely truthfully, "but at Bill's they serve alcohol in the morning, and there's a Pay and Save on the way there." At that moment I needed a handful of aspirin and then a Bloody Mary more than anyone who hadn't recently seen the flensed and unpleasantly disarticulated corpse of one of Hell's prosecutors could possibly understand.

We stretched out our breakfast 'til close to noon. Several hairs-of-the-dog-that-bit-me stabilized my head, and we mostly just read the papers, but the whole thing was beginning to feel kind of creepily comfortable. See, I actually like Monica a lot, but . . . well, nothing more than that. She always seemed to see things in our relationship that were invisible to me. Also, the mathematics of our time together seemed to work out that for every week we had fun together we spent a week later on making each other miserable. I really didn't want to set myself up for that kind of karmic payback. Things were complicated enough.

"So what's going on with you, Bobby?" she asked at one point. "You hardly talked at all last night."

"Is that why you brought me home? To talk?"

She scowled, half in jest. "Don't be that way. It was nice and you thought so too. I'm just worried about you. You seemed . . . I don't know, kind of freaky. About Grasswax and that Walker guy and everything."

The last thing I wanted to do was talk about any of that. At best it meant she was feeling protective of me again, and at worst . . . well, I didn't know what that might mean, but it bothered me that she was so interested in my recent work history. Paranoia can be caution by another name, especially when you live in the world of the unlikely full-time, the way I do.

Feeling this twitch of old habits returning was actually beginning to worry me a bit—I didn't want to become that guy again. "It's just the same old shit with some new twists," I told her as I called for the check. "I gotta book, I've got some stuff to do. Take your time. Finish your coffee."

"You're going?" She gave me a wistful smile. "Okay. It was fun. Like old times."

"Definitely." I didn't know what else to do so I bent and kissed her—on the mouth but promising nothing. "I'll probably see you tonight. At The Compasses, I mean."

"Oh, yeah," she said. "At The Compasses." I could feel her watching my back as I went out. On a hunch I waited half a minute, then doubled back past the front window at a different angle. She had her phone out and was talking, her face serious. Didn't prove anything, of course, but it didn't make me feel any better, either. And now I was *definitely* starting to feel like that guy again, the trust-nobody guy. It's not a nice way to feel, which is one major reason I gave it up.

It was a warm day for so early in the year and the waterfront was covered with downtown workers brown-bagging or just enjoying the bay breezes and watching the boats. With the return of brain-cell function I remembered that I'd promised Sam I'd take the kid off his hands the next day, which meant that, advocate work permitting, this afternoon was going to be my only chance to do some reconnaissance— I wanted to head over toward the university to check out The Water Hole and the surrounding neighborhood before the evening.

I also wanted a little time on my own to think. Some people can manage that while they're making slightly awkward conversation with an ex-lover with whom they might or might not have just started up again. I'm not one of those people.

Even if you don't know San Judas all that well you may know something about Stanford University, the Harvard of the West, alma mater of several US presidents and (although they don't talk about this quite as much) nursery of uncounted numbers of extremely unpleasant tactical weapons, including the hydrogen bomb.

Back in the middle of the nineteenth century there was only one real city in Northern California—San Francisco, which started its boom with the Gold Rush and never looked back, selling prospectors' gear to all those suckers on their way to the gold fields, then taking more money from them when they came back in exchange for all manner of services, a few of them actually legal. Across the mouth of San Francisco Bay, Oakland became the jumping-off point for those on their way to the golden hills.

Two other large towns also began to grow beside the bay, one centered around Mission San Jose at the bay's southeastern end, the other around a secondary mission named "San Judas Tadeo" beside what later became the Redwood River. See, contrary to what a lot of idiots thought then (and still do), the name San Judas has nothing to do with Judas Iscariot, betrayer of Jesus (although later on it came to fit amusingly with the growing image of the place). The city's named for St. Jude, patron saint of the hopeless, the unloved, and other lost causes—in other words, an even better fit than being named after Christ's ex-pal.

As more and more people began to need wood for boats and houses, sawmills sprung up all over the hills west of San Judas and settlers dredged the Redwood River so the logs could be brought by water to the new harbor there. Then, just when the town was really starting to grow, somebody found oil up in the Santa Cruz Range and a lot of it got shipped out down the river to San Judas and its new harbor. The boom only lasted about a decade or so, but that was enough to leave Mission San Jose and any other pretenders to the title of the Bay Area's second city in the dust.

And that's kind of been the nature of San Judas ever since—boom and bust, feast then famine. It's been an oil town, a port town, and eventually a factory town because of all the defense industries that set up here around the time of the Second World War. And a main lure for that kind of technology were all those science and engineering graduates from Stanford and the other local universities, which is why Jude, along with Berkeley and San Francisco itself, wound up at the center of the information revolution.

Leland Stanford was a Victorian-era entrepreneur—a "robber baron" to many—who became the governor of California. When his only child died of typhoid, he and Mrs. Stanford built the university in their son's honor, and for the first few years it was a remarkably forward-looking institution. Then Stanford's wife died in a fire, with the ex-Governor himself unable to save her because of a locked door. The governor heard her last terrible moments and was never the same man after that, nor was his university the same kind of open and open-hearted place it had been: No more modern, sandstone buildings, no more sweeping vistas to the beautiful western hills. Instead the university grew upward as much as out, spiking the skyline with dark, Gothic towers. The governor's gift to the state also grew more inward as well, surrounding itself with turreted walls that made it look more like the castle of an occupying army than a modern seat of learning.

Once the Camino Real, the great north-south highway that stretches from San Francisco all the way down to the far end of the bay, ran right through the university itself, but sometime in the 1920s the Stanford board of regents decided they didn't like the *hoi polloi* motoring freely through their expensive and exclusive university so they lowered the road and turned it into a long tunnel that passes under the narrowest part of the university property. If you decline to use the tunnel your choice is either line up to be examined for admittance at one of the two forbidding university gates or just turn the hell around and go back.

Perhaps because the deadly fire that killed Mrs. Stanford was rumored to have been started by a drunken servant, or perhaps because he was just a mean old bugger, Governor Stanford was also very, very down on alcohol—not a drop to be had on campus, and for years not a drop to be had anywhere *near* the campus. That's eased over the decades. Although the university itself is still famously dry, a number of drinking establishments sprang up in the shadow of the walls to serve Stanford students. Preparing to rule the world can be thirsty work, I'm told.

The Water Hole was one of these student hang-outs, nestled between the Camino Real and the university turnoff, only yards away from huge and forbidding Branner Gate, a monstrosity of black granite whose polished sheen made it look perpetually wet. At least, I had always thought of The Water Hole as a student hang-out, which was one of the reasons I'd never been inside. I once had a client who got run over in the parking lot by a drunken university professor, and helping him off to Heaven afterward was the closest to the property I'd ever been.

If Fatback's information was correct, though, there was a bit more to the place than that. In fact, if one of Hell's big hitters hung out here, that automatically made it pretty damn dangerous and the last place someone in my position should be, but here I was casing the joint like a private dick setting up a motel sting for an unhappy spouse.

I was doing it because a lot of things still didn't make sense with this whole Walker/Grasswax affair. For one thing, I wondered why my own team had so quickly and casually offered me up to the Opposition for questioning. Didn't make me feel very protected if you know what I mean, which was why I wanted a different perspective on the matter. The fact that the perspective in question belonged to a devastatingly attractive woman-creature was simply how things had worked out. That was what I was doing my best to believe, anyway, but I had to admit that despite our only momentary acquaintance, I'd had trouble keeping the glamorous Countess out of my thoughts.

Because she's made that way, I reminded myself. *On purpose, just like the wiggly little fake worm growing on one of those toothy deep-water fish.*

I'd seen the outside of the bar a zillion times, with its famously broken sign reading *"The Wate Hole."* The rest of the place was about what you'd expect of a mid-century student dive, a long, low wooden building with tiny windows that had been almost completely plastered over with old band flyers and Happy Hour two-for-the-price-of-one ads. My first surprise when I stepped through the scratched and many-times-repainted door was how big the place really was. The main room stretched back into what I had thought must be the building behind it, and though the ceiling was low and the lights were lower, it was possible to see that it was pretty crowded, especially for a weekday afternoon.

It was an odd setup for a college bar, that was clear right away. In some ways The Water Hole looked more like a nightclub, including a scarred dance floor and a small stage at one end of the room, but it was the patrons who really confused me. Usually student joints are low on ambience and even lower on mystery but big on picnic tables and pitchers of cheap beer. The Water Hole had more of the feel of your sleazy lounge rendezvous, the kind of place where businessmen in town for the weekend went looking for drunk and lonely hausfraus. Not that there weren't any students in the place, but they weren't acting very student-y, if you know what I mean. Instead of the groups of three or four or more I would have expected, the patrons were mostly huddled in pairs, but plenty of drinkers, both at the bar and in the dark narrow booths, were obviously on their own and drinking pretty seriously as well—the unsocial kind of drinking that I'd done a few times myself and which left no cheerful memories.

To be honest, I couldn't quite get a handle on anything about the place, and that was beginning to bug me. I contemplated ordering a beer from the sour, tattooed, and shaven-headed bartender, then checking out the exits and the restrooms in a conscientious manner so I'd know the layout when I came back in the evening, but for some reason I didn't relish the idea of becoming one of those solitary afternoon drinkers, even in the service of proper reconnaissance. Instead I turned around and slipped back out to the parking lot.

I still hadn't received any work calls, and I didn't want to have to deal with the questions that seeing Monica would raise, so I decided to avoid The Compasses. I stopped instead at my other place of business, the second-floor office on Arch Street that we local advocates share, a place we use to prop up our real-world identities as insurance adjusters, reporters, or whatever other guises help us to snoop around effectively as we perform our angelic chores. The only person who works there is our secretary, the angelic functionary named Alice. Like me, most of the rest of the advocates look like they're in their twenties or thirties. I'm not sure how Alice pulled duty that had her looking like she was fifty-five and lived on fast food (unless she really did live on fast food and had done this to herself) but it didn't seem like she could be very happy about it. And in fact, she never gave any indication that she *was* happy.

"Hi, Alice," I said. "Anything happening I should know about?"

She barely looked up from her computer. "Other than you screwing the pooch with that Walker thing?"

"Thanks, nice to see you too. You're the one who sent me that, right?"

She raised a penciled-on eyebrow. "Do you see anyone else here? Your big stupid buddy was offline, so I gave it to you. Then you messed it up all on your own."

All of which I already knew. "You're a treasure, Alice. Sam said he lost connection. Is that usual? Was there anything else strange about the call?"

"It happens occasionally. It's because of the weather Outside—well, it's not *weather*, exactly . . ." She shook her head, opened a drawer, and took out a bag of M&Ms. She poured herself a generous handful and put the bag away without offering me any. "As far as the call, Mr. Detective Guy Full of Questions," she said through a clicking mouthful, "it came right down from Central Dispatch, same as usual."

I left Alice typing and crunching and headed back to my place, planning to settle in with a cup of coffee and the files Fatback had sent me. It was late afternoon, and Stambaugh Street was bustling with people on their way home. Every tenant in my building seemed have entered the lobby at the same time, so I waited for another elevator instead of crushing myself into the first with everyone else.

As I walked down the fourth-floor hallway I noticed something strange—a sour, slightly alarming odor that made my eyes and nostrils itch. Before I figured it out by scent alone I reached my door and saw the source. A handprint roughly the size of a car's steering wheel had been scorched into the door, the wood blackened and charred and the paint bubbled round it—a handprint distorted by what looked like trailing scars made by long claws. My heart bumped and stuttered in my chest just like a real, terrified living person's heart, and my skin went icy cold with shock. I darted a look around, but I was alone in the corridor.

The Burning Hand. Somebody had marked my own personal door with the Burning Hand, Hell's way of letting you know that you were living on borrowed time. I'd been taught that the only people who received this sign of infernal displeasure were poor, doomed fools who'd tried to cheat the Devil himself.

Apparently someone thought yours truly was just that kind of fool.

seven

a lioness comes to drink

THE INSIDE of my apartment was as hot as an oven, sticky-hot, and pretty much a continuation of the obvious message left on the front door. Furniture was upside down, small stuff had been smashed, drawers had been pulled out and dumped, and what few papers and books I had were strewn all across the floor. Even my CDs—no, I haven't gone all-MP3 yet—had been dragged out, opened, and scattered. I looked down at the faces on the floor, Monk, Buddy Guy, Cannonball Adderley, staring up at me like a frozen crowd scene. What had the visitors been looking for?

And yes, of course it occurred to me that this had to be connected to the current mess of the missing soul and the dead prosecutor, but the fact that somebody was upset enough about it to trash my place and leave a burning symbol of their discontent on my front door didn't get me any nearer to understanding the *why* of it. The *who* wasn't real clear either, although from the blackened, Kong-size print, those guys with the pitchforks were leading contenders.

One good thing: whoever had been there wasn't smart enough to find my gun safe, and since I'm not going to explain where it's hidden, you won't find it either if you happen by some day. I don't need a gun in my daily job, and I don't usually carry, but things had just changed—drastically—so I grabbed my S&W revolver, a couple of speed loaders, and a few extra boxes of hollow points. Then I called Alice over at the office. "Tell headquarters I'm going to move out for a few days," I said.

"It's cheaper just to give in and wash the dishes," she said.

"Ha ha. Somebody tossed my place. Just tell them."

I heard her making a note, or at least banging on her keyboard. "Where you gonna be, Dollar?"

"I'll let them know when I've decided," I said.

"They won't like that." She almost sounded human. I wondered what her history might have been. "They don't like to guess. And it doesn't seem like a good time to make the bosses nervous."

"Yeah, but I don't know where I'm going yet."

"You want me to give you the safe house information? I thought you knew 'em all by heart."

"Email them. I'll pick a nice one, get cozy, and think of you."

I hung up before she told me to get bent or something and ruined the illusion that, just for a minute, she actually cared whether I did or didn't exist. Alice was right—the Mule and his supervisors were not going to like me moving out without leaving them a forwarding address, but it wasn't like they couldn't get in touch with me if they wanted. I wasn't going to one of their safe houses. Just for the moment I wanted to be the only person who knew where Bobby Dollar might lay his weary head. The Burning Hand thing had shaken me pretty good.

As I sat waiting in The Water Hole I nursed a beer and tried to figure out what had made someone so mad at me personally. It almost had to be about be the Walker thing. Even if the late Grasswax had been venal enough to want to take a shot at the folks who had witnessed his humiliation (as he'd put it) with the Martino case the day before, Sam, and especially young Clarence, would surely have been on his list ahead of me. But if it was the Walker thing, what had I done other than be on the scene when the soul in question failed to show? And what had I done after that except answer official questions from my superiors and Hell's chancellor, then request some information from Fatback? Had my visit to the pig man triggered some kind of information-search alarm? If so, that didn't narrow things down much because I'd asked him for information about lots of different stuff, including the lovely hellspawn I was hoping to meet here tonight.

Suddenly feeling a touch vulnerable, I slid along the bench until my back and left side were against the corner of the booth. Fatback's information had sent me here, and here I sat. Did my enemies know that? Had the flaming handprint across my door been meant to convince me not to do exactly what I was doing? I looked around, but though the afternoon's solitary drinkers and college students had been augmented by what looked like some after-work gatherings and a few solos grabbing a beer at the bar on their way home (most of whom were staring up at the college basketball game on the big screen) I didn't see anyone who looked out of place or seemed to be clocking me in turn. Still, I loosened my coat a little in case I had to get at my .38 in a hurry. My quarry tonight was a high-ranking minister of Hell itself, and those sort of people were not known for their sweet tempers and reasonable dispositions. Of course, they weren't known for being particularly afraid of guns, either.

Maybe ten minutes later there was a little stir that I felt more than heard. A very, very large man had just shouldered through the door, followed quickly by another even larger man. My heart sped. I had seen both of them before, although not in these earthly bodies—the Countess's bodyguards, the things with the gray, nerveless skin that had accompanied her Outside on the day Edward Walker died. Sure enough, after they stood in the doorway looking around for a moment the one in back stepped out. When he returned a couple of seconds later he was following the very creature I had been waiting for—the Countess of Cold Hands herself.

As they escorted her across the room you could tell which patrons had never seen her before by how openly and unself-consciously they stared. I didn't blame even the most obvious, since her earthly form was almost exactly the same as I had seen before and almost exactly as compelling. She was dressed a bit more discreetly tonight than the fetish schoolgirl look I'd seen before—if you could call red-streaked blonde hair, a bright pink designer sweatsuit, and large, visible diamonds discreet. She could have been the teenage daughter of an extremely wealthy Hollywood producer.

I was relieved to see that her bodyguards were smaller than they had been on the far side of the Zipper, but they were still both considerably larger than me or anyone else in the place. A couple of college dudes who looked like football players eyed them speculatively—not so much "Can we take them?" I suspect, as "Hmmm, wonder what kind of 'roids they're taking?"

The Countess walked across the room slowly but completely without self-consciousness, and even the men who weren't looking at her shivered as she went past and turned to see what had just happened. Remember how I talked about the chesty, small-dog walk? Apparently that was how she moved when she was doing "busy" and "hard at work"; here she moved more languorously and seemed even more dangerous because of it, like a lioness coming down to drink.

Obviously this particular Water Hole drew some pretty big game.

She wound up on the far side of the room from me, in another booth facing perpendicularly to mine. As soon as she slid into her seat everyone sort of lost track of her, the same way folks don't notice me and the other advocates when we open a midair Zipper—she just fell right off their mental radar. One of the bodyguards crammed himself into the booth next to her as the other one asked her something. She nodded and he headed off toward the bar.

Fortune favors the brave, I told myself and stood up. I think that kind of stuff often enough that I figure when I was alive I must have been an English teacher. Either that or just an annoying dickhead.

The beady little eyes of Bodyguard Number One, who was shaven-headed and had a spiderweb tattooed under one eye, pinned me as soon as I rose, then stayed fixed on me for my lengthy journey across the floor. I say "lengthy" because the entire twenty yards or so I was thinking there was a good chance he might recognize me and just shoot me in the gut or something. Like I've said, dying isn't the worst thing that can happen to an embodied angel, but it's certainly high on any list of painful, joyless ways to spend an evening.

Halfway across I realized I still had my beer, which showed how clearly I wasn't thinking—I was even carrying it in my shooting hand. I'd like to blame that bit of idiocy on the tension of the moment—this kind of confrontation just doesn't happen very often—but I'm afraid it was probably entirely to do with the fact that the Countess of Cold Hands was so disturbingly gorgeous, a woman for whom you might risk not just your freedom but literally your immortal soul. Yeah. She was that fine.

But not on the inside, stupid, I told myself. *Stop thinking with Little Bobby and remember that.*

I stopped in front of the table. The bald bodyguard tensed his arm-muscles but didn't move. He kept his hands out in plain view, so I did the same. One of my hands was holding a beer mug, anyway. You're right, I really hadn't thought this through too well.

"Countess," I said. "Nice to see you again."

"We've met?" The only difference between her Outside and Inside appearance, I could see now, were her eyes. Here in the so-called real world they weren't bloody red but a pale, icy blue. She smiled, but it was hard, hard, *hard*. "Remind me."

"Just the other day. Outside the Walker house."

"Walker house?" She could make even two such ordinary words sound as if I'd said something crude and suggestive. "I don't know any such place, and I don't know you."

Now it was my turn to smile. "I'm willing to believe you didn't know me before that, Countess, but I think everybody knows who was there by now. It's become kind of talked-about in certain circles. My name is Bobby Dollar."

She stared at me for a long second, chilly as a core sample pulled from the polar ice. "I'm afraid you're mistaken, Mr. Dollar. Now, if you don't mind, I'm expecting someone."

"That's okay. I'm willing to share," I said, then a hand gripped my right arm so hard that the heavy mug dropped from my nerveless fingers and fell onto the table, fountaining beer and froth.

"The lady said *go*," Number One, the guy with the web tattoo, informed me in a breathy whisper. "Now do it. Or I'll pull your arm out of—"

I didn't bother to wait and find out what he was going to pull it out of, or what he was going to do with it afterward. Instead I snatched up the dropped mug with my left hand and brought the heavy glass down as hard as I could on his fingers where they were splayed on the table. He let go of my arm and gave out a short, sharp grunt of pain that I derailed by backhanding him across the face with the mug, hard as I could swing it. As he toppled awkwardly to the floor, gushing blood from his nose, I heard footsteps right behind me. I dropped the mug and spun around; by the time I finished the turn my .38 was in my hand and pointing right at Number Two's face. He was still fumbling for his own piece. I guess he hadn't expected so much excitement at The Water Hole tonight. If it had been me running to protect my boss, I would have drawn long before I got so close, but that's because I'm not that strong compared to some of these bruisers, and I really hate pain.

"Fuck you, tough guy," said Number Two. He had a military haircut, a huge mustache, and a really deep voice. Other than that, he could have been any death row triple-murderer. "Go ahead, shoot me. She'll kill you worse than I ever could. Then she'll take you home and kill you some more."

"I don't want to shoot you, sunshine. I don't even want to damage you badly enough to interrupt your gay porn career." I turned to the Countess, who was watching with something like amusement despite the blood and beer splashed across the table and threatening to drip onto what was probably five thousand dollars worth of designer workout gear. "Well, Ma'am? Do you and I talk, or are they going to have to move the tables to mop up all the red stuff?"

She gave me a bored look, then leaned over a bit so she could see the guy on the floor. "Candy?"

Number One looked up. Blood was still bubbling out from underneath his hand, and his eyes were swelling closed. I'd done a pretty good job on his nose. "I can still kill him if you want me to, Countess," he said, grinning red.

"No, that's not necessary. Cinnamon, take Candy out to the car and stop the bleeding."

The guy looking down the barrel of my Smith & Wesson seemed disturbed for the first time. "No way! We're not leaving you!"

She frowned. "You're not doing me any good right now anyway. Go on. As you pointed out, I can take care of myself."

Grumbling like an idling big rig, Cinnamon helped his bloody pal up off the floor. During the initial moments of the fray everyone in the bar had turned to look, but now they were losing interest rapidly, as they always do when us embodied folks make a public fuss. My old mentor Leo used to call this protective effect "the Cloud of Unknowing," but I don't know where he got that.

As Cinnamon helped his friend toward the door, leaving a trail of red drips across the concrete tiles, the Countess gave me a look from which all amusement had packed up and moved out. "You've got about two minutes, angel, so sit down and start talking. Then either I'll tear your head off myself because you didn't impress me, or those two will get nervous enough to call for backup."

"Yeah. But you never got your drink."

She looked at me like I must be kidding. "That two minutes was an outside estimate." She watched me not sitting down, then the smile came back, one of the grudging, *I admire your bravery but you're still going to be dead as vaudeville* kind. I get them more often than I'd like. "It's still sitting on the bar—the one with the celery stick."

"A Bloody Mary? You're joking, right?"

She didn't like that. "If you're going to make editorial comments I'm going to pop your skull off your spine right now, Mr. Dollar."

I went to fetch her Bloody Mary. There were two beers there, too, which had been meant for the bodyguards, so I brought those back as well. I felt like I'd earned them, and now that my heart wasn't beating so fast I wanted to drink something quickly, before I realized what I'd just done. What if I'd had to shoot the second guard? At the very least I'd lose my job as a heavenly advocate, and in the midst of all this craziness about the Walker case, killing a member of the Opposition in public would probably bring much worse trouble than just a demotion to Angelic Patron of Cub Scouts or whatever.

"So," she said as I slipped into the booth and faced her across the table, "why exactly do you want to die so badly, Mr. Dollar?" Somehow bar employees had cleaned the table and floor while I was gone. Everything was so clean it was almost like a first date. "Haven't things been exciting enough already?"

"I'm not really seeking death," I said. "More like information."

"From me? What on earth can you possibly hope to learn from me? And why would I share anything with you? Need I remind you that our two organizations have been at war for millions of years?"

"Not war," I said, then took a long swallow from one of my new beers. I wondered if I'd be alive long enough to start the second one. "Remember, it's officially called a 'conflict.' Some of the bean counters on my side even like to refer to it as a 'competition.' Which would make us not enemies but . . .competitors."

She bit her lip, perhaps to keep from smiling or frowning, perhaps simply because she knew it made her look so intensely sexy that it befuddled the mind of anything with a body. "What does the competition want to know? And not that I care, but you really had better stop showing off how brave you are and get to the point. Just because you caught Candy and Cinnamon by surprise, you shouldn't think they're useless. They can make you hurt for a very, very long time without letting you die. We have whole graduate studies programs for that, where I come from."

"Oh, I know. In fact, that's one of the things I wanted to ask you. Who do you think earned their doctorate on Prosecutor Grasswax?"

Her lovely face went dead but the eyes remained as wide and innocently blue as a prairie sky. The voice was pure Mary Poppins. "Is that an accusation, Mr. Dollar? If it is, it strikes me as a very, very foolish one."

I raised my hand. "Peace, Princess—"

"Countess."

"Yeah. I'm not accusing you. Why would I want to do that even if I thought it was true? Grasswax didn't work for my side, and he certainly wasn't my friend. In fact, I thought he was a shit."

"Then perhaps *you* did it."

"Maybe. But you'll have to trust me for now when I say I doubt it, and that I'd really like to know who did."

"The whole infernal hierarchy would like to know." Her eyes narrowed. "And they're even more curious to find out what happened to his client, Edward Walker."

"Client." I laughed, but not very hard. "That's a funny way to talk about a guy Grasswax was trying to get sentenced to an eternity of being fried in flaming oil like an eggroll."

"Our prosecutor was doing his job, Mr. Dollar. I was doing my job, too. I suggest you might live a little longer—whether in or out of a body—if you just went away and did yours."

"Yeah? Well, not only was I doing my job, I was literally minding my own business until all this shit started blowing sideways." I was getting angry now, and it was beginning to suppress that prickly back-of-the-neck feeling that less experienced folks might mistake for cowardly fear. (I like to think of it as an imaginative form of caution.) The Countess had been right about one thing: I only had a few minutes at the most before her two Care Bears came back, probably with the rest of their cousins.

"It's too bad the Walker affair has inconvenienced you," she said, "but I have nothing else to share with you. And you have nothing to interest me." She was armored like a tank, a very, very attractive tank with diamond earrings and what looked like a large silver locket around her pale, smooth neck. "You ought to go away now."

The shiny stuff distracted me a little—I was under the impression that demons hated silver. "Yes, I'm sure you'd like to get back to whatever you were doing, Countess. Slumming, is my guess." I sat back, the picture of relaxation, or so I hoped. "I confess to being curious about what brings you to a place like this. I mean, sawdust-on-the-floor joints don't seem like your scene, Princess."

Now the smile was actively feral. "You're trying to irritate me, aren't you, Mr. Dollar? For your information, I like places like this. You see, I like students."

"Breaded, with cocktail sauce? Or do you just gobble them down raw like sushi?"

"Nothing so crude, Mr. Dollar." She had leaned a little closer to me without my noticing, and now her hand alighted on my thigh. I could feel the points of her nails pressing through my jeans. "I'm not a vampire or some other sad, cartoonish thing that eats people. I'm one of Hell's nobility. Despair, that's my true meat and drink. And at this age, they are so easily turned down that path." She giggled like a teenage girl whispering with a friend. "Someone I used to know told me I should aim higher. 'It's like shooting blind fish in a very small barrel,' was how he put it. But I do so love to see them cry and beg, because they start out so sure of themselves—especially the boys!"

"If you're trying to creep me out you'll have to try harder." But I was as conscious of that hand on my leg as I would have been of a poisonous spider. Although not in entirely the same way. "I really don't care how you spend your time, Countess. It just gave me a chance to meet you and ask some questions."

The nails poked into my leg a little harder. She moistened her lips, which were already dewy in the extreme. "And have you asked everything you want to ask?"

This had gotten weird very fast. Don't get me wrong—I've been around members of the Opposition's seduction brigade before, and they have mojo working for them a poor little angel boy like me can't even understand. But the Countess was something else. *Way* else. I was scared she was going to slide her hand up to my crotch and find out just how much of an act my I'm-not-impressed really was. "Okay, then, one more thing," I said. "Yesterday I came home and found that I'd been visited by the Burning Hand. Anything you can share with me about that? Did I offend somebody on your side?"

"After seeing you operate, I can't imagine how that could happen. But I highly doubt it, anyway. I suspect someone's pulled a little prank on you. The Burning Hand—well, that's a bit of an old wives' tale. Haven't heard of anyone actually getting one for years."

"Then maybe it's time to modernize the database." I pulled my phone out of my pocket and punched up a picture of my front door, then held it in front of her very pretty face. "What would you call *that*?"

Jackpot—or at least an expression crossed her face for the first time that wasn't part of her Demon Queen act. She took her hand off my leg. The weird thing was that it wasn't just surprise I saw but a hint of fear as well, which freaked me out. What could scare one of Hell's society-page regulars?

Whatever it was vanished in a moment, like the reflection of something moving. "You're half right, Mr. Dollar. That's a burning hand—but it's not *The* Burning Hand."

"What are you talking about?"

The hand dropped lightly on my leg again and squeezed ever so gently. The nails were sharp enough to poke through the denim and touch actual skin. "Back in the old days, people who tried to renege on their agreements with us would be reprimanded with the mark of a black, ashy hand on their doors . . . but the hands that made the marks were human, or at least human-sized. The tradition is very clear about that. Unless you live in a munchkin cottage, I'd say the hand that made this must have been at least as big as a polar bear's paw." She held up her own dainty little mitt—the one that wasn't prickling my thigh. Her long, sharp nails were without polish but very, very clean. "In other words, not made by anything human-sized."

I could tell there was something else she wasn't telling me, but I could also sense that she wasn't going to tell me now. A sort of wall had suddenly gone up between us. I decided to cut my losses and see if I could get out of The Water Hole without a firefight. I disengaged her grip from my leg and slid out of the booth, but just as I did so the front door swung open and several large shapes crowded through, blocking the orange sodium light from the parking lot. Reinforcements.

"Thank you, Countess," I said. "You've been more helpful than you know."

"You're cute, Dollar. If you survive the next few minutes you may call me Casimira the next time we meet." She smiled, and she was so beautiful it hurt my chest. "My friends call me 'Caz,' but I don't think you'll be around long enough to earn *that* privilege."

Damn, she was fine.

There were about five or six of them coming toward us, an entire exhibit escaped from the Big and Ugly Hall of Fame. I sprinted for the other end of the room, furious now that I hadn't taken time earlier to map the exits.

I found the men's room and levered myself out the window. Luckily they hadn't thought enough of me to leave anyone staked out in the parking lot, so by the time they'd busted the lock on the restroom door I was wiping off sweat as I pulled out onto the Camino Real. But I was most of the way back to the motel room I'd rented on the north end of town before I finally stopped thinking about her hand resting lightly on my leg.

eight

posie and g-man

I AWOKE TO the sun stabbing through the dusty blinds of the Royal Highway Motor Hotel like Norman Bates's favorite steak knife, as well as the four most famous notes of the Hallelujah Chorus chiming over and over again from my phone—the sound of waiting messages. Believe me, if it was up to me, I'd have something better (or at least more discreet) but our phones are work-issue and Nikola Tesla himself couldn't reset them. That doesn't mean that's what folks like you would hear, but it's all an angel like me gets when the phone wants you to know there's a message—HAH-lay-loo-yah. HAH-lay-loo-yah. Whoever did the programming for the House was either criminally stupid or had a very unpleasant sense of humor.

Besides all the stuff from Fatback I hadn't read yet, I had also received several nasty messages from Temuel's office wanting to know where I was staying and one text from Clarence the Trainee Angel asking when I was going to pick him up. *Shit,* I remembered, *that thing I set up with Sam.* I sat in a puddle of unpleasantly bright light looking for the time and finally spotted the motel clock proclaiming 9:22 in digital scarlet. Practically the crack of dawn. I texted the kid back with fingers that felt like uncooked sausages, telling him to meet me at noon at Oyster Bill's. No sense hurrying into the day. Besides, I had an errand I wanted to run before then, after I had self-administered some coffee.

Twenty-five minutes later, showered and with a cup of Peet's the size of a grain silo between my knees—no cup holders in a vintage Matador, which might make you wonder how people survived the seventies long enough to invent cup holders later on—I was headed down the Bayshore toward the Walker place for the third time this week. The neighborhood had more or less returned to normal after the circus of the last couple of days, the sidewalks full of smiling postal carriers and people wearing casually expensive clothes walking their casually expensive dogs. Pretty much what you'd expect on a Saturday morning in Jude's Palo Alto district.

Edward Walker's house looked like any other house on the street now except for a small island of stuffed toys and flowers and written tributes, the kind of sentimental Sargasso that quickly collects these days near the scene of any semi-public tragedy. There was a different car in the driveway today, a scuffed, nondescript Japanese sedan that didn't look like anything Walker himself would have driven. The car in which he'd died was nowhere in sight, although the garage door was closed.

I was mostly interested in what I might discover on the Outside, but the slightly odd car intrigued me, so I knocked on the door. Ordinarily in these situations I'm an insurance investigator, but that wasn't going to play well at the house of a prominent suicide, and my usual backup, the National Transportation Safety Board, didn't really make sense when the crime scene was a parked car, whether or not the engine had been running.

The young woman who opened the door could easily have walked out of someplace like The Water Hole or any other college hangout, and from practically any time in the last forty years. She had long dark hair braided with little bells and whatnot, and wore a dark, figure-camouflaging hooded sweatshirt over jeans and sandals. She squinted at me as though someone coming to the door was a very nutty idea. "Yeah?"

"Hi. My name is Robert Dollar and I work for Vista Magazine. I'm so sorry to bother you at a time like this but for some reason I couldn't reach anyone by phone. Is Mrs. Walker here?"

She looked at me as though I had asked her whether fish flew. "There isn't any Mrs. Walker. You ought to know that. My grandmother died about five years ago."

"I'm so sorry—of course." I hadn't expected to deal with real folks, and although some of Fatback's information was in a folder in my hand, I hadn't found a chance to read most of it. "So you're Mr. Walker's granddaughter. Do you think I could have a few moments of your time? We're running . . . well, it's sort of a tribute to your grandfather, and I'd like to make certain I've got the details straight. These things are always hurried, because of course no one was prepared . . ."

For a moment the irritated look dropped from her face to be replaced by sadness. She was actually quite a pretty young woman, but with a sullenness about her that made her look less than bright. "No one. You got that right." She shrugged. "Come in, I guess. Wait, shouldn't you show me some identification?"

I have more identity cards than an international smuggler and I've learned to find the right one as nimbly as a stage magician. I popped it out, and she squinted then waved me inside. She led me to a large, open living room and flopped down on the couch without giving any indication of where I should sit. The other couch was too far away, so I perched on a hassock a few feet from her and tried to look journalistic. She didn't offer me anything to drink—while she fetched it I would have cased the room as thoroughly as possible—so I did my best to examine the place while we talked. It was very clearly the living room of a man of ideas, or someone who wanted to be seen as one, anyway, with one wall of the primarily white room dominated by an immense book case. Most of what it held was books, but there were also a number of casually fabulous folk art items perched on the shelves. A few pictures hung on the walls, mostly black and white Ansel Adams prints of dramatic landscapes uncluttered by human figures. The couches had sheepskins draped on them and nice examples of Mesoamerican pottery sat on many of the surfaces. The whole thing looked expensively tasteful but also a trifle neglected—I thought I could see dust on some of the pieces.

I pulled out Fatback's report and stole a second to glance over it. There it was at the top of Walker's bio, what I should already have known—widowed, wife was named Molly. And the granddaughter was . . .

"You must be Posie, right?"

She nodded. "Like the flower."

Looking up from the bio, my eye was caught by an impressively large Mayan calendar in baked red clay that hung on the chimney behind the young woman. "That's a lovely piece," I said. "Is it genuine?"

She squinted at it, then shrugged; I was beginning to think she normally wore some kind of lenses. "I don't know. Grandma and Grandpa used to bring stuff back from all kinds of places. I think that's from Mexico or something."

Laboriously, I turned the questioning from things Posie didn't know much about to things Posie apparently knew nothing about at all—for instance, the reason her grandfather had killed himself. Not that I asked her outright.

"Such a shock to the whole community." I shook my head. "Your grandfather was so admired. He seemed like a man who had so much to live for." I lowered my voice to a respectful half-whisper. "I don't mean to pry—and this certainly won't go in the article—but was he ill?"

She shook her head. "I don't think so. But he never told us stuff like that, anyway."

"Did he have any other confidantes?"

"Other confidence?"

I wanted to groan but stood up instead. I began to examine the bookshelves, discreetly (or at least I hoped so) photographing them with my phone. "No, *confidantes*—people he talked to. Close friends, colleagues. A priest . . . ?"

"Priest!" She laughed sourly. "That's pretty funny. Grandpa hated religion. Thought it was all a bunch of shit to trick people out of their money."

I nodded. "Well, obviously it wouldn't be a priest then, but still, he must have had friends. Your grandfather was a very beloved man. Did he have anybody to share . . . difficult decisions with?" I was all but asking her who else I could talk to, but she was very slow on the uptake. I finally figured it out, though—the girl wasn't necessarily stupid, she was just stoned. As I passed her I got a distinct whiff of weed off her sweatshirt and hair.

"Not really. He had his old friends from HT, I guess."

"HT?"

I had bemused her again. "HoloTech? The company he, like, founded?"

"Yes, of course." Homework, Dollar. "I just didn't hear you clearly."

"And there was that nice old African guy. I can't remember his name."

"African guy?"

"Yeah, some kind of doctor. He used to visit Grandpa and they'd sit around talking. I saw him here a couple of times. Really nice old dude. Talked like he was from England or something, but Grandpa told me he was from Africa."

"Could you find out his name for me? He might . . . might have some unique insights to add to our article."

She rolled her eyes and stretched. "Yeah, but I can't do it now. Somebody's coming over." She looked up at the clock. "Should be here any minute."

I took the cue. As I moved toward the door I pulled a card from my wallet. "Call me or email me if you remember the African gentleman's name or anything else of interest, would you? You've been a great help."

"Sure, totally," she said. I'd heard less enthusiastic agreements, but offhand I couldn't remember when.

When I left the house I opened a Zipper and stepped through to the Outside, but the clean-up crew had been very thorough and there was nothing left to see, not a single trace of Grasswax's hideous demise or anything else useful. I stepped back into the real world and climbed into my car. It was almost time to begin my babysitting session with Clarence.

I hadn't even gone two blocks before I noticed I was being followed. The tail was so obvious that I didn't know whether to laugh or be really, really worried, because if they weren't complete incompetents then they must have wanted me to see them, and if they wanted me to see them it was because they didn't think I could do anything about it. Either way, I wasn't going to roll over. I took my time going down University Avenue so I could check out the other vehicle. It was some kind of red low-rider with too much chrome and what looked like a scoop sticking out of the hood. I decided not even the archdemons of Hell were subtle enough to be *that* conspicuous, so instead of getting back on the freeway I took him over the bridge to Ravenswood, a neighborhood about as opposite Walker's tree-lined Palo Alto as you could imagine. The Ravenswood Renaissance of the sixties was long over, and the people on the rich side of the freeway had gone back to the more familiar pastime of ignoring their eastern neighbors completely; and now poverty held sway again on the east side of Bayshore. It must have been particularly galling to the Ravenswood folks to look out and see Palo Alto's proud skyline on one side and the shining towers of Mission Shores just to the north—a bit like being the one ugly cheerleader on the squad.

Our side has got a safe house in Ravenswood, a nondescript little place in an apartment complex off Bay Avenue. The key thing is, the parking lot has an electronic gate. I keyed the numbers and drove down into the garage, then quickly drove out the back exit onto the street and circled the building. The tail car, a chopped, flame-red Pontiac GTO, was still in the driveway, halted by the gate. He saw me coming and tried to back up but I blocked him with my car, then I just sat there waiting to see what he would do next. He confirmed his amateur status by jumping out of his ride and strutting up the ramp toward me, one hand behind him. He was young, skinny, and dressed like the hip-hoppiest ghetto star you ever saw—sideways baseball cap, big chains, waistline of his pants halfway down to his knees—but he was also as white as the guy on the Quaker Oats box.

"Whatchu doin'?" he demanded. "You blockin' my car, man!"

I got out as he reached me. "Am I?"

He was clearly psyching himself up for something big and stupid: he bounced around on the balls of his feet like he had to pee, but his hand stayed behind his back. Up close I could see that he had one of those little chin beards (sparse and caterpillar-fuzzy) that always make me wonder if the guy just missed a patch.

"Don't give me no shit!" he said, bouncing even higher in his outrage. "I been followin' you!" And then, like a tired old stripper climbing from a cake, out came his piece, a 9mm. And to confirm the guy's gangsta-wannabe status he held it sideways as he pointed it at me—a recipe for inaccurate fire and a good chance of the shell stovepiping and jamming the pistol. I smiled despite myself as I spread my hands.

"Peace, dude. You got the gun, you're the boss."

"Yeah! You better recognize!" He was still bouncing, and I was a little worried he might accidentally squeeze the trigger and injure a bystander. "What were you doing at Posie's house?"

The picture was suddenly clear. I wanted to wince. "You mean you followed me all the way over here just because I was parked in your girlfriend's driveway? Scratch that, your girlfriend's *grandfather's* driveway?"

"Whatever! I'm the one asking the questions, motherfucker. And if you don't want to get your ass capped, you better just answer 'em."

"A little insecure, aren't we?" I moved one of my hands in a gentle circle. "Look, I'm going to reach into my pocket and take out one of my business cards."

"Super slow, dude." He grimaced to show me how ready he was to start my ass-capping. I felt sorry for his parents, who had clearly spent a lot of money on his very nice orthodonture and would hate the way he was grinding his teeth together. I delicately lifted the card out of my breast pocket with thumb and forefinger and held it out to him. As he stepped forward to take it I let it slip my fingers and flutter to the ground. In the half second that he stood watching it, I took the gun out of his hand then gave him a sharp smack in the middle of the forehead with it, leaving a horseshoe-shaped red mark. He tottered back a couple of steps and then fell unceremoniously on his butt in the sloping driveway, his faced screwed up like he was going to cry.

"Shit, man! What did you do that for?"

"Maybe because you were waving a gun in my face?"

"Chill, man! It's not even loaded!"

I rolled my eyes. "So you drew down on a perfect stranger without even having a bullet in the chamber?" I pocketed his gun and showed him my own. "What if I'd pulled this? Trust me—it *is* loaded. And I wouldn't wave it around before I shot you."

His eyes got big. "You would have shot me?"

I sighed. "Just get up. What's your name, kid?"

"G-Man."

"I don't mean your codename down at the Dickhead Club. What does it say on your driver's license? Your car already tells me you live at your parents' house—nobody buys that much chrome on a grocery bagger's salary unless they're saving on rent." He mumbled something. "What? Tell me again, louder. Full name."

"Garcia." He was as sullen as a third-grader caught playing with his Nintendo during class. "Garcia Windhover." He pronounced the last name like "bend over," which I thought was appropriate, because that's what people would be calling him in prison sooner or later if he stayed this stupid.

"Figures. Let me guess—your parents were hippies."

"You don't know nothing 'bout me, brah!"

"Oh, but I do. Just look at yourself—Swedes, Frisians, Poles, Scots, all those Caucasian ancestors, God only knows how many kinds of all-white salad, mixing together to make the whitest person anyone could imagine, and your greatest desire is to be a poor black man."

"Naw, man, I'm not ashamed of my roots. I'm representing the street!"

"Yeah, and your street just happens to have crossing guards at the corners and a lot of gardeners with leaf blowers." I opened the door of my car. "Wise up, kid."

He scrambled to his feet. "What about my gat?"

"I really should hang onto it—might save your life—but I'll tell you what: You see that card lying on the ground, Garcia? My number's on it, and whether you believe it or not, I'm on your side. So if you see anyone unusual around Posie's grandpa's house or notice anything the slightest bit freaky, you call me. Maybe you can earn your piece back."

His eyes got big again, and he rubbed at the dent I'd put in his forehead. "What are you—like, a detective?"

"No, son. I'm the Lord's avenging angel."

I left him thinking about that as I backed out. I hoped he didn't stand around thinking about it too long or someone was going to come and take the shiny rims off his pretty red car.

nine

a hot shadow

"DO YOU have any friends who aren't . . . who aren't like us?" Clarence asked me.

I looked up from my eggs and bacon. Oyster Bill's not only serves booze in the morning but also breakfast twenty-four hours a day. My kind of place. "You mean living people? *Real* people?"

He looked around in alarm. "You shouldn't talk so loud."

"One of the things you'll learn, kid, is that most people don't notice anything out of the ordinary even if it's *not* an angel saying it or doing it." I looked him over. Spending time with Sam hadn't changed him yet. He still dressed like an AV geek in dress shirt and khaki slacks, and even with the day approaching noon, he looked like he'd just gotten out of the shower. I've never seen a creature so clean. "Friends who aren't angels? A few. Some living folk are fun to hang out with. And some women are too nice to pass up—or at least, too convenient. But I never get very close with any of them."

"Women?" He looked startled. "You mean . . . sex? Angels having sex with the living?"

"It's not mandatory." I leaned back and signaled to the waitress for a refill on my coffee. "Jeez, kid, you make it sound creepy, like reverse necrophilia. We're all 'living', we all have bodies, it's just that some of us are in a different stage of the process." I narrowed my eyes at him. "Why do you ask? You interested in someone?"

"No!" You would have thought I'd asked him if he was planning to machine-gun a church picnic. "No, it's just all so . . . so different."

"Ah, that's right, you only just arrived here in Fleshworld." In deference to the kid's fear of being overheard, I paused until the waitress had delivered the coffee and wandered off again. "Is it that different than you expected?"

He had spilled some sugar on the table, and now he drew in it with his fingertip. "I don't know. I . . . it's strange to have a body. Again. I mean, that's true, right? Because personally I don't remember it."

"Neither do I. None of us do. It's part of the game, for some reason. Makes us better angels, I guess."

"Well, I don't get it." He looked around again, worried about celestial spies, I guess. "What's the point? If the Highest wants people to be good, why doesn't He just make them good?"

"There you go." I put down my coffee cup and sat back. The day had gone a bit gray and windy, the pennants whipping above the ferry dock. "You just said the magic word—you win a hundred bucks."

"Huh?"

"You just discovered one of the benefits of being embodied. I've been going back and forth to Heaven for years, and I don't remember once having a conversation like that up there. Nobody up there asks questions. Maybe you can't even do it without a body."

"I don't get it."

"None of us do. The ways of God are mysterious, and so on. And even if none of us remembers what we were like when we were alive, or what we believed in, obviously we know the truth now, and it's pretty much exactly what most people expected. As to the whys and wherefores, I've got a question for you."

It took him a moment. "Uh . . . yeah?"

"What makes you think there isn't more to come? Maybe we're only seeing as much of the answer as we can grasp—maybe we only know as much about the real Heaven as a three-year-old knows about quantum physics."

He looked a little shaken. "That's a weird idea, Mr. Dollar."

"I'm a weird idea kind of guy."

* * *

Things had been slow the last couple of days, but the afternoon made up for it—three calls, and I took the kid along on all of them. The first was a nice old guy in a nursing home near the 84: natural causes, a life spent as an electrician, good husband, good dad, no problems. Next we had a heart attack that took a fifty-nine-year-old car repair supervisor right on the cardio machine at the Hudson Street YMCA. After that came a sad one, a fatal household accident in Spanishtown where a young mother fell down in the shower and hit her head.

When we arrived at the first, I got a message from my superiors the moment I stepped through to the Outside.

You Are Wanted In The Celestial City, Angel Doloriel. The words rattled in my brain. There was no obvious source. *Your Archangel Wishes To Speak With You.*

I wasn't too surprised. I knew they didn't like it when one of us wasn't in regular contact, let alone when we moved house without telling them. It wasn't a crime, though. I'd check in tonight.

Both the old guy and the young woman went pretty easy. The only controversy was with the car repair guy, one Hilbert Crosley, who turned out to have embezzled a few thousand bucks from his dealership's parts department when he had been depressed about his wife's drinking. He had later begun surreptitiously to return it, although he hadn't finished paying it all back at the time of his passing. We bargained with the prosecutor, a slimy fellow (literally, and probably figuratively as well) named Puddle-of-Pus who recognized that he was going to have trouble winning even with the embezzlement—the rest of the guy's record was good—and Crosley got off with time in Purgatory.

"But he wasn't a bad guy!" Clarence told me afterward as we grabbed a burger at a roadside diner. "Why did you agree to Purgatory?"

"Because even though it was only a property crime, it was a breach of trust, and those can go pretty severely. You don't know Remiel the way I do." (Remiel was the judge who had been assigned to Crosley's case; for a being made entirely of holy light he kind of had a stick up his ass.) "Trust me—our boy will do that time in P. standing on his head."

"But these are people's lives!" Clarence said, so concerned to make his point he didn't notice the tomato and onions sliding out the back of his burger into his lap. "No, these are their whole eternities in our hands!" He looked down and frowned, then began trying to wipe the mess away with a pitifully inadequate napkin.

"Exactly," I said. "They're in our hands—in fact, that's kind of the job description. So it's better to lose small than take a risk of losing big." I did my best to explain to him that I'd tried it his way first, going after each case like a high school football coach trying to lead his underdog team to a big win, but I could tell by the way he looked at me that it just wasn't getting through—he couldn't see it. Which meant that if Clarence was really what they claimed he was, a new advocate-in-training, he'd have to learn the hard way, like the rest of us had.

See, Heaven's judges have their own ideas and don't like being lectured on how morality should work. In fact, they pretty much consider themselves to *be* the literal definition of morality, and they have the power to back that up. A series of agonizing failures taught me the most important lesson of all: Do what you can, take what you can get, try to grow scar tissue over the parts that get hurt. If you can't get the judge to see it your way, you *must* take any little victory you can get. Nobody likes to settle for Purgatory, but it beats the hell out of betting on a longshot and losing, because these are people we're gambling on—human souls. It hurts bad when I lose a case, but it hurts them much worse than it does me.

The phone didn't ring with any more work, so after our meal I swung by The Compasses, hoping to catch Sam and officially offload Junior on him, but my buddy was absent. Monica was there, and although she only smiled and said hello her whole affect was pretty weird. I wondered if she'd dropped by to see me the night before and discovered that I wasn't at home. But if so, she would probably also have noticed the monstrous charred claw-marks on my door, which seemed like the kind of thing she would have mentioned, so maybe she was just wondering why I hadn't called her since the night we spent together.

With Monica being so obviously forbearing I felt like I had a target on my back. I made short work of my drink, staying only long enough to exchange ritual insults with Sweetheart, and Walter Sanders, and some of the others. "Hey, Clarence," I asked as I pulled my jacket on, "you want a ride home?"

"I wish you'd stop calling me that," he said. "I've seen 'It's a Wonderful Life,' you know. I mean, I get it."

"And when you earn your wings we'll stop calling you Clarence and start calling you Harold or Harry, or whatever your name is supposed to be."

"Harrison," he said, sulking a little. "Harrison Ely. Yeah, I guess I'd like a ride."

It turned out that poor Clarence actually rode the bus to work when Sam didn't pick him up. An angel on one of those smog-belching city buses—can you imagine? I swear I'd walk first.

"Nice to see you, B." Monica called as I herded the kid toward the door.

"And you, beautiful. And you." But I didn't linger.

"Brittan Heights?" I asked as we drove west toward the hills. "I didn't even know there were any apartments up there. Not really that kind of neighborhood, I thought."

"I . . . uh . . . I live in a house."

"Since when does front office give a big enough allowance for a house?" My alarm bells went off again Who *was* this kid friends with?

"No, no, nothing like that, I . . ." He squirmed beside me like he wanted to throw himself out of the moving car onto the Highway 84 blacktop. "I'm renting a room."

"Renting a room? From real people?" I laughed. "You're nuts, kid. Why in the hell would you want to do that? What about when you have your own advocate practice, and you have to go in and out at weird times of the night?"

"I don't know. I'll worry about it then. They're easy to get along with and it saves me some money."

Now I knew he was insane. "Saves you money? What, you planning on buying a little place of your own someday? With a lawn and a picket fence?"

"You don't have to be rude about it. I just . . . I just believe in being thrifty." The way he said it I could tell I'd hurt his feelings somehow. I didn't much care. The whole thing was preposterous. We're not people. We don't *get* to be people. It's not our job.

We didn't talk the rest of the drive. I put on Dylan's *Blood on the Tracks* and listened to "Lily, Rosemary and the Jack of Hearts" as we wound our way up through the neat, expansive houses. Clarence told me to pull over in front of a big Spanish-style house near Crestview Park.

"Nice place," I said as he got out.

He shrugged. "They're nice people. Thanks for the ride."

It's true, I thought the kid was a sentimental idiot, but as I drove back down Brittan toward the glowing lights of the city I had an unexpected moment of envy. It must be nice to come home to something or someone occasionally—a house with other people living in it, even a pet. I've never had that, never wanted to get encumbered. I knew I wouldn't still want it by the time I reached the flats, but for that particular moment I felt a touch of something that a less self-sufficient angel might call loneliness.

The moment I walked through the door of my motel room I could feel the baking heat, as if I had left the thermostat set at a hundred and twenty-five when I went out. Then the smell hit me, so savage and so *wrong* that I took a couple of stumbling steps backward through the doorway, waving my hand in front of my face, and that was what saved me. The thing waiting in the room smashed into the half-open door, and the impact tore the top hinge out of the wall so that the door sagged crookedly in its frame. An instant later my visitor stepped on the broken door and crushed it into a splintering mess as it forced its way out onto the concrete walkway like an octopus flowing out of a tiny crevice in the rocks.

But this was no octopus, or anything else I'd ever seen. It was vaguely man-shaped but huge, almost eight feet tall, and so dark that even by the parking lot lights I could barely make it out except for spreading horns on its head and a sloping, complicated muzzle that made it look a bit like some abstract sculpture of a minotaur. Even from a few feet away the heat it threw off was painfully intense.

There was no question of trying to stand up to something like this. I turned and sprinted across the motel parking lot. I could hear it galloping right behind me, shedding bits of splintered door as it came, so I dove under somebody's sport wagon and desperately tried to claw my gun out of my waistband holster, which is no easy trick while you're lying on your belly crammed under a greasy SUV. The thing still wasn't making a noise except for its deep grunting breaths—*That's good*, I thought, *if it's breathing maybe it can be hurt*—but it knew exactly where I was, and it was very interested. It circled the wagon, then a big, hot hand suddenly swept underneath and missed my head by only by a few inches, and I swear I felt my eyebrows crisping as if someone had tried to close a waffle iron on my face.

An instant later the thing simply bent down and heaved the whole car up in the air, lifting it so that only two wheels still touched the ground. I didn't want to find out what would happen if it dropped it again with me underneath, so I rolled to one side and finally was able to pull my revolver. I emptied it into the middle of the thing, all five slugs. I can't believe I missed from that close but as far as I could tell, it did nothing but stagger the creature a bit and startle it into dropping the wagon, which bounced on its big tires as I took the opportunity to scramble farther away. We were making a lot of noise: as the echoes of my shots died, lights were coming on all over the building. I had no idea what was after me, but I didn't want any ordinary people getting mixed up in this. From what I had seen, my assailant would go through them like they were made of butter.

My decision was hastened by the huge horned shadow scrambling over the wagon toward me. Later on, the police who investigated the scene would decide that the car had been vandalized with a blowtorch and a pick-ax, but I was there—those marks were made by fingers and toes, or hooves, or whatever it ran around on. The screech of punctured metal was enough to tell me what would happen if it ever grabbed me, so I jumped up and sprinted across the parking lot and out into the lights of the busy Camino Real, fumbling for my speed loader as I dodged startled, honking motorists.

This is why I hate carrying a gun, by the way. As soon as I've got it, I suddenly keep *needing* it.

Most witness reports afterward described something like a gigantic black bear in a Halloween wig chasing a man through traffic and at one point leaping over an entire cab, which had fishtailed to a stop behind a clutch of startled drivers. A lone dissenter insisted that not only had the man *also* jumped over the cab, he was being chased not by a bear but "a giant gorilla in some kind of Viking hat." Other than that guy nobody but me seemed to have noticed the impressive sweep of horns.

I reached the other side of the Camino Real about a second and a half in front of the burning black shape. I was almost weeping with anger at my own stupidity in having stayed in the same place two nights in a row, and I was gasping for air as well, but I didn't dare stop. I was pretty certain my aim hadn't been the problem with my shoot-the-fucking-thing idea, and I didn't have a new idea yet, so I kept running until I reached the used car lot across the street. Instead of diving under another vehicle (I didn't trust the clearance on any of the economy models sitting there) I ran right toward the showroom window, feeling the thing closing on me from behind as if it were a rolling ball of lightning. A set of talons as wide across as a garden rake whooshed over my head. As I felt my hair sizzle I reflected that at least I had a pretty good idea now what had marked my door. At the last moment I juked sideways and by some miracle kept my feet, but the monstrous whatever-it-was had too much mass to turn that quickly and crashed full on into the ten-by-thirty plate glass window with a noise like a bomb going off in Chartres Cathedral.

By the time the thing dug its way out of the wreckage I was crouching on the bumper of the N 35 bus on the other side of the Camino Real, heading south. I could dimly see the shadow snorting and sniffing in the ruins of the showroom, but apparently it didn't see me clinging to the bus's rear quarter panel, struggling for breath while I bled gently down the CalTrans logo and onto the asphalt that was sliding away beneath me.

It doesn't really count as riding because I didn't buy a ticket.

ten
that frightened

I JUMPED OFF the bus in the Miramonte district at the southern end of the city. After a long conversation with the nervous desk clerk of a chain motel (and a bribe with one of the emergency twenties out of my money belt) I finally had a place to stay—"hide out" might be a better term, but I had no idea whether hiding from the thing that had just attacked me was even possible. Still, angels, demons, and even powerful malign spirits can't flaunt the rules of cosmic order—it's just that some of the rules are different for us folks than they are for you folks. If the monstrosity had a physical body, and it most definitely had (very hot, very strong, very mean—remember?) then it was operating on the physical plane. It might be able to track me by scent or something else, but in a city of a million plus it would have to get reasonably close to me first. The thing had almost certainly been pointed in my direction by some guiding intelligence, but that probably just meant it would be haunting my familiar spots. As long as I kept moving I should be all right, at least for a while. All the same (and not that it would slow something like that down for more than a couple of seconds) I put the chain on the motel room door and jammed a chair under the knob.

I had stopped at a nearby pharmacy for first-aid stuff, so after I took care of my wounds, which were fairly minor under the circumstances, I could finally leave my bandaged, Bactine-smeared body asleep on the motel bed to answer the summons from my superiors.

I wasn't really looking forward to whatever was going to happen to me upstairs and wanted to put it off as long as possible, so I took the long way in to the Celestial City. I could do this without getting in trouble because there's really no time in Heaven: when you're there is when you're there. It's all Now. Yeah, it's kind of hard to explain unless you've done it.

Anyway, since it wasn't going to make a difference to anyone but me, I took the long, slow way through the Fields, breathing the sweet airs and letting the sight of the contented faithful dancing and singing on those infinite meadows comfort me. There's a reason we angels do what we do, I sometimes tell myself (especially when the doing part has been particularly unpleasant, frightening, or painful) and in my case it's to bring deserving souls to this happy rest. Every success means another person gets to leave all misery, sickness, and old age behind and come to live here, forever young in the gardens of the Lord.

Thinking that way helped—it always does—but it didn't make all my problems go away. Didn't make the whole mess easier to understand, either.

What *was* this horned abomination that seemed so interested in ripping my head off? It had the stink of the deeper pits of Hell all over it, but it's very hard to manifest something like that in the real world—that's one of the reasons angels and demons look pretty much like regular folk when they reside on earth: it's just a lot easier to maintain something ordinary. So someone had been exerting a hideous amount of power to make that monstrous thing appear in the first place and keep it hunting me, which it had obviously been doing for at least a few days. Who wanted to hurt me that bad?

I wondered if finding out what exactly that monstrosity had been would give me a clue about who sent it. It was big and nasty, that was all I knew for sure, and it sure felt like a demon, but there was something unusual about it that kept me from being certain. It seemed old, somehow—primitive. Even the Opposition's meanest, most monstrous fetches can usually communicate, or give you the impression they could if they wanted to. The horned thing had seemed empty of any thought but violence, more like an idea brought to life than a thinking being. I'd never seen or heard of anything quite like it, but it was definitely out there and definitely interested in killing the crap out of me.

By the way, you may be wondering why I fought so hard not to get murdered when death isn't permanent for my kind. You're probably thinking, *Big deal, angel-guy, so something ugly chews up your body—you can always get another body, right?* But what you're missing is a few key facts. First of all—and this is always an important point, especially to me—painful death *really hurts*. Nobody I know wants to get eviscerated by a monster with claws like red-hot gaff hooks, even if they felt sure it was just a brief detour on their journey through eternity. Secondly, there are occasional cases where angels (or demons, for that matter) aren't or can't be resurrected. That had happened to my first mentor, Leo, and Grasswax the prosecutor had just provided another unpleasant example of the phenomenon. Nobody talks about it much, at least in Heaven, but everybody knows it happens. Every now and then an angel is destroyed and can't be brought back. The bosses always say that kind of "unsupported death" (charming euphemisms they've got, huh?) is due to the evil workings of the Opposition, but some of my colleagues over the years have whispered that it often seems to happen to the troublemakers—the kind of angels Heaven won't really miss. Sacrilege, I know, but I'm just reporting what others tell me. I will say, however, that most of those others mentioned it to me because they were worried I might turn out to be one of those "difficult" angels.

So many questions. One that had just occurred to me was, why send a monster, a massive power-drain even for a strong Hell-minion? Why not just send a couple of lowbrow demons or human familiars with Uzis? If you bring in enough firepower you can pretty much kill any earthbound angel.

That gave me a very disturbing thought. Why was I so certain the thing had been sent to kill me? An even more frightening possibility was that it was meant to capture me.

I say this because although Grasswax the prosecutor had eventually died, he had clearly been tortured first, and even when you're talking about Hell the motive for that is usually one of a very short list of things—plain old sadistic revenge, or wanting to set an example, or simply to extract information. When I considered that my current plight seemed to be tied to the Walker mystery and the subsequent fate of Grasswax (a fate which he had likely suffered because someone wanted to hear what he knew about it) I was pretty certain I didn't want that thing to take me alive even more than I didn't want it to kill me—and I *really* don't like things killing me.

Restored a little by a soothing journey through the Fields, my angelic substance no longer stretched quite to the breaking point, I let myself be drawn the rest of the way to the Celestial City without any subjective experience of time. The journey's not quite instantaneous—well, actually, it's more than instantaneous, I guess, like one of those particles that can be in more than one place. You sort of flicker in one place until you're flickering in another, and I can't say it better than that. Anyway, when I entered Temuel's office it was exactly when I was expected, but even so he seemed agitated and impatient.

"Come, Doloriel," he said. My supervisor was definitely worked up about something: his light was uneven, smeary as a Christmas tree behind a wet window. "They're waiting for us."

A moment later we were out of the maze of light known as the California Building and just as quickly out of the North American complex altogether. The Mule and I found ourselves standing before the solemn gate of a palace I've never seen, or at least that I didn't remember. (Another strange thing about Heaven is how hard it is to recall details when you're back in a mortal body: each time you visit the place it's sort of new all over again.) The vast edifice was made of pure adamant, which is a Heavenly way of saying "slabs of diamond as big as a mountain." It did indeed tower high into the heavenly sky, which is a beautiful but more transparent blue than that of earth, with stars showing through. The gleam of animate souls moving around inside could be seen through the substance of the tower's walls.

"The Anaktoron of the Third Sphere," Temuel said, and the hushed tension in his voice told me everything I didn't already know about the seat of government for the whole of Earthly matters.

"What are we supposed to do here?" I asked, but didn't get a reply. A moment later we were inside—clearly expected, too, since we didn't even have to engage with the impressively terrifying angels guarding the palace door. We appeared on one side of a great stone table in a room that looked as large as Pasadena, with windows a hundred feet high letting in heaven's pearly light. A river, an actual river, wound its way through the substance of the polished floor, bending widely around the table, and the music of the moving water was the only sound in that massive space. A quintet of brilliant shapes hovered across from us on the far side of the table—five important angels. Five *very* important angels, in fact, two who were male (in aspect), two female, and one that was neither.

"This is your Ephorate," Temuel said, then named the waiting angels from left to right. "Karael, Chamuel, Terentia, Anaita, and Raziel." Some of the names were more than familiar. I had never had the slightest urge to be called in front of any of them, much less all of them at the same time. An Ephorate is a judgement council, convened to deal with one issue. Nobody knew exactly how high angels got chosen to be ephors, but it meant that this was top-level, official business. Was I really worth that much attention? Had they summoned an Ephorate because I was going to be condemned? I didn't know, but I sure hoped not. Whatever it was, though, I had definitely been called on the carpet bigtime.

"Welcome, Doloriel," said the awesomely beautiful, merciful, and loving coruscation of light that was Terentia. She was all colors submerged in a brilliant sheen of whiteness and seemed to be the leader of this little gathering. "God loves you."

I bowed my head. It was impossible to be in a room full of so much angelic fire and not feel overwhelmed, like a child in the presence of respected elders. It was even more impossible not to be afraid. "Thank you, Mistress."

"We are concerned about events on Earth," said the astonishing youth named Karael in his armor of glittering electrum, and just the touch of his mighty thoughts almost made me swoon. His colors were darker than Terentia's, ripples of black and red gleaming through his brightness like stones in the bed of a fast-flowing stream. Karael was known all over the Celestial City. He was one of the militant angels, a veteran of the Fall, and in person he oozed power. I couldn't help wondering what complicated heavenly protocols made him take a place behind Terentia in this gathering. "We wish to hear everything that you know about the soul known as Edward Lynes Walker."

Hearing that, I felt a tiny bit less worried: Apparently this Ephorate was investigating the Walker case, not me personally. It wouldn't save me if they decided I'd screwed up, of course, but at least the focus wasn't just on Bobby D.

I told them everything I knew. Well, not every single dubious thought that had ever kindled in my secret heart, but everything else—Fatback, The Water Hole, Walker's granddaughter and her idiot boyfriend, even my meeting with the Countess of Cold Hands. I won't go so far as to say the higher angels can read minds, but I will say this: It would have taken a stronger soul than your narrator to hold anything important back while facing a group of them gathered as sworn ephors. I was damned frightened. You would be too if your immortal soul was literally on the line.

"Why would you go out of your way to speak to this Countess?" Anaita asked when I finished. "Let alone risk an incident of the sort you nearly caused?" She seemed the sweetest of all those gathered, her voice that of an innocent young girl, her appearance as delicate as a rainbow just before it fades into the sunlight, but I didn't kid myself—"sweet" is relative when you're talking about a creature who was probably spearing demons right and left in the last great war against Satan's hordes. "Why would you put yourself in such jeopardy, Angel Doloriel? You know the creatures of The Adversary mean you nothing but harm."

"Even a born liar can be useful, Mistress, if only by paying attention to the lies he chooses to tell and the way he tells them," I said politely. "I wanted more information. I was upset on behalf of Heaven and disturbed that such a thing as the missing soul could happen."

"This smacks to me of arrogance and pride." Karael's voice rumbled like a distant storm. It might have been hard to imagine Anaita smiting demons, but it was pretty obvious Karael probably smote a dozen or so before breakfast every morning, just by way of an eye opener. "You did not seek the counsel of your superiors. You did not address your concerns to Archangel Temuel or any others."

"And, now, because of your well-known stubbornness, you have become entangled with one of Heaven's dire foes." Chamuel's light was pearly and there were times when I could almost make out a man-like shape beneath the radiance, like something seen in a mist. "Someone has spoken your name to a dreadful primordial spirit—a *ghallu*, a slave of Old Night, which has put both your bodily raiment and your immortal soul, Heaven's generous gifts, in danger."

Which meant I finally knew what was after me, or at least its name, but I didn't like the "soul in danger" part very much at all.

"We are also not pleased that you changed your earthly dwelling without consulting any of those who watch over you," said Raziel, the sexless one who had been silent so far. Raziel was dark, if an angel can be dark, its light old and ruddy like a sunset. "You are a soldier of Heaven. To act without consultation suggests you do not trust the love that the Highest and the ministers of the Highest have for you."

"That troubles me, also, Doloriel," said Terentia. "Se raises a question I would have asked myself." (Heavenly speech has a way of talking about the angels that are neither male or female without reducing them to "it".) "I would hear you answer herm."

This was perhaps my most dangerous moment in front of the Ephorate, because they were absolutely right, of course. I don't trust Heaven—or at least not everyone in Heaven—to have my best interests in mind. I had developed this habit over years of petty disappointments and irritations, but sometimes it seemed to run deeper even than that, as much a part of me as the shell on a turtle or the claws on a badger.

"I . . . I was confused, Masters," I said. "That's the only defense I can offer. Caught up in time and earthly things, I judged that there would be a better moment to share everything with Heaven—as we're doing now." It was lame but it was all I could come up with, and at least there was a little truth to it. "If I've disappointed or sinned against the Highest, I beg pardon."

"It is presumptuous to think that you might disappoint He who made you," said Karael. "Did the whore of Hell say anything else to you—this Countess of Cold Hands?" He spoke her name with such withering distaste I had no doubt that if she stood helpless before him, then he would have blasted her to cinders without an instant's hesitation. "Are you certain you have told us everything?"

Karael scared me. Just by standing there so bold and beautiful he made me feel like a miserable, dirty little sinner, and at that moment I couldn't imagine telling him anything but the truth. "I have, Master. Did I do wrong?"

A pause fell over the gathering. I could dimly sense currents of thought running between the five of them but it was communication far too lofty and swift for me to understand.

Chamuel broke the silence. "Archangel Temuel, what have you to say? After all, Doloriel is your charge." Chamuel hadn't spoken much more than Raziel. His inner fires were banked low, at least to my senses, but he gave the impression of depth and solemnity: to gaze on his Heavenly form was to sense something vast and awesome lurking just out of sight.

The Mule took a moment to compose his thoughts, or at least that's what I hoped he was doing, since it was also possible my personal archangel was getting ready to throw me under the bus. "I am honored the Holy Ephorate desires my opinion," he said at last. "Doloriel's tradecraft is good. It is true that he can be one of the more headstrong spirits, but as you know, that is often the case with Heaven's servants who exist in time on the plane of Earthly existence. And as we all know, there are occasions when such traits are useful. A more composed spirit might have succumbed to the hunting demon."

"A more composed spirit might not have been pursued in the first place," pointed out Terentia—a touch unfairly, I thought, but of course I didn't say so.

"Then perhaps it is time we gathered Doloriel back into the heart of the fold," said Anaita. "Perhaps it would be a kindness to let him return to the Celestial City and exult in the closeness of the Highest as we all do."

For a moment, listening to her sweet Bo Peep voice, I really wanted that, despite everything that makes me who I am. *Yes,* I thought, *bring me back to Heaven for good. Let me live here and sink into the glow and the warmth and the certainty. No more questions, no more responsibilities, no more fear of failing a needy soul . . .* It truly seemed the nicest thing that could happen. Only for that moment, though. Then I got over it.

I said, "You're too kind, Mistress," but suddenly it all seemed different again, and I wanted nothing else in all of Creation except to get out of that ineffably beautiful, blissful place and back to stinking, dangerous, unpredictable Earth. Because that was where my work was, not up here in the shining streets and tranquil gardens of Paradise.

Perhaps the Ephorate sensed my thought in some way. All five went quiet, and the fire of their beings grew lower, or seemed to, which I guess meant they had turned away from me to speak among themselves once more. I looked over to Temuel, but he too had retreated into himself, his essential light turned down as if it had a rheostat. It seemed like I waited a very long time in that timeless place before anyone spoke again.

"Go back, Doloriel, and do what the Highest has given you to do," said the crystalline blaze of hope and solace that was Terentia. Relief washed through me—something a little less vivid than joy but still very real. "Know, however, that your fitness for that task has been questioned and that our judgement is not yet complete. Walk with caution. God loves you."

I bowed my head as the five angels reached out and touched me, one after another, little bursts of joyful fire, and then they were gone, as was the Anaktoron itself. Temuel and I abruptly found ourselves in the middle of the great thoroughfare known as the Singing Way with the sweetly murmuring crowds of Heaven eddying around us like phantoms of light and fog.

"You've had a close brush, Doloriel," Temuel said. "I don't think a second gathering of ephors will be so lenient, so try to fly a little closer to the ground from now on, will you?"

I didn't really have anything to say to that, but I mumbled some promise. Now that the danger of my personal dissolution was over, at least for the present, I was even more unnerved to realize how close to it I had been.

"One thing," Temuel said. "I didn't hear everything that passed between you and the Ephorate. Did they ask you about the Magians? Or about the name Kephas?"

Both of these were completely new to me, and I wondered if Temuel was taking the good cop role in some complicated process, working on me after the council had softened me up. "Never heard of either of them," I told him truthfully.

"Ah," he said. "No matter. Just some speculation of my own. You may disregard it."

This was all making me extremely nervous. "What's this all about? And why are they picking on me? I didn't do anything to cause any of this."

Temuel's light warmed to soothing sunrise pinks and yellows, the archangelic version of someone putting a comradely hand on your shoulder. "No, Doloriel, but sometimes when things go very wrong and even the highest are frightened, innocence is not enough for salvation."

I let this cryptic phrase echo for a moment. I was feeling a chill again, and now I really did want to get away as quickly as possible—to escape the place that every living soul on earth wanted to reach. "Are they *really* that frightened up here? Just because one soul wasn't where it was supposed to be?"

For a moment the Mule's pearly light guttered like a flame in a high wind. It took me a moment to realize he was surprised. "Of course," he said. "You don't know, do you?"

"Don't know what?"

He spoke slowly, like a grownup breaking bad news to a child. "The soul known on Earth as Edward Walker was only the first to vanish, Doloriel. Others have gone missing since then. More than a few." His voice sank to a conspiratorial whisper. "So, yes—they really are that frightened up here."

eleven

foxy foxy

"KARAEL? KARAEL, General of the Glittering Host—*that* Karael? Wow, he's a heavy hitter." Sam sounded impressed. "You really got the treatment."

"Yeah, even I've heard of him," said Clarence. The two of them were helping me clean up the wreckage of my apartment and pack it up for storage—not that I had a lot worth keeping, especially after the place had been ransacked. I'd lived there for a couple of years and a lot of people knew it. It had been the first place the *ghallu* went looking for me, which meant I was going to have to stay away from it for a while.

"Everybody knows Karael, kid." Sam took a swig of his ginger ale. "I'm not surprised they brought in someone like him, though. If that Walker guy was only the first, if other souls are going AWOL—well, shit, no wonder they're panicking up at the House."

I hadn't said anything about the other two names Temuel had floated, first because I didn't trust the kid, second because I wanted to check into them myself before muddying the waters. I'd tell Sam when I had a chance.

Meanwhile, Sam kicked at a bunch of scattered hot rod magazines that someone had dumped on the foor while searching the apartment. "You're not really keeping all this, are you, B? What are you planning to do, open a Museum of Crap someday?"

I ignored that and gathered up the magazines. Sam wasn't exactly Mister House Beautiful himself. He lived in the seedier section of

Southport, you could barely see his living room carpet under all the newspapers and pizza boxes, and his bathroom towels had sweat stains on them. "But I still don't know why someone would send a monster like that after me," I said. "Look at this place—they were searching for something. And it wasn't just that hell-beast in here, either."

Clarence looked up from where he was picking up tableware that had been scattered across the linoleum. I suppose I should have asked him to put it in the sink to be washed after being Hell-handled, but I hardly ever use any of it except to stir coffee and butter toast, anyway. "What do you mean, Bobby?" the kid asked.

"What do I mean? Look, this place is a mess, sure, but a *ghallu* is a spirit of elemental disaster the size of a small car and hot as the inside of a crematory oven. It pursues. It captures. It kills. You don't summon one of those and tell it, 'Oh, and take a look in the guy's kitchen cabinets while you're there.' That's like asking a grizzly bear to audit my tax records."

"You don't pay any taxes," Sam pointed out.

"Shut up," I acknowledged. "You understand, Junior? They want to catch me or kill me, but they also think I know something. Or that I have something they want."

Clarence suddenly looked a bit nervous. "You think they'll come back?"

"If I stayed here? Probably guaranteed. Which is why I'm going to be kicking it in some rent-by-the-hour motel tonight, and then some different but equally charming spot tomorrow night."

"Trust me—he's slept worse places," Sam said.

"Yeah, thanks for making me look good in front of the kid." With the boxes loaded into my car, the apparment looked sad (and almost tidy.) "Let's go down the block," I said. "I'll buy you boys some lunch before the phone rings and one of us has to go off and mess around with dead people again."

Sam got a call to a client in Spanishtown as we were finishing, and Clarence went with him, so I walked back to my car alone. I put my jacket on because the thin February sunshine wasn't enough to keep me comfortable. I wished the spring would hurry up and arrive. It's funny, but even regular trips to the permanently glorious weather of

Heaven doesn't change the pure pleasure of walking out your door one day and finding that warm days have arrived, that suddenly wearing a jacket makes you too hot.

I kept my eyes open as I went through Hoover Park, although I was nearly certain that the demonic beast someone had sicced on me was strictly a nighttime diversion. I told you how much energy it takes to sustain something so scary and unusual, right? It's a factor of ten more difficult to make one of those manifest in full daylight. Still, something a bit more civilized than the *ghallu* had tossed my apartment, and the horned monstrosity probably hadn't done anything as delicate as stringing up Grasswax by his own nerve fibers either, so I tried not to let myself be distracted by the heedless civilians all around me. I saw the guy waiting out in front of my building from almost a block away, which gave me plenty of time to clock him as I approached.

My car was parked farther down the street, and there was a chance I could have got into it without a confrontation, but he didn't look too intimidating. He was fairly tall but pale and thin—*really* thin. That was one of the first things I noticed. He looked like a middle school kid wearing his dad's suit. He didn't stand still, either, but jittered and dance-stepped in place, apparently not the least self-conscious, although as I watched a woman with a stroller and an old man with a bag of groceries both gave him a wide berth. And his skin was so completely white—bloodlessly white—that for a moment I had the chilling illusion his dark baggy suit might be what he'd been buried in.

It wasn't worth the trouble to try to slip past him to my car, and in fact I was a bit curious, so I kept walking toward him. When he finally heard me he spun all the way around to look at me and I realized that he was alive but more than just ordinarily pale. He was some kind of albino, although his eyes were tawny, not the more common pink. To put an interesting twist on it, he wasn't just albino but Asian, too—a combination you don't see that often, even in cosmopolitan San Judas. More importantly though, from his first words, it seemed clear that my unpigmented Asian-American friend was not entirely sane.

"Dollar Bob?" he said in a chirpy voice. "Mr. Bobby D? Dollar Man?" He stopped bouncing for a moment and frowned, his whole face creasing into a sock puppet of the mask of tragedy. "Or am I wrong again? So many people have said no today! No, no, not Dollar!"

"Who the hell are you?" My choice of words wasn't entirely random. He did have something of the look of the Opposition, but that might just have been his skin condition.

"Don't know me? Everybody knows me! All over downtown!" He giggled and did another little soft-shoe shuffle.

"Well, I don't—and I don't want to, either." But he didn't have the smell of serious danger on him, at least as far as I could tell. Still, I kept my hand in my jacket pocket where my .38 was hiding.

His eyes got big. As I said, the irises were sort of yellow-brown, the irises vertical like a cat's or a fox's eyes. Whatever he was, he was definitely in the "other" category. "Oh, but I know *you*, Mr. Bobby Dolldollar!" he exclaimed. "And I think you have something you might want to sell. I know lots of people who want to buy. I can arrange! Good business, huh? Good for everyone!"

"I don't have anything to sell." Was this guy with the Noh-mask face some kind of lost spirit who'd seen me and Sammy and the kid cleaning broken furniture out of the house and now was hoping to scam a few bucks? The creatures that fall through the cracks in the great war between Us and Them often wind up homeless, and with his too-roomy suit and his loopy dialogue this pale fellow certainly could have been one of those, but there was something about him that wouldn't let me dismiss him so easily.

"Really really truthful true?" The albino leaned way down and then squinted up at me from below. "No little something you might have found? No pretty shiny? A little flippy flappy something that needs a special helper to find a market?"

I had no idea what he was talking about, and his presence was beginning to depress me. It was bad enough that the bad guys knew my apartment—was every fairy-tale gutter-rat in Judas going to come hang out there, too? Plus, there was just something about the guy that creeped me out. Then, all of a sudden, it occurred to me that the folks who had tossed my apartment thought I knew something . . . or *had* something that they wanted. And this guy thought I might be trying to sell something.

"Just out of curiosity, pal," I said, "how much do you think you could get for a—what did you call it? A 'pretty shiny'? I mean, if someone knew where to find such a thing?"

"Oh, he would be a very rich man. Yes indeed!"

"But how do I know we're even talking about the same thing?" I was trying to find a way to get him to identify whatever he was looking for without admitting that I didn't have it and didn't know what it was. "We need to be a little more specific."

He laughed as if genuinely pleased by what I'd said and threw his scarecrow arms in the air, sleeves flapping. "If you have it, Mister B-Doll, I know people who want it. Don't need to say more than that!" He spun. Jazz hands.

I wanted to pop him one just to get him to stand still. "Look, I don't have time to mess around. I don't know you, and I don't do business with people I don't know."

He laughed again. "Okay, Bobby! You the boss! But if you change your mind and want to talk about the shiny-shiny—talk for real—just ask around. Any corner downtown! I'll find out! Fox, that's me!"

"Fox?"

"Or Foxy-boy! Mr. Fox! Foxy Foxy! They are all me and they all know me!" He grinned hugely and I noticed that at least a couple of his upper teeth were gold. An instant later he had whirled away from me and was strutting off, making his way up Stambaugh in the general direction of Main Street like the drum major of the Hiroshima Ghost Parade.

"Wait? How do I get in touch with you if I *do* want to talk?"

"Ask for me on any corner downtown!" A couple of old black guys sitting on the front step of the apartment building next door laughed and pointed as they watched him prance past.

So—yet one more weird detail to add to a large, dangerous, and very confusing picture.

I had been thinking I would check my mailbox one last time before I left, but after meeting Fox I didn't feel like going back inside the building. Not that it would have mattered—I never get anything but junk mail, anyway. I hopped in the car and went hunting for any sanctuary with cable TV and a working ice machine.

I picked a place on the Camino Real because it had a parking garage—after all, a '71 Matador with the full performance package isn't the most discreet car in the world. In fact, I haven't even seen another one around Jude with the same copper paint, let alone my checkerboard interior, so no way could I leave it out in plain view. In fact, I would have to think about ditching it entirely until the heat had blown over.

My phone continued to oblige me by not ringing, so I settled back to catch up on a few details that had been hanging fire the last couple of days. Fatback's material on the late Grasswax (the *real* Grasswax, not his earthly "Grazuvac" identity) was interesting; I skimmed it and put it aside to reread later when I had less to do, but the main thing I noticed was that he'd been around longer than most prosecutors of his rank. The material on Edward Lynes Walker was more of the stuff I'd already seen: born in 1928, started first successful company in his San Judas garage in the early 1950s, riches and fame, blah blah, split and founded HoloTech when another company he had started got too corporate, blah blah, space program, contributed lots of money to ecological causes.

All of this biographical crap reminded me I still hadn't looked through the pictures I'd taken at the Walker house the afternoon young Garcia Windhover had threatened to bust a cap in my ass. The images were still on my phone, which had somehow managed to survive in my pocket while I was being tossed around by a horned, red-hot whaddayoucallit.

There were a couple blurry shots of the Walker living room and one of Posie's shoulder and part of the Mayan calendar, but most of the pictures were of the bookcases. I enlarged the images as much as I could and read down the spines of the books, Googling when I couldn't get enough information from title and author alone. The late ELW's collection was pretty much what I would have expected from the rest of the house, lots of coffee-table art books and big, expensive picture books about science, as well as collections of photography of the West, echoing the Ansel Adams prints on the living room walls. Among the ordinary-sized books, science and the arts seemed to dominate, although there were a few novels, some of them science fiction, like Carl Sagan's *Contact*, others more mainstream stuff like Updike and John Irving. There was even a section of mysteries, the English village sort. I wondered if those had been his or his late wife's. After what his granddaughter had told me I wasn't surprised to see that Walker had no conventional religious books, although there were several volumes by Richard Dawkins, Christopher Hitchens, and even a hoary old copy of Bertrand Russell's *Why I Am Not A Christian*. All together Walker had over a dozen titles with a pretty clearly antireligious slant. Still, for a scientist that wasn't much of a surprise. Stubborn bastards, those scientists.

I was beginning to wish I'd found Walker's music collection and taken pictures of that instead. You show me what someone listens to, I'll tell you everything you want to know about his soul. (For instance, a bunch of Nickelback albums would have indicated he never had a soul in the first place.)

As I mentioned, I wasn't quite sure what I was looking for on the bookshelves—I didn't really expect to find anything titled, "Evading Heaven" or "How to Make Your Soul Disappear." I was mainly trying to get a feeling for Edward Lynes Walker beyond the dry facts that Fatback and the ordinary internet had already provided, something that might help me get a handle on why, of all the deaths in the world, his had been so different. But judging by his books at least, Walker was pretty much like millions of others who had managed to show up for their own afterlives. I had all but given up when something caught my eye.

I had enlarged a section of magazine-shaped objects that filled most of a shelf. Some of them *were* magazines, special year-end editions of things like *Chemical and Engineering News*, but most were stockholder's reports for HT and some of the other companies in which Walker had been involved. Some of these dated from several years earlier, and the section in general looked like Walker might have stuck things into it but almost never pulled anything back out. But squeezed in right between reports for Littleton Bioscience and Metaware was a slender prospectus or something similar with the words "The Magian Society" printed on its spine in tasteful italics.

Alarm bells—hell, air-raid sirens—went off in my head. Because I had just heard about Magians, and not from just anyone, either. Somebody had asked me if I had heard anything about Magians—an archangelic somebody named Temuel, my supervisor.

I did a quick, fruitless online search for Magians. I found a lot of jabber about the Three Wise Kings but nothing about any "society," so I phoned the Walker house. Posie Walker picked up about the twentieth ring, just when I had resigned myself to the answering machine.

"Hello?" She sounded a trifle baked again. I introduced myself, and she eventually remembered me. "Right. That writer guy."

"Exactly. Listen, I was curious about your grandfather's interest in the Magian Society." I said it like everybody knew who that was, although I had already discovered nobody on the internet seemed to have heard of them.

"Never heard of 'em," she said, on cue.

"That's okay. I noticed he had something of theirs when I was there, a folder—maybe you could find it for me." I gave her the bookshelf coordinates, which was a bit like trying to teach a marmoset to play chess; I doubted that she'd spent a lot of her time perusing her grandfather's books. I told her I was happy to wait.

She came back a few minutes later. "Nope. There's nothing like that."

I stifled a curse. "Did you look carefully, Ms. Walker? Between Linson Bio—"

"Yeah, just like you said. It was there, probably, 'cause there's a space, but it's not there now . . ." She trailed off, considering. "Maybe one of the cleaners took it."

Oh, yeah. The Mighty Maids just happened to borrow the one thing in the entire bookshelf I wanted to see and take it back to their office for special cleaning. "Look, could I drop by sometime and take a look around? Sometime soon? Just in case it's been, I don't know, misplaced or something. It would really help my article if I could find it."

Somebody yelled something in the background on her end. It sounded like Garcia the Gang-banger.

"I guess," she said. "Sure. But not now. Somebody's over. Later."

She hung up without waiting to hear my reply.

Despite a powerful urge to drive over there right now and break in and look for myself, I decided not to. If it hadn't been stolen from the shelf it was just misplaced, which meant it would still be there tomorrow, but breaking and entering the Walker place tonight might have dire consequences. Like I might accidentally walk in on Posie and her idiot boyfriend having sex.

It was a nice enough evening, and I would have loved to swing by The Compasses for a drink and some comradely bullshit, but it had only been twenty-four hours since the attack, and I wasn't going anywhere that my pursuer might be watching. Also, to be honest, I wasn't really in a hurry to see Monica either. Don't get me wrong, it wasn't that I wanted to avoid her—I just wanted to avoid having a conversation with her. I hadn't had time to figure out what falling into bed with Monica the other night was going to mean. Also, when I had been having the occasional moment of arousing thought, it wasn't about

Monica but a certain stunning blonde Hell-creature, and that was even more confusing. But I wouldn't want you to think I was a complete moral coward, so I would like to make clear that the *main* reason for not going to The Compasses was as follows: *Not wanting to suffer horrible, painful attack of the murderous-demon variety.*

I had emailed Fatback to see if he could find me anything about the Magian Society or the name "Kephas," but hadn't heard from him yet because midnight was still hours away. I was getting hungry, so I walked from the motel to a Mexican place I had spotted on a side street. Considering it wasn't anywhere near the worst part of Jude I felt surprisingly unsafe. Every movement at the edge of my immediate frame of vision yanked my head around, and sudden noises didn't do much for my nerves either. It wasn't just the thought of getting attacked by the *ghallu* that had me worried, either; if I was now a hot commodity that meant other people were probably willing to shop me for profit even if they didn't have anything personal against me, so suddenly it wasn't just eight-foot demons I needed to keep an eye out for but anyone who might be looking at me funny. On the streets of San Judas that can tire you out real fast.

I made it to the restaurant without incident, and to my pleasant surprise it turned out they made carnitas that actually tasted like something you might get in Mexico, and I mean that in the best possible way. It looked like the kind of establishment where they'd have a DJ on weekends, but on a weeknight it was almost deserted and quiet enough to think. As I ate I knocked back a couple of Negra Modelos and looked over the research material. I discovered some interesting things about the late Edward Walker I hadn't known, including the fact he was a member of American Atheists and had even spoken at a few of their conventions. It still didn't get me any closer to what had happened, of course—as far as Heaven is concerned, an atheist's soul is just like any other nutbar's. If they lived a decent life, we take 'em.

I also did a little more searching for Magians online. Turns out the term doesn't just mean the guys out of the "We Three Kings" song but also covers Zoroastrian priests from Persia. Either way, though, it seemed to have too much to do with religion to interest someone like Walker. Could the name "Magians" have some other meaning, I wondered—alchemical or something? Could it be some kind of fraternal organization of scientists? I Googled as I worked my way through dinner but didn't turn up anything.

Somewhere during my second beer I looked up and noticed that a guy sitting at the bar was watching me, but he glanced away when he saw me looking back. He appeared to be an ordinary working guy in work boots and a trucker cap, probably Mexican or Central American by ancestry. At any other time I would have figured he'd just been looking me over out of idle curiosity, but tonight I was thinking about things differently. I caught him staring again a couple of minutes later and gave him a hard glance in return. He dropped his eyes quickly, but I could see a tiny sheen of sweat on his neck. He didn't look like someone who thought I was kind of cute. He looked like someone who'd recognized me, and that probably didn't mean anything good. That's the downside of having friends in odd places—other people who hang out in those odd places start to recognize you.

If I stayed long enough I felt pretty sure he'd find an excuse to step outside and call someone, so I beat him to the punch, finishing my beer with a long swallow and leaving my money on the table. As I headed for the door I swung wide to the bar and caught the guy by surprise. As he stared up at me I leaned toward him and whispered, "If anyone's coming after me, they better come hard and strong, got me? *Duro y fuerte. Porque yo soy un ángel de Dios.*"

I left him staring, his mouth hanging open. I had either given one of Hell's helpers fair warning or scared the crap out of some guy who'd developed a little crush on a stranger.

I walked back with my eyes wide open just in case he'd informed someone of my whereabouts before I noticed him, but I got back without incident. As I reached the motel my phone rang.

"Is this Mr. Dollar, yo? It's G-Man—remember?"

"G-Man as in Garcia? As in, I took away your piece and rapped your skull with it? Yeah, I remember you, chummy. What do you want?"

He sounded like he'd really psyched himself up for this. "You said . . . you said maybe I could get my strap back?"

"*Gun*, Garcia. A Palo Alto kid can't call it a 'strap' without sounding like a total douche. You got some information for me?"

Now he just sounded hurt. "Yeah, okay. Sorry. If I tell you something, can I get my—my gun back?"

"I don't know. What do you want to tell me?"

"Well, Posie . . . I was talking to Posie . . . she's my girlfriend, right? And she said when you came over you were interested in some African guy her grandfather knew?"

"Yeah, I am." Although this Magian thing was what really had my interest now. "So? Did you find out his name?"

"Sort of. But even better, man—he was here."

"What? What are you talking about? Where?"

"Here at Posie's house—I mean her granddad's house. That African guy was here. She didn't know he was coming or anything, he just showed up. He hung around for a long time, talking to Posie and stuff. She made him tea, even. He was here when you called before. Anyway, he just left a few minutes ago."

"He was there *when I called*?" It was very difficult not to shout, but I was on a public street. "And you waited until now to tell me?" I had a sudden, very strong suspicion about why this African gentleman might have dropped by and also why Posie hadn't been able to find the folder. "Jesus, why did you wait so long?"

"Hey, man, I didn't want to give anything away! Like that you were looking for him! I know all about this private detective shit, yo. So I waited until he left."

"God save me." I headed for the stairs down to the motel garage. "Stay there, both of you. I'll be right over."

"Well? Do I get my piece back?"

"Oh, I'm going to give it to you, all right—same way I did last time. I'm going to smack your dumbass head with it." I hung up on him and climbed into my car.

twelve
black windows

AS I hurried toward the Palo Alto district I thought about all the questions I still didn't have answers for. I needed to know more about the Magians for one thing, a lot more than I could find on my own, but it was hours too early to call Fatback unless I just wanted to listen to him grunt and squeal. (I've already got plenty of friends who can do *that* for me, especially if I catch them before they've had coffee.)

Still, things were moving fast enough that I was beginning to think I needed to go visit one of my other sources. Fatback was very good at what he did, so he was usually my first choice, but there were others in and around San Judas with a different and maybe deeper insight into what went on in the Opposition camp. The Broken Boy and the Sollyhull Sisters sprang to mind, but the Broken Boy was expensive, and hard to work with at the best of times—he had problems that made my new friend Foxy Foxy seem as together as the head of the local Rotary Club—so I decided I'd give the sisters a try first. Not now, though. Now I was back on University Avenue again, turning onto Walker's quiet, expensive side street. I was beginning to get sick of the smell of stately old trees and trimmed hedges.

"Wow," said Posie, opening the door. She was wearing a baggy caftan, the kind of thing hippy chicks used as sleepwear back in 1973. Posie had clearly missed her natural era. "He really did call you! I didn't know you and G even knew each other!"

"Yeah, we're practically white soul brothers. I understand the African gentleman you mentioned before, dropped in for a visit tonight."

She nodded as she led me down the hall toward the living room. "He just showed up. He's nice. I never really talked to him before."

"What did he want?"

"Oh, he wanted to thank us for a contribution my grandpa made to his charity. They're building some kind of school or . . . or hospital or something." She flapped her hand. "I didn't really catch all of it. G was tiptoeing around like Super Spy Squad. It was really distracting."

"Shut up," said Garcia, appearing from the kitchen with a box of Cheez-Its in his hands and crumbs in his little chin beard. "I was helping Mr. Dollar—right? I was, wasn't I?"

A little more help like his and I'd be demoted to appearing to nuns in visions. "Did your visitor say anything else, Ms. Walker? Did he leave any literature, anything? What was his name?" There was a chance the guy was perfectly legitimate—I never had anything on him in the first place except that Posie remembered him coming to visit her grandfather—but his timing was a little suspicious, showing up the same night I found out the Magian Society folder was gone.

"Mubari or Nabari or something," said Posie. "Something weird."

"With all due respect, you're killing me here," I said. "Did he give you a card or something else that might have a name, an address, anything?"

"Not this time. I think G scared him—he kept asking the poor guy all these stupid questions."

"They weren't stupid!" Garcia was full of righteous indignation. "I just asked him what his deal was."

I winced. If the poor guy was legit he couldn't have enjoyed that. If he wasn't . . . well, let's just say he was now definitely aware he was under suspicion. "Hold on, slow down. Ms. Walker, a second ago you said, 'Not this time.' Does that mean he gave you a card or something another time he was here?"

"I think so, yeah."

I did my best to remain calm. "Any possibility it's still around? That you could find it?"

"It might be in the crud drawer. That's where the rubber bands from the newspaper and, like, twist ties and all the useless stuff like that goes." She smiled beatifically, as if this breakthrough in domestic order was hers and hers alone.

I smiled back as charmingly as I could manage. "Any chance you could go see if it's there, Ms. Walker?" Because if this guy *was* a ringer he obviously wouldn't have left anything tonight. He had probably come just to vacuum up the Magian Society folder and any other loose ends, and he wouldn't be coming back, either. "It would really help my article on your granddad."

Two minutes later, after a great deal of rummaging noises and mumbled curses, Posie Walker reappeared in triumph waving a white cardboard rectangle. "Found it!"

I tried not to look too eager as I reached out for it. G-Man was watching me with the kind of hero-worshipping attention that I knew was going to cause trouble somewhere up the line. The card itself was simple—just a few lines in the same neat black italics as the folder I'd photographed:

The Rev. Dr. Moses Habari
The Magian Society
4442 East Charleston Road, Suite D, San Judas, CA 94043

There was a phone number too, which I immediately dialed. No longer in service, of course. "How long ago did you say he left?"

"'Bout half an hour," Garcia informed me. "You gonna go after him? Can I tag?"

I briefly considered telling him my real feelings, but decided I might need something from him or Posie later on. "No, I need you to stay here in case he gets in touch again. And if he does, *please don't do anything weird*." I gave him my sternest look. "Just call me, understand? Discreetly?"

"Under control, Mr. Dollar." He all but saluted. A couple of days ago he had been waving a gun in my face, now this dumbass was ready to follow me around like a baby duck. I don't know, sometimes I think I'm an idiot magnet.

I was back on the Bayshore a few minutes later, this time heading toward Southport. I knew East Charleston Road fairly well because it wasn't that far from where Sam lived, a neighborhood that had fallen on tough times twice, first in the seventies when the cargo-handling industry took a hit from competition across the bay, then again twenty years later when Shoreline Amusement Park closed for good. What remained were little business parks, storage lockers, and party supply warehouses, as well as a few apartment buildings and stores catering to a local population of retired longshoremen, general rummies, and of course the occasional angel.

As I made my way down Charleston toward the bay I could see the skeletal remains of Shoreline Park off to my right, the great fretwork arch of the Whirlaway coaster draped across the face of the waxing moon like a spiderweb. People were always coming up with new projects that were going to turn the little manmade island back into a dynamo of the local economy—hotels, office complexes, even one plan for a mid-bay golf course—but somehow they all came to nothing, and the abandoned amusement park just kept getting rustier and more decrepit. Nowadays it mainly got used as a location for low-budget zombie apocalypse movies.

4442 East Charleston was pretty much what I'd figured it would be, one of those single-story warehouse condos for small wholesalers and light retail, the business equivalent of the Island of Misfit Toys. Suite D was empty and shuttered, also as I expected. I should have brought my break-in tools (again, none of your business) but they were in one of the packing boxes from my apartment, and I hadn't had the time to find them. Anyway, it was impossible to tell from outside when anyone had last occupied the office suite, but just for due diligence I knocked loudly several times.

No response from the Magian Society folks, but a dissheveled guy with several days' growth of beard finally came out of the C space next door and asked me who I was looking for. I wondered if his wife had kicked him out and he'd moved into his shop (which turned out to be true). He ran a little grinding business, specializing in the sharpening of some kind of exotic industrial cutting blades, and was quite willing to talk—a little too willing. He told me within the first minute that he'd never seen the tenants of Suite D, had no idea what they did or sold, and had often wondered if anyone was using the space at all, but it took me another ten minutes to get away from him, and I had to admire some of his machinery and reject several offers of a beer first.

All the way back across the city to my motel I rolled the newest bits around in my mind. I had confirmation of a connection between the African gentleman and the Magian Society, and I had a name for him, or at least a pseudonym. Also, judging by how quickly he'd scuttled over to cover his tracks at the Walker place, I was pretty sure that he knew I was looking for him. I had got the name of the landlord for the Charleston address from the grinder guy and decided that might be a place to start tomorrow, if luck kept the local deaths down to a minimum, so I had some free time.

Of course, no sooner did I think this than the phone rang, summoning me to a heart attack in a Spanishtown apartment building.

The deceased, who seemed to be the beloved patriarch of a large Honduran-American family, eventually turned out to be a nasty old bastard who defeated my best efforts to paint him as a product of his culture and era. He hadn't actually killed or raped anyone, but his record was poor, and I was lucky to get him off with about a thousand years in Purgatory. I couldn't help hoping it would do him some good, because even as his soul stood looking at his own corpse and his dry-eyed family, he was complaining that he deserved better. He was still bitching when the light took him.

Anyway, it was a nasty grind, and by the time I stepped out of the Zipper and back into real-world Spanishtown, it was nearly two in the morning. (Time continues to pass Inside while you're Outside, if I didn't already mention that, although not always at exactly the same rate.) All I wanted to do was get back to my motel, pour a drink, and call Fatback, who would have cycled to man-brain-and-pig-body by now, then fall into bed. But I was also on edge due to recent events, so when I heard a noise at the other end of the client's apartment garage, I stopped in my tracks and yanked out my .38. Yes, my pulse was elevated. You damn betcha.

"Just to let you know, whoever you are," I announced loudly, "I'm tired, nervous, and armed. Let's avoid a serious mistake, shall we? Come out where I can see you."

The figure that stepped out of the shadows was so big that for a freaky moment I feared the worst, but I quickly saw this shape was far more human than the *ghallu* that had chased me. With some relief I recognized my old friend, the Countess's Bodyguard Number One.

"I wish we had some more time, Dollar," he said. "I'd love to see you try to stop me with that popgun before I folded you up like a napkin."

"Yeah, it's a shame we don't have time to try that, you big cutie," I said. "Seriously, if you want to waltz around, come back when I'm not so tired and we'll do it properly. Because right now I want to go to bed so bad that I'll just put a few slugs in your skull, which will at least keep you out of my hair long enough for me to get some shut-eye."

"You talk big, halo boy."

"Look, what do you want?" I wasn't kidding—I really was willing to shoot him just to get into bed sooner.

"Somebody wants to talk to you. She's waiting."

My heart sped. It couldn't be good to have an archdemon looking for you in the middle of the night, but for some reason I still found it exciting in a sick kind of way. "All right. One thing, though, Carob? Wait—Cocoa, was it?"

He wasn't amused. "It's Candy."

"Oh, sorry, right. I just wanted to know—where's your buddy with the porn 'stache?"

"Cinnamon? He's driving the car."

"I hope so. Because please notice where I'm holding my gun. If someone suddenly appears out of the bushes I'm going to blow your dick off on general principles."

Fortunately for Candy he was telling the truth. As we emerged from the apartment building garage, I saw a long car with black windows idling under a streetlight. The driver's window was open, and Cinnamon was sitting there in all his cookie-dustered glory. He sneered at me as Candy opened the back door and gestured for me to get in.

I didn't like turning my back on Candy—didn't like it at all—so I shoved my gun against his belly as I leaned down to look inside. The Countess gazed back at me. Her eyes were big as a doe's under the dome light, but none of Bambi's relations ever had a gleam like that. Satisfied that at least Candy and Cinnamon weren't on some kind of freelance revenge trip, I slid in. The door thumped shut behind me, making my ears pop.

"Hiya, Countess," I said. "Or does you following me around at this time of the night mean we're good enough friends that I can start calling you Ca—"

I didn't finish my sentence because she slapped me so hard it nearly dislocated my jaw. I stared at her for a moment, stunned. "Hang on . . . !" I began, then she smacked me again, and this time I felt her nails dig into my cheek like fishhooks. When little lights stopped flashing in front of my eyes I reached up and dabbed at the wetness I felt there. Yep, blood. "What the hell was that for?" I asked.

"I knew you were self-absorbed and self-satisfied, Mr. Dollar." The dome light was still on; she was showing a little color high on her cheeks, something I hadn't seen before. You'll probably think me hopelessly shallow when I confess that I liked it, despite the pain I'd had to endure to see it. "What I didn't realize is that you were also suicidal."

"I have no idea what you're talking about," I said.

"Oh, I think you do."

"On the contrary, and I feel like I know less and less every second." What was with this woman?—no, this *demon*, I reminded myself. I couldn't figure her out at all. Most of the denizens of Hell I meet make it very clear they wish they could immediately start killing you in a complex, painful way and are only prevented from doing so by the Tartarean Convention, but I couldn't figure out what the Countess wanted at all. "Why don't you ask me some questions next time before you start hurting me?"

"You think that hurt? Believe me, if I ever decide to inflict pain on you, Dollar, you'll know."

"Look, just tell me what's going on." Bodyguard Two had just climbed out from behind the wheel to share a smoke with Bodyguard One under the streetlight, so we were alone in the car. "Is this something to do with that Foxy character?"

"The little Japanese freak?" She leaned back in the seat. She was wearing a black dress, very short, and showing a lot of long, smooth leg. I dragged my attention back up to her face. *It's not real, Bobby,* I reminded myself. *Strip away the illusion, and she probably looks like some kind of giant slug.* "No," she said, "this is about you, angel. Word is all over the street that you've got hold of something big—and I'm not talking about the street you can see from your cruddy little apartment."

"Ah. You've seen it, then. I'm planning to redecorate—you know, ferns, Scandinavian Modern furniture in natural woods . . ."

"Shut up. I'm talking about the word on the Via Dolorosa." Which was one name for the main drag of Pandaemonium, the capital of Hell. "That you've got hold of something important and you're looking for a buyer. A once-in-an-epoch piece of merchandise."

"But I don't—!"

"Shut *up*. And they're also whispering all over Dis Pater Square and the rest of the city that you got this something important from *me*. Which means on top of everything else I have Chancellor Urgulap and his investigation poking into all my affairs, making my life miserable. I am *not happy*."

That stopped me dead for a second. I looked at her and for the first time saw not an impossibly beautiful temptress or an evil spirit in disguise but somebody who might just be as worried about the current state of play as I was. And I sure didn't envy anybody who had that horrible melted giant bug I'd met at Walker's place breathing down her neck.

"Okay, lady," I said. "You've had your say. Now listen to mine." I held my hand up to forestall an interruption and to my amazement it worked. "I don't know anything about any special something except that a dancing albino Asian asked me today if I wanted to sell it, and you seem to think I've been bragging that I have it. But like I said, I don't even know what I'm supposed to have, and if I've got it, I'm not aware of it. *Hang on*—I'm not done." I raised my hand again when she started to speak, but instead of slapping her as she'd done to me I reached forward and gently touched my finger to her red, red lips. I don't know exactly why I did it, I just did. She knocked my hand aside, but in a strange, uncaring way quite different from the way she'd slugged me just a minute earlier. "Right," I said. "Now, here's the next part. You remember the scorchmark I showed you—that handprint something burned into my door? Well, now I've seen that something up close and in person. In fact it tried to kill me last night, and nearly succeeded. When you saw that picture, I could tell it meant something to you—you've seen something like it before, haven't you? So instead of busting my chops again, why don't you show a little good faith and tell me what *you* know for a change? Something's got you upset, Countess—let's see if we can do each other some good. Is *all* this craziness about the Walker case?"

She stared at me for a long time, and all of a sudden the inspiration that had carried me along deserted me. What did I think I was doing here? I couldn't trust this tarted-up hellbitch even if she decided to trust me, and she would never trust me. Not to mention what would happen if my bosses found out I was sitting in a car in the middle of the night volunteering to share information with the Countess of Cold

Hands, one of Hell's fixers. The next summons I got would be to a heavenly court martial (if they didn't just incinerate me without a trial). This kind of shit just wasn't done without archangelic supervision, and I had already been warned to stay on the straight and narrow. But things had started moving too fast for me, and I was tired of playing blind man's bluff, weary of trying to figure out the shape of what was going on by feel alone.

"It's not all about the Walker case," she said slowly. "But Walker has got my masters shaken up."

"Really? It's not just something they've done to drive Heaven crazy?"

She shook her head. "Doesn't seem to be. As far as I can tell, they're really worried. And there have been more souls lost since that happened."

I felt a little chime of reassurance. I knew I was probably crazy for even entertaining the possibility, but maybe she really was being straight with me—or as straight as she knew. "I've heard that too. But if both sides are freaking out, where did Walker go? Where did any of them go?"

She pulled a compact from her purse and gave herself a quick once-over in the mirror. "Don't know," she said. "And to be honest, I don't care, even though I've been questioned about it nonstop ever since it happened. I've got enough problems of my own."

"Like what?"

Her eyes flashed, and I'm not saying that poetically: something sparked red in the depths. "None of your fucking business, Dollar."

"Okay, fair enough. But what about the thing that burned the crap out of my apartment door?"

"It's a *ghallu*," she said, sounding like an English Home Counties schoolgirl reciting what she'd learned in a particularly dreary class, "a living piece of Old Night, which is another word for Chaos, in case you crashed and burned your afterlife exams. Expensive to summon, nearly impossible to stop. And, yes, I've seen that mark before."

"Where? And who sent it after me?"

"The answer to the first is, again, none of your business, Dollar. As to the second, I don't know, but it's bad news. If you really don't know what's going on with any of this, I strongly suggest you get out of the way, as far away and for as long as possible. No good can come of it."

Now it was my turn to stare. For the first time since the conversation started I didn't believe what she was saying, at least the part about not knowing who sent the *ghallu*. Still, she had been amazingly open, so I decided not to push my luck. Well, not *too* much.

"Okay, then, Countess. Only one more question, I guess. What about us?"

Her eyes opened wide. "What?" But she sounded more surprised than angry. "What's that supposed to mean, angel?"

"We're helping each other, right? Well, what if I find out something you should know? I'm not just going to hang around The Water Hole on the off chance you'll wander in to pick up a couple of pre-meds to go."

"Is that really what we're doing?" She was definitely amused in a kind of biting-something-sour way. "Helping each other? As far as I can see, the only person helping anyone is me. What could you possibly do for me in return?"

"Let's not rush things. Just in case it comes up, how do I get in touch?"

She laughed, suddenly and with apparent sincerity. "You really are a piece of work, Bobby Dollar. You have a very high estimation of your own importance."

"Beg your pardon, sister, but it's your car I'm sitting in, not the other way around. You wanted to talk to me. *And* knock me around a bit." My jaw was still sore.

"Very well." She pulled a business card from her purse, wrote something on it with a very nice fountain pen. "Call this in an emergency. Leave a message. I'll get hold of you."

"Thank you, Countess." I still wasn't quite sure what I had got into, but it was definitely something unusual.

Suddenly a smile, tight and secretive. "Oh, I think you can call me Caz, now," she said. "Until you get yourself killed, anyway. Sleep tight."

Which was definitely a dismissal. I slid toward the door, then paused. "I've been meaning to ask you—where does your name come from?"

"Casimira? It's Polish . . ."

"No, your other name—the Countess of Cold Hands."

She leaned forward and cupped my face in her slender fingers. The skin was as icy as a fish's belly. "You know what they say," she said, and a strange, sad expression crossed her face. "Cold hands—cold heart." The door opened behind me as if by magic, but it was only big Candy, who helped me out none too gently.

"Goodnight, boys," I called as he and his plug-ugly pal climbed back into the black car. "Dream of me."

The long, low car with black windows rolled silently away and I stumbled toward my car and the drive back to my motel.

thirteen
leviathan on a hook

AS LATE as I got to bed, as tired, scared, and pissed off as I was, you'd have thought that just this once the universe might cut me some slack. You'd have been wrong. My phone rang again at five-thirty in the morning and, although I ignored it, kept ringing every two minutes until I gave up and rolled onto the floor, then crawled across the unfamiliar motel room on my hands and knees to answer it. It wasn't a Heaven-related number, so I was even more certain it couldn't be anything worth waking up for.

"Who wants to die?"

"It's me, Bobby." The pig man.

"It's really, really goddamned early, George, in case you didn't notice."

"Nobody knows that better than me. You want to talk about the time? I got about ten minutes left until the sun's up and then all you're going to get is oink, oink, oink."

"Sorry, George. Go ahead."

"Okay, first there's 'Kephas.' It's ancient Aramaic and it means 'rock.' It's what Jesus actually named Peter. You know, 'You are Peter, and upon this rock I will build my church.' There's tons of mentions on various Bible sites but only in that context. I haven't found anything interesting or out of the ordinary about Magians yet . . . but *you're* hot as a pistol, Mr. D. Lot of people want to know about you. According to my sources, secondary queries with your name in them have tripled in the last few days."

"What are 'secondary queries'?"

"That's someone other than me asking the questions."

Helplessness tugged at me, the leading edge of panic, and I did my best to slap it away. "Why me, George? What is it that everyone wants to know? And who's asking?"

"As to who, it's mostly folks who operate on the edges between the two sides. Information users, mostly. I can't figure out yet what's got people so interested except that some folks have been talking about you and others want to know why. There's a lot of stuff all over .ky."

It was too damn early. "Dot K Y? I'm big news on a sexual lubricant site?"

"No, that's just the domain name—means Cayman Islands. Lot of the paranormal folk use their internet domain because the accounts can't be traced. Anyway, my business is all about information chasing its own tail, but it's even harder than usual to get hold of anything substantial on this; I'm chasing a rumor without knowing what the rumor is, see? But I promise I'll let you know as soon as I have anything specific."

"Thanks, George. You're a good man. Anything on the monstrosity that's after me? Tall, dark and horny?"

"Oh, shit, yeah—of course. I'm really sorry you have to deal with that crap, Bobby."

"Yeah, George, I am too." I appreciated him, but I wasn't at my most patient. "Any helpful details?"

"Again, not very much. They're not common. 'Allu' or 'ghallu' is the closest match I can find."

"I've got confirmation on that already. Some kind of hireling spirit. Very old, pre-Christian."

"Yeah. And it's bad news."

"I knew that, too."

"The problem is, they don't show up very often, so nobody's got much real information more recent than the nineteenth century. Only somebody with a lot of clout can put one of those babies to work."

"Damn it, George, I already heard all this—I need to know what to *do* about it! How do you kill one, or at least dismiss it?"

"I don't know, Bobby. The last confirmed sighting was back in the nineteen eighties in Syria."

"Well, I confirmed one trying to set my ass on fire as it chased me down the Camino Real a couple of nights ago, so I think I need a better answer than that."

There was a long pause. When he spoke again, something strange had happened to his voice. "I . . . I'm . . ."

"George? You okay?"

"Unh. Unh." He was reduced to grunting now. I peered at my window and saw a gray gleam between the curtains. Daybreak. *"Unhhh. . . ."* The next grunt had a little squeal in it—I guess the last human part of him didn't like letting go.

"Well, thanks for calling, George." I hung up and crawled back into bed, which seemed like as good a place to die as any other.

Just to make sure I didn't get too much sleep, Alice sent me a client at about eight o'clock. I had to scramble out of the motel without breakfast and hurry down to Sequoia Hospital, where I at least had the luck to represent a lovely elderly lady who had spent most of her life going to church and taking care of her family and also most of her neighborhood, like Mother Teresa without the lust for publicity. Seeing her go peacefully and happily into the light reminded me that a lot of what I do is to make sure good people get the reward they deserve.

When I was done it was almost lunchtime. I hadn't been to The Compasses for a couple of days and I was feeling nostalgic so I called the place. Chico set the phone out on the bar and made it a conference call with the members of the Choir who were there—Walter Sanders, Sweetheart, Young Elvis, and a few others. No Monica, no Sam.

"What's happening, Bobby?" Kool Filter asked. He had a voice like Louie Armstrong trying not to cough, and he almost always sounded amused. "Heard some ugly old shit is chasing you around."

"Nothing I can't handle." Which was an outright lie, but I hate people feeling sorry for me like a cat hates bathwater. "Seen Sam?"

"He was in last night," reported Young Elvis. He got that name because of his hair, by the way. I have never seen any living human being spend as much time fucking with his hair as this angel does. There's a permanent solidified mist of hairspray on The Compasses' bathroom mirror because of him. It's a pretty spectacular 'do, though, I have to admit—like the King in his leather-jacketed prime. Our boy likes to wear that rockabilly shit, too, Spanish heels, the works.

"Hey, do any of you happen to know where I can find the Sollyhull Sisters these days?"

Kool chortled. "Shit, you *are* a glutton for punisment, B. I think somebody said they were haunting some diner across town."

"Superior Grill, off the 84," Walter Sanders said in his sniffy way. "At least they were there a week ago. Ruined my otherwise perfectly mediocre lunch."

I thanked them and signed off. I missed hanging out with the Whole Sick Choir, but I wasn't going to see them for at least a few days, that was obvious. If my visit to the Magian Society's landlord didn't take too long, and nothing else intervened or tried to kill me, I figured I might be able to consult the sisters that evening. They could tell me things even Fatback couldn't, and about now I was feeling a desperate need for new information.

As I threw on my jacket to go out my phone rang again. It was Monica.

"Well, hello, stranger," she said, but if you had licked her tone of voice your tongue would have been frozen to it until the fire department came to get you off. "I just walked in to The Compasses and the boys said I barely missed you. How's life?"

"Yeah, great, sort of." I couldn't avoid it any longer, that was clear. "You have a minute to talk?"

I could almost *hear* the lifted eyebrow. "A whole minute?" she said. "This *is* my lucky day."

I hoped she was sitting by herself instead of in the middle of the Choir. Nothing like a dysfunctional tavern family to make an emotional scene even more embarrassing.

"Look, I know I've been kind of distracted lately," I began.

"Don't underestimate yourself, Bobby darling. The truth is, you've been an utter shit."

I opened my mouth to argue, then said, "Yeah. Yeah, you're right."

"What is it with you?" Now I could hear how deep the unhappiness went. "We had a crazy night—so what? You think that means I expect us to get married or something? Hello? I'm an immortal just like you are. If anybody understands letting someone have their space, I do. Not to mention that you made your need for that space very clear a long time ago."

"I know. I just . . ." That's why I hate cell phones. The door to the outside world was only a few feet away but it didn't make any difference: I was connected and could not honorably disconnect until the conversation was over. And I was too old for the *bad reception—I'm losing you* dodge. I sighed. "Honestly, Monica, honey, things really *have* been complicated. With demons trying to murder me and all. But basically you're right. I did a terrible job. I actually had a nice time with you that night, and the next morning, too . . . but I got in my own way. I even hope we can do it again sometime. But I was afraid you'd—"

"Take it more seriously than you." Some of the bitterness was gone this time. "Possibly. But not anymore, now that I've seen that you're still a prick when you get panicky. And any future Naber-Dollar collaborations will go forward only with that in mind." She took a drink of something, swallowed. "Because I don't want to lose you as a friend, Bobby. I really mean that. You've always been an idiot, but you make me laugh."

"I don't want to lose you, either, Monica. As a friend, I mean. Or . . . or whatever we are, sometimes. So I don't know exactly what we're agreeing—but it's a bargain, right?"

"Right. Just try not to be such an asshole."

I was still jumpy about everything else but a little less guilty about Monica as I began my research on who owned the 4442 East Charleston property. This was the kind of legwork I could do myself, which was just as well because the Sollyhulls didn't do real-world stuff, and Fatback wasn't going to be of any use to anyone except the local sows for another eleven hours or so.

As I suspected, a quick check of title deeds, county tax records, and other fun stuff confirmed what I already suspected: the landlord Grinder Guy gave me was a holding company, just a cutout for the real owner of the property. And that was only the first holding company of several, as it turned out. Somebody had buried the facts pretty deeply, but I'm a curious guy who likes to get answers, so I know my way around a tedious paper trail better than most. An hour of work in the county file dungeons, a few small bribes, and I finally had what I wanted—the identity of the true and ultimate owner of the address listed on Habari's Magian Society business card. It was a bit of an eye opener.

There was still some afternoon remaining so I headed to the other side of the Palo Alto district to follow up—not the garden suburbs this time, but the tall and shiny buildings of Page Mill Square along the Camino Real, just a little south of the Stanford campus. In only a couple of short decades the office towers there had climbed above even the Wells Fargo building and the other proud stalwarts of Jude's old downtown, and the one I was headed toward was one of the tallest of them, Five Page Mill, otherwise known as the Vald Credit Building.

The most interesting thing was not that a billion-dollar institution like Vald Credit was the ultimate landlord for a little hole-in-the-wall operation like the Magians, but how much trouble someone had taken to hide that fact in a chain of ownership as long as my arm. I mean, I suppose it could have been coincidental—obviously a business empire that big must own a lot of stuff—but another thing that made it interesting was that Vald Credit was owned by one guy, and pretty much everyone in San Judas knew about him.

It wasn't that Kenneth Vald had become rich in any unusual way: he had made a little money, then used that money to make some more, and so on and so on. He hadn't even done anything particularly awful along the way, by billionaire standards, though nobody makes a globe-girdling fortune without stepping on a few toes. No, he was famous precisely because he and his riches were so visible. He was a man who enjoyed being wealthy in the most public possible way: parties, public exposure, expensive toys, and expensive women. Vald acted like someone who'd made a deal with the devil and was going to enjoy every instant of it until the loan came due. My colleagues and I had been convinced for a long time that there was more than a hint of sulphur to Vald's resumé.

Of course, one of the things about powerful people like Ken Vald is that you don't just waltz in and get an appointment to see them. In fact, I wasn't going get an appointment no matter what I did—at least, not as long as I went about it the ordinary way. So I wasn't going to bother with the ordinary.

Yes, the whole thing was probably stupid from the start. I should have gone back and done a full-scale prep on Vald before I went anywhere near the place. That was what I had been taught, and if I'd sent that along with a full report to Heaven it might even have got me off the hook with my superiors. But right that moment I was curious enough to cut some corners and nervous enough about my current dangerous situation not to care if it was kind of stupid. Plus, there was also the buzz of being on to something: it seemed pretty damn significant that the Edward Walker case, which had put all of Heaven and Hell in an uproar, should be connected, however remotely, to the office of such a very wealthy and seemingly arrogant man.

Actually, that was another reason not to just walk right in, now that I think about it.

A little rain was falling when I left my car in a restaurant parking lot across the Camino Real from Page Mill Square. I knew that the underground parking lot shared by the buildings around the square could be locked down with a single call, and I didn't want to be stuck in there if I pissed anyone off, because I was already guessing I might piss *someone* off before the afternoon was over, I just didn't know yet how many or how badly.

A lot of both as it turned out.

The lobby of number Five was pretty much what I would have expected, workers streaming in and out, messengers with packages, maintenance guys trundling carts. A big guard desk dominated the front end of the lobby with five guys in uniforms; a smaller desk sat at the other end of the lobby, and everywhere I looked I saw security cameras. I also noticed that they weren't letting anyone go through without an employee badge and a visual inspection. Even the bike messengers had to leave their packages at the desk, probably so they could go through an x-ray machine. Anyway, security was pretty darn tight. I loitered for a while as if I was waiting for someone, checking my watch from time to time, and wandered in and out of the sundries store that sold gum and cigarettes and checked that out too.

Number Five appeared to be your average office tower in most ways, although the employees seemed a little more reserved than what you'd usually see in a big company, more like the kind of vibe you'd expect from workers in a foreign embassy in an unfriendly city. Still, as I've mentioned, I was pretty hyped up so I told myself I might be imagining things. Then something happened that I most definitely *didn't* imagine: a group of obvious security guys emerged from one of the service elevators in matching dark glasses, ear-pieces, and suits with gun bulges. The desk guards greeted them respectfully as they went past on their way to the main entrance. They obviously worked there and looked like the usual collection of muscle unleavened by sense of humor, but something about the one in front was extremely familiar, especially his unibrow and thick, close-cropped dark hair. He glanced in my direction without seeing me as he led his men through the front doors, and suddenly I recognized him even in his people-skin. He had just too much beast in his face to look one hundred percent human, his hairline too low, his nose too wide across the bridge. It was Howlingfell, the guy who had been Grasswax's muscle the night Clarence saved the Martino lady from getting sent to Hell. The guy whose neck I had sort of kneeled on.

I watched him disappear out onto the sidewalk and decided that there was no way coincidence could be stretched *that* far. I definitely needed to learn more about Vald Credit, and the best way might be paying a visit to the executive suite while Howlingfell and his security team were out of the building. I knew it wasn't the most subtle play, but as I may have told you, when I get stressed I tend to drop back into old habits. I wanted answers, and failing that, I wanted people to know I was pissed.

I decided my best bet would be the smaller guard station at the less-used back entrance, where only two men were on duty. I stood around a few minutes more until one of the guards had gone off to the restroom, then I walked up to the other one just as he finished running his barcode reader over someone's badge.

"Excuse me," I said, "but I think you'd better come look at this elevator. Something's seriously wrong. Someone could get hurt."

He hesitated for a second, glancing around to see if his partner was coming back, but then grunted in a bad-tempered way and got up from his booth. He looked like he might have been an athlete about a decade ago, but he'd been sitting down too much since then.

"Which elevator?" he said as he followed me toward the rear elevator bank, one hand resting on the butt of his taser in a very impressive way.

"This one," I said, punching a button.

It opened, and he peered inside. It was empty. "What's wrong with it?" he asked.

"Well," I said, pressing the barrel of my .38 against his spine, "it's going to have your guts all over it in a second if you don't get in."

He grunted again, this time in shock. I nudged him forward. As the elevator door closed behind us he said, "What the hell is . . . ?"

I clocked him behind the ear with the handle of my revolver. The butt was rubberized so I hit him pretty hard, and he slumped to the floor without another word, though I did my best not to cause permanent damage on the slim chance he was an innocent patsy instead of accredited Hell-minion—which was far more likely if this place was as important as I was beginning to suspect. I slipped his ID card into the elevator slot, pressed the 40th floor button, and we started up. I looked at his name badge then took the walkie-talkie off his shoulder and keyed it on.

"This is Daley in the lobby," I announced, trying to sound like an excited nine dollars an hour. "Somebody just ran out the back to the rear parking lot carrying a woman's purse. I think it's a robbery! I'm in pursuit!" I keyed it off and attached it to his belt again.

Luckily no one was waiting for an elevator on the 40th floor. I dragged Daley down to the restroom, then into one of the stalls where I propped him up. I dumped his walkie-talkie into the toilet of the next stall so it wouldn't disturb his slumber, and also so he wouldn't be able to alert anybody too quickly if he came to before I left. I also checked to make sure he was breathing okay, just in case he turned out to be an actual person. Yeah, I'm that soft—I'm an angel, remember?

And this is where you came in.

I already explained what happened next. I reached the top floor of Five Page Mill and encountered Vald's demon-secretary, who flaunted most versions of expected business etiquette by leaping across her desk and trying to rip me apart with her claws and teeth. I shot her twice in the face, which caused a lot of damage but didn't slow her down much, and I also broke her jaw so badly that it swung like a door coming off its hinges, but she was still coming after me. It was when she got me down on the floor and began trying hard to tear my head right off the body it belonged on that it became clear I was losing the fight.

When you've only got seconds to live you don't fuck around with etiquette. If you're fighting a guy you hit him in the nuts as hard as you can. If you're fighting a she-demon who is wrapped around you like a constrictor and trying to bite off your face, and you can't reach anything else, you punch her in the tit. It caught her by surprise just enough to make her rear back with a snort of rage, at which point I got my hand free, reached up, and yanked hard at the strings of bloody flesh hanging from her wounded face, peeling them most of the way down. Thank goodness that even borrowed mortal bodies have nerves, because the pain was enough to distract her long enough for me to fight my way free, panting and covered with blood, some of it hers but not all. I've had fights that made me feel better about myself.

I scrambled my way back across the outer office as she lurched after me, still trying to locate me through the tatters of flesh blocking her vision. When she realized I must be trapped against the floor-to-ceiling window she leaped toward me, arms wide and snarling, a faceless, hateful thing. I didn't want those red nails sinking into me again, so I shoved my gun against the plate glass and fired twice before I spun out of her way. The safety glass spiderwebbed, then leaped outward in a sparkle of little irregular pieces as she hit it and crashed through.

I waited a few seconds, then leaned out into the cold air to check out the body in the tasteful silk power suit lying motionless on a rooftop about a hundred feet below. She was about as dead as demons get, or at least her real-world body was, and that was the part that would get me arrested.

Shit, Bobby Dollar, I thought, *what have you got yourself into now?*

It was way too late to turn back. I shouldered through the door to the spacious inner office, gun held high. I couldn't remember exactly how many times I'd shot the she-demon, and even if I was lucky there couldn't be more than one bullet still left in the chamber, but I was damned if I was going to let anyone know that. Not that the man waiting for me looked very scared of my .38. He turned slowly away from the window where he had been looking down at the remains of his secretary. Kenneth Vald was handsome as a Spanish grandee out of a Velasquez painting.

"So, you couldn't make an appointment like anyone else?" he asked.

"Very funny." I moved sideways until I had his huge teak desk between him and me. He was maybe in his early forties at most, dressed in the casual-est of business casual, a blue Lacoste polo shirt and khaki slacks, expensive loafers without socks. He was pleasantly tanned, had white-blonde hair that was less sticky but just as impressively full as Young Elvis's, and a neatly trimmed goatee. He looked like a talent agent who would represent the Hitler Youth.

"What do you know about the Magian Society, Mr. Vald?" I asked him.

He frowned just a little bit. "Just like that? Get you, you come in and kill my assistant—do you know how long it takes to train a really good executive PA?—then demand information. Why should I talk to you? I'm sure you've arranged some little diversion but it's only a matter of time until security gets here. Oh, and if you think you're going to scare me with that toy gun—well, go ahead." He pointed right to the alligator over his heart. "Put a couple right there. See if it even slows me down while I twist your head off."

He took a step toward his desk. I didn't want him getting anywhere near it, so I steadied my revolver. "Fine. But if I shoot you in the face, at the very least it's going to ruin your weekend, Ken. And I have another even better reason you should behave yourself."

"Oh? What might that be?"

"Because I don't think you want everyone in Pandaemonium to know about your connection to the Magian Society." I watched him carefully (I still didn't know if he was a sold soul or an actual, paid-up member of the Opposition) but his face gave nothing away. "See, my guess is that you've got more than a few friends downstairs, Ken—and I don't mean in the lobby of number Five. Oh, and the Celestial City might be interested in your activities too, so remember, if anything happens to me they're *all* going to know, because I arranged things that way."

"What, that old *if my lawyer doesn't hear from me he'll go to the authorites* wheeze?" He looked me over for a long, speculative moment. "Cute," he said at last. "And what do you think this is going to get you? Wings? Because you must be an angel, or at least an ex."

Which I confess freaked me out a bit, because I'd never heard of such a thing as an ex-angel, or at least not any new ones since the Fall. I was beginning to think this guy was no ordinary sinner. Listening too closely to what demons say is a famous rookie mistake, however, and whatever else I might be, I'm no rookie. "Does it matter?" I asked. "I just want information. If you give it to me and it's real, then I'll walk away and everyone's happy."

"Everyone? What about poor Holly? She was the pitcher on our company softball team." He took a few steps back toward the window and looked out and down again. "Ah, the police are here. Looks like somebody noticed her body." He turned around and smiled at me. "What's your name, angel? Who is it I'm going to see dragged down to the deepest pits of Erebus?"

"I'm not telling you my name unless you tell me yours." There are rules about these things, you see. "But I don't care that much about you, really. I just want to know about the Magians. Now hurry up, Ken. If your guards get here you're going to be in more trouble than I'll be in, remember?"

He sighed and shook his head, then spread his arms in a gesture of amused resignation. Something I can only call an aura of power began to radiate from him, strong as the heat of the sun on a hungover morning, strong enough to make my eyes blink and my head ache. The master of Five Page Mill was golden and self-assured as a lion on the veldt. "Tell you my name? You mean you really don't know? Do you think that if you find out you'll wield some kind of control over me?" He laughed like he truly was enjoying himself, as if I had shown up just to please him. "I'm Eligor the Horseman, you wretched upstart—one of the Grand Dukes of Hell."

Oh, shit. That was all I could think, over and over like a skipping CD. *Oh, shit. Oh, shit.* Eligor was one of the really big ones. I had tossed in my little baited hook, and I had snagged Leviathan.

"I fought beside the Lightbringer at the walls of Heaven." His voice seemed to get louder with every moment. "I was cast down when He was cast down. I have shared His exile since the beginning. But you—you're nothing. A fly." With that he began to grow, shadows of both glaring light and total darkness stretching around him, his face blossoming into something grotesque and horrifying beyond description, until he towered above me crowned in flames and cloaked in shadow and the room itself seemed shrunken to the size of a grave.

"And do you know what else?" His voice pressed in on me from all sides, louder even than my heart's blood as it rushed through my veins. "I don't believe your story, little angel. I don't think you've made any arrangements at all. No, I'd guess you're the improvisational type—that you're here by yourself without any backup plan at all. And that's how you're going to die, too. *Alone.*"

He stretched out his hand toward me. I couldn't move. Dimly, dimly through the thundering of my arteries I could hear the guards banging on the office's outer door, breaking in, but I couldn't turn, couldn't see anything but Eligor's triumphant, terrifying face.

fourteen
friends in low places

ELIGOR'S LONG, icy fingers wrapped my head. Again I was in the presence of something that could tear my mortal body apart like bread dough, but this time it had already caught me. The founder of Vald Credit lifted me at arm's length until my feet were kicking several inches above the floor and my neck felt like chewed taffy.

"Go ahead," I told him, determined not to go out begging. It probably sounded a lot like *Grrruhrhrdd,* since his hand was crushing my features into a shape they weren't meant to take. "Kill me." *Krrrmrr.*

"Oh, definitely. Sooner rather than later." He smiled. There were sharp things in his mouth that didn't even look remotely like teeth. "But first, I'm going to call up a couple of hard, pipe-hittin' Nergalis and we're going to go to work on you until we find out who you are and why you came storming into my office with this Magian Society bullshit."

Still dangling me in mid-air like a prize trout he muted his glamour and shrank back to looking like Kenneth Vald once more, but his eyes remained distinctly goatlike, pus-yellow with horizontal slots for pupils. This was about as bad as things could get. Eligor may not have been Old Scratch himself, but he was high in the Hellish nobility, with strength and abilities to match. They don't really have a firm hierarchy down there, but I couldn't kid myself—he was a member of the All-Star Team and I was one of Heaven's lowliest bench-warmers.

The demon lord fluttered the fingers of his free hand and the nearer office door abruptly sprang open. Out of the corner of my eye I saw a half-dozen or more armed guards dressed like SWAT commandos tumble through and into the office. One was so surprised by the door's sudden unlocking that as he fell he discharged his M4 with a deafening rattle. Bits of ceiling rained down around us for several seconds as the guards scrambled to their feet and surrounded me with a ring of automatic weapons, although it scarcely seemed necessary since I was still hanging helplessly in midair and no threat to anything except my own dry underwear.

Several of the plainclothes security guys shoved in after the armored men. The leader of these had his gun in one hand and a phone in the other. It was Howlingfell. "Boss," he said, "—I mean Your Grace—we got a problem!"

"I've got the problem right here," said Eligor, bouncing me gently up and down. I swear I could hear my neck vertebrae popping like popcorn. "I want you to get me some of those nasty Shahr-e Sukhteh fuckers who like to play with needles and fire. We're going to find out who this little winged rat is and who sent him."

"Oh, shit," said Howlingfell. "I think I know that guy." He pushed his way through the ring of guards and got right up in my face, standing on tiptoes so he could examine me as I struggled in Eligor's unbreakable grip. Even in his human body he was no prize: not only was he ugly, he had breath like rotting dog food. After a moment he showed his teeth in a tongue-lolling grin. "Yeah, that's Bobby Dollar. I met him a coupla times—he's one of those advocates." If he remembered me, I was pretty sure he also remembered my foot on his windpipe.

I smiled back, then spat at him, hoping he might go for me despite his boss's presence and accidentally kill me (this definitely seemed like one of those situations where dying had to be better than the alternative) but although the gob of spittle landed on his cheek, Howly never had the chance to do anything but step back, because suddenly Eligor roared like a wounded lion and flung me to the ground.

"Bobby Dollar?" his master bellowed. "You mean this is *Doloriel*? The little pimp who *stole from me*?"

This shit was just getting worse and worse. So that thing I was supposed to have (but didn't actually possess) belonged to one of the Grand Dukes of Hell? To the same archdemon who had just captured me with the ease of a man scooping up an escaped hamster and had decided to set some sadistic Middle Eastern demons on me before he even knew who I was? This was just fucking peachy.

"Tell me where it is, punk. Right now." Eligor leaned down and yanked me back into the air, this time with hands clamped on each arm, and held me in front of his face. He smelled a lot better than Howlingfell, but for a moment I could see into the endless abyss behind those black-slot eyes, and it nearly stopped my heart. Eligor wasn't Hell's only grand duke, but there aren't many and they are all horrifyingly dangerous. Like the stupid dick I am, I had started a bar fight with a stranger who turned out to be a World Heavyweight Champ. "If you tell me right now," he said, "maybe I'll just peel your face off and let you live like that for a while, chained to my desk."

"I c-can bring it to you. I swear I can—if you let me go. Otherwise you don't get shit out of me."

"Oh, I'll get *everything* out of you, you little winged pimple." The demon lord was having trouble keeping his Kenneth Vald face on: it was rippling as if it might get too hot and just melt away. The experience was a bit like sitting in the control room of a nuclear power plant in mid-disaster—fascinating in that you only get to watch something like that once in your life, and it's probably also going to be the last thing you'll ever see. "Sweat, blood, shit, and piss to begin with," Eligor snarled, "—oh, a *lot* of blood. Then eventually every cell of your body will slowly be turned into liquid and squeezed out onto the floor of my recreation room." He dropped me again. I fell hard but managed to crawl back up onto my knees. Might as well die with my head above floor level, I figured. (Don't ask me why—it just seemed better somehow.)

"But, Master," said Howlingfell, "you can't—I mean, not now!"

Vald/Eligor turned toward him, head pivoting slowly like a king cobra gauging optimum striking distance. "I *can't* . . .?"

Howlingfell went pale and began squirming. I thought he was going to throw himself to the floor beside me and show Eligor his belly. "No, it's because of the cops! There's about forty of them down in the lobby." He waved his phone. "They said there's a fugitive up here—they must have meant this Dollar guy. He's wanted for murdering Grasswax, the prosecutor—I mean Grazuvac. They were afraid he might have taken you hostage. It was all I could do to get them to wait five minutes and let me and my men check things out!"

Eligor snorted. "Cocksuckers. As if some minor-leaguer's going to . . ." He shook his head in irritation. "Look, just tell them we killed the little shit already, and they can come pick up the body pretty soon. That'll give us time to—"

Astonishingly, Howlingfell interrupted. He had bigger balls than I thought, although judging by the look on Eligor's face he might not have them for long. "But it's been more than five minutes, Master. They're already on the way up. Talk to the guy in charge of them, Your Grace—he won't listen to me!"

"Give me that fucking phone." Eligor reached out and snatched it from Howlingfell's hand. "Is someone there? This is Kenneth Vald speaking. Officer, I don't know who you are, but I demand you contact Deputy Chief Bryant and he'll tell you . . ." He paused for a moment. "Bryant? That's you? What the hell is going on? How dare you enter my building without . . ." There was another kind of anger in his voice now and, for at least this moment, he had forgotten about me. I stared blearily around the room but didn't see any immediate hope of escape. My revolver, which might or might not have been empty, had fallen to the ground when the Grand Duke grabbed me, then had been kicked aside somewhere by one of his guards. Unlike the window in the outer office, the one in here was still whole, and without a gun I had doubts I could break the safety glass, even if I could somehow get through the ring of guards pointing their assault rifles at me.

"What do you mean you're outranked? I don't care!" Duke Eligor was beginning to look a bit bothered: his hair and whiskers were still the same pale, pale gold, but his skin had gone the color of new brick. "Well, screw you and your higher authority, Bryant! I'm going to cut the little bastard to pieces, and you can have what's left when you get there. So? I don't *care* if this is a public frequency! Anyway, who's even going to know if you tell them the guy was already . . ." He frowned, listening, then pointed at Howlingfell. "Go look out the window."

The minion went to the window. "What do you want to know?"

"Are there guys with sniper rifles and cameras on the roof of the Courier Building?" Eligor asked. "Looking in the window here?"

"Yes, Master," Howlingfell said. "A lot of them. Do I have to keep standing here? What if they think I'm him?"

Eligor raised the phone again. "Who did this shit to me, Bryant? Because that's a pretty damn big coincidence. I want a name." His slotted eyes narrowed. "Oh, really? All right, you can take the suspect. Bring your men in and I'll have my boys stand down." He clicked off the phone and turned to Howlingfell. His expression could have removed paint from a battleship hull. "We're going to let them have him. Too much shit to clean up, otherwise."

Howlingfell scuttled over. As he dragged me up off the floor he gave my arm a not-too-friendly squeeze just to let me know he remembered our previous meeting. I swear the bones squeaked as they rubbed together. "But if you want to question him, Master, can't we just take him Outside? Then you'll have all the time you want. As long as he's alive and still breathing when we turn him over to the cops. . . ."

Eligor cursed, or at least that's what I assume he did. I couldn't understand the words, but at the sound of his sharp exclamation a wind suddenly rose that made the windows shudder and several of the papers on his long teak desk caught fire. "Did I advertise for stupid? Because that's the only way you could have been the top candidate." He glared. Howlingfell cringed. "You *can't* take one of our kind out of Time unwillingly without turning the whole apple cart upside down. That's a major breach of the Conventions—it'll set off alarms from the top floor of Creation down to the basement, alert his overlords *and* mine, and probably start a war. Do you think that's a good idea, you fucking idiot? *Do you?*"

"No, Master!"

I would have sworn the security chief was about to urinate submissively.

"And you, angel," said Eligor, turning to me. "Don't think you're safe even with the police. You can guess how many friends we've got in prison." He laughed, but he sure didn't sound happy. "You've got something of mine and not only am I going to get it back, you're going to suffer like you never even imagined suffering. You thought you could treat Eligor the Horseman like some kind of street bitch, did you? I'll see you again . . . real soon."

And before I could even reply to any of his charming promises he kicked me in the balls and then in the head as I crumpled forward, sending me somewhere that even angels go if you hit them hard enough.

I won't bore you with the details of being dragged across the San Judas Hall of Justice parking garage, half-stupefied, handcuffed, and throbbing painfully between my legs, then being tossed into a holding cell to wait, bruised and bloody, without benefit of either a lawyer or medical attention. Stronger than normal body or not, I was in a world of serious hurt. About half an hour later, when I was able to sit upright on my own without puking, two SJPD officers came and led me to the booking desk. The cops there might as well have been processing a shadow—they barely looked at me, spoke to me only enough to direct me through the required photos and fingerprinting, then dumped me back into the holding tank. It was odd that I had a cell to myself in the middle of the day when the San Judas County Correctional System was so notoriously overcrowded. It was also strange that someone being arrested for a newsworthy murder should have been walked into the Hall of Justice without a single reporter present, especially when a police tactical squad had been staked out on the roof of the San Judas Courier, a building full of journalists, while everything went down right in front of them in the penthouse office of one of the richest men in America.

At first I had been relieved just to be alive and out of Five Page Mill Square, but I was beginning to wonder if I had simply been helped out of the frying pan and into something a little warmer. Not to mention that my groin and my head still ached so miserably from Eligor kicking me that it felt like the best possible solution would be separating the two wounded areas as far as possible, by decapitation. I banged on the door and demanded a lawyer or a telephone call (of course they'd confiscated my phone) but was thoroughly ignored.

At last, just when I was imagining they'd have to feed me something soon and wondering if I could hold it down, a quartet of cops in full riot gear came in to get me. Somebody had apparently decided I was dangerous, which was precisely why I went with them like the sweetest lamb you ever saw. *Never do anything expected* is my motto, especially when you don't know how much trouble you're in, which I didn't, except I knew there was a lot of it. Eligor, one of the Opposition's major beasts, thought I'd been stealing from him, and somebody with even more clout than Eligor had just had me arrested. Oh, and in case I didn't explain earlier, those Zippers we angels use don't lead anywhere except out of normal time., so you're still in the same place. I wasn't getting out of jail that way.

The cops led me across the facility to a part I'd never seen before.

(Yes, I've been in the Hall of Justice a time or two. "None of your business" is the next answer.) It was an interrogation room, but although there was a single heavy steel table bolted to the floor in the center, there were no two-way mirrors for observation, nor, in fact, anything on the walls at all except an old poster about how to perform CPR. The walls themselves were chipped and pitted, the paint scraped away in spots by what might have been fingernails, which didn't bear much thinking about. I decided a few off-the-record interrogations might have taken place there back in the day, or maybe even earlier that week, and my stomach began to curl up into a hard knot. I was wordlessly directed to a folding chair on one side of the metal table, then the cops retired to the back wall, inscrutable as robots in their plexiglas face masks and helmets, and for about three or four minutes we all just waited in silence. I spent the time imagining impressive ways to escape, but I knew that none of them would work. I'm pretty tough but I'm not going to beat four cops with body-armor, tasers, and batons if they've had any training, especially not after the punishing way Kenny Vald and the *ghallu* had knocked me around recently.

Suddenly the door opened and the cops all straightened a bit, although they had been pretty much at attention already. The tall, dark-haired woman who walked in was not someone I immediately recognized, though she had one of those semi-familiar faces I felt I ought to know. She was maybe in her early fifties, wore a very boring, very serious dark business suit, and had a handsome, intelligent face with a strong nose.

"Robert Dollar?" she asked, looking down at a sheaf of papers in her hand, then up at me, as if I was different than what she'd expected.

"Yes, ma'am," I said. "At your service."

"Spare me anything cute, Mr. Dollar." She slid into the chair across from me, then handed me a package of wet wipes. "Clean yourself up. I'm Congresswoman Jennifer Taccone. And you are a lucky man."

"Tell that to my scrotum, Representative," I said. My face was stinging as I wiped away the dried blood, and I was tired of playing Mary's little lamb. "Because the bastard on the top floor of the Vald building kicked me there pretty hard, and no matter what any of his thugs or the SJPD said I didn't do anything wrong." Unless you objected to killing demons, of course, but I was relying on Eligor to clean up the mess I'd made of his secretary. He didn't want publicity, and he didn't want me in jail. He'd made it clear he had more personal plans for me.

"I hope that's true, Mr. Dollar," she said. "Because somebody has gone very, very far out on a limb for you. You are no longer just an ordinary smart-mouthed irritation, you have become an extremely high-priced favor—the biggest I've ever done."

Who had that kind of clout? A sudden thought made my stomach flip-flop. "You're not handing me back to Kenneth Vald, are you?"

A cold stare. "Mr. Vald is no longer involved with this matter. And in a moment I won't be, either."

"I really have no idea what you're talking about."

"That's good, too," the congresswoman said, "because after you leave here you're going to completely forget any of this ever happened . . . and that most definitely includes this little chat." She shot me a hard, unpleasant look. "You and I have never met. Remember that."

"I'm leaving?"

"When I walk out of this room the guards will walk out behind me, Mr. Dollar. You will then wait until you have counted to at least one hundred before you follow. The door will be unlocked. If you turn left and walk to the elevator it will take you down to the employee parking garage. There are a number of exits from there. Once you leave this property, I will no longer know or care what happens to you. Clear?"

I was beginning to remember more things about Congresswoman Taccone now, and one of them was that she wasn't just an ordinary politician. She had seats on some of the most important committees in Washington, and if the Democrats got back in control she was the horse some people were backing to finish in the money, either as House Whip or even Speaker. All of which made me wonder: who had the muscle to bend *her?*

Still, only an idiot would have been counting the teeth on this particular gift horse. "All clear," I told her. "Thank you, Ma'am. Thank you very much."

"Right." She pushed my phone and my empty revolver across the table to me. "Then our business is done." As I holstered my gun and slipped the phone into my pocket she stood and gave the cops behind me a look. They shuffled past me, all that gear rattling as they followed her out the door.

Well, I thought, *this is definitely some weird, weird shit.* I counted to a hundred and then headed for the door, half-expecting to find it locked and the whole thing some bizarre infernal prank, a bit of morale-stomping before they got down to interrogating me properly, but the door was open and the hallway outside deserted. I tried to look as much like an unhurried and innocent person as I could, but it didn't seem to matter. The couple of other civic employees I encountered barely glanced at me, although I must have looked like I'd lost a fight against a guy with a snow shovel.

Same thing in the garage—cars rolled past me without the drivers even looking hard, a parade of stolid looking cop-types in their civilian rides, SUVs and sedans that looked like unmarked police cars. Instead of coming out on Broadway I went up the stairs on the Marshall Street side. It was dark, the lamps hung with Carnival bunting for the upcoming parade, the streets busy with people leaving work, but I still hoped I could find a cab without having to stand around too long in the open—I was very conscious that my gun had no bullets in it. As soon as I reached the curb, though, a long, black car pulled up alongside me, and the passenger-side window slid down. The passenger seat was empty. Nervous, as you can well imagine, I leaned down to peer into the dark interior and saw a shadow behind the wheel and a hint of hair as pale and shiny as Karael's armor.

"You are very predictable, Mr. Dollar," the Countess said from the driver's seat. "I suggest you climb in before someone notices you. No—the back, not the front."

"So what are you doing here?" I asked when we were rolling. "You always troll outside the Justice building looking to pick up newly released criminals?"

"Who do you think got you released, you idiot?" This wasn't anything like the last time we met, when I could briefly convince myself that she could sort of tolerate me, if not actually like me. "I called in my biggest favor. For you. And I'm regretting it already."

"Whoa—*you* were the one who called in the Congresswoman? How do you know someone like her?"

"From law school." She kept her eyes on the road.

"You were in law school?"

She made a hissing noise. "No, fool, I just like students. I told you."

I let this slide. "So why did you do it? You don't owe me anything. And what is this thing everyone thinks I have?"

"You don't need to know the answer to either of those. In fact, you're better off not knowing, so instead of asking me rude questions like the little pretend-gumshoe you think you are, you might just thank me for keeping you from being turned into a flesh-and-blood accordion like our friend Grasswax and leave it at that."

"Hey, sister, he wasn't any friend of mine."

"You're right about that, Dollar, because he landed you right in the shit." She turned onto Jefferson. It was strange to see her driving her own car. "In fact, I'll give you one for free—something that even Chancellor Urgulap and his inquisition don't know. Grasswax was the one who ratted you out. He was the one who told Eligor that you had the thing Eligor wants."

"That bastard! That gill-faced bastard! I don't even know what the damn thing is—why would Grasswax blame it on me?"

"Oh, maybe because they were pulling all his guts and wiring out at the time, and it really hurt, and he thought if he gave them a name they might stop." She slowed as she approached a red light. I was watching out the rear window now, my eyes open for anyone who might be following us. "Maybe because he didn't think anyone would miss you, and he already hated your guts because you screwed him in a case the day before?"

"Shit, I didn't have anything to do with that!" I had a sudden thought. "Hey, why are you driving? Where's Sweetie and Honeybuns?"

"If you're talking about my bodyguards, the situation is going to be a little different from now on," she said. "For me as well as for you. Because things around here have gone very seriously pear-shaped. Where are you staying?"

"Huh? I don't know. I need to find someplace. Can you take me back to get my car? I left it across the street from Page Mill Square . . ."

She turned and gave me a hard stare. With the streetlights gleaming behind her pale golden hair she looked like a pissed-off Piero della Francesca portrait. "If you think I'm going anywhere near there you're dumber than I thought you were, Dollar, and I don't think that's theologically possible."

"Shit. Okay, turn around, then, and take me down Veterans. I'll grab a room in the Holiday Inn or something. I'll get my car back tomorrow." I slumped back in my seat, overwhelmed and exhausted. "So if Grasswax got me into all this, I still don't understand why it's *you* getting me out of it, Countess. I mean, I know I'm charming and handsome and everything, but . . ."

"Spare me your bullshit, Dollar." She turned right, then at the next block turned right again. "I have my reasons, and none of them have anything to do with your meaning anything to anyone."

"Okay, Countess . . . no, Casimira. That's your name, right? Okay, like you said, no more bullshit. I think the person who needs to do the explaining now is *you*. Because not only don't you and I work for the same side, we're deadly enemies. Stay with me now. Somebody stole something from Eligor, right? And the Grand Duke or whatever he's called, he's not happy. He thinks it's Grasswax the prosecutor who did it, and so Eligor and his boys pull a bunch of stuff out of Grasswax that's not supposed to be removed—at least not without anesthetic—and then the late advocate tells them he *doesn't* have this whatever-it-is, he gave it to *me*. Which is an absolute lie because I've never had it and don't even know what it's supposed to be. But why should any of that matter to *you*, Casimira?" I was talking to the back of her head so I couldn't tell if I was accomplishing anything. "No, I'm going to call you 'Caz' because it's shorter—like my temper's getting. Go ahead, Caz, tell me why Miss Cold Hands, Cold Heart is helping out an angel who even most of the other angels don't like very much?"

I waited out the silence. At last she turned onto Veterans Boulevard, a mess of neon and cookie-cutter commercial buildings—car lots, shopping centers and office complexes, all of them glowing with what looked like desperation, as if terrified they wouldn't be noticed. "I'll tell you one reason," she finally said. "You remember that thing Eligor's missing? Well, I'm the one who took it. And I was only safe as long as the Grand Duke thought I had it. And he doesn't think that anymore."

I swallowed all of the dozen or so questions that burbled up, picked the one that seemed most germane. "So who *does* have it?"

"Grasswax did—for a while. But obviously he got rid of it." She pulled into the Holiday Inn driveway. "And nobody knows where or to whom. Your stop, Dollar."

I considered walking around to the driver's side and asking her if maybe we should get a drink and talk about this some more, but as soon as I closed my door she was gone, rolling down the driveway and then pulling out into the flow of lights on Veterans like a fish tossed back alive into a swift river.

fifteen
dead yampy

"SO WHAT have we learned?" Sam asked me as we waited for our coffee. "Don't march into strange buildings and kill secretaries?" He squinted up at the menu board. "Do you think one of these is that expensive kind crapped out by a weasel?"

"All of them, judging by the prices," I said.

Clarence's face stretched in horror, and he looked like he was seriously considering dumping his caramel macchiato in the garbage. "Eew, what? You're joking, right?"

"He's not joking," I said. "You never heard that? Where did you live when you were alive, in a clothes hamper?" But I wasn't in the mood for banter, not even with an inviting target like the kid. I turned back to Sam. "The whole thing kind of snowballed on me."

"Yeah," he growled. "Remember what they say about the sort of chances a snowball has when dealing with the infernal powers? You dumbshit. Why didn't you call me?"

"I wouldn't know about what I did when I was alive," Clarence said loudly. A couple of the other people waiting for their drinks turned to look at him. He colored. "I mean, how would I know?" he said more quietly. "I don't even know that I *was* alive."

I did my best to ignore him. "Okay, Sam, you're right, I should have called you. I was just getting a little desperate, I guess—trying to make something happen. I've got the boys and girls upstairs breathing all over me and down here a bighorn something-or-other seems to want to take off my whole head and probably suck stuff out of my neck hole. And now I've got Vald Credit kicking me in the junk as well, so can we get off the street, please? I feel like someone's going to recognize me any moment."

"Relax, B," Sam said. "You're with me. The bad guys know us and they leave us alone!" He continued singing "I Get Around" tunelessly to himself.

"I mean, how do we know any of the story our bosses told us is even true?" Clarence asked, still off on his own little tangent. "Maybe it's like *The Matrix*, and the computers are controlling our minds!"

"Nice faith," I told him. "Nothing's even *tried* to eat you and you've already given up on the Divine Plan?"

Sam rolled his eyes. "Just assume you're being lied to by everyone, kid. That always works for me."

Sam's double espresso and my latte finally arrived, and we walked out. With its motels and mini malls, Veterans Boulevard in the sunlight was like a little slice of the Anaheim resort district—yes, that charming. We climbed into Sam's boredom wagon, and he drove me to the restaurant where I'd left my Matador parked. "Here you go," I said to the kid, handing him the keys. "You said you'd like to drive it, so we'll meet you in Mayfield Station parking lot."

"Really?" Clarence said, his eyes big. But as he got out both orbs went little and mistrustful again. "Hang on, you just want me to do this in case somebody's been watching the car, waiting for you to come get it."

"Exactly."

"But what if they try to grab me?" He looked like he was about to climb back in through the driver's side window.

"Then we'll come and help," Sam told him. "Go on, don't be a pussy—you're an angel of the Lord, remember?"

He went, reluctantly.

"Not really very nice, using the kid," Sam told me a few moments later. Despite all the things he says he's a bit of a softy.

"Trust me, they don't want him. Anything really dangerous probably won't even *react* to him."

We watched Clarence open the door, looking around as if any moment a bunch of paratrooping demons were going to come shrieking down out of the sky, but none appeared. He got in and started the engine. Nothing exploded. He rolled out of the parking lot and headed north. We waited to see if anyone was following, then set out after him.

"Looks like the Lords of Hell refused to believe you were stupid enough to drive your own car," Sam said, "because I can't believe they wouldn't have been able to find that garish piece of shit if they'd bothered looking."

"Naw, they just knew I'd be coming with backup this time. You know, a couple of local tough guys."

"Yeah, me and the Tiniest Angel. Oh, and that female demon who's got a crush on you. By the way, I can't believe she did all that for you." He turned down California Avenue, heading for the station. "She must have mistaken you for me."

"You wish. It's my natural charm—even Hell itself isn't immune." But I didn't really want to talk about her even with Sam. The Countess was a bit too complicated a subject. "Speaking of Clarence, how's the kid doing? Any hope for him as an advocate?"

"Well, as you saw, he gets whiny and he's going through a bit of an existential crisis," Sam said. "Like we all do. But he's not all bad. If he really is a snitch for the House, they've used worse." Sam had always been convinced that we were surrounded by our bosses' spies. He was probably right but I couldn't really live that way myself. "By the way," he asked, "what are your ideas for the afternoon? Not planning on storming the gates of Tartarus or anything, are you?"

I frowned. "If nobody dies on my watch today, I thought I'd see if I can talk to the Sollyhulls, get a few more answers. I'm sure not going to figure out this puzzle with the pieces I've got so far."

"Hey, that would be perfect for the kid," Sam said. "You could take him along, couldn't you? He's always asking about the big picture—you know that kind of stuff bores the shit out of me. And I've got some other things I'd like to get done without having to answer questions the whole time." His voice rose to an imitation of his young protegé: *"Sam, why don't the nice Buddhists go to Heaven?"*

"Don't they?"

"Fuck if I know. I'm just telling you: questions, questions, questions. Like someone else I used to know." He glanced over at me. "That would be you."

"Yeah, I got it, Mr. Sentimental. Everybody's like that at first. You probably were, too, Sammy-boy."

"I have never, for one instant, been a millimeter less than cool. Look, just take him off my hands for the afternoon, will you? Because I swear, B, he ain't a bad kid, but I'll go back to drinking if I don't get some time away from him."

This from a man who'd previously boozed two bodies to death, so it wasn't a completely idle threat.

"But doesn't this stuff bother you, Bobby?" Clarence asked me as we left the drugstore parking lot. I stashed the Thrifty bag in my jacket pocket and took the ramp onto the 84, headed west. In the last decade or so, a lot of tall buildings had sprung up around what had been the old Woodside Expressway, but when the traffic was moving slowly you could still see between them to the flatlands of Spanishtown on either side, block after block of two- and three-story apartment buildings. "I mean, that there are so many questions about what we do—questions without answers?"

"I got enough of those already, Junior, and mine are going to get me killed if I don't answer 'em, so I don't really have time for the other kind. Look, like I said, it turned out that there really is a Heaven, there really is a Hell, and this is what happens after we die. What's so hard about that?"

He scowled. "You don't get what I'm saying."

I hit the brakes hard as some moron tried to catch the yellow at Valota Road, missed it by three seconds, and would have t-boned me if I hadn't seen him coming and waited to start into the intersection. "I hope when you kill yourself they send Young Elvis to plead your case, asshole!" I yelled after him. "No, check this, Clarence—I *do* get it. Because I had more questions than you when I started, and I still ask questions all the time. But some things we may just never know. As living beings, humans don't understand completely how the universe works, and as angels there's still stuff that hasn't been revealed to us yet. I decided I can live with that." Which was not entirely true. I was pretty sick of unanswered questions, but you can only bang your head against so many walls before you either rethink your approach or knock your brains out once and for all.

"But what about the religious thing? Why is it that the whole operation is run by Christians and Jews? Were they right about everything all along? Were the Buddhists and—and the Ba'hai, and Muslims and everyone else wrong? That just seems so . . . American."

I laughed as I swung into the coffee shop parking lot. "Hold on, kid. Who's saying everyone else is wrong? Who's saying the Christians or the Jews are right?"

"What do you mean? It's obvious that if . . ."

"*Nothing's* obvious," I said, cutting him off. "Have you bumped into Moses or Jesus hanging around upstairs? You haven't, have you? We see what we see, and that isn't much." I sighed. "Look, kid, for all we know the Highest—the one who gives us all the orders—also calls Himself Allah, or Ahura Mazda, or Jade Emperor or even Brahma. Maybe we've been told we're 'angels' because that's all we can understand, even after we're dead. We don't really know *anything*, and as you should have learned by now, you can't trust the way things look, either." I got out of the car. "You're about to learn *that* lesson all over again."

He got out, still frowning like he wanted to argue some more. "Who are these people I'm going to see, anyway?"

I shook my head. "First, you're just tagging along, a quiet observer. Second of all, they're not people. Third, you may not see anything at all—unless they decide they like you."

"Huh?"

"Just shut up for a change, okay? Let's get some lunch."

I could understand Walter Sanders' less than enthusiastic review of the Superior Grill when we got inside. The place was your garden-variety greasy spoon with menus printed in the seventies and waitresses who looked like they had been working there a lot longer than that. Even the pies behind the glass counter had a slightly embalmed look, like the corpses of Communist leaders on public display. Our waitress resembled Wallace Beery in one of his prizefighter movies—definitely the punch-drunk phase of the story. She didn't seem all that crazy about having to serve anybody, but took our orders without actual argument, hung the slip on the roundy-roundy thing, then went back to talking to the other waitress (who could have passed for Lon Chaney Jr. with a beehive hair-do).

"I don't get it," Clarence whispered to me. "We're the only ones in the place. When are your friends supposed to get here?"

"Why, bab?" asked the cream pitcher, its top opening and closing like a tiny silver mouth. "Are you thinking about asking one of the waitresses out instead?" The chuckle that followed was a little coarser than the silvery-bell variety one usually expects from invisible spirits. Clarence let out a yelp like a dog whose tail has just found its way under a foot and was halfway to the front door before I could convince him to come back. At the other end of the long room the waitresses looked up without interest, then went back to discussing particle physics or whatever else was keeping them from bringing me a glass of water.

"*Who said that?*" Clarence asked me, eyes wide.

"I did, bab," said the cream pitcher in a broad West Midlands dialect. "Didn't mean to put the wind up you."

"She did, though," said the coffee thermos, its own lid also bouncing up and down as it spoke, like a cheap overseas cartoon. "She loves it when they jump."

I rolled my eyes. Both sisters enjoyed this sort of childishness way more than they should have after all so many years of afterlife. "This is Haraheliel, ladies," I said. "But we call him Clarence. Clarence, these are the Sollyhull Sisters, Betty and Doris. They know everybody who used to be anybody."

"He looks like a nice young one," said the cream pitcher. "Not an old grump like you, Bobby-love."

"Oh, but our Bob's got reason to be grumpy, doesn't he?" said the coffee pot. "Look at his face—the poor dear's all over cuts and bruises!"

The bell above the door tinkled and a couple of delivery drivers in uniform walked in. They waited a minute for the waitresses to finish up their review of quantum field theory, then when that didn't happen, they chose a booth not far from ours and sat down.

"Is this a trick?" asked Clarence in a loud whisper, still looking around for the source of the bodiless voices. "Who's doing this?"

"He's not thick, is he?" Betty asked. "I mean any more than normal, young-lad thick?"

"Oh, is he one of those unfortunates?" her sister said. "That's a shame."

"Just new," I told the ladies. "Betty and Doris are earthbound spirits," I explained to Clarence. "They exist both here and the spiritual plane, although it's more like they're just visiting here. Where they come from is sort of another part of Outside—through the Zippers, except it's actually part of Purgatory. I think." I shrugged. "It's confusing."

"What he means is that we're ghosts," said Doris proudly. "The real thing, us. 'Cept we've got no place of our own to haunt. Once we lost the bungalow where we grew up, we just floated around. Eventually we floated all the way over here!"

"Bloody Norah, she makes it sound easy!" said Betty. "We haunted a second-class stateroom on the *Franconia* for two whole years before we could get off again! That running water is nasty stuff for ghosts—everyone knows that—but who would have guessed that the ocean counted too?"

"Oh, and then we were in New York for a while," her sister continued. The two voices seemed very close to the ears, and the ladies loved to jump back and forth from side to side, as though someone was playing with the mixing board of reality. Even for somebody like me who *was* supposed to try this stuff at home, it could be quite disorienting. "Too cold, that was. That's why we come out here!"

"Ghosts get cold . . . ?" Clarence sounded like he was not getting the kind of answers about the supernatural world that he had expected.

"Just conceptual-like," said Doris. "But it still stings a bit when it's winter."

"Oh, and you never liked that, our Dor, did you?"

"No, you're right, bab, I day'n't."

"If you ladies are finished with your reminiscences," I said, "perhaps we could do a little business."

The coffee pot rattled, bouncing the lid and belching out a little drift of steam. "Ooh, wotcher got?"

I took the bag out of my pocket and set it on the table just as the waitress arrived with our water, a mere fifteen minutes or so after we'd entered the diner. When she was gone again I pulled out the telltale bottle. Now the cream pitcher began quivering too. "Oh, lovely!" said Betty. "Doris, look! Yardley's English lavender!"

"Have a quick sniff," I said and took off the cap. The lids of both pot and pitcher popped open as whatever was inside them rose invisibly and, presumably, hovered above the perfume bottle.

"Dunt it just take you back," said Doris dreamily (and still invisibly.) By this time the delivery guys sitting a couple of tables away had noticed the rather potent smell of lavender drifting over and, by their expressions, were wondering what the hell Clarence and I were doing.

"Reminds me of going down the dance hall on a Saturday night," crooned Betty, then groaned as I put the cap back on the bottle. "Oh, you cruel sod! What did you do that for?"

"Because I need information, ladies, and I need it badly. Several not very nice people and some even less nice things are trying to kill me. I want to know what you can tell me about any of them."

"Do we have to keep talking to the pitchers?" asked Clarence. "I mean, where are they now? Can *you* see them? 'Cause I can't."

"He is a strange one, in't he?" said Doris. "Poor thing."

"Count yourself lucky, bab," Betty told him. "If you don't like us in the cream pitcher, it could be worse. Sometimes we get into the sarnies. That'd make you lose weight, woont it? Your bacon bap talking back to you?"

"Sarnie?" the rookie said helplessly. "Bap?"

"Sandwiches," I translated. "You ready to listen, ladies?"

"First let us get comfy, like," Doris said, and suddenly they were both there. Well, not *there*, not in the three-dimensional sense, but present and visible in a filmy sort of way, two slightly purply-blue, mostly transparent and fairly podgy middle-aged ladies in what I've always assumed were outfits from the 1940s: dark dresses, heavy cloth coats, and hats. We were sitting in a four-person booth so one of them was next to each of us, Betty beside Clarence, and Doris next to me. Clarence tried to look like it didn't bother him at all, but he also kept sliding away until he struck up against the wall of the booth.

"Mardy little bugger, isn't he?" said Betty. Her hat was festooned with artificial flowers. "Cheer up, lad—it might never happen!"

As the waitress returned with our food, I explained the last few days to them all. I had to trim out some details I wasn't sure I wanted to share with the kid, but I was able to lay out the most important bits. When I finished, the Sollyhull Sisters seemed to be listening carefully. The first question, though, made me wonder.

"Do you remember that boy from Erdington we were at school with?" asked Doris. "The one who had nasty crawly things in his pocket?"

"That Hamish? I was just thinking of him too," her sister said.

"He was like that, wasn't he? Trying to hide things from teacher, but she always sussed it out."

"You two are not going to get even another sniff of that Yardley if you don't start helping me," I said sternly.

"We are, pigeon, we are," said Betty, rippling a little with impatience. "So just shut it and listen. This Hamish used to have things in his pockets he shouldn't—snakes, beetles, once he had a live mouse, can you believe it?—but he was his own worst enemy, wasn't he, our Dor? He truly was, he always made a fuss whenever the teacher looked at him, squirming and looking away from her so she always knew when he was up to no good. It was as good as saying, 'I've got something I shouldn't!' "

"Am I supposed to understand this?" I asked.

"Don't be thick, pigeon," Doris told me. "It dunt become you. She's saying that you can see things better when you're face to face with someone. Most folk can't help showing what they're thinking if you're 'round them long enough."

"Right." Betty nodded as though that had made sense.

"Meaning what? Look, ladies, I've almost had my skin ripped off my body several times in the last couple of days. I may not look it, but I'm scared. Can you just talk plainly for me?"

Doris sighed. "Put it about that you *do* have this thing. See who shows up to dicker for it. That'll lead to conversation."

"But I don't care about the people who want to buy it, I want to find the missing thing—the thing itself—because if he doesn't get his thing back, one of the major lords of Hell is going to remove all my nerves and organs. And there's no way that can turn out well."

"We're just trying to help, love. You don't even know what it is that got stolen. But if you put it out that you *do* have it and then see what you get offered for it you might find out. That would make it a lot easier to find the thing, now wouldn't it? Knowing what kind of a thing it is?"

"Actually," said Clarence, "that makes sense."

"Yeah," I told him, "the kind of sense that will get me killed in new ways I haven't even imagined yet. And here I was just worrying about the old ways." I pushed my plate away. Suddenly I didn't feel much like finishing my Belgian waffle, although usually I can choke down anything with sugar in or on it, no matter how beat up I am. "Speaking of the old ways of me getting killed, ladies, any insights about my horned friend, the *ghallu*? Because I have a feeling I haven't seen the last of it."

Doris frowned and nodded sympathetically. "Oh, that's a bad one, pigeon. We've been asking all of our friends on the other side for the last few minutes, but nobody likes to talk about such things, even those old enough to remember. Them *ghallu*, they're dead yampy—completely mad. They'll eat their way through a mountain just to break a rabbit's neck on other side."

"Thanks for those words of colloquial wisdom," I said. "What can I do to stop it?"

"Not much, bab," said Betty. "A spell of dismissal, but you'd have to get the same fella who summoned it to dismiss it as well."

"Great. I'm pretty sure that's not going to happen, because the fella who summoned it is probably the same Eligor, King Bad Ass of Hell Corners, who wants me so interestingly dead." I said it a little more emphatically than I should have, perhaps, and I heard one of the delivery drivers drop a spoon.

"Sssshhhh!" Betty wiggled her stubby fingers. "Don't say the fella's name out loud."

The two delivery drivers finally got up to go. They'd been watching Clarence and me talking for several minutes, and of course we had only occasionally been talking to each other, the rest of the time to empty spaces in the booth. It seemed to have disconcerted the drivers; they left a pile of money on their table and inched past us wearing unconvincing smiles.

"Ooh, I fancy that second one a bit," Betty said. "He's got a nice bum."

Doris hooted with laughter. "You old slapper!"

"Focus, ladies, please." My head was beginning to hurt. The Sollyhulls are decent enough for dead people, but trying to get anything out of them requires the patience of a saint. "*Ghallu*, remember? As in, how do I kill it?"

"We don't know, love," said Doris. "Silver works on some demons, but on these big, old ones, well . . ." She trailed off.

"Maybe if you popped it one right in the heart with a silver bullet," said Betty—trying to sound like Jimmy Cagney, I guessed, but it didn't make it any more convincing. "Or popped it four or five, more likely, and it wasn't well . . ."

"Believe me, I'll try silver, but judging by past experience it's a bit like trying to aim a rubber band at a tiger while it's busy trying to knock your head off." I moved around in my seat to unkink my bruised and aching back, then took a last swallow of my coffee. "Anything else, ladies? About the *ghallu* or any other subject?"

"Oh, yes, one," Doris said. "Your Grasswax fella? That prosecutor?"

"I remember him well—his outside *and* his insides."

"We used to hear a bit of him," said Betty as if she'd started the sentence. Sometimes it seemed like they were one person, the way they finished each other's thoughts, but I guess that's what happens when you've been living together (or living and dead together) for over a hundred years. "He had a gambling problem. That's what we heard."

I waited. "That's all? He was from Hell, ladies—of course he had vices. I don't think you're allowed to live there unless you do. Not having vices would *be* a vice, if you get what I mean. So what of it?"

Betty frowned, a thin, nearly transparent line on her even more transparent face. "We told you, Bobby love, don't get stroppy. People who have the gambling fever tend to owe people things. Money. Favors. We just thought we'd mention it."

I stared at them for a moment, and they looked back at me expectantly. "Right," I said. It wasn't like I'd come up with anything better on my own. "Thank you, ladies. I'll think it all over. Come on, Clarence."

As the kid sat wondering how to get out of his seat without sliding through the ghost of Betty Sollyhull, I took the bag back out of my pocket, removed the bottle of English Lavender, and discreetly poured it on the floor. As the almost asphyxiating smell of the stuff rose around me I dropped an extra twenty on top of our bill. As we reached the door I called to the waitress.

"I'm afraid I've spilled one of my perfume samples on the floor. Sorry to make work for you, but I've got to run. I've left some extra money."

The Sollyhull sisters had risen up like clouds of steam in sensible shoes, becoming less and less substantial as they flew back and forth above the table until at last I could no longer see them. But as I led the kid to the door we could still hear them, giggling like schoolgirls.

"Oh, that's lovely. Lovely! Takes me right back!"

"Do you remember that boy Tom Kippers who used to take you to the pictures? The one who always carried barley sugar?"

"Barley sugar! What I wouldn't give for some of that right now! Oh, Doris, what a lovely thought!"

As we headed for the car Clarence asked me, "How did they die?"

"I think they set their house on fire. Something like that. Killed their parents, too, but I don't think they meant to die themselves—just didn't get out fast enough or something. Pretty famous case in Birmingham."

"What? Did they do it on purpose?" the kid asked, horrified.

I closed my door and buckled myself in. "They died a long time ago—like I said, it was a famous case. You only haunt things when you're working off certain very severe Purgatorial deals, the kind that keep souls from going straight to hell." I shrugged. "They probably wouldn't still be hanging around if it had been an accident, would they?"

The rookie didn't say much on the way back into downtown.

sixteen
brady doesn't believe

ANOTHER NIGHT, another cheap motel. So far, I was staying ahead of trouble, both from the Opposition and from my own people, but I couldn't figure out how my little adventure in Eligor's office tower hadn't come to the attention of my superiors. I didn't expect the Grand Duke himself to report it, even though it was a ridiculously indiscreet breach of every convention there was, right back to Tartarus, but the whole Magian Society connection to Vald Credit suggested Eligor did have something to hide. He was quite high up, after all, so I supposed one of his underlings could have been the one sheltering the Magians, but I was fairly certain that the connections between a Hell-founded megacorporation, the slippery Reverend Doctor Habari, and Grasswax's former bodyguard couldn't *all* be accidental. For one thing, why would Howlingfell take time off from working for Eligor to pull a low-level duty protecting a mere prosecutor unless the Grand Duke wanted it that way? But the odds were that folks on both sides would eventually hear about my trip to Five Page Mill, and my bosses would find out soon after that. I could only imagine what the Ephorate would think of my little adventure, but my educated guess was 'not much.'

So when I got woken up at the ComfortRest Inn at four in the morning with a client call, summoned to an accident scene on the freeway up near Mission Shores, I suspected I might hear from the Celestial City while I was Outside. And I did.

The client wasn't anything unusual, a woman on her way to her job, driving all the way in from Morgan Hill. She'd fallen asleep at the wheel, drifted, hit the center divider, and flipped over. Luckily it had been early enough in the morning that the freeway was largely empty and no one else had been killed. Her guardian angel explained that the deceased was a nice, hard-working sort, a fifty-something grandmother whose defense wouldn't provide much of a challenge, but I didn't have long to enjoy that before the judge appeared in a glare of inscrutability and informed me that my superiors were requesting my presence in Heaven after we finished.

The last thing I wanted to do was face those five shiny, powerful beings across a table again, this time trying to explain why my idea of a low profile included shooting up somebody's office, but I didn't bother to tell that to the Principality who delivered the message. Firstly, it wouldn't have done any good, and second, it might have spoiled poor Gloria Dubose's chance at Heaven. I may be crazy, but I'm not a bastard. Not most of the time, anyway.

So I did my duty for God and Choir and then headed back toward the unevenly disinfected premises of the ComfortRest, but when I reached the motel I didn't feel like trying to go back to sleep, and I certainly wasn't in a hurry to visit my front office. As I've said before, Time is different in Heaven, so I didn't think they'd care too much if I waited until night came around when I would sleep again. Until then, I'd just keep myself caffeinated and vertical. So I went and downed about four cups of dishwater-strength coffee at a 24-hour coffee shop and tried to decide what I was going to do next.

The more I thought about it the more I liked the Sollyhull Sisters' advice about pretending to put Eligor's whatever-it-might-be up for auction. I mean, it was a spectacularly stupid, spectacularly dangerous thing to do, but it wasn't as if I had a lot of time to come up with something more subtle. My superiors were probably about to rip off my halo and drum me out of the corps, and a certain red-hot monstrosity with horns was out there somewhere looking for me—along with the rest of Eligor's minions, probably—slowed only by the fact that I was moving around a lot and sleeping in motels. (It's times like this when I wonder what the higher angels who organized all this were thinking when they gave us earthbound underlings bodies that needed to be fed and watered and rested just as if we were real people.)

So it seemed like I might as well poke things along. If I was going to wind up demoted (or worse) then I intended to go out like a crazy man, kicking and screaming and setting shit on fire all the way.

I parked downtown, not too far from Beeger Square. It was getting into the morning now, and I was beginning to think about a late breakfast to ease the headachy buzz of too much coffee, so I tried Sam but got no reply. On the off chance he was sitting in The Compasses and had turned his phone off, I called the bar phone. Chico said he hadn't been in but that Monica had just walked in and wanted the phone. I didn't even have a chance to react to that before she was in my ear.

"Don't come in, Bobby."

"Huh?" was what I replied, or something equally dazzling.

"If you were going to come to The Compasses, don't," she said.

"I wasn't going to, but is this some weird way of saying you're still pissed off at me?"

"How could anyone ever be pissed off at a sweetheart like you?" The sarcasm was so thick it actually made the phone heavy in my hand. "No, seriously, B, it's weird around here. There are people lounging around outside the building, homeless folks, street crazies . . ."

"And this is new?"

"Shut up. I know the regulars, and these aren't them. They're watching the place—they take turns so it's not too obvious. Someone's definitely got an eye on The Compasses, so how much would you be willing to bet it's *not* you they're watching for?"

"You're right, I wouldn't touch that action. That's why I wasn't planning to come in anytime soon." I sighed. Eligor must have found out that after the arrest I'd walked right out the back door of County. Was I going to be living on the run indefinitely? Permanently? Because you don't outlast one of the Lords of Hell in a grudge-match.

"And there's more," she said. "We've had a couple of more no-show clients, if you know what I mean. Like your Walker guy."

"Hang on—you mean here in San Judas?"

"One for Sanders, one for Jimmy the Table. I'll send you some information about those clients when I can, but basically it was the same as with yours—everybody present except the guest of honor."

I cursed silently. If there were already more vanishing souls just in San Judas that might mean more everywhere. It was beginning to look like an epidemic. "Thanks for the information, beautiful. I owe you."

"More than you'll ever know, Dollar. Dinner and drinks might pay back a little of it. Let me know when there's a break in your schedule of being attacked." She paused when she normally would have hung up, then added: "Be careful, Bobby. Really. This stuff is getting scary-weird."

If the bad guys were keeping watch for me at The Compasses then obviously Beeger Square was out, but I still needed a corner somewhere in the middle of downtown, because that's where Foxy the White-Nosed Reindeer had told me to ask for him. I headed back down Broadway until I got to Beech, where the pedestrian traffic was still thick, then popped over to Marshall, not far from the Kaiser Health tower. Only a couple of days to Carnival now and the decorations were all up, streetlights and traffic lights swathed in tinsel. They'd have finished erecting the stage and the reviewing stands in Beeger Square and hung the special colored lights, but God only knew when I'd get to see them.

I watched the nearest corner for a few minutes but nobody seemed to be lingering except the guy crouched against the base of the traffic light with the cardboard "HOMLESS NEED HELP GOD BLESS YOU" sign. I gave him twenty dollars to get something to eat and he thanked me and ambled off toward the coffee shop on the far corner. As soon as he was gone I took a breath, feeling increasingly stupid, and said, *"Fox."*

Nothing happened. I tried again, *"Mister Fox"* this time, and over the next few minutes even worked my way up to *"Foxy Foxy,"* but still without luck. I was about to give up, deciding I had been too tricky trying to summon him that way, that he really *had* meant I should ask for him like an ordinary street person, among people hanging around on corners, but I had one more idea and was determined to try it before packing it in. In a lull after the pedestrian green light emptied my corner, I opened a Zipper—just a small one—put my mouth against it, and whispered *"Fox"* into the timeless spaces of Outside.

"Dollar Man!" someone cried from just behind my right ear, startling me badly. I spun around, and there he was in all his pale glory, his baggy dark suit augmented by a truly ghastly knit scarf of alternating pink and black stripes. With his untanned skin and his continual prancing he looked like the sacrificial lamb the goth kids might send out first to distract the school bullies while the rest made a run for it. "You call for Foxy!" he said cheerfully. "Is it love, true love?"

Another group of pedestrians was assembling on the corner, waiting for the light to change, but none of them paid us any attention. I couldn't tell whether that was angelic glamour protecting us or just the fact that downtown Jude has plenty of residents who looked and acted like Mr. Fox. Did I mention that we closed the state mental hospital a few years ago and threw most of the patients out into the streets?

"So you come to do business, Mr. Bob Dollar?" He spread his long white fingers. "You decide to sell, or you interested in some of Foxy Foxy's other products? I have the best, all sizes, all smells, all the time!"

I really wanted to get this over with quickly: Every moment I spent standing on a downtown corner I felt like I had a big target painted on my back. Or maybe a price tag. "You said you had . . . buyers," I said quietly. "For that . . . *thing*. I've decided I'd like to have a little auction. Do it all at once. Get my price and then get rid of it."

"Ah." Fox smiled broadly, showing some gold. He looked like a live-action anime character. "Getting a little hot in Bobby-town, yes? Is it, yes? Perhaps the grand duke's moo-cow going clip-clop in your china shop?"

I smiled back, but it wasn't a happy one. "Just tell me, can you arrange it?" So my pale new friend knew about the *ghallu*. He clearly knew a few things. Who was this guy? I couldn't figure out if he was one of Hell's banished—you run into them—or an undead hanger-on like the Sollyhulls, or something else equally weird that I just hadn't heard of yet. "Can you?"

"Can do, flyboy!" he said cheerfully. He grinned like the host of one of those Japanese game shows where they make the contestants eat centipedes. "Can do! I'll set it up, you bring the thing, and we'll all swing, swing, swing."

"Okay. But one more thing—*no demons*, got it? Nobody from Hell. I smell any horns, I walk."

"Heard and obeyed, Dollar Bob!"

"Okay. When should I get hold of you again?" I turned sharply at a noise, but it had nothing to do with me—a car had almost run over a late-breaking pedestrian in the crosswalk, and the driver was now venting his rage through his open window.

"No need, my new friend," Fox said cheerfully. "I'll find you and let you know when the big meet and greet will be!"

"I'm not sure you'll be able to find me that easy," I began, but when

I turned back to him there was no longer anybody on the corner with me except the homeless guy, who was just returning with a cinnamon bun and a cup of coffee, his sign tucked under his arm.

"Gotta go back to work," he said as if apologizing.

"Did you see where that guy went? Pale-skinned Asian guy in a dumb-ass scarf?"

The man only shook his head. "No offense, man, but you weren't talking to anyone when I got here . . . just yourself."

I had a choice of errands to occupy me while I waited however long it would take for Fox to set up the auction. As I drove back to the motel I called Fatback and left a voicemail adding Foxy Foxy and Grand Duke Eligor to the list of things I wanted to know more about. I was giving George so much work I was going to need to top up his retainer out of my motel-shrunk bank account. I also left a message with my friend Orban the gunsmith telling him what I was going to need from him, then ducked into a drug store and bought myself more shaving stuff and toiletries because it looked like I was going to be staying in motels for a while, and I was beginning to get a little lackluster in the grooming department. I mean, if *you* died, you wouldn't want a heavenly advocate who looked like he'd just tried to use his six months' sobriety chip to buy a drink, would you?

The small stuff dealt with, I headed down toward Southport with the car windows open, hoping the bay air would blow a little life back into me. I only had until tonight to get more answers, then I'd have to go in and face my masters—and that was really what they were, weren't they? I called them bosses or employers, but unless you're in the mob or an army under fire your bosses can't usually kill you when they get pissed at you, and no other bosses but mine and my opponents' can have your soul jerked out of your body and sent to the deepest fiery pits to suffer for eternity. Unless you work for Walmart.

Anyway, I did my best to enjoy the cool but not too cool air, since I didn't know when I might get to appreciate it again. I followed Charleston Road out to the little office park I'd already visited, the place where the Magian Society had rented their storefront. This time I had my breaking and entering tools in the trunk because I was going to toss the place, if there was anything left to toss.

As I pulled into the driveway of the parking lot for 4442 another car was pulling out, a clunky old sedan which might once have been pearly gray but now was scratched to shit and had a fine tracing of rust around all the trim. I looked at the driver as I passed, wondering if it might be my friend the grinder guy from Suite C, but the person who looked back at me was a middle-aged black man with a round face, gray hair, and—as soon as he saw me—a look of extreme shock on his face. I mean he pinned me *immediately,* like he'd just been looking at a picture of me. Habari. Had to be. His tires squealed as he pressed the pedal all the way to the floor, and the big old rusty boat fishtailed for a moment before it caught the road and roared away. His back seat was full of boxes—the guy even had rolled-up stuff hanging out the windows like some kind of fly-by-night carpet salesman.

I was caught in the narrow driveway and made the mistake of trying to make my U in a single turn, which meant I had to go up the high curb on one side of the driveway where I got stuck for a second. When I finally got all my wheels back on the level I took off after him as quickly as I could, but that big boat had more under the hood than I would have guessed: he was already a few hundred yards or so ahead of me, heading back up Charleston.

I won't bore you with the details—you want a car chase, wait 'til they make a film out of my life. I almost caught up to him after about a quarter of a mile, but he was swerving all over the narrow road, and there were enough other cars nearby that I didn't want to risk causing an accident. I almost caught him again on Rengstorff Avenue on the far side of Bayshore. I forced him over toward the other lane, then we hit a red light, and he was pinned by the cars in front of him. I was too, but he was in the far left lane, and the crazy bastard drove right over the center divider, leaving part of his muffler pipe on the ground, then disappeared back over the freeway toward the eastern side. Despite all the smoke and noise he was putting out, by the time the light changed and I could go after him, I couldn't find a trace anywhere.

I drove back to the Magian Society and let myself in, but Habari had cleaned the place out. Nothing left but cut phone wires and electrical cords hanging out of the sockets. It was an empty cave now, just drywall, industrial carpeting and concrete—not even an insurance company calendar left on the walls.

I cursed myself up one side and down the other for waiting too long before coming back. I had let myself get caught up in everything else, although admittedly *everything else* included almost getting killed and being arrested by an SJPD S.W.A.T. team. But still, I shouldn't have left it. I had only missed getting the slippery bastard by a few minutes. I ached to have him there with me in that deserted office so I could ask him a few pointed questions, but that wasn't going to happen, was it?

I headed back toward the busier parts of town.

I was really missing The Compasses. Avoiding my favored hang-out would have been tough at the best of times, but for a guy who also had to move from motel to motel it was miserable. I was banned from most of my friends, my home, everything. I was angry that this had happened to me—furious—and, of course, I was scared, too, but also just plain bored. In fact, it was a bit like being in combat.

I picked my stop for the night early, a budget place near the Bayshore, then sat watching a preseason Giants game on the television and nursing a beer. Sam returned my call but said he had a client that was probably going to take him a while. I would even have been willing to spend an evening hanging around with Clarence, but Sam said the kid had gone home for the night. In a fit of *ennui* I even called him but he didn't answer his phone. I wondered if the kid was having dinner with his adopted family, cozy and, for a little while, feeling almost human.

When my own phone rang a bit later and it was Alice sending me a client, I was as pleased by the news of someone else's death as I'd just about ever been. Horrible, I know, but I'm being honest—I was that desperate for something to do besides watch a bunch of minor league players I didn't know getting their brief shot at the bigs.

The victim turned out to be a kid from Stanford who'd fallen out of his dorm window, so I flashed one of my fake IDs at the Teller Gate guards and drove onto the campus. The dormitory in question was at the western end of the school where the trees were thick and the hills leaned close overhead, which gave the spot kind of a Sleepy Hollow feel. I left my car in one of the lots and walked the rest of the way in, showing a press badge to anyone who seemed doubtful about my right to be there but otherwise trying not to be noticed. I did it well enough that by the time I reached the dormitory itself, an island of flashing lights in the middle of the darkness, I might as well have been invisible. I strolled past the outermost barricade of Stanford campus police vehicles, three regular cruisers, and several golf-carty things blocking the driveway. The house was festooned with bunting and hand-painted signs—apparently a Mardi Gras party had been the evening's entertainment. I glanced briefly at the tent being erected over the body of the unfortunate student, then opened a Zipper and stepped Outside.

It was a relief to see the dead kid's soul actually waiting there, dressed in a stained toga and tangled strings of shiny parade beads, probably looking pretty much as he had in life (although undoubtedly better than he did in death after falling head first off the roof of a four-story building onto pavement). He had one of those haircuts that always irritates me, one where the hair on either side has been brushed together in the middle like some kind of dolphin fin. It turns the wearer into a pinhead—not a good look for anyone.

"Brady Tillotson," I said. "God loves you."

"What is this shit?" he asked, glaring as though I might have engineered his fall, although by the smashed bottles lying near the now shrouded body I guessed his passing was more likely what would be called "misadventure," which is legal shorthand for "death by stupid."

"You're dead, Brady. I'm sorry, but I'll do my best to make this go smoothly for you. I'm Doloriel, your heavenly advocate." I didn't see his guardian angel yet, or the Opposition, so I gave him a quick rundown of what was going to happen.

He seemed less than impressed. He was a big, handsome kid and looked and acted like he usually got his way by one means or another. "You're shitting me, right? I don't believe in any of that crap."

"Well, it believes in *you*, Brady, so it doesn't matter much what you think."

"Fuck that. I'm leaving." And he turned around and stumbled off into the darkness. Death usually sobered people right up but there were exceptions. I wasn't too worried about him getting away, though: One thing about being Outside is that it isn't a place, it's the timelessness that belongs to a place—an eternal moment, I guess you'd say. It's tied to the people who are physically in that moment, observing it, so the farther away you get from what you could see during that original moment, the less real it is, until eventually you're left in the dark with a few familiar sounds. Then, after the sounds go quiet, you usually find yourself hurrying back toward the main bit of the moment again. See, there's nowhere else to go. Otherwise, all the angels and devils would be popping in and out of Outside like it was a Star Trek beam-me-up device, spying on each other through the Zippers. It doesn't work that way. Anyhow, what I'm telling you is that Brady Tillotson wasn't going anywhere.

His guardian showed up a couple of moments later, a fizz of light named Gefen. Rotwood the prosecutor showed up shortly thereafter, a demon so old and gnarled he might have been painting Hell when the Devil himself first moved in. I'd appeared against Rotwood before—he knew his stuff and some of the judges seemed to like his familiarity with the rules, but there were scarier prosecutors out there.

"This won't be easy," said Gefen quietly as the prosecutor conferenced with his own infernal version of a guardian angel.

"Why do you say that?" I asked.

"Because our client is a shit."

It was only a short time longer in that timeless place before the judge flared into our presence. It was my old buddy Xathanatron, the Principality who had sent Silvia Martino to Heaven the night Clarence had first tagged along.

Angel Doloriel, it said to me, *You Are Again Summoned To The Celestial City.* There was a pause, then: *It Seems I Must Add "Secretary To The Advocate" To The List Of My Titles.*

This was a joke, boss-angel style, and so I laughed in a way I hoped sounded at least slightly sincere. "That's very funny, Your Honor. Thank you for passing the message along. I hope we won't keep you long tonight."

It Is All The Same—The Interruption Of My Contemplation Has Already Occurred. I couldn't help noticing he still had that charming, democratic touch.

I finished huddling with Gefen just as my dead student stumbled back into our presence, toga flapping like the sails on the Marie Celeste. He looked a little more sober now but just as pissed off. The guardian angel's full report was longer than his initial remark but came to the same thing: Brady Tillotson was a drunkard, a bully, and as close to being a date-rapist as you can get without actually stepping over the line and using drugs or gross physical force, but certainly the kind of guy who liked his women too drunk to understand the issues of consent properly. He cheated on his studies—he was a starting linebacker on the football team and people were always around to "help" him pass his classes—he stole from friends, and was also one of those people who even years out of high school still got a real kick out of bullying other students. In other words, a shit. What made my job even tougher, though, was that he wasn't cooperating.

"I don't think any of this is right," he kept saying way too loudly. "Who do I complain to? I didn't sign up for this. I don't fucking believe in any of it. It's crap. There aren't any angels. It's a lie."

The judge didn't say anything about this unending whine of complaint, but it couldn't have been helping. I did everything I could to come up with mitigating circumstances—Brady Tillotson's youth, his parents' divorce, the fact that junior high school and high school coaches and teachers had never disciplined him because he was a star athlete—but I was not at my best because I'd taken a bit of a dislike to the kid myself. He would definitely be getting a long stretch in Purgatory, but I have to admit I thought he deserved it.

Near the end, when we'd summed up and Xathanatron had dropped into a glittering silence to consider the arguments, Brady suddenly turned to me, and for the first time all the anger and resistance had left his face. Post-mortem sobriety had caught up with him

"Oh my God," he said. "This is real. This is real! I'm dead!"

"I'm afraid so," I told him. "But things can get better than this. . . ."

"What's going on here? Why are you . . . ? Oh, Jesus—shit, I'm never going to see my mom again." His face went slack with grief, and a tear welled up and trembled on his lower lid. "Never . . ."

Xathanatron spoke. *The Sentence Is Damnation*, was all the judge said, then vanished.

Rotwood clapped his withered hands together once in pleasure before he also vanished. A vortex began to swirl around Brady Tillotson and although he fought against it, already he was beginning to be pulled apart and sucked downward.

"No!" he cried. His eyes were terrible. "Don't let them. Please, please, please! This isn't supposed to happen—you were supposed to save me! Aaah! Huuhhhh! *Aaaaaaaah*!" Brady's shrieks kept changing pitch because his face was melting, warping obscenely as he took on the dreadful shape he would wear Down There forever. Then he was gone.

I drove very slowly back across the city, stopping on the way at a bar I didn't remember ever seeing before and couldn't have found again if

I had to. I downed two fast drinks, then realized I probably shouldn't push my luck, even though I badly needed to get smashed, and get that way very soon. Too many nasty people were looking for me to risk ending up in a drunk tank or stumbling around in some parking lot in the dark. I got back into my car, stopped at a liquor store on the Camino Real and bought a bottle of vodka and a bag of ice, then headed back to my motel.

Before I got too obliterated I called in to the office and got Alice's voice mail.

"Tell the bosses that Bobby Dollar isn't coming into the Celestial City tonight," I instructed the silence. "Because I don't want to have to listen to any more lectures about doing my job. Tell them that. And tell them if they really want me they can come get me. Otherwise I'm going to stay here and keep doing what I'm doing, the best way I know how."

I was halfway through the bottle before I stopped hearing that college kid screaming like a burning child as he tumbled down into the darkness.

seventeen

economical with the truth

I GOT UP the next morning with a head that felt like the ball from some brutal medieval game, the kind where at least a couple of peasants died every time. But even the horrible throbbing couldn't make me forget the not-very-bright thing I'd done the night before—basically told Heaven to go fuck itself. So why wasn't I standing up in front of a celestial firing squad or whatever it was that happened to bad angels?

I toyed with the hope that Alice had tried to save me by not passing my message along, but I couldn't make myself believe it. Another possibility was that up there in the timelessness of Heaven they just hadn't yet got around to pressing the "Blow Up Bobby Dollar" button, but as far as I'd seen, Heaven didn't tend to wait around before meting out corrections and general holy vengeance.

So I was left with the two most likely answers: Heaven didn't care that much what trouble I got into, so Heaven was going to wait and let me hang myself, or Heaven actually approved of what I was doing and, presumably, whatever I was going to do in the near future. Which would have been pretty funny because I didn't have even a clue as to what I should do next.

I put on a pair of sunglasses so I could hobble to the motel manager's office and get myself a couple of cups of cheap coffee to take back to the curtained, comfortable darkness of my room. A few aspirin, a few more aspirin, then I was almost ready to face the day and what it might bring. First, though, I had some self-defense business to take care of. I'd lost my Smith & Wesson in Five Page Mill, and this didn't seem like a good time to be walking around unarmed.

Orban the gunsmith picked up on about the tenth ring. "Speak." He has an eastern European accent and the rasp of a man with a porcupine lodged in his throat. He told me once he was shot in the neck during the First World War and it's never been right since. I believed him. You would, too.

"Bobby Dollar here. I need some silver."

"Hmmm." A noise like someone dragging a stick along a picket fence. "Bullets or something else?"

"Bullets. But I need to talk to you about it. You around today?"

"Two o'clock," he said, then hung up.

Orban's factory was out at the end of Pier 22—one of the Salt Piers. Thirty or forty years ago the southern end of the port of San Judas was owned by the Leslie Salt Company. They harvested salt from the bay water and piled it into mountains to dry, a range of miniature Alps looming over the not-quite-Tyrolean splendors of Belle Haven and Ravenswood. The salt-harvesting people changed to a different technique in the nineties that used less space, so they sold off a bunch of the land at the southernmost end. Most of it became a nature preserve, but some of the piers where they used to load the salt onto container ships were repurposed into shops and apartments. The dingiest of them at one end were sold as live/work spaces. A lot of artists got in with grants from the city, but a few small manufacturers like Orban got in too. He wanted somewhere he could make noise at any hour of the day or night.

He made a lot of it, too. Today I could hear his machinery and the clangs of hammers all the way out at the entrance to the cracked asphalt expanse of the parking lot, which was mostly full this time of the day, but would be nearly as empty as the Gobi desert by midnight. Orban had created quite a thriving little concern here at the end of Pier 22, a collection of long, low buildings full of metal-grinding and bending and riveting machinery and God knew what else, manned largely by black and Hispanic workers. At the near end stood another set of benches set up for handwork, where lots of white guys with beards, who looked like they should be out with the anti-government militia on weekends, sat fiddling with various bits of guns—measuring, filing, polishing. Out of sight at the far end was the room full of sand-filled buckets that Orban used as a firing range. Beyond that, outside, was what the gunsmith called his veranda, a metal platform that stuck out over the water. He kept a couple of chairs out there so he could sit and look across the bay all the way to the Newark Ferry Port, atmosphere permitting.

The master gunmaker himself had a short grizzled beard and hair that grew naturally in a thick monk's tonsure. Just looking at him you'd guess a fit sixty-five years old, but according to him, he'd been around about five centuries longer than that. Orban got on the wrong side of Heaven back in the fifteenth century because of something that happened at the siege of Constantinople, (or so he'd told me one night over a couple of glasses of strong red wine, while we waited for one of his assistants to finishing customizing some weaponry for me). Since Heaven would never take him back, he said, and he didn't want to go to Hell, he had simply decided not to die.

Don't bother to ask—I'm just telling you what he told me.

Orban had his back to me but looked up as I reached the makeshift counter, as though he had actually heard me over the clanging, slamming din. He was wearing some special eyepieces that made him look like a robot crab. He slid them back onto his forehead and stood up, which didn't take long. He's not very tall.

"What do you want, Dollar? Make it fast—I have real customers to take care of, you know."

"Yeah, nice to see you too. I need some help and advice. Oh, and bullets. Silver bullets." I told him what was after me and everything I knew about it, but he shook his head the whole time I was talking like I was saying it all wrong. "What?" I asked. "Silver no good against one of those?"

"Only if it's special."

"Special how? Blessed by a priest?"

He made a face like he'd bitten a lemon. "Priests no good. This thing chasing you is older than the Jews, let alone the bloody Christians. Come."

I kept asking him questions as he led me across the fluorescent-lit expanse of the long, extremely noisy room, but he couldn't define "special", except that he couldn't supply it. That gave me a chill, and I hadn't been particulary warm before: Orban's place doesn't have a secondary ceiling beneath the roof, just a fretwork of beams, so it was cold in there most of the year. Maybe that's why the gunsmith still looked pretty good for five hundred plus.

He stopped to discuss my order with a swarthy guy in an apron. "How much you want?" Orban asked me. "Going to cost ten dollars per piece just for the silver—it's high now. Give you a hundred at fifteen a round complete—that's a good price for custom work."

Man, I thought, saving my life was going to be expensive, and Heaven didn't pay us much. "Then give me a hundred of 'em, I guess. I don't know how long this is going to go on." Orban always treated me fairly, but I still wasn't thrilled. The new ammunition was going to blow a large wad of my emergency funds, and I was pretty sure my bosses weren't going to expense me for the extra motels and silver monster-killers.

Once Orban finished going over the technical specs with his assistant he led me out to his rusty veranda. It was mid-afternoon, and the water was full of working vessels, most of them small since we were a good distance south of the working part of the port, and most of what surrounded us was shallow water and estuaries. "Sit," he said, pointing to one of the rickety chairs and lifting a bottle of wine off the huge wooden wire spool he used for a table. "You want some Bull's Blood?"

I usually liked the stuff just fine, but not today. In fact, just the thought after the previous night's binge made something bulge painfully behind my eyeballs. "No, thanks. But don't let me stop you."

He shrugged and poured himself a full tumbler. "So you have got yourself in some serious shit," he said after he'd taken a swallow. "That's no good, that horned fellow. I knew a man at Adrianople who saw one take a bad priest. Not a pretty sight. The man who saw it, his hair turned white all over."

"Do you know anything about it that might help me?"

Orban ran his fingers through his beard. "The horns say it is from India or Mesopotamia—they loved their bulls and buffalo, those old river people, and that's the kind of dark spirits they call up. But I heard the Egyptians knew this *ghallu* bastard and thought it was their god Set. They couldn't kill it either." He frowned. "Tell you truth, Dollar, I don't think I ever heard about someone killing one."

"Thanks. You're really cheering me up," I said. "Did you bring me back here just for a pep talk, or did you have some other help to offer?

You said the silver bullets needed to be special if there's going to be any chance—special, but not blessed. Special how?"

"Don't know." He shrugged again and took a long swallow of the Egri. "Just know what I read in manuals." I should mention that manuals of the sort Orban referred to are pretty obscure, since as far as I know, things like where to shoot a chimaera and the best ammunition to use on various sorts of undead don't make it into the standard Smith & Wesson user's guides. "But I'll do some thinking, and I'll tell you if I come up with anything."

"Great. Okay, here's a weird one. Anything to be done when facing off against a Grand Duke of Hell?"

"Say your prayers." He snorted. "You sure don't kill one of those—not with any weapon *I* work on, anyway. Just make them angry." Orban took a long drink. "Do you want to wait for your bullets? It will take most of the day."

Disappointed, I got up. I hadn't really counted on Orban having anything useful in the way of advice, but I had still hoped. "Nah. Can't wait. Too many irons in the fire." I thought about where I was. "Not literally, of course. I mean I've got a lot of things to do."

He wiped his lip with the back of his hand and gave me a dry look. "I understand metaphor, Dollar."

"Sorry." Sometimes it's hard to forget that even the really old ones have been living in the present as long as the rest of us have, it's just a smaller percentage of their total experience. I shook his hand, which was as rough as his voice. "Do you want me to give you a deposit?"

He made a face. "Normally, I say no. You are good for the money. But with a *ghallu* after you. . . ?" He nodded. "Yeah, give me check for half when we go back inside." But he still wore an odd expression, and it took him a moment to speak again. "I thought you were out of this kind of business, Dollar. It's been a long time since those days. I thought you were advocate now—nice safe job. Why is something like this after you?"

"Somebody said something that wasn't true to somebody who isn't nice. That's basically it."

"Keep your eyes open, Dollar," Orban called after me as I left. "You always were the kind of stupid bastard that attracted trouble." But he said it in a nice way.

* * *

All right, all right, I admit I haven't been completely honest about everything. I haven't lied—I'm an angel, remember?—but I have been, in the famous words of a British politician, a bit economical with the truth. Yes, I did have another job before I became a heavenly advocate. That's where I met Sam. Orban, too. And my old mentor, Leo? That was where he did his mentoring. But to explain I have to go back a bit.

Like most other angels (or at least most of those I've talked to) I first woke to the light of the Celestial City. In a way I was born there—not as an infant, knowing nothing, but as something else entirely, an angelic being with the general but non-specific knowledge of a human adult. I wish I could tell you now exactly what I did and didn't know at first, but those memories have been muddied and confused by all that's happened since.

Over the course of what seemed like a few years I became more and more aware of what was going on around me in Heaven as well as back on Earth (although I hadn't yet visited my old home). Somehow, though, I still knew I belonged down there, or had belonged there once. Yeah, like a lot of heavenly stuff, it's hard to explain. And after a while I became aware that things were expected of me, that I wasn't merely around to enjoy growing up, like a pampered child, but had a duty to take my foreordained place on the walls of Heaven, defending it against the constant threat of the Opposition. The Highest and His Adversary had been in conflict since the earliest days, since shortly after light and dark were separated, and the only reason there was anything like peace now was because of the protocols they had established. And Earth was neutral territory, open to both sides—an open city, like Casablanca during WWII. But Earth was also the main battlefield.

And as I grew in Heaven and became more and more aware of my duty, I was also being observed and shunted (in the most subtle of ways and by authorities I never knew) toward the role for which they thought I would be best suited, an Angel of the Lord's Vengeance—a member of a Counterstrike Unit. The Highest's ambition for me was finally revealed, and I was sent to Earth to begin my long training process.

If, as I assume, I lived my pre-angelic life on Earth, I returned there from Heaven in the early 90s. It was strange beyond belief to leave the Celestial City and inhabit a meat body, to feel the firing of nerves and the pumping of blood, to be covered in a garment of living flesh. On Earth, everything around me seemed so *present*, the things I saw and felt right on top of me, almost overwhelming my strange, frail human senses. Sunsets and sunrises could make me weak with joy, and the stars suddenly seemed distant and mysterious.

My first waystation in this new life was a walled camp out in the California desert north of Barstow. Camp Zion—now *that* was an interesting place, but I'll save most of those stories for another time. I will say, however, that if Earthly sunsets were painfully intense, being sent down from the cool, comforting shimmer of heaven to the baking, shit-colored mud of the Mojave was staggering in a completely different way.

From the moment I walked into Zion my education was in the hands of my staff sergeant (as you'd probably call him—his heavenly title is more like the Greek *lochagos*, the leader of a small band of warriors, which was why we called him "Leo the Loke"). Leo was African-American, or at least his earthbound body was; he had a flat, knowing stare that could make any of us stammer, and he was nimble as a dancer but strong enough to crush rocks in his fingers that the rest of us could barely lift with both hands. The "us" in question were the unit's new recruits, half a dozen in all. (Although we hadn't become friends yet, my buddy Sam was one of the squad's veterans.) We were now part of Counterstrike Unit (or "CU") *Lyrae*, named after a constellation and informally called the Harps.

Don't get me wrong, the other rookies and I weren't just being trained like army guys are trained, running obstacle courses and firing guns—or at least that was only a small part of what we were learning. We were Angels of Vengeance, after all, so what we studied more than anything else was the Opposition—their habits, strengths, and weaknesses, how they preyed on the innocents of Earth, and what we were allowed to do about it. As I mentioned, Earth is a very complicated place for the forces of Heaven and Hell: the appearance of neutrality between the two sides has to be preserved at all times, even if underneath we all know it's complete bullshit.

Anyway, since I'm trying to keep a long story short, I learned my job as part of a twenty-five angel unit, two dozen men and women and our leader. Leo the Loke had two corporals. Sam—or Sammariel as we called him then—was one of them. Sam scared the shit out of us, to be honest. He's always had big Earth bodies, and he's built like Jack Dempsey or one of those old boxer guys, big arms, big torso. He talked slow, thought fast, and could make you squirm in shame with only a couple of well-chosen words. Later on I found out he could make you laugh just as easily. I also didn't find out until later that when I met him he was already rethinking his career choice and (perhaps not coincidentally) busily drinking his earthbound body to death.

After about a year and a half we graduated from training to actual work—counterstrike, which meant we went into situations that had gone wrong and did our best to put them right and also, quietly, to send a very strong message to the other side that such things would not be tolerated. I have no idea what was going on in other CUs, but CU *Lyrae* was strictly reactive.

I'll gloss over the nearly eight years, Earth-time, that I spent as an Angel of Vengeance. Suffice to say that some of it was exhilarating, much of it terrifying, quite a lot disgusting, and almost all of it dangerous. Our territory, like my advocacy beat these days, was mostly San Judas, although we ranged as far afield as the Pacific Ocean on the other side of the mountains, or occasionally to other parts of Northern California. After all, the Lord's vengeance has no limits, so what's a county line or two? That was something Leo used to say. Another favorite of his: "The only thing dumber than angels are the dumb bastards who think you can train 'em." He was a good man when he wasn't making you want to disappear from self-loathing over something stupid you'd done. I wish I knew if anything was still left of him, soul-wise. It'd be nice to think we might meet again someday in some higher Heaven.

As to how I came to leave the Harps—well, I couldn't exactly tell you. That's because I don't remember it. One day I woke up in a CU hospital facility. The last thing I remembered was that we had been sent after a particularly nasty gang of drug cowboys that Leo said was Opposition-backed and which had a lot of Belle Haven and Ravenswood under its sway. According to Sam, who was there with me in the hospital when I woke up, I was ambushed, and two of the earthbound angels with me were blown to pieces on the spot, but the bad guys took me back to their warehouse base to question me. By the time Sam and Leo and the rest found me, I had been in their hands for about three days, and the body I was wearing was extremely dead. With some luck they managed to get me back to base and into another body, but I still wasn't right for a long time—Hell can inflict damage that isn't just physical. You can see why the thought of Grasswax's last hours had some impact on me.

Anyway, after that my superiors decided I was in no fit shape to continue in the Harps. Although I begged to stay on in some other capacity, they instead offered me a transfer back to the Celestial City, to heal and be retrained. But I didn't want to go back. I liked Earth. In some weird way I still can't fully explain I felt comfortable there in a way I hadn't exactly felt in Heaven. So I inquired about jobs in San Judas and was told that there were openings for advocates.

I saw Leo in Jude a few times after that—he'd drop by The Compasses and we'd have some laughs, but of course he couldn't tell me what he was doing since I was no longer cleared. Sam and I stayed friends, too, although we weren't as close as we later became. Then Leo died.

I don't know the details very well, and I still don't like to think about it. As I may have mentioned, it wasn't him dying that was hard to take, and it sure wasn't surprising—he had a dangerous job—but the fact that he couldn't be resurrected, and that some people suggested it was because he'd made enemies upstairs. Which nobody wanted to believe, because . . . well, where did that leave the rest of us?

Not too long after Leo's death Sam quit the Harps and came to work for the advocates as well. He told me he'd been thinking about it long before I was invalided out, but losing Leo had been the final straw. He had a lot to say about his reasons, although he shied away from specific details except to say that some of the jobs he'd done had been really, really bad. Worse than anything I'd ever seen.

Okay, so now you can guess the answers to some of those things you've probably been wondering, like why I know a gunsmith as weird as Orban, and how I met some of my more obscure friends. And, of course, why I wanted nothing more at this moment than somehow to escape the whole mess I was in as quickly and painlessly as possible.

I was driving west when the phone rang, heading for the Camino Real to shop for a new motel—people pay way less attention to you when you check in during the daytime—and noticing that the Carnival decorations seemed to have spread out of downtown and all across the city. I squinted at the phone. It wasn't a number I recognized.

"Go," I said.

"Top flight! Excellent to reach you, Mr. Bobby! And to find you not yet dead!" It was Fox, the albino jitterbug.

"How the hell did you get this number?"

He only giggled. "No time for such, Dollar-man! You wanted meeting? You want big auction? Price is Right? Studio audience? You got it!"

"Are you saying it's on?"

"Tomorrow night. Midnight." He hummed a snatch of music to himself, but I couldn't make it out. "Be there or be square, Mr. Bobby!"

"Be where?"

"Don't know yet. But I promise—I call as soon as I know."

"You didn't tell them I'm bringing . . . the thing they're interested in, right? Because that's not going to happen. I want to agree on a price, *then* I'll arrange the delivery."

"Don't worry, Dollar-Bob, don't worry. Everything will be right in the rain."

Before I could ask him if he meant "right *as* rain," he was gone. So now on top of all the other shit I had to deal with, I had twenty-four hours to figure out how to conduct an auction with a bunch of criminals or worse for something I had never seen and couldn't even name.

We sure know how to have fun in San Judas.

eighteen
poison darts and fiji mermaids

I'VE ALWAYS preferred the city at night. I believe that San Judas, or any city, belongs to the people who sleep there. Or maybe they don't sleep—some don't—but they *live* there. Everybody else is just a tourist.

Venice, Italy, for instance, pulls in a million tourists for their own Carnival season but the actual local population is only a couple of hundred thousand. Lot of empty canals and streets at night, especially when you get away from the big hotels, and the residents pretty much have it to themselves when tourist season slows during the winter.

Jude has character—everybody agrees on that. It also has that thing I like best about a city: You can never own it, but if you treat it with respect it will eventually invite you in and make you one of its true citizens. But like I said, you've got to live there. If you're never around after the bars close, or at the other end of the night as the early workers get up to start another day and the coffee shops and news agents raise their security gates, then you don't really know the place, do you?

Anyway, that's the city I love, the nighttime city, but unfortunately that was the part I couldn't really enjoy at the moment because so many different people and things that liked darkness wanted to hurt me.

Still, I was feeling a tiny bit better. I'd stopped back in to see Orban at the end of the day and now had a hundred rounds of high-quality .38 caliber silver ammunition, thirty of which I'd already transferred into speed loaders, making for some very heavy pockets. Orban had also loaned me a car, one of several he kept around the place, and my

Matador was now hidden out behind the pier where Orban kept some of his bigger projects under tarps. (I was parked next to an M41 Walker Bulldog and couldn't help wondering if the tank was meant for a local client.) So now I was out tooling around in a lumbering decades-old Pontiac Bonneville that had about three-quarters of its armoring job finished. Who the hell puts armor on an ancient whale like that? Must have been where the owner lost his virginity or something was all I could figure. Anyway, driving the thing was like piloting a cabin cruiser in a shallow inlet, but at least it was sturdy. Oh, and I felt much, *much* less conspicuous now. I love my whip, but it's only a notch more anonymous than the Batmobile.

Before going back to Orban's I'd checked into my motel-du-jour and taken a nap, which had helped my hangover a little bit. I'd also had dinner and a couple of cups of coffee, and now I was out driving. It clears my head and helps me think, especially when I open the windows and let the air knock me around a little. I definitely needed the oxygen that night, so I took the Woodside Highway up into the hills and tooled south along Skyline, looking down through the gaps in the tree line to see the scatter of ground-hugging stars that is a city by night.

I know it's going to sound particularly bizarre coming from an angel, but I've always had an almost mystical feeling about San Judas. It's a strange town in a lot of ways, not as cosmopolitan as San Francisco or as funky-ethnic as Oakland, and with a long, checkered history of economic bubbles and collapses. Despite the presence of Stanford it's not really considered a world-class city, but there's something about the place that got into my blood and has just stayed there. I can imagine living somewhere else but not permanently. I like the smell of the bay, I like the hills at night, I like the old downtown buildings with their now slightly shamefaced Gilded Age opulence, I like the alleyways and hidden courtyards and whitewashed churches of Old Spanishtown. I like the bars at the waterfront and the stories you hear in them. Jude is like one of those favorite books where you find something new every time you open it.

You can't get much in the way of radio up on Skyline unless you have satellite. The Pontiac wasn't finished with its conversion yet so it had nothing but a cassette player, of all things. Still, I wanted music badly, and I'm not much of a singer so I pulled over at a vista point and fumbled around in the box of ancient tapes on the floor of the shotgun side until I found a collection of Gregorian Chants, which made better thinking-music than the impossible alternatives (which ran to the likes of Loggins and Messina and *Chicago VI*). The tape actually played, which surprised me—it must have been in the car for decades. I wondered if someone had died in this four-wheeled sleigh back in the mid-seventies and just lay there mummifying along with his stupid tapes until Orban cleaned out the interior.

Accompanied now by melodiously moaning monks I reached misty Santa Cruz and turned around, still waiting for everything to fall into place, for the secret design to be revealed at last, or at least for the universe to give me a hint about what to do next, but the universe was keeping its mouth shut. I came back the slow way through the redwoods via Highway 9. By the time I got back to the top of the Woodside Highway I was so deeply tangled in my own thoughts that the sudden ring of my phone almost startled me into driving that big old car off the road. I was hoping it wasn't a client, and this time I got lucky: it was Fatback, which meant it must be after midnight. I was surprised at how quickly the time had slipped away.

"Mr. D, that you?"

"I'm here, George." I started down the hill. "Not too many miles away from you, actually."

"You want to drop by? I think Javier's got a few beers in the refrigerator."

I'd had a nice hot shower before I came out and the thought of getting my clothes full of that smell didn't really appeal. Also, I still needed to think. "I've got a client I have to go see, George—sorry. I'll see you again before too long."

"Yeah." He sounded wistful. "It's always nice to have visitors." He seemed to hear himself because he quickly became businesslike. "Hey, D, you sure are piling up the work for me here. That Walker guy, Grasswax, Habari, what else? Oh, yeah, the albino, Eligor, your *ghallu*-thing, your Magian Society, and now you want to know about all these new dead guys?"

I was guessing by "new dead guys" he meant the owners of the latest missing souls. "Well, if you had someone working for you during the daylight hours you wouldn't find all this crap waiting for you when you come back from Pigtown." I immediately wished I hadn't said it—it sounded mean-spirited—but if it bothered George he didn't give any sign.

"Yeah, right. Like I'm going to hire another full-time employee on the piddly amounts *you* pay me, Bobby. This is the first work you've given me in at least a couple of months. Just because people are trying to kill you, suddenly everything's rush, rush, rush."

"Very funny. Look, all those new guys are . . ." I paused. "I'm having trouble remembering, George—did I tell you what's going on?"

"What, you mean with more missing souls? Yeah, creepy. And these are them?"

"These are *some* of them," I said. Monica had sent me a list that now had five names on it. "Just the locals."

"Wow." He seemed genuinely impressed. "So it's happening other places?"

"As far as I know. But they must be hushing it up—in fact, if you haven't heard about it, both sides must be hushing it up like crazy."

"Heard lots of rumors, but the psy-ops boys from both sides are smart, Bobby. They don't try to deny or undermine a story like that, they just put out even more rumors, more and more until the original signal disappears almost entirely in the noise."

"Well, I need whatever I can get on the new guys." I had decided that since it was no longer just Edward Walker's soul that was missing it might be useful to know what he had in common with the newest cases, if anything. "And did you find any more about the Magians or, what was it, Kephas?"

"Nothing you couldn't have found out yourself, except that I finally turned up a few obscure references to the Magian Society, mostly in backchat on various religious discussion sites. All I can tell is that they seem to be some kind of charitable organization or something, and they have links to some other groups—*Der Dritte Weg* out of Berlin and something called the Shaw Philosophical Trust in London and Dublin. But what their connections are and what any of them actually *do*—boy, that's a lot harder to tell."

I sighed. To think I had been face to face with that guy Habari and his hastily-loaded car full of Magian Society memorabilia. "Okay, thanks. Obviously, let me know if you get anything else."

"Right. Oh, and the word on the street is that not only did your pal Grasswax have a gambling problem, he was in deep and in bad."

"Why does everybody keep calling that miserable dead demon bastard my pal? Never mind, just go on, explain."

"Well, you know your other friend . . ." He had the good grace to pause and start over. "You know that guy Eligor who right now doesn't like you so much? And you know how he's a really high muckamuck in Hell? Well, the guy Grasswax owed his gambling debts to? He's even higher up the ladder than Eligor."

"Huh?"

"That's what I'm picking up here and there. Sitri is his name, Prince Sitri. A prince of Hell. Apparently he's a gambler too, but he doesn't lose very often, and he really hates it when people welsh on him."

"Sitri?" I knew the name, of course, but not well. He was big, okay, in more ways than one. My head was swimming. Did this mean there was someone even higher in Hell's ranks than Eligor who might want my head as well? "I can't say I remember much about him. What do 'prince' and 'duke' even mean down there, anyway?" I asked.

"Power, mostly," Fatback told me. "How much of Hell belongs to them. And they all hate each other." He chuckled. "They'd probably have beat you guys a long time ago, otherwise."

"Probably. So the late Grasswax was in hock to this prince? For what? Money? Souls?"

"Don't know, Mr. D. But the articles I've been reading make it look like Sitri isn't the kind of demon you want to keep waiting too long for his winnings, whatever they are. Eater of the dead, Satan's foul hunter, scourge of wayward souls, etc."

"Yeah, like I said, I've heard his name. But I don't know much about him, so dig me up anything that looks useful, will you? Man, this shit just keeps getting deeper."

I was about to hang up when he said, "Oh,wait, Bobby! One more thing!"

"Yeah?"

"This thing you're supposed to have? That got stolen from Eligor? Well, I ran across a couple of individuals talking about it. Some bad, weird folk on a private channel in a members-only network you don't even want to know about, but they're the real thing, Bobby, trust me. Anyway, they didn't name it, but one of them called it 'the Horseman's little souvenir' and the other one said, 'it's not an ordinary one, remember—it's a *gold* one.' But I've never heard even a whisper about it anywhere else, and that comment was between two parties who thought they were having a secure exchange."

"Let me get this straight. They said, 'Not an ordinary one—a gold one'?"

"Right."

"Okay. I'll think that over too." But it didn't exactly make me feel more confident about the phony auction I was facing in twenty-four hours. "Thanks again, George. Take care of yourself."

"Oh, you know me. Happy as a pig in . . . well, you know."

"You and me are both swimming in the same stuff right now, old pal. I'm glad at least one of us is enjoying it."

I had two advocate clients the next morning, one right after the other, and no sign from Heaven that they were treating me any differently than before I sent them my grumpy little message about how I was quitting. Which just showed me how much I mattered in the halls of Heaven. I suppose the business-as-usual was a good thing since it kept me distracted from the night of open bidding and merriment ahead. I still didn't have an idea about what I was going to do or how I was going to do it, and I was beginning to wonder if I'd let the Sollyhull Sisters talk me into something I was going to painfully regret. Still, I was getting very, very tired of sleeping in a different room every night like Stalin avoiding assassination, and I was even more tired of looking over my shoulder for the *ghallu,* which had been quiet so long now I was beginning to wonder whether the stalking was meant to be as much psychological as physical. Was Eligor trying to get me to panic and reveal where his "souvenir" was hidden? Good luck, since I didn't know myself.

Sam met me for a late, late lunch. He was letting Clarence handle his first solo call.

"I didn't want to stand over him, B. I let him argue the last one, and the kid did pretty well. This one looked like a no-brainer, slam-dunk, all those clichés. He was a church deacon, and the guardian said he was actually as advertised, an all-around good guy."

"Who did the Opposition send?"

"That weedy little dude who looks like he's wearing glasses, what's his name? Beetlespew?"

"The one that looks like Urkel in a bug suit?"

"That's the guy."

As we finished and Sam called for the check, my phone rang.

"Mr. Dollar? Mr. Robert?"

"Yeah, it's me, Fox." I had forgotten to ask Fatback if he'd turned up anything on my new albino friend; I reminded myself to take another pass through the material he'd sent me over the last couple of days. My first readings are always hasty, looking for things that jump out immediately. I owed myself a more deliberate study. "Are we still on? You got a location for me?"

"Oh, yes, most truthfully! We are, as you say, completely and totally still on. Do you know the Islanders Hall, Dollar Bob? King Street off of Jefferson?"

"That place has been closed for years."

"The finest sort of spot for a midnight meeting, then, don't you think?" He chuckled in a really irritating way. I could almost picture the little *merengue* he must be doing. "So we shall not be disturbed! Meet me a few minutes ahead of time, and I will guide you to our appointed spot." And then he was gone.

"Trap," said Sam when I told him what I was doing. "And a pretty obvious one. You know you're not going by yourself. Even you aren't that stupid."

"Are you volunteering?"

"Somebody's gotta keep you from getting blown up, chum. I know the place. I'll meet you there at quarter 'til, out front by the parrot." He swung his big body out of the booth. "And I'll be carrying. I suggest you do the same."

I was profoundly grateful to think that Sam would be there with me, but I wasn't going to admit that to him—bad for his humility. "I'll try to remember, Sammy-boy, but I was thinking I might just pick up a stick or a couple of rocks when I got there."

He slid me the check that had just been dropped on our table by a passing waitress. "You'd better pay. You probably won't survive to get the next one."

The rest of the day went pretty quickly. I had another client, a case I lost through no fault of my own—the guy was a total bastard, an unreformed drunken wife-beater who'd died by falling off his own roof after his wife locked him out. (He was trying to get back inside via the skylight so he could "teach her a lesson," as he thought of it.) Seeing him go down the drain didn't affect me near as badly as seeing Brady the jock get his sentence, but it still made me wonder who exactly was in charge. Guys like this client, well, that's exactly who Hell was made for, that seemed clear—but forever? Did people really get sent off to flail screaming in pits of molten lava and blazing feces *forever*? I was pretty sure that even the drunken wife-beater didn't deserve to burn for longer than the stars themselves.

I mean, that's a really long time.

When evening came I left my latest motel room to go get a late dinner. After a leisurely meal and a cup of coffee I headed toward the place where it was all going to go down, feeling all the things you feel when you're wearing an extremely tense human body. Perhaps I should have had things planned more carefully in terms of the auction itself, but I'd survived this far by trusting my instincts, and I didn't have time to become a new person overnight. I wasn't going to produce the object in question anyway, I'd made that pretty clear, so nobody should be planning to rob me. I wasn't going to say anything stupid and give the game away and neither would Sam. Other than that, I'd just have to see what happened, pay close attention to who showed up and what they said.

I parked on King at the Jefferson end about a block or so from Islanders Hall and spent a while just watching the street as people came back from social evenings or walked their dogs before bed. Years ago that neighborhood used to be an almost entirely residential section of late nineteenth century brick buildings turned into apartments, but now there are stores and coffee shops on several of the corners and even a local bar; still, by eleven-thirty the sidewalks were all but deserted. I left Orban's battle-wagon unlocked, wagering the odds of getting ripped off were smaller than the likelihood I might need to make a fast getaway, then headed for the dark bulk of Islanders Hall.

The Independent Order of Islanders was one of those fraternal organizations like the Masons and the Elks that thrived during the beginning and middle of the last century, but unlike the Elks and the rest, the Islanders as a group sort of died out, and their hall closed about a decade or so back. It gets rented out for occasional functions but not generally the sort that begin at midnight. Most of the property is surrounded by an old iron picket fence meant to keep people away from the building but there's a little porch in front that's open to the street, with benches and hedges and a long-dry Benny Bufano fountain in the shape of a very plump parrot. That's where I expected to find Sam, since it was about quarter 'til, but he wasn't there.

I waited nearly fifteen minutes, checking my phone intermittently for messages, but there was no sign of him, nor did he answer his own phone. I was just about to take a short walk down to the streetlight to see if he might be coming when the gate creaked open behind me and my pale friend Fox was there, shimmying like the ghost of a nautch dancer. The weird thing was that the gate had been chained and locked, and I'd never heard a clink.

"Right on time, D-Man! Right on the money! Come in—many are waiting!"

I didn't like the sound of that. "How many? And how did they get in? I've been here all the time."

"Dollar Bob, you don't think clever Foxy picks a burrow with only one entrance, do you?" He laughed and did a quick shuffle, then led me through the gate, up the front steps and inside.

Islanders Hall is a genuinely unsettling place, especially after dark. The organization had a South Seas theme, and the downstairs lobby played that up big, with tapestries of pounded bark stretched along the walls and carved masks leering from the shadows (many of which could pass for Infernal prosecutors I'd met in the flesh) as well as other more exotic displays like clutches of poison arrows and poisonous darts, feathered costumes, shrunken heads, and even a Fiji mermaid in a glass case. The Fiji mermaid was an infamous kind of sailor's souvenir, usually the mummified corpse of a monkey sewed onto the body of a fish, but the face on the one in the Islanders Hall case looked more like a dessicated child than an ape. I didn't look at it very long, though. To be honest, the filmy, fishskin eyes gave me the creeps.

At the back of the lobby, beneath a full-sized Hawaiian battle canoe that dangled on chains from the ceiling, complete with a paddling group of ancient mannequins in feathered warrior drag, stood the door to the main hall. I followed Foxy inside as if he were a will-of-the-wisp. As we entered the large, shadowy room everybody turned to look at me; perhaps two dozen folk in all, most standing at silent attention. Since many of the attendees wore dark colors the first impression I had was a sea of bodiless faces. I recognized a few of them as Fox led me past, but only a few. He whispered the names of some of the others. Three shaven-headed white guys in dark pajamas were from the European branch of a Japanese Aleister Crowley cult. While I puzzled that one out he pointed out two fellows in ostentatious Catholic clerical garb who were apparently members of Opus Dei. There was also a man Foxy named "Mr. Green," who looked absolutely normal except for the antique smoked glass box he held in his hands, which was just about the size of a bowling ball, and which he kept lifting to shoulder height as though he was helping it to look at things.

More than a dozen others were waiting with them, including those I recognized, like the fifteen-year-old girl with a Bluetooth headset who looked as if she had just stopped in on her way home from junior high school. That was Edie Parmenter, one of the most trusted sensitives in Northern California; she had an almost infallible knack for identifying psychic phenomena. I couldn't help wondering who'd hired her. Also, what her parents thought about her being out this late. Besides a few other usual suspects, known dealers in *objets d'occultes* whom I'd guessed would be here, Fox pointed out Coptic priests, some representatives of the Russian Mystery Circus, and a trio of women so tall that for a moment I thought they might be wearing some kind of Carnival costumes with false heads. Fox whispered that they were Scythian priestesses—"truly real Amazons, dear Bobby!" as he put it. It was quite a stunning array of weirdness, but it still didn't tell me anything about what it was I was supposed to be selling.

Fox clapped once. "Gentlemen. Ladies. Before the bidding commences, a word from the sponsor of proceedings, Mr. Dollar."

Something north of forty eyes watched me as I took a step forward. I slipped my hand into my coat out of habit and touched my revolver just to assure myself it was still there, still full of silver. I really, *really* wished Sam was with me, but I was also a bit worried about him. He'd never let me down before.

"I won't waste much of your time." My voice echoed and quickly died. I noticed for the first time that there were life-size wooden frigate birds hanging from the high ceiling like frozen phantoms. "You know what I've got. I'm here to answer questions, and then I'll take bids. I'll make arrangements for transfer with the winner."

"But why can we not examine the object?" demanded one of the Copts. "How can we be expected to bid on something that we cannot see?"

I took a breath. I had pretty much expected that as the first question, but I was glad to hear the word "object," which I would use from now on. "You'll have a chance to examine the object before any payment is made, trust me, but I'm not going to set up inspections for every Tom, Dick, and Youlios who wants one. Please remember, my possession of the object in question is still slightly . . . controversial." I smiled. Nobody laughed.

Edie Parmenter, who'd been talking into her Bluetooth, looked up and said, "One hundred thousand." She had a slight lisp.

A murmur ran through the others. "Do you know for a fact it's real?" called out one of the Euro-Japanese Crowleyites.

I took a small risk. "It is. Not all that glitters is gold, if you get what I mean, but this absolutely, definitely is."

The Crowleyites nodded. "One hundred fifty thousand," one of them said.

Fox stepped in then and began to orchestrate the bidding as if it were an ordinary auction (except very few of those are usually run by tap-dancing albinos) and the bidding quickly climbed beyond six hundred thousand. Box-man, Edie Parmenter on behalf of her absent principal, and the Opus Dei guys took the lead, with occasional brave stabs from the Crowleyites and one or two of the occult object dealers. I was guessing things would slow down for good and settle near a million, which was pretty amazing for something nobody had actually been able to examine, and possession of which, as my own experience attested, could easily get you killed. And I *still* didn't have an idea what I was selling. What was I going to do when someone was actually ready to hand over the money?

I didn't have long to worry about that. As little Foxy Foxy wheedled a new bid out of the Catholics for three-quarters of a million dollars I heard something bang against the door behind me. For half an instant I had the horrible, funny idea that it would be Sam showing up late, guns drawn and blazing even though I didn't need saving, but a moment later the entire door splintered around the latch and swung inward and a couple of objects not much bigger than tennis balls bounced through into the hall. I covered my eyes, and a half-second later they exploded loudly, blinding anyone who hadn't looked away and not doing my ears much good either, thank you. Smoke was filling the hall as a group of armed men rushed in. I threw myself onto the ground, and the hall's single overhead light abruptly went out. People were shouting in anger or fear or both, then the shouts turned to screams as guns began firing, muzzle-flare strobing the room as the walls echoed with the ratcheting of automatic weapons.

nineteen
one night only

AS THE guns started blazing in the darkened hall it occurred to me that if anyone was the likely target of this raid, it was me; even if these men weren't Eligor's, they almost certainly belonged to someone who wanted what I was supposed to have. I needed to get out of there. Sure, I felt bad about the other auction participants getting shot at, but I was even more worried about what was going to happen to Heaven's least favorite angel.

I fired back at the armed shock troops, then rolled to another spot so they couldn't get me by aiming at my flashes. More shots crackled out. I reloaded, then returned fire again, cursing all the time that I had to use silver bullets at ten dollars a round on what were probably cheap-jack, low-level mercenaries. I'd already wasted something like a hundred bucks just firing into the darkness, and it pissed me off.

"I turn off the lights, Dollar Bob!" a voice whispered in my ear during a brief lull in the gunfire. I admit I squeaked like a startled puppy. It was Fox, who had proved many times over how easily he could sneak up on me. "But they find the switch soon, I think, so maybe you better vamoose, podner."

"Yeah, this whole auction thing kind of went to hell, didn't it?"

My crypto-Asian friend laughed quietly. "Hee! Don't worry, we finish our business another time, Mr. D-Bob. Go now—crawl to the back of the hall, behind the totem poles."

He was referring to a forest of New Guinea carvings I had noticed earlier, each pole so extravagantly decorated and carefully burnished that they looked like melting psychedelic candles. In the intermittent flashes of muzzle fire I could make out the poles standing a few yards away across no-man's-land, pale as a copse of birch trees, so I began my commando-crawl, belly against the parquet and extremely grateful that I was wearing dark clothing. Once a line of automatic rifle slugs stitched their way along the floor just in front of me, missing my face by mere inches and showering me with stinging slivers. I also had to crawl over two bodies that were in my way, one of them in stiff clerical robes, but I finally made it into the totem forest without taking a bullet. A couple of seconds later I found the heavy fire curtain at the back of the room and the exit door hidden behind it. It was locked, but I rose to a crouch, waited for another loud burst of gunfire before kicking the door open, then dove through, hitting and rolling on the far side and fetching myself a nasty thump on the head against the iron railings of the hall's covered back porch. I dragged myself upright in the dim light, swaying and woozy, and realized I was now on the opposite side of the building from my car. I was just about to jump down and try to lose myself in one of the neighboring buildings when I heard voices both behind me from inside the hall and also coming toward me from the front, getting louder.

There was no direction to run where I wouldn't be out in plain sight for several seconds, an easy kill shot for men with automatic rifles, and although I took a moment to reload my .38, there was no way I was going to try blasting it out gangster-style with a bunch of armed assault troops. Instead I broke the light bulb above my head with my gun butt, then shoved the pistol into my pocket and leaped up to catch the overhang of the porch, which was not much bigger than the top of an old-fashioned phone booth. I managed to swing my legs up and pressed myself belly-first into the dark space above the door just as the first people appeared from around the front of the building. It sounded like some of the auction guests running away, but I didn't bother to look, since I was busy straining my muscles to keep myself hidden. An instant later the door crashed open beneath me and a trio of armed men lurched out and met several of their fellows coming around from the front of the hall. One of the three beneath me was talking into a headset, but he pushed it away from his mouth to growl at the other four.

"Haven't found him inside but they're still sweeping the building. The bastard's probably running, but we'll catch him before he gets far. Move out and deploy down the street along either side, and I'll get you some backup. Go! *Go!*"

I recognized the leader's voice—my hairy old chum Howlingfell, who began talking on his headset again as his men hustled off in military quick-step. I waited until the last of the assault team had rounded the far corner before I interrupted his conversation by swinging down and booting him as hard as I could, both heels against his nasty flat head. He was wearing an aramid fiber assault helmet; I didn't crush his skull but it wasn't for lack of trying. As he crumpled to the ground I dropped on him, planting my knee on his throat for the second time in a week or so as I shoved my .38 against his belly.

"Remember me, Howly?"

"Fuck you, Dollar," he gasped, then made a retching noise. I was glad to hear I'd kicked him as hard as I'd meant to. "You're as good as dead."

"I already *am* dead, stupid. That's how you get to be an angel." I pushed down harder on his neck. "How many men have you got out there?" He just stared at me so I prodded him with the gun. "Remember our past meetings? I sure do. I treasure every golden minute. Why were you babysitting Grasswax when you work for Eligor? If you're really his security chief, you're too high-ranking to be a prosecutor's bodyguard."

He stared at me, his single eyebrow drawn down in a scowling V. "I'm not telling you shit, Dollar. I told you, you're a dead man—the *real* kind of dead, like Grasswax. The Grand Duke is going to eat your heart."

"Maybe, but if you don't tell me what I want to know you won't be around to enjoy it." I was bluffing though, and he probably knew it—I didn't have the time to shake him down for information.

He definitely knew it. "Have a nice ride down to Hell, Dollar," he rasped past the pressure of my knee on his compressed throat. "Go ahead and kill me—my boss'll just get me another body."

"Really?" I straightened up but still keeping my foot squarely on his windpipe. "Do you think he'll bother if I just blow off your nuts?" I paused to savor the expression on his bestial face briefly, then gave him a couple of silver hollow-points in the general crotch area before I turned and ran toward the front of the building, reloading as I went. Howlingfell's screams of agony sounded loud as an air raid siren behind me. Every member of his assault team still on the premises would be spilling out the doors of Islanders Hall within half a minute.

Just before I reached the front of the building I veered off and scrambled over the high iron fence, catching my pants leg and ripping it on the spikes at the top. Yanked off balance, I came down tumbling and flailing and crashed right into an angular, painful shadow that appeared out of nowhere, sending both of us flying. I sprang up, revolver in hand and braced to run or shoot, but it was only Edie Parmenter, sprawled in the street with her bicycle lying beside her, its wheels still spinning. Horrified, I leaped forward to lift her onto her feet and give her back her bicycle.

"Edie, get out of here!" I whispered. "Hurry up!"

"It's okay," she said, as calmly as if we had met in front of her boarding school instead of while being chased by armed troops. "I live real close. I'll be fine. They don't want me." As she climbed back on her bicycle she asked, "Is it safe? The feather?"

For a moment I didn't know what she was talking about, then suddenly the light went on. "Don't worry," I said. "I didn't bring it. Be careful!"

"You too, Mr. Dollar," she said as she pedaled off into the darkness.

I didn't have much time to savor the revelation that Eligor's object was apparently some kind of feather, because I could hear Howlingfell screaming orders from the back porch of Islanders Hall and his soldiers' rapid footsteps getting closer. I jumped up and started scorching leather toward where I'd left my car, doing my best to keep out from under any streetlights as I sprinted out of King and onto Jefferson. I spotted my loaner a few dozen yards down and headed toward it, and although I could hear many voices in the street behind me now, I was thinking I might actually manage to reach it, and had even started to fumble in my pants pocket for the keys—no easy feat when you're running, looking over your shoulder, and holding a revolver in your other hand—when somebody screamed my name.

"Bobby! Look out!"

Everything that happened next seemed to take place in a single kaleidoscopic swirl of light and darkness, a muddle of flaring streetlights, clawing shadows, and things that shouldn't exist but *did*, right where I didn't want them. A blazing hot blackness snapped past my face with such force that if I hadn't slowed at the shouted warning it would have knocked my head right off like I was a carnival sideshow game. It was the *ghallu*. The rotten, burning, bastard thing had been waiting for me and had almost got me. The voice had been Sam's.

I stumbled as I avoided the creature's flailing swipe, which missed so narrowly that the hairs on my head crackled and curled from the heat, then I took a few more steps without ever really getting my balance. Finally, surrendering to gravity, I fell and rolled, smacking some part of myself hard against the asphalt with every revolution, until I came to a stop halfway onto Jefferson Avenue and still several yards from the Pontiac Orban had loaned me. There weren't many other cars on the street this time of night, but they all had to swerve abruptly to avoid hitting me. The drivers only located their horns afterward, blatting indignantly as they straightened out and went on their way, apparently never noticing the huge black shape pounding after me.

I hadn't dropped my gun until the last roll so it hadn't gone far, but as I scrambled after it I still doubted I'd reach it in time—the *ghallu* was right behind me. Then Sam, bless him, leaped out into the street from behind my car and opened fire on the monstrosity, emptying a whole clip from his automatic into the thing. Whatever kind of loads he was packing didn't seem to hurt it at all, but it startled the creature a little and it hesitated before continuing after me, which gave me time to reach my own gun, roll, and start firing.

I pulled the trigger three times before I hit an empty chamber, and I swear all three silver hollow-points hit that big ugly bastard right in the torso, but the *ghallu* only stood up straight like an angry bear and bellowed in pain or maybe just irritation. It was the first cry I'd heard it make—a booming roar that made my ears pop and set off car alarms up and down the block. The gunfire must have already awakened everybody in the neighborhood, but now windows started slamming open up and down Jefferson as people peered out to see who was jackhammer-murdering an African lion in front of the Arco Station. The *ghallu* shook its misshapen, horned head and then started toward me again. Meanwhile, I had already given up on the idea of trying to reload in the street and was sprinting toward my car.

"It's unlocked!" I screamed at Sam. "Get the hell in!"

I yanked the door open and threw myself behind the wheel even as my buddy came crashing in from the passenger side. I tossed him my .38 and a speed loader as I cranked the ignition, grateful beyond expressing that I hadn't dropped the keys and equally thankful that Orban's old bomb had decent plugs. It caught on the first rev and I threw it into reverse, skidding backward just as the thing threw itself onto the armored hood. We crashed into the car parked behind us but the *ghallu* hung on. For just a moment I could see something of its face through the windshield, a sight I will probably never be lucky enough to forget—insane hatred sketched in fire, features that rippled and ran like a slow liquid, and a beard composed of writhing, headless snakes. It stared back at me like a burning mask of Hammurabi, with just enough human symmetry to make it inexpressibly alien. The *ghallu* was primitive, I remembered, and that was its power; it came from some even deeper, darker pit than Hell itself.

The beast raised fists like black sledgehammers. I knew it was going to punch its way through the hood and destroy the engine, stranding us, so I gunned the engine and threw the Pontiac into drive, slamming into the car parked in front of me as hard as I could, trying to nutcracker the monster between the vehicles. The thing bellowed and thrashed but didn't seem badly hurt. I grabbed the gun-butt that Sam was pressing into my hand and emptied my weapon into the *ghallu* as it scrabbled to tear itself loose. It bellowed again, and I swear I heard some pain in the cry this time, but although I'd knocked it off my hood it was quickly pulling free from the tangle of the other car's bumper.

"Let's get out of here!" yelled Sam. I didn't need to be told.

The Bonneville screeched backward, tires smoking. The *ghallu* dropped to one knee, then shoved itself upright, pressing down on the other car so hard that the whole chassis collapsed and one of the wheels popped off and skidded across Jefferson Avenue. I didn't wait around to see what kind of shape the monstrosity was in—I could tell it wasn't badly hurt. Seven or eight silver rounds in the thing and it was still up and running, as I quickly saw in my rear-view mirror—loping after us like some horrible carbon-black ape, dodging between the honking cars on Jefferson as I pushed the pedal to the floorboard.

Sam leaned out the window and fired a couple of shots back at the thing.

"If those aren't silver, don't bother," I shouted over the roar of the V8. "And even if they are, it probably won't slow it down much. What the hell happened to you?"

"What happened to me?" he shouted back. "*That thing* happened to me! I was a couple of minutes late, and it was waiting outside the building. Damn near caught me, but I managed to get down a manhole where it couldn't follow me. I got back out in time to see you running toward me, so I figured it might be laying for you."

"Thanks. *Shit!*" I swerved to avoid a group of merrymakers in Carnival costumes who had just staggered out of a liquor store and right into the street. I don't know what happened to them when the *ghallu* went past, and I didn't want to look back, but I did hear screams. I accelerated, but I could still see that immense shadow loping along the rain-slicked streets behind us at a terrifying clip. And now brake lights were going on in front of me—a big back-up of cars ahead at the Camino Real. "It's still right behind us. Where are we going to go?"

"Office or The Compasses," said Sam. "They've both got wards that should keep that thing out. Nothing else will." He was loading my gun again. "You get these from Orban?"

"Yeah. But they don't seem to be doing much good."

"Nice work, though." He squinted, then bit down on one of them. "That's good silver."

"It better be. I've shot off about four hundred bucks' worth already, and I haven't killed fuck-all except some of Eligor's assault squad guys." I gave Sam a quick rundown on what had happened inside Islanders Hall. By the time I'd finished I could see the Camino Real in front of us and not only was the light still red, the road between us and the Alhambra Building, home of The Compasses, was gridlocked.

"Turn right before we get there," Sam said. "Shit, I just remembered—they had the parade tonight! The whole downtown is going to be like this."

I slalomed the Pontiac right onto Adams, fishtailing so widely that I almost lost control of the car, sending a group of costumed pedestrians shouting and leaping for the stairs of the Victorian houses that lined the street. Once I was clear of them I risked a glance back and saw the *ghallu* digging around the corner behind me like a hound after a rabbit.

I don't like being the rabbit.

When I got to the T-junction with Oak Avenue at the end I yanked us back toward the Camino Real, cutting the corner so sharply that we went up over the curb at about fifty miles an hour, the two left side wheels off the ground for a couple of seconds before we slammed down again, bouncing like a low-rider. The barriers were still up at the Camino Real end of the street but only a few cars were in the intersection, so I crashed the yellow caution gates at speed and dragged the emergency tape out into the wide street, the ends flapping like pennants behind me. For about a second and a half it looked like a power surge had hit a bumper car ride as I pinballed between vehicles, damaging a couple badly but mercifully not hurting any of the drivers or passengers as far as I could tell. We smashed through the barrier on the other side and zigzagged over to Main Street before heading toward the heart of downtown. I knew we'd never get around the whole parade route before the thing caught us, and I didn't want to risk crashing the barriers again. I was just grateful the parade itself was over.

Downtown was crawling with post-parade revelers. Most of them reeled in drunken groups, but others were in their cars now, cruising slowly up and down the streets that hadn't been blocked off, still looking for amusement or action even at one in the morning. San Judas combines several carnival traditions—I saw rainmakers in Mayan hats and the Elders of Guymas in their long robes and pointy beards as well as the Knights of Numa and the Ravenswood Krewes and all kinds of other Mardi-Gras-inspired partiers. Just by the mess and the merrymakers still swarming the downtown streets, it looked like it had been a hell of a parade. I wish I'd been there instead of being shot at in Islanders Hall.

I nearly killed a pair of stiltwalkers as I crossed the railroad tracks at speed, but though I missed them the *ghallu* didn't, tearing the legs right out from under them and sending them flying.

What I saw in my rear-view mirror was getting increasingly hallucinatory, but the view ahead wasn't much better. We were coming up fast on the downtown barriers, and that was where the serious mayhem was going to start—cop cars and firetrucks were lined up everywhere, red and blue lights spinning, and even the armored Bonneville wasn't going to crash through them without hurting a lot of people, not to mention what would happen to Sam and me if we got tangled up in a wreck long enough for the *ghallu* to catch us. We were going to have to ditch the Bonneville and try to get to The Compasses on foot.

But even as I thought this, the monstrosity *did* catch us: a ghastly hollow thumping as it leaped up onto the trunk was followed by the most painful groaning, gnashing sound I ever heard—the sound of a very large demonic summoning trying to yank the top off an armored sedan to get at the fleshy treats inside. I was counting my blessings: if we'd been in my Matador not only would the creature have reached us by now, it would have really screwed up the paint job, too.

The aluminum oxynitride driver's side window, which was meant to resist anything up to armor-piercing rounds, shattered into a spider-webbed hole as a hot black claw smashed through, intent on yanking my head out of the car whether or not it was still attached to my body. I ducked even as I slammed on the brakes so that I bashed my face against the hard old steering wheel, then realized stopping with the monster on top of the car had not been my best idea. The *ghallu* was trying to rip through the reinforced metal of the roof while still trying to catch my head in its other great taloned hand and pop it like a boiled grape; even as I strained my neck to stay out of its reach I could see little wisps of smoke or steam dancing on the thing's carbon-black skin. Sam still had my gun, and I was beginning to lose faith in the idea of silver bullets anyway, at least for this particular horror, so instead I did what they taught me at Leo the Loke's Emergency Driving School: When something's on your roof, knock if off. Still holding my head at an absurd and extremely painful angle, I floored the car and steered straight for the nearest building.

"What are you . . . ?" was all Sam had time to shout before we hit the curb, bounced into the air and hurtled into the wall of the Main Street branch of Wells Fargo Bank like a runaway missile, sending bricks and plaster flying everywhere (and not treating us passengers much better). A huge piece of rebar came through the windshield like Van Helsing's money shot and passed neatly between Sam's head and mine as we bounced around with the impact, the pointy end of it lancing the back seat like a tuck-and-roll boil. I prayed fervently that the *ghallu*'s head had been bashed in, but I doubted it; if close to a dozen silver rounds in the torso couldn't stop it then a little thing like a bank building wasn't going to do the job.

There is nothing quite so terrible as fleeing something that you know is more than a match for you. The helplessness, the way the strength just runs out of your limbs like sand . . . you feel yourself getting colder and slower by the moment. Your worst fears rise in triumph.

I didn't bother to check on Sam—I could hear him struggling to get out on his own side. I just kicked my door open and sprinted in the direction of Beeger Square, shouldering my way through inebriated and oblivious revelers. There was no chance to look back, nor did I want to. I knew the fetch would be right behind us like a distorted, smoldering shadow, eyes narrowed to slits, mouth like a hole torn in a curtain. I knew it was only a few moments until our weak earthly flesh finally let us down.

Sam pulled abreast of me, his overcoat flapping crazily as he ran. I'd never seen him move so fast, like a big farm horse on a steep downhill slope—everything was moving at the same time, and there was no way it was going to stop by itself.

"Garage!" he gasped. He was holding something out in front of him. For a moment I thought it was a gun and that he was going to shoot some of the drunken idiots blocking our way, but it was a remote door-opener, and he was pressing that button over and over as if he were a rat left too long in a gratification experiment. We leaped and scuttled between two deserted police cars and under a wooden barrier, then sprinted down Main toward the Alhambra Building at the end. Beyond it, Beeger Square was still packed with people, and I had a momentary, nightmarish vision of leading the monstrous thing into the crowd where it would rip up all those innocent folk like a power mower going through a brood of Easter chicks.

"Driveway!" Sam shouted. He skidded into a sharp right turn and pelted down the cement ramp of the Alhambra's garage. To my immense relief the remote had worked: the gate was open and the way clear. Even as we reached it, Sam thumbed the remote again and the gate started down.

As we scrambled through the closing gap I risked a look back and saw the *ghallu* reach the top of the driveway. It hesitated for a moment, visibly confused, then realized we were no longer running in front of it. It whirled and leaped down the sloping concrete after us like a giant black frog. To my immense relief it slammed against the metal gate and bounced back, then lowered itself like a cringing dog and stared at the bars with a hiss that sounded of frustration and, of all things, pain.

"The wards," Sam said as he bent double, gasping for air. "The wards are holding him. God really does love us."

I could no longer see out to the city lights—the *ghallu* was blocking the whole of the metal fence and it didn't look like it was planning to go away. "Yeah—for how long? Come on. Let's get upstairs."

The monster had begun stamping and huffing its way all along the base and sides of the gate as if trying to find a weak spot in whatever charms or holy names held it at bay. Tired as I was, I still had no urge to stand in the cold lights of the garage waiting for the elevator while that unholy thing stared red murder at us, so I led Sam toward the stairs. After a few carefully selected words of disagreement, he followed.

We staggered out onto the fourth floor and down the hallway to The Compasses. A slightly faded sign next to the front door proclaimed, "Tonight—One Night Only! Gabriel and His Hot Trumpet at the Living End!" Chico's put that sign out every day for years—somebody's joke from way back when, now a tradition. It's also a tradition that the front door is always open during business hours.

I ended that one.

"Hey, Dollar, what are you doing?" Chico shouted from behind the bar as I slammed the thing and threw the bolt. "We got fire regulations! The Opposition call in complaints all the time just to get us hassled—!"

"No time. Bad shit outside." I looked around. There were only a few other people in the place: Young Elvis and Jimmy the Table camped at the bar along with Kool Filter and an angel friend of his named Teddy Nebraska who I didn't know very well. It wasn't quite the doomsday survival crew I would have chosen; Jimmy the Table is built along the lines of George from the Seinfeld show, and Kool looks like he's just stepped off the Duff Breweries tour. Nebraska at least looked like he had some smarts—he was strapped and was already reaching for his piece at my announcement. I allowed myself to wonder for an idle second what *he* did before he became an advocate.

"What's going on?" Chico was no slouch either; he was already digging under the bar. "What is it?"

"Demon called a *ghallu*. Big, hot as hell, and *old*," I said. "Holy water won't work. Silver—a little, maybe. That's what I'm using, anyway. Beyond that I'm out of ideas."

"Okay," Chico said, straightening up. "Sam, you pushing silver or lead?"

"All I got's Brand X."

"Then catch." Chico straightened up and lobbed Sam a pump-action Mossberg and a couple of boxes of shells. Sam caught them and started loading the magazine. Chico bent again and stood up with the ugliest-looking weapon I've seen in a while—a massive black shotgun with a round drum like an old-fashioned tommy gun.

"AA12," Chico said. I think he must have been in the vengeance business too, once upon a time, but he never talks about it. Still, I hadn't seen him this happy since the Davis verdict riots. "Automatic shottie. This will fuck some supernatural shit *up*."

"Oh my God. What are you firing?"

"Silver nitrate—that's silver salt for you lay brothers," Chico told me with a very disturbing smile on his usually stoic Aztec face. "Gonna spread some pain."

His own gun now loaded, Sam had started tipping over freestanding tables and shoving them against The Compasses' front door. I ran to help him. At just that moment Monica came out of the ladies' room with Annie Pilgrim, another co-worker I hadn't seen much of late. For just the barest microsecond I wondered whether they been double-dating with Kool and Nebraska. And then I thought, Who the hell cares?

Monica's eyes went very wide as they turned from Chico and his monstrous gun to me. "Bobby, what are. . . ?"

"That *ghallu* thing that was after me? It's outside trying to sniff its way through the wards. Any idea how strong they are?" Monica was our unofficial historian and knew a lot more about the Alhambra Building than I did.

"Strong." She thought about it for a moment. "Does it fly?"

"The *ghallu?* Not as far as I've ever seen, but it sure can run—why?"

"Because the wards are strongest around the base of the building, of course, on the doors and windows on the ground floor." She frowned, thinking. "And I'm pretty sure the roof is warded as well. But I'm not so certain about everything else."

"What does that mean?" Suddenly I had a cold, cold feeling around my heart. "Monica, that thing can jump like a flea—a giant, two-thousand-degrees-hot, man-eating flea."

"Push!" Sam shouted at me. We had almost completely buried the front door behind a pile of tables eight-feet high. It might not keep the *ghallu* out for long but it would keep it exposed as it smashed its way through—enough time for Chico and Sam and me to put a bunch of silver in it, anyway.

"It's just that I'm not so certain about the upstairs windows . . ." was all Monica had time to say before the lights suddenly went out, and something huge came through the big glass rectangle behind us like a runaway jet plane, spraying glass and bricks everywhere, its blackness big enough to obliterate the very stars of the sky.

twenty
wards and wheels

ONCE AGAIN I was stuck in a dark room with guns booming all around me. At least this time I wasn't the one being shot at.

Chico rested his front grip on the top of the bar and hosed down the hulking shadow that had come through the window, his gun on deafening full auto, strobing the darkness with muzzle flare. Beside me Sam fired the Mossberg slowly and methodically, trying to put as much of each load into the target as possible. I could hear Teddy Nebraska and Annie and Monica and Jimmy yelling, but the guns made too much noise for me to understand what they were saying. I'm guessing it was something on the order of "Oh, shit, what is *that*?"

The *ghallu* didn't like Chico's silver nitrate at all, which was probably all that was keeping us alive. Like rock salt from a farmer's old bird gun it clearly stung more than it wounded, but from the howling and thrashing of the *ghallu* it stung a *lot*. How much it disliked the silver salt became clear a second later when it leaped right past me and bashed a smoking hole in the middle of The Compasses' ancient mahogany bar in an attempt to get Chico. I didn't see what happened to the bartender after he dove to the side but for at least the moment his weapon had been silenced.

"Annie, follow me!" Monica shouted as the *ghallu* dug through the wreckage of the bar like some monster badger trying to claw its prey out of the earth. I didn't know what Monica was up to—running for her life, I hoped—but I needed to cover her, so I stepped forward with my revolver leveled, and as the thing turned its nasty, inhuman mask of a face toward the running women I started firing. The fetch swatted at the flashes and reared back from what I presume was the annoying pitter-patter of my little silver bullets on its skin. I hit an empty chamber and dove to one side to avoid being skewered by a spike of shattered bartop the size of a surfboard that the *ghallu* flung at me. I was seriously rethinking my little five-shot Smith & Wesson, which emptied in seconds. I hadn't been forced into this kind of military rate of fire in a very long while, but right now I wished I had something with a more generous magazine. Like maybe a silver-throwing antiaircraft gun.

Sam had dug his way backward into the mound of chairs and desks we had stacked, which were now blocking our only exit, and from this improvised defensive position was laying down fire as fast as he could pump the Mossberg. I knew Chico had only tossed him a couple of boxes of shells, so he was going to run out soon. On the other side of the bar, and true to his name, Jimmy had turned over a table and he and Nebraska and Kool were barricaded behind it in one of the booths. I figured they were probably firing plain old lead, but even the *ghallu* still had to be made out of some kind of flesh and blood, since it was here on Earth vigorously breaking things: a shitload of regular bullets couldn't hurt our cause any and might do some good as an annoyance. Young Elvis lay in a well-coiffed heap behind them, knocked silly by a piece of flying debris, but there was no sign of Monica and Annie in the main room, which made me feel a little better—maybe they would survive this unholy clusterfuck to tell everybody else what had happened. Then I could hope that somewhere up the line someone might pay Eligor back for letting his monstrous servant rip up The Compasses. I mean, the place was practically a sovereign embassy . . . !

The monster tore away chunks of the bar now, trying to get to Chico and his semi-automatic shotgun as the bartender fired the AA12 in ear-splitting drumrolls. Sam straightened up in his improvised blind and began peppering the creature's back to distract it from killing Chico. He did his job well enough that the thing decided to do something about Sam instead.

The *ghallu* turned with a roar I felt as much as heard, a burst of pressure and heat that smelled like boiling sewage, then it flung a huge broken slab of the heavy mahogany bar at Sam. It hit like a missile and sent most of the tables flying as if they were bowling pins, silencing my buddy and his Mossberg. The impact knocked me down as well, and I knew I'd be limping later when the adrenaline faded. Before I could go help Sam the *ghallu* leaped toward the spot and began digging through the wreckage, roaring like a Harley that had lost its muffler. Even from a few feet away I could feel the heat radiating from it as if it were a dark sun. Worried that Sam might be unconscious and unable to defend himself, I stood up and gave the ugly bastard the rest of my silver rounds right in the side of its inhuman head. As my hammer fell on the last shell, and the flash of light caught that dreadful half-face turning toward me, twisted with near-mindless rage, I suddenly realized that we had this whole thing wrong: Sam and I had come here for the safety of the wards, but whatever Heaven had devised to protect The Compasses had come up short against this ancient hobgoblin. The bar was no longer a place of refuge, it was a trap with no way out but a fifty-foot drop or a deadly bottleneck in the stairway or the elevator.

More importantly, though, the monster was after *me*, not Sam or any of the others, so if they couldn't help me kill it—and if Chico's awesome silver-salt machine gun wasn't going to do it, nothing else would—then I needed to get out. Otherwise my friends would die too, and what would be the point of that?

Of course, this was all completely academic because the *ghallu* had just refocused itself on me, a soft squishy thing with an empty revolver, standing only a couple of yards away. It dropped the shattered table it had just lifted, then sprang toward me like a cat on a lame mouse.

A stream of water smashed into the *ghallu* and knocked the thing stumbling to one side. It soaked me too but I hardly noticed that. The creature bellowed in anger and—hallelujah!—serious pain, enveloped in clouds of hissing, billowing steam. Police spotlights were now shining through the broken window from the street below, but even by their glare all I could see of our attacker was a writhing, black shape, a shadow within a shadow.

Monica and Annie Pilgrim stood in the doorway of the hall leading to the restroom, struggling to aim a giant fire hose as if they were wrestling a live anaconda, hammering away at the demon with something like a hundred pounds of water per square inch. The steam clouds were getting thicker and thicker but the creature hadn't lost its footing and, in fact, appeared to be wading against the thunderous flow of the hose toward the source.

It had been a wonderful idea but it wasn't enough water to completely cool the creature, or even enough force to slow it down very much. It was enough, however, to give me a single desperate idea and the chance to operate on it. As the room slowly turned into a boiling hot sauna, and the monster bellowed and gurgled and fought back against the hose, I leaped over the bar and dug through the wreckage until I found the bar hoses for soda water and tonic. I ripped off the nearest one, faucet and all, then crawled through the wreckage to the wall, feeling with my hands until I found a heavy extension cord, which I pulled loose from the socket. I could hear Chico groaning somewhere in the rubble.

"Chico?" I called. "You okay, man?"

"Some broken ribs, I think. I need to reload but I can't find the rest of the fucking shells!"

"I'm getting out of here—I think it'll follow me if I do." I jammed the siphon hose into my belt, grabbed the extension cord, then straightened up and sloshed as quickly as I could past the splashing, thrashing giant and toward the shattered window. I was almost blinded by the thick clouds of steam, but fortunately so was the *ghallu*, and I managed to slither past just beyond its reach. The water around my ankles was already getting uncomfortably warm from the demon's heat as I reached the jukebox and looped the extension cord around it, keeping an end in each hand like a logger climbing a big tree. It was almost certainly too far down to the street to jump without breaking an ankle—our angel bodies are tough but not magically invulnerable—but I was hoping to lessen the distance with this little trick. I climbed onto the window sill, kicking long slivers of glass out of the frame, then when the creature's angry bellowing quieted for a moment I shouted, "Monica—take the hose off it!"

"Are you crazy?"

"Trust me!"

The stream of water shifted to the side and the *ghallu* straightened. For an instant I could see something of what it looked like undistorted by heat, its skin dark, knotted and shiny, like something out of one of Billy Blake's most apocalyptic etchings. The pressure suddenly gone, the *ghallu* actually stumbled; before it could regain its balance and go after the two female angels who had made it so angry, I bellowed as loud as I could, *"Hey, you! Yeah, you—big, hot and stupid!"*

As the steaming thing turned toward me, I leaped off the window backward, one end of the heavy-duty extension cord in each hand like a giant jump rope. I had a moment of freefall, then a painful jounce that almost yanked my arms out of their sockets. I didn't have long to suffer, though: my weight on the loop of electrical cord tipped the juke box over, a result I hadn't expected, so instead of having a moment to ready myself for the rest of the drop I simply bounced once in midair and then kept falling.

I hit the ground with a painful jolt to both legs, but did my best to parachute-roll and disperse the force. As I lay panting on the ground feeling for anything interesting like compound fractures, I saw the *ghallu* staring down from the shattered window above me, haloed in the water from the hose that Annie and Monica had trained on it once more. The thing stood almost motionless despite all that pressure, looking for me . . . or sniffing for me. Police officers and firefighters were all over the sidewalk and street around me, clearly called in on what they thought was some kind of armed robbery of the Alhambra Building gone very wrong—another reason I had to get the monster away quickly, before it massacred them all. I rolled over, scrambled to my feet, and ran limping away from the flashing lights into Beeger Square with people yelling after me and a few policemen even trying to catch me.

That wasn't going to happen.

As I reached the middle of the square I heard the first startled screams from the late-night crowds, and I knew the *ghallu* was after me again. That was one less thing to feel bad about—at least I was taking it away from my friends—but if the next part of my hasty plan didn't work, I definitely wasn't going to make it to Ash Wednesday this year.

A couple of teenagers riding double on a motorcycle almost knocked me over in their hurry to escape the square, self-selecting themselves as key ingredients in Part Two of my plan: I knew that if I didn't get back into some kind of vehicle I wasn't even going to make it to the far side of the plaza before the demon pulled all my bits off. I ran after the motorcycle kids and caught them in a few strides. I yanked the one in the back off his seat, then jumped up behind the driver and, before he realized quite what was going on, lifted him up and tossed him over too. I leaned down over the handlebars and fumbled the bike into second gear—it was a newish Yamaha, and I hadn't ridden one in a while—then yelled back at its driver where he lay on the ground, "Tell me you got insurance. You do, right?"

He said something I couldn't quite make out—I told myself it was, *"Yes, plenty!"* Then I gave it all the throttle I could, and it leaped ahead. The engine was surprisingly strong; the front wheel came up off the ground for a moment, but I leaned way forward and brought it down, then blasted across the square as fast as I could, weaving in and out of startled revelers who were beginning to panic and run in different directions—perhaps because of me, perhaps because of the giant, steaming, horned terror that was chasing me.

I almost dumped the bike getting out between a couple of official vehicles on the far side of Beeger Square but regained my balance and accelerated again along Main Street as I left the crowds behind. I was aiming for the open-air Riverside Shopping Center since it would be closed for the night, and I couldn't really afford to dodge pedestrians much longer. The *ghallu* was just behind me, something I could hear even though I didn't dare risk a look back at the speeds I was traveling. Up and down curbs and through pedestrian alleys not meant to be traversed at sixty miles an hour—I was coming damn close to killing myself and sparing the ancient demon-thing all the trouble. But somehow I bounced up an inactive escalator without popping a tire and made it to the upper esplanade of the Riverside Center. Now I risked a look back and saw the black shape coming up the escalator behind me. It had dried and was already ablaze again, flames licking its silhouette, gleaming red eyes fixed remorselessly on me.

The upper level of the Riverside Center has shops all along one side, but the other side is open to the manicured bank of the Redwood River below. I needed to get to the far end of the shopping center where the water widened and deepened, but the roof was full of cement planters and benches and little kiosks that sold waffle cones and candy and other useful things, padlocked now, so I had to ease up on the throttle enough to slalom through them all. I could actually hear the slap of the *ghallu*'s feet on the esplanade behind me, still in close pursuit. The monster was all but tireless, but I definitely was not.

There was no way to jump the iron fence at the end of the esplanade, so I did the only thing I could: at the last second, with the fence ten yards away, then five, four, three yards, I clambered up and stood on the seat, spreading my arms, then jumped as high as I could.

The Yamaha smashed into the fence at something over forty miles an hour with an explosive, grinding clang. Carried forward by momentum, I flew through a shower of sparks as a whole length of iron pickets tore free with the motorcycle still tangled in them like a dophin in a net. The broken fence tumbled awkwardly down the embankment, carrying the bike with it. I watched it in almost slow-motion clarity, because I was plunging through the air toward the green water far below.

I hit the water in the clumsiest, most painful cannonball dive imaginable—really, I've seen people land burning aircraft more gracefully. But the important thing was what happened next: I splashed down into the river at a place where it was deep enough to absorb the energy of my fall. I also somehow managed to stay conscious. When I stopped moving and began to float to the surface again I pulled the bar's siphon hose from my belt and ripped off the little faucet, then put the end of the hose in my mouth. I held my breath as long as I could as I drifted up, then poked the other end of the hose above the surface. When I reached a place where I could put my feet on the bottom and still get the tip of the hose out of the water, I stopped moving and tried just to stay still.

I was well out into the middle of the river, and I didn't think that anything that had howled so much at being hosed down would wade out into so much water if it couldn't even see me. I was hoping being underwater would hide my smell, too.

It had been a desperate plan, and one of the things I hadn't had a chance to consider was what it would feel like to be submerged in fifty-degree water, breathing through a plastic tube. It wasn't so bad for the first couple of minutes, but even with my stronger-than-human constitution I was shivering so badly by the ten-minute point that I began debating whether it was really worse to be captured or killed by that creature than to die of exposure in a river full of cold water.

I gave it one more minute, then crept slowly into the shallows and staggered ashore on the cement bank at a spot hidden under a pedestrian bridge, soaked and shivering. No sign of the *ghallu*, but I didn't move any further until I saw that the police and other emergency workers were gathering along the esplanade where the bike had gone through the wrought iron fence, pointing to the spot where everything had hit the water. Some of the twisted wreckage protruded above the surface. I figured they'd be sending in divers to look for my body soon, so I clambered out on the far side of the bridge and did my best to squeeze most of the water from my clothes, hoping that when I was done I'd just look like a bum who'd had a hard, hard night. Cold and miserable? Don't ask.

I called Sam but nobody picked up, so I left a terse message to let him know I was alive. I hoped he was the same, but the creature had hit him very, very hard, and I was worried. I tried Monica, too, but also without luck. I was seriously worried that my incompetence might have gotten all my closest friends and colleagues killed, but I couldn't worry long because I knew for a fact that the *ghallu* was still out there somewhere, that I had no car and no silver bullets, and that by now Eligor must have spies all over town.

As I huddled there shivering I couldn't even raise Clarence the trainee, which made me wonder if everyone was just avoiding me out of self-preservation. I didn't want to try to walk dripping down brightly lit Veterans in search of a motel, and I didn't know of even a homeless shelter I could get into at this time of night. Which left me but one option.

I called the number I never really thought I'd use. Nobody answered that one either, but I left a message.

Fifteen minutes later the big black car pulled to the side of Veterans near the place where, still drizzling river water, I was crouching out of sight of the road. I scrambled up the embankment and, keeping my head low, opened the passenger side door. As I pulled myself in, something hard and extremely gunlike pushed against my forehead.

"You realize this taxi ride isn't free, don't you, Dollar?" The Countess of Cold Hands had a very steady grip on the pistol, no tremor. "Either you're going to tell me everything you know and everything you think you know, or they're going to find a floater that looks like you in the Redwood River tomorrow morning."

It's hard to argue with the barrel of an automatic pressing against your glabella. "You have my angelic word on it."

"Lovely," she said with perhaps just a hint of sarcasm. "Buckle up." She removed the barrel from my forehead but kept it pointing toward me. It was a big Czech 9mm with what looked like silver plating, I was guessing platinum or chrome. Very flashy, though.

She stared her disapproval as I arranged myself wetly on the leather upholstery, then she swung the big car out onto Veterans. "You smell like pond scum and duck shit, Dollar. I'm guessing you might have found yourself in over your head."

"Ha ha." The unamused way I said it was slightly undercut by my violent shivering. "Could you turn up the heat?"

"I'm not sure you can take it any hotter," she said, but dialed it up a couple of notches anyway as she nosed through traffic, the gleaming automatic now tucked between her thighs. "And after you tell me what I want to know, where will I be taking you?"

"Right now Hell itself would make a nice change."

She frowned. "You have no idea how unfunny that is."

twenty-one
knife fight in a harem

I HAVEN'T MET that many women, human or angelic, who actually like to drive. In my experience they seem to be much more pragmatic about the whole thing than we are. For most males, driving is an extension of their masculinity; they have little fantasy scenarios going all the time—races, chases, and dramatic combat with other drivers. Females, on the other hand, generally seem to view driving as something you do to get somewhere. I know, crazy.

As we sped away from the scene of my most recent escape from the *ghallu*, I noted with interest that the Countess of Cold Hands was not one of that usual type. She was aggressive, and she drove fast, but with a self-assured inattention, too. She also drove mostly one-handed, but that might have been because her not-so-dainty CZ 75 automatic was in her left hand now, resting on her thigh but pointing in my direction.

"So why did you have a chauffeur before? Because you seem to like doing this."

"You mean Cinnamon? Most of the time I've got better things to do than drive. But as I told you before, things have changed—I've been forced to downsize a bit." She knifed between two trucks and then slid neatly to the right into the exit lane. We had been on the Bayshore, but as we pulled off and headed west on University my Dollar-sense started tingling. I thought for a moment we might be heading toward the Walker place, home to Posie and her idiot boyfriend, and I wondered if I was about to find out I had been a bigger sap than I already thought I was—that the Countess had set me up from the beginning for some reason I couldn't yet see. But then again, why would she need a reason? We were on different sides, weren't we? We were blood enemies.

Just as I was planning my escape (or my counterattack, if that sounds more manly) she made a sharp turn off the main thoroughfare toward the brightly lit but seedy little district known as Whisky Gulch, an oasis just outside the legal limits of the Stanford family's anti-booze crusade. It had been the hub of the local jazz scene in the 1950s and revived briefly with a couple of discos in the seventies, but had fallen on hard times since then. Still, some of the clubs like The Glo-Worm had been there since the Great Depression, and scarcely a one hadn't seen some important San Judas citizen arrested or shot on its premises over the years. It was funny to think that this den of revelry and bad behavior stood so close to the manicured, leaf-blowered streets of Edward L. Walker and his neighbors.

"Slouch down," she said suddenly as we tooled down the main drag. "Too many eyes on this street."

"This car has got tinted windows."

"I'm not worrying about human eyes."

I slid down until my head was level with the glove compartment. From this close proximity I couldn't help looking over at my driver, who I realized for the first time was not wearing some kind of exotic wrap-around dress but a silk dressing gown. It had slid entirely off her left leg, and I watched her slender but muscular thigh and calf muscles bunch and relax as she worked the accelerator and brake pedals. It was very interesting.

"Keep your eyes to yourself, Wings," she said after some moments.

"You really don't want me to look? I thought you lady demons were all about seduction."

"What you don't know about lady demons would fill several books too long for you to read, Dollar."

I laughed despite myself, despite my broken ribs and the gun pointing at me. "Whatever. Where are you taking me?"

"Someplace to get you dried off and less conspicuous while I think about where to dump you. And so you'll have a chance to tell me what you know in private."

"And that would be. . . ?"

"Don't you ever just shut up?"

I get that a lot.

We drove through a dark neighborhood of tall apartment buildings, not the nice kind they had out on University Avenue with their gleaming frontages and doormen in uniforms but the kind where people dried their washing on their balconies, and broken children's toys slowly turned into bleached fossils on patches of crabgrass-studded dirt that had once been lawns. The sidewalks were empty, of course—it was well after two in the morning—but the litter suggested they were usually full of people with nothing much to do. Our tires crunched through bottle glass as we turned into a downsloping driveway.

"I'm spending a lot more time than I'd like in underground garages these days," I said as she nosed the big car down the ramp into a five- or six-story apartment building that, as far as I could see, was indistinguishable from its neighbors along the quiet, dark, depressed-looking street.

"You won't be in this one long." She passed several empty parking spaces and drove right toward the back wall of the garage. As we approached it she reached up and thumbed a device on her sunshade; the entire wall lifted up like a magic trick. We drove through and it slid quietly down behind us again.

"Whoa." I was impressed. "How did you find this?"

"It's mine. I had it built. And all the contractors are dead." She gave me a look—I honestly couldn't tell if she was joking or not. "Going to keep your mouth shut about it?"

"You're taking me to your place?" I had a moment of what I imagine is teenage excitement—"imagine" because I can't remember the actual thing and "teenage" because suddenly I felt like I was growing hair all over my body and could no longer create articulate speech. I'm telling you, it may have been pheromones or just Hell's nastiest magic, but the Countess of Cold Hands could have made an actual stiff stiff. If you know what I mean.

"Yes, it's my place, but it's not the only one I have so don't think you can sell me out. It's a very small piece of information. And you're not the only one who has it."

That had several strange resonances, but I didn't bother to follow up as we got out of the car. "Thanks. You have a way of making a guy feel right at home." I followed her up a dark, narrow stairway from her hidden parking spot. "Speaking of, are you still pointing that gun at me?"

"What do you think?"

"Yeah, I figured."

She unlocked the door at the top of the stairs—I couldn't help noticing the door itself was as heavy as the kind they use in government air raid shelters—then led me into a really surprising place.

Surprise number one was when she flipped the switch and light bloomed everywhere, a half-rainbow of muted reds, yellows, and sunset oranges. The apartment had no windows at all as far as I could see, as if we were underground, which we weren't. The other surprise was that, based on how the Countess dressed and talked, I would have expected some kind of serious stark modernism or at least a sort of bohemian informality. Instead, her hideaway looked like some antique version of a sultan's harem—you could almost imagine it as the setting for some romance novel about a sultan's seraglio. The walls were covered by streaming gauze, with little lights set in alcoves or hung on the walls glowing through the fabric. A huge bronze mirror stood in a corner, draped with what looked like very expensive versions of Carnival beads, and across from it stood a curtained bed. The filmy red draperies were drawn and several layers deep, so I couldn't make out what the bed itself looked like, but just being near it carried a strong erotic charge.

Bad angel, I told myself. *Stupid angel. Snares of the enemy, remember?*

I realized I was staring at the bed. Instead of reveling in this demonstration of the effect she had even on a battle-hardened enemy, my hostess seemed irritated and maybe even a bit embarrassed.

"Nice place," I said. "Who was your decorator, Cecil B. DeMille?"

"I happen to like it." She sounded angry. "If you want a shower the bathroom's through there." She pointed at a door half-hidden by more filmy drapery, then settled herself in an overstuffed antique chair in front of an equally old-fashioned writing desk, the picture only spoiled by the open laptop on top of it and the nest of cords snaking out from beneath. "You should be able to find some clothes that will fit you in the closet. Take anything you want." She turned to her monitor screen as if I had ceased to exist.

I couldn't figure out anything about this woman.

No, I reminded myself. *Not a woman. Maybe once upon a time, but not for a while. She's part of the ruling class of Hell—a demon, sworn to destruction and the perversion of everything good, and if she's helping you, it's only because it suits her. Don't trust a single thing she says or does.*

Still, when I stepped out of the tiled, gloriously hot shower and began rummaging through the carpeted walk-in closet, I wasn't thrilled to find an entire row of hangers full of khakis, expensive bespoke sports coats, slacks, and collarless dress shirts, as well as polo shirts in all the colors of a blooming tropical forest. It made my gut clench, because I'd met someone with just this kind of wealthy-preppie taste recently. A Grand Duke of Hell, to be precise. I checked the monogram on the inside pocket of one of the coats. As I suspected, it was KV—Kenneth Vald.

I picked out what was least offensive to my eye, black slacks and a white button shirt, and returned to the main room. "Nice closet. Whose clothes?"

"None of your business, Dollar."

"Are you sure about that? Maybe it's someone I know."

"I'm asking the questions, remember. Unless you'd like to leave now, but this isn't a great area at this time of the night—especially if you're a wanted man on foot."

Stalemate. I fell into a chair not far from her desk and solaced myself by digging my toes into the thick, fleecy rug and thinking how much better this was than crouching in a cold river breathing through a tube that smelled of tonic water. "Okay, Countess, I definitely owe you one. What do you want to know?"

"Everything." She pinned me with those pale blue eyes. I couldn't help remembering the ones she'd had the first time I saw her—scarlet as an Amsterdam whore's window. "Tell me everything that's happened to you since you've been caught up in this."

"And if I do, will you answer some questions of mine?"

"No guarantees, Dollar. Like you said, you owe me."

So I told her where I'd been and what I'd done. I might have shaved off an uncomfortable rough edge here or there, and I certainly didn't go into minute detail about how badly the *ghallu* had scared me. I also kept a few facts about Heaven and The Compasses secret too—after all, I was just paying back a favor, not selling out my side of the ancient war. I didn't stop to point out where I was leaving things unsaid because I could tell she knew, and the Countess had the good grace not to task me on any of them until I got to the most recent stuff I'd heard from my friend Fatback.

"Grasswax had gambling debts with Prince Sitri? Are you certain? Who told you?"

"Now it's my turn to say none of your business." I wasn't going to give up my sources. Not that it would be so hard for her to find out—lots of folks knew about the pig man and his grudge against Hell. Still, it was a matter of principle. Yes, I do have a few. "What's the big deal?"

"Because, you pillock, I told you already that I gave the . . . thing to Grasswax. To hide. He owed me and I knew things about him, things he didn't want known by the powers above him. But somehow I didn't hear he was in debt to Prince Sitri. The slimy little bastard!"

"Sitri or Grasswax?"

"Grasswax! He must have been more afraid of Sitri than he was of me." She got up and began to pace. "What's Sitri's interest in all this?"

I would be lying if I didn't say that part of me enjoyed watching her walk back and forth in front of me. She had kicked off the slippers she'd donned to pick me up, and watching her pale calves, ankles, and feet was mesmerizing. Distracting, too.

"Hang on, I don't get any of this." I looked at something else for a moment to regather my thoughts. "You must have taken a big risk stealing something from Eligor. Why would you give it to a weasel like Grasswax?"

"Because I was being followed, and I had to get rid of it! Because the . . . the thing . . ."

"You can go ahead and call it 'the feather' now."

This last shot had been fired somewhat offhandedly, just to see the effect, which was pretty impressive: Her eyes widened in what I almost could have sworn was helpless fear. "How did you find out?"

Since I didn't want to get Edie Parmenter in trouble I only said, "A little bird told me—but that's not the issue. I know all about it." Which was one of the least truthful things I'd said all day. I still had no idea what a golden feather might be and why Eligor or anyone else should be so worked up about it, but just then I wanted her to think I knew more than I did. "I need to know everything else. Come on, Countess, help me fill in the details. You were being followed. You had this incredibly valuable thing—so you gave it to Grasswax? A lying, treacherous bastard who's not only a demon from Hell to begin with but also a *lawyer*? Why would you do that?"

"Why? Because I thought I had a hold over him. I promised that if he'd keep it safe, I'd destroy some evidence I had on him."

"Why did you have something on him? What was it?"

She was clearly getting frustrated with me. "It doesn't matter! Don't you understand, you idiot? Where I come from, *everybody* has something on *everybody*. That's how we survive. Everyone spies on everyone and cheats on everyone, and everyone makes deals. That's how we climb up out of the mud and the shit and the molten lava and make a little freedom, create a little life for ourselves. . . ."

"Like here in San Judas," I said. "Where you've created this pretty little pied-a-terre for yourself."

"This place?" She looked around with scorn on her face. "One of a dozen. I used to have houses all over the place. Not just in California, either."

"So what happened?"

She looked at me like I was not just an idiot but the intentional kind, although there was also something strange beneath it, a simmering anger I hadn't seen before. "You haven't figured it out yet? Some gumshoe you are, Dollar."

"I'm not a gumshoe, I keep telling you that. That's *your* fantasy. I'm just a guy trying to do his job and stay alive. Right now, staying alive *is* my job. Yeah, I think I know what happened. Because it isn't just blackmail that can buy freedom is it? It's also doing favors—all kinds of favors—for the right people. Important people, like Kenneth Vald, otherwise known as Grand Duke Eligor. Your sugar-daddy."

She tossed her head and her white-blonde hair fanned and then fell straight again. "You can put it that way if it makes you feel good. I'm sure you wouldn't believe I actually fell for him."

"Yeah, you're right—I wouldn't. But I'm a big boy, so I understand. He's powerful. He's *very* powerful. Rich as Bill Gates but probably a lot more interesting, what with the eternal damnation and the sixty legions in Hell and all that. Yeah, I can definitely understand why a tough, smart little cookie like you set your sights on someone like that. What I *don't* understand is why you decided to steal from him. That's just asking for trouble. And why a golden feather?"

She stopped pacing then and stared at me with such cold fury that I swear I could feel myself crystallizing from the cellular level out. "Stole from him. Oh, yeah, I decided that instead of staying the contented mistress of one of the most powerful creatures on this whole green earth, I'd just rip him off. That's exactly the kind of thing you'd expect from a nasty little *thing* like me, isn't it?"

"It doesn't matter what I think," I said. "But I do want answers."

She turned away from me then and walked to the antique desk, yanked out the drawer and began rummaging in it. "I should have known," she said, but in a low voice that sounded strangled and odd. "I should have known. Should. Have. Known."

"Look, spare me the *Snake Pit* act, or Lady Macbeth, or whatever you're doing here," I said, walking up behind her. "I don't care why any of it happened, and I'm certainly not judging you. If I'd been condemned to Hell I don't think I'd be worrying a lot about what I did afterward either. But I still need to know what you did and why, since I seem to be on the hook for it with your boyfriend." I put my hand on her shoulder, but even through the robe the chill of her skin was startling enough to make me pull back, and that was what saved me. She whirled. The huge, curved knife in her hand hissed past my jugular, nicking me despite my reflexive lunge backward. The weapon was one of those long Gurkha blades called a *kukri,* and little Casimira clearly knew how to use it.

I reached up to my throat just in case I had underestimated the damage and was bleeding to death, but when I took my hand away there was only a thin smear of blood. "What the hell . . . ?"

"You bastard," she said in the strained voice of someone talking to herself. "Not judging me, are you?" She took another backhand swipe, this time at my belly, and I jumped away just in time, but as soon as I landed she was on me again. I grabbed at her arm but she slipped under it. She actually got the point of her knife against my gut but a *kukri* is much better for slashing than stabbing and I managed to spin away to the side, suffering nothing worse than another shallow cut. Still, I was already in bad shape from my multiple run-ins with the *ghallu,* and I knew this was not just a squabble with an unhappy female—the Countess was as strong as I was, a lot angrier, and she was the one holding the sharp object.

"Stop now," I said. "I'm not kidding!" I was looking around for something to defend myself with, but in this Turkish boudoir of an apartment I couldn't find anything more useful than a chair, so I promptly grabbed one and held it before me. It occurred to me that if I'd also had a whip I might have a chance of taming this tigress, but I didn't feel I could do much with a heavy piece of furniture except what I was doing—clumsily trying to keep her at bay.

She came after me again, low and with her hands wide, starting with a feint at my face. When I lifted the chair to block her she kicked out and got me in the shin hard enough to make me lose my balance and stumble sideways. She was right on top of me as I fought to regain my footing but I hammered her small pale foot with the leg of the chair, then as she hissed and took her weight off it, I managed to keep the chair from overbalancing me long enough to sweep her other leg out from under her. As she tumbled to the floor I very briefly considered hitting her with the heavy piece of furniture, but even though she'd just tried to slit my gorge, I sensed there was something strange going on: She fought like someone defending herself, even though she was the one who'd attacked me. Her eyes were distant, too, even desperate, full of what a more poetic angel might call resigned horror. Not the emotions you expect from a veteran hell-beast doing her best to exsanguinate you.

As the Countess hit the floor I leaped on top of her, paying close attention to the long-bladed *kukri* that for the moment was under her. As she rolled away and slashed at my face with it, catching my cheek and ear, I managed to grab hold of her knife-arm and carry it past me. I slammed it against the floor and promptly threw my body on top of it, pinning her wrist so that she couldn't reach me to slash me—at least not with her knife. She managed to give me a good scratching with her other hand, then half an instant later, she somehow pulled her legs up and threw them around my neck. Despite the slenderness of those smooth white pins, within seconds she managed to cut off most of the blood trying to get to my brain. Things were going black, and everything that was Bobby Dollar began to disappear down a tunnel into roaring depths. I wasn't entirely certain what was going on with the Countess and her crazy attack, but I had a strong feeling that if I passed out I might not wake up again, so I did the only thing left to me to do—I punched her in the head as hard as I could. It bounced her skull off the carpeted floor and for a moment shook loose the astonishing grip of her legs around my neck. I took advantage of the reprieve to gulp in as much air as I could, then grabbed her knife arm and started twisting until at last, as she snarled and spat and grimaced at me with what looked a great deal like insane hatred, I finally got her to open her fingers and drop the blade to the floor. I knocked the big knife as far away as I could, but that moment of changed balance gave her the chance to slide partway out from under me. Then all of a sudden she was somehow on my back instead, pulling my hair in the most painful way imaginable while she used her other hand to hit me over and over again on my already bloody right ear.

I reached up with both hands and caught her behind the neck, then yanked her forward over my head and shoulders so that she cracked her forehead against the floor once more—which, even through the cushioning of the carpet, had to be getting uncomfortable for her. The she-demon didn't hesitate, though, immediately snaking her legs around me once more, tightening them this time just under my floating ribs, which she then proceeded to do her best to break while I did what I could to get her off of me. Neither of us quite succeeded, but we were both inflicting a great deal of pain on each other. The fight had become something like a wrestling match between two crazy drunks, neither of us really sure who was winning, or why we were fighting, or even very concerned about such trivia—all we could do was keep trying to snap each other in half.

I finally got her under me again, and although she had one leg over my shoulder, the knee of the other in my solar plexus, and was busily punching at my face with her hands, I managed to ignore the pain long enough to get the bar of my forearm down across her windpipe. I held it there, ignoring the hard blows she was giving me except to let my head roll with them, diffusing as much of the force as possible. After half a minute the fists became open hands, then the slaps became a strengthless grabbing and scratching. At last her arms went limp, and she sagged. I didn't want to kill her—even if she was determined to do me in, she still had information I needed—but I stayed on top of her, and though I eased the pressure on her throat so she could breathe I didn't remove my arm.

For perhaps twenty seconds she lay beneath me, panting shallowly. Blood was dripping from my ear and face onto her cheek, where it mixed with her own, then ran down her jaw and soaked the carpet beneath her with a spreading red stain. Her eyes flickered open and for a moment she stared at me like an animal stares, without knowledge of anything beyond its own fighting instincts, but then that pale blue stare focused on me, and her mouth opened in a lazy grin. There was blood between her teeth and all over her lips. She pushed her belly up against me, and for a moment I thought she was trying to escape me again, but she stayed there, her pelvis pressing hard and insistent against me.

"If you're not going to kill me, angel," she said, "then let's think of something else to do while I'm still all worked up."

twenty-two
cold hands

I'VE NEVER kissed a hellbeast before. I know that sounds like the beginning of an ex-wife joke, but it's true. I've been with waitresses and biker chicks, middle-aged broads with a long tale to tell, and barely-legals just starting to discover their own story. I've also had more than a few flings with women of the angelic persuasion, not to mention those odd, sexless but intense, pre-teen-type relationships that you have in Heaven. Did I mention there's no sex there? Yeah, put it into the "but that's another story" category. I had even come close to something intimate a few times with members of the Opposition, but only because I didn't know what they were; I'd always figured it out in time. But until now, I had never had cause to knowingly kiss a demon.

Wow.

I don't mean to make it sound romantic, because it wasn't—not really. Not at first. One moment I was lying on top of this crazy thing that was trying to murder me, the next moment we were rolling around on the floor again, but this time without the distraction of bladed weapons. Only as we bumped up against her writing desk did it occur to me I didn't know where she'd put her gun when we first came in, or whether she had some even nastier weapon than her *kukri* stashed in that drawer—a tactical tomahawk or a Turkish *yataghan* or some other godawful exotic thing—but the Countess no longer seemed to be interested in killing me, at least not in any conventional way.

I don't want you to think I had completely forgotten an angelic lifetime of hatred and distrust. Alarms bells were going off in my head that would have deafened me if they'd been real, but at that moment I just didn't care.

Casimira's robe was already half off, and we were both slippery with blood and sweat. Her mouth tasted hot as Tabasco but her skin was shockingly cold to the touch. We were pressed together so hard it seemed like we might simply pass through each other; I could feel her nipples against my chest, hard as silver bullets. My mouth was full of the salty tang of blood, but it tasted good. It tasted *right*. I didn't know if it was infernal magic or plain old chemistry, but it was getting more and more difficult to think and more and more difficult to care about that fact.

"Hold on," I said, drawing back. We were lying side by side near the bed now, although "lying" is way too passive a word: She had one long, smooth leg wrapped around me, both arms around my neck, and her face so close to mine I couldn't see much of anything except her blue eyes. At least I thought her eyes were still blue, but in the dim harem light they could have turned red again and I wouldn't have known. In fact, we could have fallen through the floor and tumbled all the way into Tartarus during the last few minutes and I probably wouldn't have noticed. "Wait a minute. Just . . . what are we doing here?"

She leaned forward and licked a smear of blood off my chest, then smiled at me with it still glistening on her tongue. "They don't teach you much in Heaven, do they?"

"I mean what are we doing, you and me? We're not . . . we're supposed to be . . ."

She pulled herself up until she could kiss my forehead—a surprisingly gentle kiss, almost ritualistic, lips as chilly as a marble statue's—then slid back down until her pelvis was lodged against mine again, pressing, rubbing. "I don't care!" She sounded almost drunk, halfway between tears and laughter. "I don't care about any of that, Bobby. Not now. This is our time. Whatever happens later . . ." She didn't finish, but lifted her face to be kissed—that beautiful, treacherous, untrustworthy face—and suddenly I no longer cared either. Not about my bleeding cuts and cracked ribs, not my friends or my angelic tribe, my place in the great conflict, anything. If the *ghallu* itself had kicked down the door, blazing and roaring, I would have done my best to ignore it. I lowered my face to hers and felt my last reservations melt.

Although our mouths almost never left each other's mouths and skin it didn't take me long to ease her out of the torn nightgown, exposing her small white breasts and the delicate cathedral of her ribcage, to coax the filmy white strip of nothing off her hips and down her legs until she was utterly naked, pale and splendid. She helped me remove my own clothes, pulling and dragging at things without patience until we both laughed at what a muddle we'd made, but even as we laughed we continued to press as much of our skin together as we could, feverish and hurried. We slithered against each other, kissing, licking, biting, tasting salty blood and sweat. Casimira was almost wordless, making little noises of surprise or mock-protest as something was pulled away from her tender attentions, then growling with pleasure as something else was given to her instead. We were both covered with small, stinging wounds, many of which we'd given to each other, but for that time, in that windowless room, even the pain of those injuries seemed only to broaden the range of our pleasure.

Her skin was cold as the belly of a fish, smooth and dry in the few places my own sweaty skin hadn't rubbed against her, and with just the faintest tang of blood and sea-musk curling through the sweetness of her scent like a snake in a garden. As I pressed my face against the skin of her stomach I had, for a moment—and only a moment—the sudden sensation that Casimira was some kind of animate corpse, that I had been tricked into loving a dead thing. I pulled back in shock, but one look at the frightened need on her face told me what was happening between us was far more complicated than any mere horror, any mere trick or stratagem of the long war. We were different creatures from different worlds, but at that moment we both wanted the same thing, even though we were neither of us certain exactly what that might mean.

She was built like a ballet dancer, no fat anywhere, her breasts small as a very young woman's, with amaranth-colored buds on the tips as firm and cold as ice cream still hard from the freezer. A delicate shimmer of fine pale hair descended in an almost invisible line from her navel and across her flat lower stomach to the delicate swelling of her pubis, where it joined the tiny puff of near-whiteness that hid the cleft.

As I held her legs apart to look at her there, the muscles of her thighs quivered and she made a noise as if she fought back tears. She pulled herself upright in what seemed more than ever like desperation, put her hands flat against my chest to shove me backward, then took my cock in her mouth and did things to me with her startlingly cool tongue that I still cannot quite explain or even remember clearly, but the sensation was enough to make me fall back on the floor and lay there for long moments, unable to do anything except let it happen and hope it would never stop. Her hands kept moving the whole time, stroking, cradling, her chilly, tender fingers everywhere, distracting and delightful.

Soon enough, though, she lifted herself up on one elbow, holding me in her hand and squeezing gently, her eyes glinting with mischief. "More? Or do you need a rest?"

I answered the only way I was capable of at that moment: I rolled over and wrestled her to the floor again, then began to lick and kiss and nibble my way from her face to her toes and back up again, stopping somewhere in the middle of the second traverse to nose my head between her thighs. She yanked down one of the filmy curtains surrounding the bed and let it settle over us, then took an end of it and looped it slowly and lovingly around my neck, using it as a bridle to speed me up or slow me down as I indulged myself in her astonishing, wonderful wetness. I heard her cry out my name until even that last word disappeared into less articulate sounds. But as much as I loved the taste of her, the cold skin and the warm, salty damp, I couldn't wait long—in fact, I couldn't wait any longer. As she lay catching her breath, I sat up between her thighs and began to position myself over her, but she was not going to let me do it, not yet. She rolled me onto my back, putting a finger over my mouth to silence my questions, and then squatted on her heels above me, teasing my hardness with her own silky softness, rubbing back and forth without allowing me to penetrate, until I was almost as desperate as in the most frightening moments of our struggle, with her knife pressed against me. Then, as if we still struggled, I suddenly summoned my remaining strength and wrestled her onto her back. This time I was the one who stabbed at her, and she was the one who gasped out a cry that sounded like agony. Cold, cold, her skin was so cold . . . but inside she was hot as a furnace.

I cried out then, too, shocked and amazed and overwhelmed that it could be like this—that anything could be like this.

"He's never been here," she said as we lay on her bed later, naked and sweaty. "He doesn't know about this place."

"I guessed, actually. Wouldn't be a very good hiding place if he knew it, and he's the one you're hiding from, right?"

She nodded. I couldn't help staring at her flawless features, her schoolgirl face and ancient eyes, and wondering again what she really looked like, but somehow it didn't matter as much to me as it had before. "Not just hiding from. Running away from."

"What do you mean? And if he's never been here, why do you have clothes for him here?"

"Because I had the same contractors build it who did all the rest of our . . . hideaways. And to keep them from being suspicious I did everything the same, including stocking the closets with his clothes. I handled all the bills, and he doesn't care how much things cost, anyway. He's a duke of Hell—money is like water to him, he turns on his faucets and it pours out. So I had them build this one just for me. I decorated it myself. I know you think it's ghastly."

"No," I said, "not at all. Just . . . surprising. Not what I would have expected."

"It was something I dreamed of when I was a girl. Don't worry, we also had the boring Aspen cabin with the fabulous view and the boring Manhattan penthouse on Central Park West, and even a boring little chalet in Gstaad. But this one is *mine*. So if you spoil the secret and make me give it up I swear I'll kill you, Bobby Dollar."

For a moment the tone of her voice made me raise up on my elbow to see if she was kidding. She didn't look like she was. "Did you really . . . fall for him? Like you said?"

She shrugged and rolled onto her side to root in a bedside drawer. She took out a slim golden case and removed a cigarette, then offered the case to me.

"No, thanks. Had to give it up years ago."

She lit up anyway, then settled back on her pillow and watched the smoke lift lazily toward the surprisingly high ceiling. "I don't know, maybe you were right. Maybe I didn't fall for *him* so much as

I fell for what he had, what he could do—what someone like him could mean to someone like me." She frowned. "I don't really want to talk about it."

"Then you don't have to, Casimira."

"Caz. Nobody's called me Casimira much for a couple of hundred years."

I looked at her. My surprise must have shown.

"Yes, I'm old," she said. "I've been around a while. How about you?"

"We never know, and they sure don't tell us. I don't remember any farther back than the 1990s, which is when I first got to Earth."

She dragged on her cigarette, let a plume of smoke geyser upward. "Lucky."

"What are you talking about?"

"Never mind." She put the cigarette out in an ashtray on her bedside table, grinding it dead with surprising force. "I didn't mean to get you into this, but I'm sorry anyway."

Even now, after all that had happened between us, I still found myself reflexively mistrustful. Who ever heard of a demon *apologizing*? Was she laying it on too thick? Had I just fallen for the oldest con job since the apple? "From what you've said it wasn't your fault," I offered. "It was Grasswax's."

"Yes, but if I hadn't tried to leave Eligor—if I hadn't stolen from him so I'd have some protection against him—"

"Slow down, Caz. You stole from him *because* you left him? Not the other way around?"

For just a moment I saw the return of that sharp flare of anger, but then it passed and something infinitely sadder crept into her eyes. "He wouldn't have let me go any other way, Bobby. Once something belongs to him, it's his forever. He's that way even with his living possessions—no, even *more* with the ones that are alive. Someone like me, who's likely to live as long as he does and would be a permanent reproach to him . . . well, he'd much rather destroy me than let me go, whether he still wanted me or not."

"So you stole this . . . feather. To blackmail him into leaving you alone?" I was mostly guessing since I still had no idea what the feather actually was but didn't want to reveal the depths of my ignorance. I was relieved when she nodded.

"I guess you could say that. But I don't want to think about him any more—about any of it. You're here. I'm here. We may never have this moment again." She shook her head. "What am I saying? We *won't* have this moment ever again." She smiled a hard little smile. "Obviously we were never meant to be."

I was badly torn between wanting to tell her I'd never leave her, which was truly how I felt at that moment, and wondering still if this was just some elaborate scam—if I had fallen hook, line, and sinker for a cynical ploy from a self-serving demoness. I certainly knew which side the oddsmakers would have chosen, but looking at those wide, almost tearful eyes it was hard to let my more critical self do its job. "Whatever we are or whatever we're meant to be, you're right—we have right now," I said, and pulled her toward me so I could kiss her neck. She rolled closer, then fastened herself against me so that I could feel the wetness we had made together pressed warmly against my leg.

"Oooh," she said, reaching down and giving me a squeeze. "It appears your chariot is no longer swinging low, Mr. Dollar." Her voice dropped down to a husky rasp. "What do you say, Wings? Would you like to . . . carry me home again?"

Caz was asleep, her hair spread in a white-gold fan across the crimson pillowcase, her back nearly as slender as a child's. I could count every knob of her vertebrae and watch the muscles move beneath the skin every time she changed position.

I crawled out of bed to take a shower. As I dried off I tried to call Sam and the others but couldn't get a signal. Perhaps the walls of Caz's hideaway had been constructed to block transmissions. After seeing her secret agent garage, I could believe it. Whatever the case, I was going to have to get in touch with somebody on my side soon, just to make sure Sam and Monica were all right, if nothing else. And I knew it wouldn't hurt me to get away from the Countess for a while. Any objectivity I might once have had about her was long gone, and even though there was still so much I didn't know about her and so many reasons for me not to trust her, I couldn't help looking at her as she slept and feeling a clutch in my chest I hadn't felt for a long time. In fact, I didn't think I had *ever* felt quite like this. That would have been scary enough with any woman, but with this one it seemed damned near suicidal.

As if she could read my troubled thoughts, Caz began to twitch a little in her sleep, then to whimper. She rolled over and pushed feebly at something that wasn't there, then scrabbled at her pillow in a way that reminded me so much of what she'd done to my cheek a couple of hours earlier during our struggle that I reached up to touch the tender, healing scrapes.

"No," she said faintly, "no, no!" She was struggling harder now but the nightmare still seemed grip her tightly. I sat down on the bed next to her and gently lifted her eyelids with my fingertips, still mistrustful enough to think it might be a trick, but her pupils did not contract, which they should have done even in a dim room. Instead she grabbed at my hands, slapped at them and fought against me, but so weakly I could tell that she was still deep in her oppressive dream. Her cries became more articulate, and now tears ran from her shuttered lids and down her cheek.

"Caz!" I said, shaking her. "Caz, wake up! It's just a nightmare. You're having a bad dream." I couldn't believe I was saying something like this to one of Hell's minions, but I couldn't just sit by and watch her suffer either. Nothing I did seemed to help, though, and at last I pulled her out of the bed and stood her on her feet, holding her tight to keep her from falling. This seemed to drag her back to some kind of consciousness, although I regretted the decision almost immediately because as soon as she got her balance she attacked me with nearly as much savagery as before, although this time it was clear she didn't know who I was. I defended myself, doing my best not to hurt her, and after a short struggle she became less frenetic in her movements. She came slowly back to herself as though surfacing from deep waters.

"What . . . ?" She looked around at what must have been the familiar sights of her windowless room, then down at her own slim, naked form. "Why . . . ?"

"I really hope you remember why you don't have any clothes on, Caz, because if you don't I'm going to have a tough time convincing you."

She looked up at me, her eyes troubled. "Don't ever joke about that, Bobby. We're here. Of course it all happened. I just didn't know why I was . . ." She shook her head.

"You were having a nightmare. I tried to wake you up, but I couldn't."

Her eyes suddenly filled but did not overspill. It was precisely those tears, which should have set all my alarm bells jangling, that finally made me stop doubting her. They had been so fast to rise—surely nobody, not even a trained actress, could come thrashing up from sleep and make a real physical body jump through hoops that way. "It wasn't a nightmare," she said. "It was a memory."

She climbed back into the bed, pulling the covers up to her waist. With her youthful, wide-eyed face and long white-gold hair cascading over her naked shoulders she might have been a portrait of Alice that Reverend Dodgson would have kept locked away and shown to no one—not even God.

"It was him. I was dreaming about him," she said, closing her eyes with a shudder.

"Eligor?"

She laughed. "No, the first 'him' in my life. The man who owned me. The man I killed." I didn't say a word—I didn't dare—but she must have sensed something in my silence. Her eyes opened, and she gave me a crooked grin. "You didn't think I got sent to Hell by mistake, do you? Believe me, Bobby, I earned every single moment of my damnation."

"You don't have to talk about it if you don't want to. But if you do, I'll listen."

"There's not a lot to say. It was a long time ago. He was an important man, the *hrabia*—the count, we'd say now. His name was Pawel, and his family owned most of the land around Lublin."

"Poland." Now I finally understood that whisper of middle-European under the British schoolgirl diction. "When was this?"

"Do you really want to know?" She smiled, but it was a bitter one. "I hope you like older women. *Much* older. Let's put it this way—you know about the Renaissance? Well, it was before that."

I didn't say anything. Something was happening here, something as powerful and inevitable as a storm, but I had already decided to hunker down and let it wash over me.

"They gave me to him," she said. "That's how they did things in those days. I was scarcely fifteen years old. Practically an old maid!" She laughed. It hurt to hear it. "And Count Pawel looked every inch the part. He was tall, handsome, a brave soldier, and a firm ruler. He was also twisted inside, twisted and bent and broken." She shuddered. "He still is. Even in Hell he's considered dangerous."

"You have to . . . see him?"

She shook her head. "Any business between us is long over. He's happier persecuting the dead than he ever was on Earth. But for a while, when we were both alive, I was his favorite plaything."

"You don't have to—"

She lifted a hand. "I want to. You . . . you deserve to know the truth. But come and sit next to me. It would be nice to have someone near."

I sat beside her and took her hand. I could sense she didn't want to be looked at, so I leaned back and stared at the ceiling and the draperies as they swayed gently in the breeze of the air-conditioning.

"He was a monster. Some are discovered, but some are never known except by their victims. He was one of those sort; the subtle, clever kind of monster. Never killed anyone powerful, never tormented anyone who could fight back—although, since he was a high nobleman, he had a wide array of victims to choose from, of course.

"With me it was different. Yes, he raped me over and over, but that was nothing unusual for the time. I was his wife, and he owned me. A little thing like reluctance bordering on terror only added savor for him, and as my terror grew so did his enjoyment. He went out of his way to find things that would frighten me and hurt me. And he hurt others in front of me, especially women . . . and girls. The servants were no more than furniture—no, they were no more than animals. Either way, they were possessions, and unlike Elizabeth Báthory or Gilles de Rais, he was just careful enough with his crimes that no one ever felt the need to stop him.

"And if God had not punished me enough, I also had to live with his mother Justyna, the dowager countess, a harridan who never killed anyone but in her own way was every bit as cold and cruel as her son. Worse, in some ways, because she understood some of the subtler cruelties only other women know how to use. She employed them gleefully, too. My family were only minor nobility, and she never thought I was good enough for her Pawel.

"I gave that monster and his bitch mother two heirs, both boys, and I lived each day of my life in dread. If any of the servants showed me any sympathy or kindness beyond the strict performance of their duties Pawel or his mother went out of their way to punish them. Justyna all but snatched my own boys away from me and raised them herself to be certain they grew up to be Pawel's sons and nothing of mine . . ." She trailed off, then took a deep breath and resumed.

"And one night it was finally all too much. I won't trouble you with details, but my husband had recently killed a sweet little servant girl I favored, and only that day I had seen her buried in our churchyard. He came to me that evening and, as he took me, showed me a lock of her hair that he had cut from her head in the coffin, and which he had put into a locket to give me, 'So that you may keep your little peasant girl with you always,' he told me. So that I would remember always how he had snatched her from me and killed her, was what he meant. So I would know that he could take from me anything I cared about—and that he would always do so.

"I don't know what happened to me, except that I simply couldn't take any more. When he fell asleep I slit his throat with his own knife. As he thrashed in his own blood, I stabbed him over and over in his chest and back and face, and continued to stab him long after he was dead. Then, covered in dripping red like some horrible phantom, I went and dragged the two boys out of their bed—they could scarcely have been six and seven years old—and brought them in to see the wreckage of their father. I was laughing hysterically and could not stop. 'Here's a present from me so you'll remember him always!' I kept saying, or so I'm told. They ran away in terror, but not before I tried to kill them both as well, wanting now to dam the whole river of Pawel's cursed blood once and for all.

"When I was alone again I tried to pray but my hands were numb and my heart was like ice in my chest, as though my crime had stolen all the heat out of my body.

"The boys brought back their grandmother and the guards. They found me sitting beside Pawel's body, sunk up to the wrists in his deepest, widest wounds, blood soaking my arms to the elbows. I tried to explain what I was doing but they pulled me away from him, screaming that I had desecrated his body. I wasn't trying to hurt him any more—I only wanted to warm my hands, because they were so cold."

She turned to look at me. I could scarcely stand to see the agony there. "And now, dear Bobby, you finally know where my name comes from."

She looked away again. "I was convicted of murder, of course, and after much torture I confessed to witchcraft as well, because why else would a woman kill such a fine husband and then try to destroy his children, too, unless she was possessed by Satan himself?" She was winding down now, her head nodding like an exhausted child in the back seat of a car. "I was not treated leniently by the authorities, either in this world or the next—but that's no surprise, is it? Count Pawel hadn't done anything to me that most husbands do not do, in spirit if not in fact. If I'd had a clever advocate like you, perhaps I would have received a lesser sentence than eternity in the pits of fire. But I didn't."

I didn't know what to say. I realized I had been silent for long moments. "Nothing . . . there's nothing. . . ." I stammered. "You didn't deserve . . ."

"Hush." She sat up a little and laid her finger against my lips. "It's all over now. What did Marlowe write? 'But that was in another country. And besides, the wench is dead.'"

"Caz . . ."

"Don't. I told you, that wench is dead. Come and love this one . . . while we can still love."

And what else was left to me in my horror and my sorrow except to do as she asked?

twenty-three
assorted blasphemies

WE HAD fallen asleep, and again I woke first, or thought I had. I lay with Caz's head pillowed in the crook of my arm and stared up at the ceiling. The light hadn't changed but now the swirl of flame-colored draperies and the dim light behind them gave the space above me the feel of sunrise, even though outside, in the real world, it must have been much later in the morning than that.

I took my phone off the bedside table and tried to call Sam again but couldn't get a signal. It occurred to me that I might be missing a bunch of incoming calls; that I might be missing actual clients. Even worse, if I was missing calls from my bosses in the Celestial City, coupled with the damage the *ghallu* had done the night before, they might think my body was dead or critically injured, and only the Highest could guess what kind of crazy snafu might come from that. If I had possessed any sense at all I would have been out of Casimira's hideaway hours ago and doing my best to reestablish contact with Heaven.

I was about to put the phone down when Caz stirred. "You can't use your cell here," she said sleepily.

"I figured that out."

"If you really need to call someone, use the landline. Just make sure you're not calling anyone who'd want to trace the call."

Landline. I felt like an idiot. I found the slim receiver sitting on its stand on the desk.

"You look good with no clothes on, Wings," she said.

"Thanks. I worked my way through angel college as a go-go dancer."

"Liar."

"Delivering obscene birthday-grams." I was only half paying attention—I had got an actual dial tone this time. To my surprise, though, it wasn't Sam who picked it up on the second ring.

"Sam Riley's phone."

"Monica? Is that you?"

"Bobby? You're alive!" She actually sounded pleased. "Where are you?"

"Nevermind, how's Sam? How are you, for that matter?"

"Sam's not good, but he'll pull through. We're here with him at Sequoia emergency—me and Jimmy and Annie. He got broken up pretty badly . . ."

A pang of guilt and sorrow stabbed my gut. "I'll come right over."

"No!" I could imagine all the other people in the waiting room turning at her loud exclamation. When Monica spoke again it was in a near-whisper. "Unless you killed the thing with the horns, somehow. Which I doubt."

"No such luck. It was all I could do just to get away."

"Then don't come near here. The last thing anyone needs is to have that two-ton monstrosity come smashing through the hospital looking for you."

Which meant I was being ordered to stay away from my best friend's bedside—my best friend who had been smashed up trying to help me. "Okay. I see the logic even if I don't like it. Is Sam awake? Can I talk to him?"

"He's way, way under, Bobby. His brain was swelling so they induced a coma. I don't know how the fixers from upstairs are going to explain this one—The Compasses looks like someone drove a train through it. On the fourth floor. Chico's over there now, wrapped up in bandages like Claude Rains, swearing at the water damage. I was pretty proud of the hose, actually."

"As you should be—that was a nifty idea. Don't worry about the cover story too much. They can say a single-engine plane crashed into it—probably already have. I've seen them use that one before. The Clean-Up Squad keeps smashed-up plane and car parts and all kinds of useful shit like that in a warehouse in Millbrae."

"Like they say, my Father's house has many mansions."

"And you're really okay, Monica? Really? Not too badly hurt?"

"I'm a bit bruised, but I'll live. How did you get away?"

"I'll tell you another time. At the moment I've got stuff to do. Like in the movies— 'Now it's personal!' Or something like that."

"Just don't do anything stupid. I . . . we were all worried about you, Bobby. I thought . . ."

I didn't want her to say anything she'd regret later, especially not with the Countess lying naked in bed behind me, listening. Not that Caz would hear what Monica said, but it just seemed wrong somehow. "Thanks, but I'm okay." I changed the subject. "How about Clarence? Has he been in? Does he know about Sam?"

"How could he not know, Bobby? The Compasses has a hole in it, and the whole block is knotted up in crime-scene tape."

"Okay. If you see the kid before I reach him, tell him I want to talk to him. Give everybody my best—and my apologies for getting them into this shit. I'll stay in touch. And take care of yourself."

"You too, Bobby."

I made one more quick call, this one to Alice at the office. Other than what happened to poor Sam, my luck had been very good: I hadn't missed a client while I'd been offline, although I did have a message from my superiors telling me that I needed to speak to a minister (the official name for a fixer, as you may remember) about the events in downtown the previous night. I said I would (and I was telling the truth—you don't dodge one of those) then I asked her to steer any clients to one of the other advocates for the next twenty-four hours while I recuperated. I got off the line before anything else came up.

It looked like Caz had fallen asleep again, but as I climbed in next to her she said, "You have to go, don't you?"

"Before too long, yeah—I probably do." I stared at the gleaming oval on its chain around her neck, then reached out and touched it gently. "Is that it? Is that the locket your husband gave you?"

She opened her eyes. "Yes. It's all I have left of little Anna, my maid. She was only eleven when that bastard killed her."

"It looks like it's made out of silver."

"It is."

"But doesn't it burn you? I thought silver . . ."

She reached up and pushed the locket to the side. Where it had rested, an angry red mark disfigured Caz's white skin. Even as I watched it began to fade.

"Does it burn?" she asked. "Every moment of every day. That helps me remember." And the way she said it gave me chills all over again. Her voice turned softer. "Do you have to leave right now, Bobby? Or do we have a little more time . . . ?"

I wanted to—God, how I wanted to—but first things first: I had made a decision while I was on the phone. It scared me, but I was determined. "Listen, I have a couple of questions to ask you."

"Be my guest." She reached down and began to play with my wedding kit, as Leo used to call it. Very distracting.

"Not when you're doing that. I can't concentrate. Come on, stop tha— *ouch*!" She had wickedly sharp fingernails. "Bad girl!"

"Well, duh."

"Look, I'm going to do something first that's probably really, really stupid. I'm going to tell you the truth."

Suddenly she became very still. "Really?"

"Yes, really. Here it comes. I have never, from the beginning, known what you took from Eligor. I told you that before. That was true. What's also true is that I *still* don't know. I found out it was a golden feather—how I found out doesn't matter—but I have no idea what that means. I can't imagine one of Hell's major players gets worked up over any mere piece of jewelry. He must be able to get his hands on all the gold he wants. It has to be something more."

She was lying on her side facing me. Her hand slid up to her own throat as if for protection. "Go on."

"So what *is* this thing? I'm tired of bluffing, Caz. You've been straight with me as far as I can tell. I've been wandering in the wilderness for a long time. What's this about? Why all the fuss over a feather?"

She raised herself higher on the pillows. The blankets slid away from the upper half of her slim torso like waves retreating from a beach. Even if it was an illusion, she was so beautiful that it was all I could do not to reach out and pull her to me.

"You're right, Bobby," she said slowly, her hand still at her throat. "Gold and jewels don't have much meaning to . . . to people like us. In some rare cases, the value could be sentimental." She lifted her hand away, revealing the locket. "Like this has meaning to me. A few dollars worth of silver but I've worn it for five hundred years. Would I raise a *ghallu* to get it back? I don't know. I don't know if I'm strong enough—but I'd consider it, I swear I would."

"Eligor doesn't strike me as the sentimental type."

"I'm just saying that there can be other reasons to covet something."

"So the feather has some special meaning to Eligor?"

"To anyone who knows what it is—really, to anyone who sees it. It's hard not to recognize it when it's in front of you."

"I'm not following, Caz."

"Then you're being a bit slow, Bobby. Where does a feather come from?"

"A bird."

"Now you're overthinking. Simpler. Where does a feather come from?"

I gave it a moment, then took a breath as it came to me. "A wing," I said at last.

"And what has wings? Birds and bees and . . .?"

I shook my head. "No. Not here on Earth. Not in the real world. Look, Caz, I should know, I'm an angel myself. We don't have wings here."

"*You* don't, Bobby. Because you're Earthbound. You're minor-league, if you'll pardon me for saying—a foot soldier. But when the higher angels manifest here . . . well, *they* keep their heavenly attributes. If they're important enough, that is. If they're high enough up the ladder."

I felt like she'd punched me in the face again. "So you're saying that what Eligor had was a feather from an important angel? You really believe that?"

"Believe it? I held it, Bobby. I stole it out of Eligor's safe and smuggled it out of the building—with a little look-the-other-way help from some bribed security guards. And if you'd seen the feather, you'd know I was right about it."

"Yeah, but I haven't seen it—and that's the problem. Everybody thinks I have it but me. And eventually that's going to get me killed."

Her face changed then, blue eyes widening in such a convincing display of guilt and sorrow that for the first time in a while I wondered again whether I had been a fool to trust her at all. "I honestly didn't mean this to happen to you, Bobby. It was my play, but it went wrong.

I trusted Grasswax—not very far, but far enough for him to betray me, as it turned out."

"Explain."

"I had to get rid of it—I told you, I was being watched. And followed. As soon as Eligor knew his prize was gone, he knew what I'd done. He knew that I had it, and that I wouldn't be afraid to use it against him."

"What does *that* mean?"

"Look, you don't just pluck a feather out of one of the Powers or Principalities," she said. "And they don't molt, either. Eligor had that feather for a reason."

I was beginning to see the light. "A pledge, or a marker. And I'm guessing that somewhere in Heaven someone's got something of Eligor's stashed away in a desk drawer, too, which would prove to Eligor's side that he'd been messing around making deals he wasn't supposed to make. That way if either one betrays the secret, he goes down as well. All the way down." I saw how it fit together, but I still had an awful lot of questions. "So one of my bosses and the grand duke must have made a bargain . . . but a bargain about what? What secret would be worth that kind of risk?"

She shrugged. "If I knew—or if I even had the feather—I wouldn't be hiding out right now."

"Because if that gold plume belongs to one of the higher angels, the rest of the higher angels could probably tell who it came from." I whistled. "Man, this shit is bigger and crazier than I even guessed. Tell me the details about Grasswax. When did you give it to him, and when did it go missing?"

"I gave it to him the day before he died."

"The day Sam and the kid opposed him over that Marino woman."

"I suppose. And the next day he told me he'd hidden it—that he'd let me know where it was when we could talk in private." A startled look crossed her face. "You were there! When he told me that, I mean."

"At the Walker house? When we all found out about the missing soul? Seems a bit weird that would be a coincidence—the two biggest things to happen around here in years both going on at the same time." I paused to chew things over. "Is that when Grasswax told you he'd got rid of the feather?"

"Yes, when I showed up. I was in a foul mood about the whole

Walker thing because I thought Grasswax had done something stupid to draw attention to himself at exactly the time we didn't need it. I didn't realize how much bigger it was than that. And I didn't get a chance to talk to him again before they killed him." Her mouth pulled into a grim line. "He was a nasty, treacherous bastard who was going to rip me off, but even he didn't deserve to go *that* way."

"Are you sure he was going to betray you? Maybe he just didn't get the chance to tell you where he stashed it before—"

"He had a perfectly good chance. I tried to have a private talk with him just afterward—I still had the excuse of debriefing him on the Walker thing, so it wouldn't have attracted attention. But he shined me on, told me he had something crucial to take care of, making sure the feather was safe. Really he was going to offer it to Sitri, I'd bet now, to buy himself out of his gambling debts. But Eligor must have got to him first."

I did my best not to dwell on the ugly memories this brought up, of Grasswax's remains unstrung and festooned across Edward Walker's backyard. "So that means the missing feather isn't just Eligor's problem, is it? Whoever it came from has to be just as worried about it as he is. Maybe even more. Any idea at all who it might be? A name Eligor might have mentioned?"

"In front of me?" She was scornful. "He wouldn't take that risk. Where I come from nobody trusts anyone, with good reason. I only knew he had something important in the safe because I eavesdropped on one of his conversations."

"And that conversation . . . ?"

"Part of one. It was a few weeks ago. He was on the phone, and I heard him say, 'I don't care. I've still got your boss's voucher in my safe, and we're going to do everything just the way we agreed. If anything goes wrong I can blow you all up so completely even the Highest won't be able to find you.'"

"'Your boss's voucher' . . . so he was talking to an underling. Which means our mystery angel has at least one person working for him or her—or herm, I guess—down here on Earth."

"You have a look in your eyes I don't like," she said, quite abruptly. "Like you're about to leave."

"My best friend is in the emergency room, Caz. Damn near dead because of Eligor's pet nightmare. And I've just realized that everything I've said to any of my comrades here or in Heaven may have already got back to Eligor's secret partner, so who knows how much damage I've caused that way? I need to think."

"But when you leave, we'll never have this again."

"What do you mean, Caz? Do you think I'm just using you for information?" I looked at her, tried to make out the secrets I could see hiding in the depths of her gaze. "Don't you believe this means something to me, too?"

She shook her head as if it were too heavy for her slender neck. "I don't know, Bobby. I've never been in this situation."

"I haven't either."

"Then just stay a little longer. One more hour." She reached out, touched the tips of her fingers to my naked chest, then dragged her nails ever so gently down through the curls of hair toward my belly. "Give me just a little more of you, a few more memories. The nights are very long sometimes, even here in the real world, Bobby. It's better than . . . than other places I've been, but the centuries have been lonely." She got her arms around my neck and pulled herself up so that her dry, cold skin slid over me like a chilly breeze, making pretty much everything stir and stand on end.

"Ooh," she said, lifting her face close to mine. "Feel that—Lazarus has risen."

"Don't blaspheme," I said, then kissed her cool lips until they parted, and her hot tongue touched mine. "We're above that now." And I meant it.

"Oh, yes," she said. "Oh, yes."

twenty-four
slumber party

CAZ WAS still sleeping when I left. Gently detaching myself from those slender limbs while ignoring her half-conscious murmurs of protest, climbing out of that warm bed that smelled of our sex—it truly was one of the hardest things I ever did. *When you leave, we'll never have this again.* Was she right? If we both survived, would we spend the rest of our lives regretting this or wishing it could happen again? Could it happen again? I didn't even want to think about what the penalty might be for consorting with the enemy in such a very, very specific and (as far as my bosses would be concerned) objectionable way.

And could I even believe it myself? She was a demon, a minion of Hell itself. What could love truly mean to her?

It didn't keep me from hurting as I walked away, though. Didn't help at all.

After I found a cab I went to see Orban, not just because I needed to replace my lost gun, left somewhere at the bottom of the Redwood River, but because I owed him the courtesy of a face to face when I told him what had happened to the Bonneville he'd lent me. Also, the errand would distract me from what I'd just left behind. Orban wasn't happy, of course. His accent got even stronger when he was in a bad mood: I have never been called a "deekhad" so many times in such a short span of time in my angelic life.

"How could you do that? That is my favorite, that car! Do you know how hard I look for parts? Nineteen seventy-one! How expensive? Almost two hundred dollars just for one sun visor latch! You bring back my sun visor latches? You bring back *anything*?"

Eventually he calmed down—in this case, "eventually" meaning after a half hour of fussing, fuming, and spitting, plus two glasses of Egri. I had one or two with him since it was lunchtime. I mean, why the hell not? I also promised I'd get the Bonneville back from impound and (somehow) pay for the damages, so eventually we changed the subject.

Tapping out my bank account and letting him hold the pink slip to my beloved Matador allowed me to drive away from Orban's in another loaner, this one a far less glamorous and slightly less well-armored old diesel Mercedes the color of shower caulk. More useful, at least under present circumstances, was an FN Five-Seven pistol, a Belgian automatic with a twenty-shot magazine. (Yes, I know, technically it's spelled "Five-SeveN" with a capital "N" at the end, but I've got no patience with that kind of cute whoopty-doo.) I had also sprung for another hundred silver rounds, which Orban had made up for the original buyer of the Five-Seven.

"That guy was too dead to pick them up when they are finished, so I let you have them cheap," he said. "You can get a kit to make a thirty-shot magazine for the Five-Seven, but I don't trust. Too tricky. Stick with twenty. Twenty is plenty." He smiled in his beard. "Ha! Orban makes a rhyme."

I left the poet of firepower standing behind his counter and headed back across town, bound for Five Page Mill in the huffing, rattling Benz.

I'd been thinking about the things Caz had told me ever since I'd left her, and much as I wanted to trust her—much as I *needed* to believe what she'd said, since I'd broken so many rules being with her—I still had some nagging doubts, and I had decided to do some checking.

I parked a few rows back from the front of Number Five, put on some sunglasses and an old Giants cap that one of Orban's mechanics left in the back seat of the Benz, then settled back to watch who went in and out of Vald Credit. I saw Howlingfell pop out a couple of times like a cuckoo on a clock, always leading at least two other security guys, but I just stayed in my car and watched. The last thing I wanted was another shootout in Page Mill Square. Late in the afternoon I abandoned my surveillance long enough to drive to a nearby deli for a turkey sandwich and cup of coffee to go, then returned to the parking lot, ready now for a long siege.

As five o'clock passed most of the Vald Credit employees and many other workers from the plaza's buildings spilled out of the high-rises and headed for the street and the bus stops. Vald Credit had its own parking lot under the building, which also began to empty, but the public lot was still full of customers for the shops on the lower floors of most of the buildings, so I didn't feel any need to move.

At last, closer to seven than to six, my wait paid off: Howlingfell walked out of the building by himself and stood for a moment looking expectantly from one side to the other before a long, sleek car pulled up and he got in.

I followed at a respectable distance, the tail made easier by the fact that it was getting dark, and the Camino Real was crowded with commuter traffic. When the car pulled into a place called Il Milanese, a couple of miles down the main drag, Howlingfell went in by himself and the driver stayed outside in the parking lot, just as I had hoped. I watched the driver put on the dome light to read a magazine, then I took a minute to scribble a note on a piece of paper, seal it in an envelope, and pocket it before I went inside.

It was an interesting place, full of swoopy modern decor and black and white photos of nineteenth century Italians, the men in high collars and the women mostly in voluminous black dresses, as if they had spent the entire century in mourning. The wall that fronted on the Camino Real was made of glass, and I wondered if the place might once have been a twenty-four-hour coffee shop. The counter with its roll of revolving stools confirmed my guess, but these days the guys in trucker hats had been replaced with young professionals eating bar snacks and drinking vodka and Red Bull.

Howlingfell was in the restaurant's back room, his low, animal brow furrowed as he surveyed the wine list. He didn't jump or even look particularly surprised when I slid into the other side of the booth, but his hand slipped off the table, and I knew he was reaching for his gun.

"Don't do anything stupid, Howly," I said. "I'm just here to talk."

"Stupid?" He scowled at me, which made him look even more like something you'd find in your chicken shed with a limp hen hanging from its jaws. "You're the one who just did something stupid." He slowly lifted his hand and set it on the table so the flat black automatic he was holding lay sideways, pointing at me, with his finger still on its trigger. Then he carefully draped his napkin over hand and gun to hide them from the folks in the other booths. "Why do you want to spoil my dinner, Dollar? What'd I ever do to you?"

"Less than I've done to you, to be perfectly honest. Remember when I stepped on your neck? Good times, good times. Ah, ah, ah, stay relaxed! I've got a big old gun of my own pointing at you under the table. Let's not turn this into a contest to see how much silver we can put into each other."

"Silver. You think I'm afraid of silver? You tried that already." His lip curled. "You missed my balls by a couple of inches, but it's still going to take me weeks to heal down there, and I heal fast. My girlfriends are all pissed at you. Not to mention that it *really fucking hurt.* In fact, I don't think I'm going to listen to any of your bullshit—I think I'm just going to blow your face off!"

"Don't. I'm not threatening you with silver this time, pal. I'm threatening you with something a lot worse." I looked up. The waiter was coming toward us. I hoped nobody got startled.

The napkin over Howlingfell's gun hand twitched a little, but for the moment everything stayed in place. "Worse? Like what?"

"Like your boss. Hang on."

The waiter took two waters off a tray and put them in front of us. "Hi, my name is Eric, and I'll be your server," he said with cheerful disinterest in whatever weird vibe was going back and forth between us, which he couldn't have helped but notice. "Can I get you gentlemen anything?"

"Vodka rocks for me," I said. "I'll just have some breadsticks, but my friend probably wants dinner."

"I'll order later," Howlingfell snarled. "Just bring me a glass of Chianti. The Castello dei Rampolla."

As the waiter glided away I smiled at my unwilling host. "So, have you really learned to like fancy wines? Pretty good for a kid who grew up on the scorching sidewalks of the Via Dolorosa, Howly. Or do you just like to put anything in your mouth as long as it's wet and red?"

"Shut up, Dollar. You have something to say about my boss, then say it fast. I'm sick of your face."

"Okay, fair enough." I took a breadstick and crunched off the end of it, my other hand still out of sight beneath the table. "I'm going to tell you a little story. About how your boss's ex-girlfriend ripped him off. And how *you* helped her do it."

"What the fuck are you talking about?" He half stood and the napkin over his gun started to slide, but after a moment he controlled himself and sat down again. A few people turned to look at us. "You lying cocksucker!" he said in a loud whisper. "I didn't know anything about that!"

I was taking a big risk that he might just start a firefight right there in the restaurant, but the last, small part of me that still had any sense needed to know that Caz had been telling me the truth. Outside of the Grand Duke, Howlingfell was the only person still around to confirm her story, and I already knew that threats weren't going to make him talk to me—after all, here he was in a restaurant less than twenty-four hours after I had put a couple of silver slugs into his pelvis, inches from his jewels, so obviously he was one tough bastard. The only thing he was scared of would be the same thing that scared me—his pissed-off, crazy, murderous boss Eligor.

"Honestly, Fuzzy," I told him, "for your own sake, don't do anything stupid 'til you hear me out."

He showed me lots of teeth. "The stupid thing would be letting you walk out of here."

I smiled back. "You can decide for yourself, but here's what you need to know first. My information says that if the Grand Duke catches up with the Countess she's going to say the two of you were in it together; that she only walked out with Eligor's . . . personal property"—I had a sudden attack of discretion because I didn't know whether Howlingfell knew what had been stolen—"because you deliberately looked the other way."

"Lying whore!" I thought he was going to pop a vein. His face began to take on the color of a zesty marinara. "I didn't know anything about it! She got to one of my crew. . . ."

"So it was just a coincidence that the grand duke's chief of security was slumming as a mere prosecutor's bodyguard?" I affected a superior laugh. "Right. You were keeping an eye on your investment."

"Fuck you, angel. Eligor was the one who put me on Grasswax in the first place! I was watching him because the boss knew he was in it with that bitch, somehow." Howlingfell was beginning to lose control.

The idea of his boss blaming him for the theft really scared him, and he wasn't thinking carefully, which was what I had been hoping. "This is all made-up crap. Do you really think this is enough to get you off the boss's shit list?" The napkin was definitely moving, which meant his hand was twitching as he got a better grip on his gun.

"Ah, ah," I said. "You don't really want to make all that noise in here, do you, Howly? You *like* this place, remember? Not to mention that after you miss me several times and I get away, you'll have to explain to the police why you accidentally shot all these nice people."

Howlingfell picked up his butter knife and ran his thumb down its smooth edge, his hairy hand trembling ever so slightly. "I don't need my gun to do you, angel. I could kill you just fine with this. Or my bare hands."

"I don't know why nobody wants to hang out with you, Howly. You're *fun*." I stood up, then—carefully, so as not to alarm him—and took out the note I had written before coming in. "I'm going to be on my way now. Before you call for reinforcements, or even decide to try to butter me to death on your own, I strongly suggest you read this. But only if you value your continued torture-less existence. As you keep pointing out to me, your boss is a bad character to cross." I set the envelope down on the edge of the table as I turned. Seems I wasn't too careful and the envelope fell onto the floor. As he watched me, eyes almost glowing with hatred, I headed for the door. I confess that my muscles were tensed since I was half-expecting to get shot in the back.

I looked back and saw him lean down to pluck the envelope from the floor so I hurried out of the restaurant. As he tore it open and read the words, *"Stay away from the osso bucco, I hear it's not very good tonight,"* I was climbing into my car.

By the time Howlingfell burst out the front door of Il Milanese with his gun out and a face like an enraged, shaved pit bull, ready to blow me to tatters, I was already speeding away down the Camino Real.

My dangerous due diligence performed—so far Caz's story about Grasswax and the feather was holding up—I got on with the rest of my list. First I phoned Clarence. I still had my doubts about him, but I'd thought of a way to kill two birds with one stone.

"Wow, Bobby, are you okay?" he asked when he picked up. "What happened? I saw The Compasses . . . !"

"Yeah, yeah, it was all very exciting. Most fun I've had since Grampa Dollar confused the gasoline and the corn liquor. Are you at home?"

"Um, yeah. I mean, I will be in a few minutes. I was just at a restaurant. My roommates are out tonight."

I had no idea what that meant. "I was just in a fine dining establishment myself, but I didn't eat anything but breadsticks so I may pick something up on the way. I'll see you in about half an hour."

"But . . . !"

I hung up before he wasted my time trying to talk me out of it.

Cruising across town in the Benz was less than exciting. I've never liked diesels. They root and snort like Fatback looking for a truffle, and they're about as fast to respond as the complaints department of a major corporation. Still, it beat the hell out of walking, so I rolled down the windows and did my best to enjoy the evening. I grabbed a couple of tacos at a fast food drive-through and ate them as I drove, dropping bits of tortilla shell and tomato into my lap and onto Orban's floorboards. I wondered where the *ghallu* was now—was it hunting for me this moment, or did it only go where it was sent?

As I headed up Whipple toward Brittan Heights I passed the angled white bulk of Sequoia Hospital and thought about Sam lying there in emergency, stuck full of tubes and with nothing to do (if he was conscious) except listen to Jimmy the Table's boring stories about the good old days in Spanishtown, when Jimmy had first been an advocate back in the seventies. I wouldn't wish that on anyone, let alone my poor buddy who couldn't even get up and walk away, and for a moment I was strongly tempted to pay Sam a surprise visit. The temptation only lasted a moment, though: I was feeling pretty good because my bluff had worked on Howlingfell, but I also knew I really shouldn't push my luck.

I had previously dropped Clarence off in front of the big house up in the heights, but this time I had to get out and look for the front door, which was harder to find than you'd have guessed. I finally found *a* door, and after I'd been knocking for a while Clarence showed up.

"Wow, so . . . you're here." He was wearing gray, old-fashioned sweats, like he'd been working out, and white running shoes. I'd rather die than wear white running shoes. In fact, it might even be what killed me in the first place. Maybe I'm an angel today because the white running shoe mafia bumped me off.

"Is this your tribute to Rocky Balboa?" I asked him.

He looked down at his clothes. "I guess. Come on in."

He didn't have any beer, but he got me a soft drink out of a refrigerator that was almost as big as my apartment. The house was huge too, one of those Frank Lloyd Wright-ish things, all wood and tile and concrete, mostly open plan so you could see from one room into a couple of others without moving. One of the bigger rooms was even open to the sky, although you could close it off with sliding doors in bad weather and make it into an interior courtyard. I wondered again about Clarence's roommates. They must be rich valley kids with high-paying jobs, but they also must have a maid service because the place was quite clean.

We sat in the kitchen, and I told him about everything that happened right up until I crawled out of the Redwood River and called Caz, because that was obviously not only my own business but totally against the rules and thus not the kind of thing I was going to discuss with a new and almost unknown quantity like this kid. I still sort of liked him, though, even though I didn't trust him, which was a fairly familiar situation for me. (Because I don't really trust anyone, get it?)

"I saw Chico's gun one other time," Clarence said as I rehashed the Gunfight at the Compasses Corral. "That machine-gun thing. Wow." He sounded like Piglet talking about Christopher Robin's blue braces. "He asked me to take a tray of drinks off him while he answered the phone, and I saw it stashed behind the bar. That thing is huge!"

"And it still barely slowed that bastard of a *ghallu* down," I said. "So I'm having to rethink the whole thing. Meanwhile, I need your help with something."

A certain trapped-animal look crossed his face. "Really? Like . . . like what?" I could see he was imagining being deputized and dragged into a new shootout with the Nightmare from Nineveh. "Because I . . . I've got a lot of stuff to . . ."

"Shut up, you have nothing. I talked to Alice and made sure you have the night off. We're going to upstairs."

He involuntarily looked toward the staircase.

"Not *that* upstairs, Clarence. To the Big House on the Hill. Headquarters. *Heaven*." A noise from the other side of the room made me grab for my piece, but before I got it out Junior leaped out of his chair and skittered between me and whoever was coming in the side door. (I found out later it led in from the driveway.) A nicely dressed Caucasian couple of a little past retirement age stopped in the doorway.

"Oh, hello, Harrison," the woman said to Junior. She was handsome in a slightly hippie-chic way, an old Northern California liberal with money. "We didn't mean to startle you and your friend. The movie was terrible and Burt had a headache."

"The movie gave me a headache," said the man, presumably Burt. "It was the kind of thing that Sheila likes, but it leaves me cold. Subtitles, people staring, nothing happens at the end."

"We didn't see the end, so how do you know?" Sheila asked pointedly, then smiled at us to show they were acting out old, familiar roles.

"I saw enough of it. I *know*." He headed across the kitchen. "I'm going upstairs. You coming, Sheil?"

She looked at us. "He was right," she said in a stage whisper. "It wasn't very good. But he always thinks foreign films are going to be bad, so I don't want to give him the satisfaction." Out loud, she said, "Yes, Burt, I'm coming." She turned in the doorway. "Oh, when I was at the store today I saw some of that cereal you like, Harrison—the one with the grain and nuts and dried fruit. So I got a couple of boxes."

"Thanks, Sheila," said Clarence, looking as though he wanted to slide through the floor and disappear.

"Well, I remember you liked it," she said brightly. "Help yourself to anything, boys. Goodnight!"

He was still watching the door long after she'd disappeared, probably because he didn't want to see the expression of incredulity on my face. "You're kidding me," I said. "Those are your *roommates?*"

"What? They're nice people."

"Did you go out shopping for a mom and dad? Or did you answer an advertisement? 'Wanted, surrogate child for older couple'?"

He colored very impressively. "Lay off, Dollar. You're not funny."

I started laughing. It took me a while to stop. "Okay, sorry. Nevermind. I've got more important things to do with you than argue about your weird domestic arrangements." I leaned over and slapped him on the shoulder in my chummiest manner. "After all, we're going to have a slumber party tonight."

"Slumber . . ."

"In other words, I'm sleeping over and we're going to Heaven together."

"Ssshhhh!" He looked absolutely panicked. "Jeez, what if they hear you? Can you imagine how that would sound?"

I chortled again. "Pretty funny, now that you mention it. And it's going to get worse, too, because I'm going to bunk down in your room. Just find me a spare blanket and a pillow. Maybe we'll even tell ghost stories."

"You're going to sleep in my room? Isn't that . . . kind of gay?"

"No. If I suggested we play Twister in our underpants, *that* would be kind of gay. Now shut up and find me a blanket and lead me to your room. You do have your own room, don't you? You don't sleep in a crib at the foot of Sheila and Burt's bed or anything?" I know I was being a bit nasty to the kid, but I still didn't trust him and I was interested see if I could get him riled up past his haplessness act.

He only stared morosely. "You think you're funny, Bobby, but you're not."

"I do like to see a junior angel sulk," I told him. "It smells like victory. Now drink up all your milk and then let's get to bed. Little Clarence has a busy night ahead of him."

twenty-five
misremembered

THE KID and I met up in the Fields of Glory. Clarence was late and appeared over the brow of a green Elysian hill, waving his hands like a semaphore nostalgist. I wasn't happy about the delay. It wasn't so much the waiting, it was just that it left me thinking time, and thinking time meant thinking about Caz. I didn't want to do that just at the moment, not least because I already missed her fiercely. The subject was simply too confusing, and it also made the miserable handful of options I had suddenly seem ten times worse. Either I had betrayed Heaven or I had fallen in love with someone so impossible for me that she made Dante's untouchable Beatrice look like a Vegas street hooker.

"Sorry!" the kid said. "I had trouble falling asleep!"

"We've got a long walk. You've been here before?"

He straightened in indignation. "Of course! More than once!"

I was amused in spite of myself. It really was like dealing with a kid. He might be a complete and total traitor for all I knew, dropped into the Whole Sick Choir by my superiors to report back my every anti-Heaven grumble, but if his earnest goofiness was a complete front it was a very good one. I kept wanting to like him, and I couldn't help wondering what kind of trouble that was going to get me into. Had Caesar enjoyed teasing Brutus right up until his best pal stabbed him?

We set out together through the brilliant green fields beneath the invisible sun that warmed everything in Heaven. One thing I did like about Clarence was that he asked as many questions as I did. The thing

I *didn't* like is that he asked them all out loud. He was curious, as always, about how things operated behind the scenes for our angelic business on Earth. He even asked me how the Zippers and Outside work, which is kind of like asking a Juggalo to explain magnetism.

"Okay, you don't know how they work," he persisted, "but can anyone do it besides an advocate? And what if someone closed it behind you? Would you be stuck there?"

"Any angel can do it—even you. Hasn't Sam showed you how yet?"

"He said he would, but he hasn't got around to it."

Probably trying to minimize the trouble you can cause, I thought but didn't say. "I'm sure he will."

"I hope he's okay. He looked terrible! Tubes up his nose and down his throat . . ."

I felt more than a bit guilty that I hadn't visited Sam in the hospital, even though I'd been told not to show up. "As far as getting trapped Outside—no, it can't happen, not without causing an interafter incident. The rules are very strict. They must have spent a huge part of the Convention just arguing about how all that had to be regulated."

"Inter . . . after?"

I smiled. The phrase had been one of Leo's. "Friend of mine made that up—he was a friend of Sam's, too. Inter-afterlife. Between them and us."

"And when you say 'Convention,' you mean the Tartarean Convention, right? Where we got together with the Opposition back in the beginning and made up the rules?"

"Yeah. Once it was clear that the Highest was banishing Satan's crew but not destroying them, then everybody had to agree how the game was going to play out." I remembered something. "You can't *force* anybody to go Outside, either, or take them there against their will. That actually saved my life recently."

"I know. With Eligor, in his office."

I squinted at him. "How did you know that?"

"Because you told me, remember? Come on, Bobby, you're getting paranoid. When we were getting coffee that time with Sam?"

"Oh. Yeah." But it knocked me back a little, and so we continued for a while in silence.

I've been glossing over the journey through the Fields, but I really shouldn't because it's quite an experience. I mean, believe me, mortals would line up for miles and pay Disneyland prices just to stroll for a few hundred yards. The most amazing thing is the colors, the way they glow and snap and sparkle. People who have experienced peyote or magic mushrooms or LSD might have some inkling of how, when you're tripping, the colors of everything seem to intensify, almost to throb with inner light. The difference with Heaven is that there's never the harshness that happens with psychedelic drugs, let alone the potential for a bad trip. In fact, a hike through the hills and meadows that surround the Celestial City is pretty much by definition the opposite of a bad trip.

Now, of course I don't know anything about peyote or any of those others myself. After all, I'm an angel, and even an angel who was stuck in a desert training camp with a bunch of other bored angels wearing human bodies for the first time would never experiment with drinking and illegal drugs and other such bad human habits. It just wouldn't happen. You see that, don't you?

Anyway, since I had decided to be a little more reticent with Clarence, I had time to appreciate again the peculiar beauty of the Fields, as well as the parts that were just plain peculiar. For one thing, although there were people all around—the Blessed, perhaps, certainly the souls of the happy departed—it was very hard to reach any of them. The Fields were dreamlike, as was the Celestial City itself, but the nature of this particular dream was that it was easy to reach *things*, like a shady grove or invitingly grassy hillock, but people were always farther away than they seemed: You could get to them, but if they appeared to be a few hundred feet away to begin with it might take what felt in Earthly terms like a quarter of an hour to do it. I don't know whether that was just the unique physics of Heaven or because the Highest didn't want people's afterlives interrupted too easily. Not that you ever got much out of people when you talked to them in the Fields, anyway. They often seemed half-asleep, cheerful and willing to answer you, but lost in memories of the lives they had lived or the afterlife they were currently living, and only capable of paying partial attention. Sometimes, in the early days, when I was still asking my questions out loud, I would leave the Fields of Heaven feeling like a creepy grownup who'd been hanging around a children's playground.

But the rest of the Fields offer themselves up much more easily than the inhabitants do. The sun shines all the time, but—again, like a dream—if you walk into the darker places, the shadowed corners and forested glens, you quickly find that it's much like night in some trustworthy, beautiful, and benign nature spot. You discover places that seem to be right out of your own fondest memories, although of course, if you're someone like me or Clarence, you have no memories to match them with, just that *feeling*. Everywhere you go it's like that: unfamiliar but unthreatening, or familiar but still mysterious, as if *déjà vu* was in the very air you breathed. And like the City, being in the Fields of Heaven feels right. It feels *good*. Every time I pass through I tell myself, *I need to see more of this. I need to learn more. Maybe I could be happy here. Maybe.*

But all things come to an end, even the endless Fields. Eventually you reach a high place where you can discern the shimmering walls of the City in the distance. For most people this would be the highlight of any trip, but for me it always comes with the smallest internal shiver of disquiet. I've never really felt like I belonged in Heaven. Every time I come here, even when summoned by high authorities, even on those rare occasions when I've been praised, I still feel as though I'm in danger of being found out.

Found out about what? I don't know. I wish I did.

"So why did you want me to come with you?" Clarence asked as we made our way through the great gate and into the murmuring flow of angelic inhabitants that always crowd the streets. (By the way, although the streets are not really all paved in gold, there are certainly parts that seem to be, but it's a gold that's pleasant to the touch, yielding as firm earth, with few of the real qualities of gold except beauty.) "Is it something about Sam?"

"Why would you think that?"

He shrugged. He was already acting a little distracted, caught up in the infectious good cheer of Heaven. I could feel it myself but I was struggling hard to hold onto my sense of purpose, as I always did when I went back. I've found that if I go about it in the same way that a drunk undertakes a complicated task—concentrate, concentrate, concentrate—I can just about manage. Then I pass under a tree full of blossoms, each one shining from within like a fairy subdivision, and I have to start over.

"Why? I don't know," he said. "I guess because Sam's in the hospital 'cause he got hurt helping you against that *ghallu* thing. And because Sam's kind of my boss."

"Not a bad guess. But no, not really. I wanted you because you used to work in the Records Hall, right?"

For the first time since we entered the City his cheerful calm retreated a bit. He wrinkled his forehead as though I had just spoken the name of a particularly unpleasant ex-girlfriend of his—not that I believed he'd had many of those, unpleasant or otherwise. "Really?" he said. "But, I haven't worked there for a while. . . ."

"Not too far back, really. A few weeks, Earth time, plus your stretch in training before they sent you down—which obviously wasn't long, at least, based on how little you know."

He blushed. I'd never seen anyone blush in Heaven. It was charming in a pathetic sort of way. "Am I really that bad?"

"You know how nature makes babies helpless so we don't want to eat them? Well, even Eligor's horned monster would probably just pick you up and ruffle your hair and play a game of got-your-nose." He looked so shamefaced I almost felt bad, but I was determined to test him. "But there's plenty you *can* do to help out, and this is one of them. Let's head over to Records and I'll tell you."

We drifted across Merciful Square and down the Eternal Way with its endless white columns. Angels passed us constantly, but some of the highest simply appeared and disappeared, not bothering with approximations of Earthly life. I suspected these might be the ones who had never been mortals. Every now and then I could make out the shape of golden wings inside a high angel's glow, and it reminded me that one of the Celestial City's very important citizens might well be a traitor. I distracted myself by pointing out some of the more esoteric sites to Clarence.

"And that's the Panepistimion," I said. "It's where they learn to work with the Dominions of the Second Sphere. I don't really understand what that means, but it has something to do with the machinery of the universe."

"See, that's the problem with Sam," Junior said abruptly. "He never tells me anything. Not like you do."

I bristled a little. "Sam's got his own way of doing things. Don't underestimate him."

"I don't, but sometimes I wish he wouldn't . . . I don't know, hold me at arm's length so much. Half the questions I ask I don't even get answers. Not even, 'Shut up, I'm not going to tell you'! Maybe you could ask him to talk to me a little more, Bobby."

I laughed, but now I wasn't feeling quite so protective toward the kid. "Look, if he answers even half your questions you must keep him talking twenty-four seven. He's trying to train you, and he's going to do it his way. If you wind up as even half the advocate Sammariel is, you can be very, very proud of yourself."

Clarence looked at me carefully. He was very present now, as if the discussion had helped him shake off some of the free-floating joy of Heaven. "He always sticks up for you, too. That Elvis guy said something about you once, nothing too bad even, and I thought Sam was going to hit him in the face."

Now I did laugh. "Yeah, well, Young Elvis can be a bit of a bitch. And Sam and I go back a long way. Has he told you . . . ?"

"That you guys were in the Counterstrike Force together? Yeah. You were Harpers or something."

"Harps, youngster. CU Lyrae. That's not the kind of connection you forget, and those aren't the kind of friends you turn your back on. I'll tell you a quick story." We were approaching the street of shining, cloud-piercing buildings in which the Records Hall was to be found. "I was on point once on a SALT mission in Spanishtown—"

"SALT?"

"Yeah—Secure And Level Target. Which means burn it to the foundations and purify the ground with silver nitrate. We were going into a desanctified church that a group of Deniables had made their base of operations—"

"Deniables?"

"Are you going to let me tell the story, kid? Deniables are demons who've supposedly gone rogue. The Opposition is still running them, of course, but they can claim they're out of control, acting on their own. And these bastards were doing some bad, bad shit in that part of Spanishtown. Three possessions among children in the neighborhood, a rash of suicides, and a big increase in drunken fights, stabbings, family violence, you name it. They were peddling despair, and they were building their clientele by the hour.

"Anyway, I was point and Sam was our top-kick that night when we broke into San Juan Soldado. It was a bad fight, and I don't really want to talk about it here—doesn't quite seem right. We had pretty much wrapped it up, though, until we broke into the final chamber, the old sacristy . . . but they had a Deathwatch hiding there. You probably want to interrupt again. Or do you know what those are?"

Clarence shook his head.

"It's a demon who looks like a man, but who's made up of . . . well, bugs, or things that look like bugs. Beetles usually, which is where the name comes from. We already had the area enclosed with wards, so the Deathwatch wasn't going anywhere, but he wasn't going to surrender, either. All the pieces of him flew apart and swarmed me." I paused for a moment. I hadn't talked about it in a while, and it still made my stomach clench. "Oh, one thing I forgot to tell you about those bugs—they're poison. Every single one of them sinks its little jaws into you and the pain is . . . well, there's no describing it, really. Time just stops. The pain is everything. All you can do is scream and thrash, if you can even hold it together enough to do that.

"Anyway, do you know what Sam did when the Deathwatch got me? He grabbed me and wrapped his arms around me like a drunken frat boy hug. A bunch of them jumped off me and onto him, and he staggered away, carrying them with him. Then he shouted at the guy with the flamethrower to hose him down."

"What?" Clarence looked like he was going to be sick. It raised an interesting question—did anyone ever throw up in Heaven? "What do you mean . . . ?"

"You heard me. He told the guy to hose him down with the flamethrower."

"But how could Sam survive that? How could his body survive it, I mean?"

"It couldn't, of course. But he was showing me what to do. So when the guy turned the flames on him I jumped into it too, just like it was a warm shower." I sounded glib, but it all came back as I said it, that endless, shrieking, agonizing moment that in some ways, especially during sleepless nights, had never ended. Time does not always move forward, no matter what they tell you. That kind of agony equals eternity, and that's how long the memory would be with me. They also say that you never really remember pain. That's bullshit too.

"You . . . you burned up?"

It took me a moment to push it away. "Yeah. It was the only way to stop it, the only way to kill those fucking beetles. But it was fairly quick, believe it or not—a few bad seconds, then it was all over."

Clarence was looking around as though hoping to find evidence somewhere nearby that I was making it all up. "So, w-why didn't Sam just use the flamethrower on you? Why did he let himself . . . ?"

"Because he was our leader. Nothing like this had happened to us before, and he wanted us to see that Heaven was behind us. Also that he wouldn't ask anything of us he wouldn't do to himself. Believe me, everybody remembered. Wherever they are now, they *still* remember, I promise. I did, too—when I woke up in a new body, that is. Sam and I spent a while in Rebirth—see, it takes some time to get used to the new body when you go out violently like that. And while we were there . . . well, that's when we got to be friends." It was also the time Sam started doggedly drinking his new body to death, but I didn't tell the kid that. None of his business.

Something about the stark horror on Clarence's face almost made me sorry to have told him the Deathwatch story. He looked like a whipped puppy. I glanced up and saw the first of the Halls of Records looming in front of us, a literal ivory tower covered with gold and silver scrollwork, a massive needle without a haystack. It was quite interesting on the inside, too, but I wasn't going to be seeing it, at least not today. If I even stepped inside I might as well have set off an alarm throughout the Celestial City announcing "Bobby Dollar's back in town."

"Here's what I want," I told him, and recited the list of half a dozen names, beginning with the Rev. Dr. Moses Habari. "Get me whatever you can find on all of them. Everything of interest."

"But I can't bring the records out!" he said, horrified. "I'm not even supposed to go back there after being transferred!"

"You still have friends there, I'm sure," I said. "Sam must have taught you at least a *little* by now, Junior. Schmooze them up. If you can't bring me copies just memorize them—remember, you're an *angel.* I'll meet you when you're done. Go on, get to it, or I'll have to report you for loitering."

He stared at me as I turned away. When I looked back he was slouching toward the door of the Records Hall like he'd been called to the principal's office.

I headed off to the building where the fixers hang out to explain what exactly had made The Compasses fall down go boom.

The Mule looked up from his work, if that was what the ball of cold fire in front of him represented. The face inside the angelic glow changed expression, but it was hard to tell from what to what. Archangels aren't anywhere near as inhuman as Principalities, but they're still hard to read. "Angel Doloriel!" His tone was guardedly friendly. "God loves you! What a surprise. Are you well?"

Well, not actually. I'm in love with one of Satan's little helpers, and one of his poker buddies is trying to kill me—and that's if I'm lucky. But even in Heaven, that's a question I seldom answer honestly. "Yes, I am, Archangel Temuel, thank you for asking."

"The Ministry of Inquiry wants to talk to you. Have you communicated with them?

"Just finished up with them before I came here. But I also wanted to check in with you. Do you have a moment to spare?"

He hesitated an almost undetectable instant, but I was looking for it. "Of course. Let's go out. Do you like Contemplation Park?"

"Lovely spot." *Does he know how deep I'm in*? I wondered. *Has he somehow heard about Caz?* Why else would he want to take me somewhere beyond the reach of eavesdroppers?

My next thought was even creepier. *Does such a place even exist in Heaven?*

We made that strange Heavenly transition between *inside* and *outside*, the one where you kind of just melt your way through everything in a matter of moments, then walked in a more normal fashion through the crowds to Contemplation Park. (The folks in the City are busier and more focused than the folks in the Fields. They're also off in their own worlds, but their worlds seem to be part of *now*. If you stop them and ask them something they'll even directly answer your question, if they can. In some ways they're almost like people in an ordinary city, but there's still that vagueness I've never quite been able to penetrate, and that sense of undifferentiating happiness that just . . . well, it makes me nervous. I can't help it.)

An idea struck me—one that I realized I would have to give some serious consideration: *What if I'm not the only one who feels this way?* It was important, somehow, my instincts told me, though I didn't know why. I prayed I'd be able to remember it later, since many things that happened in Heaven seemed to melt away like dreams back on Earth.

"So things are still a bit difficult for you, I hear," the Mule told me as we traveled along the flower-edged paths. I saw a group of children playing on top of one of the grassy knolls, a charming sight until I began to wonder how they'd died, and why it had happened to them so soon in life.

I am one badly screwed-up angel, there's no question about it.

"Difficult. Yes, you could say that. Did you get my message, Archangel, that I needed a few days without clients? Is that possible?"

Temuel did whatever archangels do when they nod their heads. I can understand it but I can't describe it. "Yes. And although not everyone was happy about it, you've been given some leeway, at least for the present. I think it's because of the summit conference."

"The what?"

"Ah. Then you haven't heard." The song of a solitary bird, oddly haunting, twittered through the park, and it made me aware for the first time how quiet it was in this part of Heaven. "The conference will be about the matter of the missing souls, of course. We have been given to understand that the Highest is disturbed. The Opposition claim they know nothing more about it than we do. It's a vanishingly small chance they're telling the truth, but a meeting has been agreed anyway. You will be invited to attend, of course, Angel Doloriel." His calm voice took on a momentary edge. "It will not be the sort of invitation that can be turned down."

"Why me?"

"Because you were the first advocate this happened to, although by now you have a great deal of company. And since that unfortunate hour you have also been pursued by a malign spirit, which may be related, or may not." A change in Temuel's glow led me to guess he was showing me a half-smile. "After all, you have made a few enemies in your years on Earth, Doloriel."

I politely ignored this. "Please tell me the whole truth, Archangel Temuel. Is this a real inquiry or are they simply looking for scapegoats? Because as the first poor bastard this happened to I see myself as a likely candidate to get tied to the post."

"It's a large, important inquiry, and I believe the intent is honest. Whatever our superiors think of you, this is a problem that cannot simply be blamed on someone—it must be solved." Temuel's attention turned slowly past me, and I wondered what he was thinking. He seemed to be looking out over the misty vastness of the park toward the distant gleam of the Empyrean. Temuel was opaque to me, and not just because he was an archangel. I simply had never been able to get a fix on him. "I think unless there is something else you need of me, we should go back now," he said. "Rest assured that for a few more days I will do my best to give you the freedom you feel you need on Earth. But do not—what is that old expression? Do not push your luck."

That had the sound of something you didn't want to be told twice. Unfortunately, I'd heard it several times already just in the last little while. "Thank you, Archangel. When is this summit conference happening? And do you know who'll be there?"

"Who will be there? Everyone of importance in the matter, I suspect—from both sides, too. Nobody can afford to be seen ignoring this. As to when—soon. You will be given the rest of the details when they're available."

It was a real joy to know all my enemies would be together with me in one place. Was I just being paranoid again, or was Heaven doing its best to get me bumped off? "Oh, one last thing," I said as we drifted back toward the California building and Temuel's office. "Do you remember when you asked me to keep an eye on the new advocate, Haraheliel? The one Sam has been training?"

I swear when I said that, the Mule's glow dwindled—for a moment I even thought I saw the edges of it flutter, like flames in a sudden wind—but then everything was as it had been. "No. I do not remember that."

For a moment I could only stand there with my angelic mouth hanging open. I've never known one of my superiors to forget *anything*. "Hang on," I said, "maybe I'm confusing things somehow. I'm talking about Haraheliel—the one we call 'Clarence,' but that's just a joke. His earthly name is Harrison Ely, and he's been working with Sam. When I was here before you asked me—"

"No." I hadn't heard the Mule so stern. Ever. "You are mistaken."

"But . . . !"

"You are mistaken, Angel Doloriel. Do you understand? I'm afraid you have misremembered. Such a conversation never took place."

He left me standing there all by myself, completely surrounded by angels.

twenty-six
the pride that goeth

I DREAMED I was reaching out for Caz. The dream should have been sweet or sexy or full of Catholic guilt or something, but instead I was scrabbling in dirt like a dog as she was being pulled away from me down a hole into dark, crumbling earth. At last she was gone, and though I scratched frantically all I could hear were muffled screams. I woke up in my Earthly body, streaming sweat, and for long moments my limbs felt like they belonged to somebody else.

Earthbound angels dream, but not very often. I almost never do, but occasionally a disturbing experience brings one on, and Temuel's response counted as just that. I've always had a kneejerk distrust of Heaven, especially when it came to whether or not they had Bobby Dollar's best interests in mind, and although my superiors could be stingy with the truth I'd never known any of them to lie straight to my face. I mean, could they even *do* that? They were important angels of the Lord! But unless the Mule had forgotten an extremely important conversation with me, something angels definitely don't do, he was baldfacedly denying something that we both knew had happened.

There was a third option, of course: I might have lost my mind, or at least the parts that I'd always counted on, my memory and my sense of logic. That wasn't a possibility I could afford to entertain very seriously, since I had become more and more isolated from my Heavenly support system in recent days. My best friend was in the hospital, maybe in a coma, my favorite hangout was wrecked, and my bosses were pissed off at me. If I couldn't trust my own judgement I was in real trouble.

Morning light was filtering in on me through the curtains of Clarence's rented basement room. Well, I say rented, but it looked a lot like the kind of room an adult son might have waiting for him in his parents' house, always ready for a visit. A fancy (and dust-free) model of a biplane dangled from the ceiling on a nearly invisible thread, a Giants team poster hung on the wall, and the bookcase was crammed with science fiction and sports and travel books. Even the bed where Clarence's currently untenanted body lay looked as though it had once belonged to a child. The coverlet was decorated with the logo of the San Judas Jacks, a local minor-league basketball franchise that had gone under some years ago.

But just because Clarence's soul was still in Heaven didn't mean his body was dead. Our masters had arranged things much more sensibly than that, and the kid gave every sign (and sound) of merely being asleep. I lay waiting for him to wake up, and while I did, I ran through everything that had happened to me on this last strange trip Upstairs. I knew I had particularly wanted to remember the idea that I might not be the only one with authority problems, but as often happens, whatever had made it seem so significant at the time had not remained attached to the concept. Still, it was something to mull over while I listened to Clarence's quiet snoring.

I thought about calling Caz. I'd actually thought about it a lot in the last twenty-four hours, but I didn't know what to say to her. Hell, I didn't even know how I *felt*. Well, actually, I did, but that was part of the problem—I wasn't supposed to feel that way about someone from the other side.

"Where's the coffee?" I said when Clarence's eyes began to flutter open.

He groaned. "Come on, man, give me a minute!"

"A minute? Angel, please. I've been lying here waiting and listening to you wheeze like an asthmatic basset hound for at least half an hour. You should get checked for whatever that is. Sleep apnea. You sounded like you were trying to swallow your tongue."

"Really?" Alarmed, he sat up.

"No. But I'm glad your heart's actually beating now. Find me coffee, and then tell me what you discovered in the Records Hall."

"You're an asshole, Bobby."

"Just trying to do the Lord's holy work."

He led me upstairs to the kitchen and got something going in a French press that looked appropriately black and strong. "Are you going to be pissed off at me if I didn't find all the stuff you wanted?" he asked.

"Depends. Talk."

He looked like a kid who was certain he'd be grounded for a month. "It's just . . . well, except for that Patrillo guy, there *wasn't* anything on any of the rest of those names."

"Really?" I gave him a stern look, but inside I was pleased. He'd passed the test, as well as confirming what I'd guessed about the names. Jose Maria Patrillo, head of some Christian charity called the Sixth Angel Foundation, was the only person whose name I'd given the kid that *wasn't* one of the names Fatback had told me showed up in connection with the Magian Society. As I'd suspected, Clarence hadn't been able to find any records on Habari or any of the others, just the ringer, Patrillo, which meant the Magian-related names all had to be pseudonyms. "Really, kid? You couldn't find *anything* on the others? Nothing at all? Not even rumors?"

"It doesn't work like that!" He looked upset at being doubted. Really it was what I had expected to hear, and I was happy to have the confirmation. It also made me feel better about Clarence's truthfulness, although by no means did it prove he was legit. "This isn't like an internet search or something," he explained as I did my best to act as though I didn't already know. "The Records are about real people, see. I found all kinds of stuff on that Patrillo guy, but all the other names—that Habari and the Germans, those others—they just don't give anything back. They're not among the living right now, if they ever were."

"Which is probably because they *aren't* real people," I said. "Cool your jets, kid. I believe that's all you found, and I don't think anyone else would have found anything more, but—"

I didn't get a chance to finish because just that moment Sheila, Clarence's roommate/surrogate mom, walked into the kitchen. She was wearing slippers and a dark green velour housecoat. "Good morning, Harrison," she fluted as she came in, then stopped, clearly a little surprised to see me. "Oh! Did your friend stay over?" Her look was confusion mixed with an unwillingness to intrude on what she obviously considered private matters.

"Yes, ma'am," I said cheerfully. "We were up so late playing Twister that I just crashed out on Harrison's floor." I turned to the kid, who had spluttered coffee down his front. "You okay, buddy?"

"Twister?" she said doubtfully.

"Yeah, it's a card game. A variant on Two-Man Stud. Hope you don't mind me spending the night. It got a bit late to drive home."

"Of course I don't mind," she said. "Do you fellows want some breakfast?"

"He might," I said, standing up. "I need to get to work. See you, Harrison. Thanks for the game."

Clarence looked as though he wished the *ghallu* had got me after all.

I only knew part of the reason that Eligor had sent his pet monster after me; I knew why he thought I had the golden feather, but not why Grasswax had blamed it on me, or exactly what kind of weird bargain the feather signified. But one thing I'd decided was that it was too much of a coincidence that Grasswax, Caz, Eligor, and I should all be involved somehow with both the disappearing souls and the disappearing feather, especially since it was now looking like it had all gone down on the same day. In fact, I was becoming more and more certain that the feather had some bearing on the whole missing-souls mess that started with Edward Walker's death. I also wanted to know why Walker and the others had been souljacked in the first place. Were they just random victims? But if so, why would Walker have been checked out so closely ahead of time, including personal visits from Habari? Was Habari working *with* the soul-stealers or against them?

The fact that the Rev. Dr. Habari and the others from apparently Magian-related groups seemed to have no independent existence only strengthened my belief in a link between Eligor's feather and the missing souls. The Magian paper trail leading to Eligor suggested that, whether or not he was the author of the Great Soul Snatch, the grand duke clearly had something to hide about his role in the whole apocalyptic mess. It also made me realize that I needed to get a better handle on the souls who had already disappeared, or at least find out enough about them to look for patterns. I needed to speed things up, and I had very little hope that the summit conference between Heaven and Hell was going to come up with answers that would help me—not with so many asses to cover, both those bearing tails and otherwise.

When I hit the Camino Real I found myself a coffee shop that looked just busy enough that I wouldn't be the only patron and ordered a late breakfast, then pulled up all the memos Fatback had sent me about the individuals in San Judas whose souls Monica had told me were among the missing. It wasn't the first time I'd looked the information over but it had been more than a few days, and I was hoping something new would jump out at me.

Even the atheist angle, which was quite strong with Walker and a few others, didn't hold up all the way through. Several of the missing souls belonged to men who seemed to have a fairly ordinary connection to religion, and one of them was even a well-known Christian minister, leader of a successful, modern, evangelical church that was big among the lapsed Catholics of Spanishtown. On the surface, the missing souls seemed to be a pretty random lot.

I had worked through hash browns, bacon, my second cup of coffee, and was poking at the fruit cup when I finally realized I'd been spending my time looking for secondary connections like neighborhoods and workplaces and committees and even children's schools without giving any attention to perhaps the most important thing they all had in common—their deaths. Walker was a suicide. Rubios, the minister, had fallen from an office balcony when a railing had given way. An esteemed Stanford researcher had slipped off a BART platform in front of a moving train with nobody nearby. The police had concluded her death was nothing but a tragic accident. The rest? Two suicides and three more natural deaths.

So there was my first question—three suicides? Wasn't that an abnormally large ratio out of seven otherwise random deaths? Had they all really chosen to take their own lives? One of the suicides had been very ill, which made it less likely that foul play was involved, but it certainly didn't rule it out.

But if Eligor or some other strategist in Hell had come up with a way to snatch the souls of the departed right under our angelic noses, why would they need to make it look like anything? Dead folks were shuffling off the mortal coil every hour, and both sides had thousands of operatives just to process those transitions to the afterlife. Why bother to hurry a few folk out of their mortal bodies just to snatch their souls? Unless some kind of special death was necessary before the soul in question could be hijacked. Was that where someone like the elusive Habari came in? To "help" the chosen out of their bodies, whether they wanted to go or not? But the Reverend Doctor seemed to have spent a lot of time hanging around with Edward L. Walker for someone whose job was simply to commit a murder. Even if it was necessary to give the mark something before he or she died—some kind of soul-collector or equally science-fictional device—it seemed like it would have been easier to have a professional pickpocket plant the thing on them before they were killed instead of sending someone like Moses Habari to pal around with the intended victim for weeks ahead of time.

No, clearly I still didn't have enough information to make sense out of the disappearing dead, or even to begin to. I sure couldn't guess what the method was, and I didn't have a clue as to the motive, either. Why steal souls and try to hide it? Not that the Opposition wouldn't have loved to be able to do it, but when there's only two players in the game, and one of them always cheats anyway, why would they bother to keep their advantage a secret? There *were* only two players in the game, weren't there . . . ?

I shuffled through the information Fatback had sent me on the deaths, all the forensics and reports from first responders, but still nothing jumped out at me except the waste of all these significant lives, many of them over before they should have been, no matter what the reason.

Then something *did* jump out at me. In fact, it damn near knocked me down and screamed "Boo!" in my face. *Significant lives.* The methods of leaving those lives may have seemed random and the lives themselves may not have had any connections with each other, but one thing *did* link them—they were all significant people.

As this struck me, I felt a prickle run up my spine. Scientists, educators, entrepreneurs, and even a minister. I scanned the list again, and now that I was looking for it, it screamed out at me: they weren't all as rich as Edward Walker by any means, but they were all accomplished people who had made their way in the world and done so very successfully. Proud people, and with good reason to be. Bright, determined, and probably articulate.

Proud people.

Struck by a sudden hunch I dialed a number I hadn't called in a while—the Walker house. I was in luck: Garcia Windhover answered the phone.

"Yo. G-Man talking at you."

"Bobby Dollar here. I need you to do me a favor."

"Sweet! I'm all over it, boss."

Boss? Did he think he was my deputy now? Or worse, my assistant? "Uh, okay. Well, if Posie's there with you I need you to get her out of the house for about two hours. Can you do that? You see, I'm worried. I think she might be in danger at her place." I explained to you how sometimes even angels like me have to stretch the truth, didn't I? "Give me a couple of hours, and I'll let you know when it's safe to go back." I explained it would be best if he could get her out of the neighborhood entirely for the afternoon.

He promised he'd give it a shot. "I'll tell her it's like a bomb threat or something."

It wasn't a very good excuse, but obviously she wasn't the most discerning young lady, either. I decided not to micromanage. "Thanks . . . G-Man. I'll be in touch in a couple of hours."

Was I feeling guilty? Good question, but I wasn't putting him and Posie in danger—the contrary, if anything. I was heading for the Walker house, and the farther they stayed away from me the better their chances of a long, happy life, since I was a bit of a disaster magnet at the moment.

I left Orban's loaner Benz around the corner from the Walker place and let myself into the yard through the side gate. The house was empty, which meant G-Man had done his job. I hadn't bothered to ask him to leave the house unlocked for me because of the terrifying possibility that if he knew I was going to be there he might sneak back to try to help me. Anyway, anybody who was in the Harps can pick a lock with his eyes closed and his hands tied. I wasn't trying to make things interesting, so I was inside in a minute or so. The house hadn't changed much, except that more dust had gathered on the books and *objets d'art* since my last visit. I got the feeling that Posie was squatting in the place more than inhabiting it. Perhaps it was going to be sold, which made it even more important that I find what I was looking for today.

There was one problem, though: I didn't actually *know* what I was looking for. As I'd reviewed Fatback's material on the local victims, I had become more and more certain that someone like Edward Lynes Walker, a successful, well-known man, wouldn't just kill himself without even trying to explain it, unless he was very, very depressed, if for no other purpose than the apology many suicides left. But Walker had no history of depression, and judging from the coverage of his death, it seemed that everybody who knew him had been astonished that he had taken his own life. It's damn hard to prove a negative, of course, and the absence of a note certainly didn't indicate murder. But if I *did* find a suicide note that others had missed, or anything that would shed some light on his frame of mind in his last days, I might be able at least to eliminate foul play and narrow my focus to what had happened after he died.

My only lucky break was that most of Edward Walker's working life seemed confined to the room he had probably called a "study," but which a later generation would have called an office; a big, sunny upstairs bedroom oriented around a handsome antique writing desk, on which his computer, a fairly expensive Dell Precision, still sat. The walls were lined with bookcases except for a low table on one side of the door and two large metal filing cabinets on the other. I didn't bother checking the computer, and not only because the police lab and probably his lawyer would have already examined it thoroughly. Although he was no doubt very technologically literate, Walker seemed to me like the old-school kind of guy who would always have a hard copy of anything important. In fact, if he was concerned enough about snoopy hackers he might not even have committed it to electronic memory. After all, Edward Lynes Walker had been born into the last analog generation.

There are two different ways to toss a room: the kind where you know what you're looking for and the kind where you don't. The first kind is easier because you can immediately eliminate a lot of things. For instance, if you're looking for a picnic basket you don't need to spend a lot of time searching in envelopes. I didn't have that luxury, so I started pulling things out of cabinet drawers as quickly as I could and setting them on the floor. After about half an hour the carpet looked like the downtown San Judas skyline crafted from piles of paper and beige cardboard, and I sat down and began working my way through.

I pulled out every sheet of paper in all of those files, one sheet at a time, and examined each one, albeit briefly. For an otherwise lazy guy

I'm pretty thorough, but at the end of the first two hours of hard grafting I hadn't come across anything out of the ordinary, although after having looked at thousands of snippets of Walker's life I was beginning to feel as if I was finally getting to know him. For one thing, just reading his business correspondence made it clear that he was no sucker. He might have had an overly keen belief in his own undefeatable good sense (which I have found is often true with engineering types) but I was equally certain he wouldn't have bought any pitch without proof. The atheism first suggested by his books seemed to arise not out of a dislike of religion per se, but from a feeling that anything that couldn't be scientifically proved wasn't worth wasting time on. Did that make him more of an agnostic than an atheist? Walker certainly hadn't been religious, no matter how you sliced it. If by some chance his disappearance had been voluntary, why would someone who didn't believe in an afterlife decide to play hide-and-go-seek with Heavenly authorities?

More than two hours had now gone by. Posie might convince her boyfriend to bring her home any time, but I wasn't ready to give up. I hurried through all the books in the office, pulling each from its shelf and inspecting it for stray envelopes or pieces of paper tucked inside, without luck. It took a long time but I was being thorough. I got all the books back into place and the room tidied just as I heard a car pull into the driveway. I wasn't panicked—I knew I could make Dozy Posie believe just about anything, and I couldn't imagine G-Man putting up much of an intellectual struggle either, but I didn't want to push my luck in case I had to get back into the house again, although I wasn't sure it would be worth it. After all, I'd failed to find what I was looking for despite a pretty thorough search, so I was beginning to doubt the sudden certainty that had set me off, a hunch that had seemed very powerful just a few hours earlier.

I hurried down the stairs and stopped dead, staring. I had completely forgotten the books in the living room shelves, most of which were art books, business manifestos, and a few novels. But right in front of me were several rows of religious material—well, antireligious, mostly—that now seemed to me like as good place to leave a suicide note as in his office. But I could hear keys rattling in the door, which meant I couldn't stay. I'd have to come back another time.

Then I saw it, down near the bottom of the nearest bookshelf, between one of Dawkins' books and Mark Twain's *Letters From the Earth*—the black leather, gilded spine of a King James Bible. As they used to sing on *Sesame Street*, "One of these things is not like the others." The front door was opening, so I just reached out and grabbed. Then the angel with the stolen bible under his coat (that would be me) sprinted through the kitchen to the back door and escaped into the yard, only seconds ahead of the bible owner's granddaughter and her faux-gangster boyfriend.

twenty-seven

the atheist's bible

I DROVE A little farther into Palo Alto, then stopped in a quiet residential street. As soon as I took out the heavy, leather-bound bible I could see that something had been pressed inside the pages, a rather fat envelope. I was lucky it hadn't dropped out during my hasty exit. The writing on it said only "To be opened after my death," in handwriting that looked like what I'd seen of a few samples of Walker's.

Jackpot. And everybody missed it but me!

I used a tissue to open the envelope, in case I needed to leave it for the police to find, and handled it the same way. Inside were at least a dozen sheets typed on thin, old-fashioned paper, which made the document seem more antique than its date only a couple of weeks back and a few days before Edward Walker's death. I took a quick look around to make certain I was alone on the quiet side street, then started to read.

To Whom It May Concern,

This is not a will, but it is a last testament of sorts. The contents should have no bearing on any of my personal affairs but I doubt the legal profession would agree with me. That is why I haven't trusted it to my attorneys. If any of my dear friends were still alive I would have given it to one of them. Sadly, that choice is no longer available to me.

Still, it is a risk to write this at all. What I am about to relate will be unbelievable to many, if not most who hear of it. However, I can assure whoever is reading this that there is nothing wrong with my mind and that I have had proofs that have more than satisfied me of everything I set out here.

Here is what I now know, which I have seen proven beyond the possibility of debate. There is life after death. The soul does exist without the body. And although most of the narrow, interfering rules of the world's organized religions are just as wrong as I always thought they were, when it comes to the basic facts I must admit that they were right and my fellow doubters and I were wrong. There is a Heaven and there is a Hell.

I attended a conference of the Atheist Alliance International in Los Angeles where I gave one of my infrequent but heartfelt lectures on the mischief caused in the world in general and America in particular by the adherents of organized religion, whether Christian, Jew, Islamist, or any number of other flavors of Theism. Afterward I was approached by a small dark-skinned man with gray hair whom I took at first to be African American. After hearing him speak I decided he might actually be African or Afro-Caribbean, since he had what sounded to my ears like a slight British accent. He told me he had enjoyed what I had to say and wished to speak to me about it. Amused and intrigued by his air of importance, I said yes.

Over coffee my new acquaintance began to ask questions, not so much about what I had said to the conference as to my actual beliefs. Did I think that God was impossible or just unlikely? Why did humans keep returning to the belief in something beyond themselves, century after century?

I could not quite understand what he was getting at, although when he finally produced a business card that read "Reverend Doctor Moses Habari" I was pretty sure I understood. I suggested that he was one of those ministers who trolls for converts in seemingly unlikely places, and that although I was not as hostile to spirituality as some of the people here, I was certainly not in attendance because I needed reinforcement of shaky beliefs (or rather non-beliefs). He laughed and said I was only partially wrong, but that what he was looking for was not men and women of weak principles who could be bent by fear into belief but instead those who could hold onto their skepticism and integrity even in the face of frightening revelations.

The word "revelation," of course, filled me with distrust, as it is one of the many code-phrases for Christian end of the world fantasies, but I did not mind the doctor's quiet, friendly company, and so we talked amiably about many things other than religion, and at his request I agreed that we would stay in touch.

For a year or so that was the precise limit of our relationship, an occasional letter. He wrote to tell me he was involved with something very important, which he wanted to show me one day, and I told him of how I kept myself busy with work. Molly had died a couple of years earlier and in all honesty I was a bit at loose ends, but I never emphasized this to Dr. Habari. Still, he must have decided that I would be ideal for his project, because although our friendship continued as a casual sort of thing, with a letter passing between us every month or month and a half, he also began to send me articles that I thought were purely political in nature, about the Third Way movement in Europe and other parts of the world, a fairly well-known attempt to find a middle ground between left-wing and right-wing political agendas.

Well, one thing I had to say about the late Edward Walker was that he certainly appeared to be lucid. He was awfully wordy, though, so I skipped lightly over the next couple of pages about Habari's interests in politics and social organization, so that I could get to what I thought of—rather ironically, as it turned out—as the good stuff.

But the day came when Dr. Habari no longer referred to his grand project in vague, sweeping generalities about "religious freedom" and "finding a new way forward," and began to talk about it as a very real thing that was now underway, and which he thought would be, as he put it, "ideal for someone like you, my dear Edward." I had been friends with Habari long enough that I no longer thought he was flacking for converts to his low-key brand of Christianity, and so I agreed to talk to him about it in more depth. "Even better, my dear Edward," he said, "I shall give you a demonstration." I had no idea what that meant. I anticipated a trip to a local outreach center or some other charitable endeavor. Even the religious folk who despair of converting me still sometimes hope to get some money out of me. A well-to-do widower makes a likely candidate for charities of all stripes.

Instead Habari came to my house one day in April, two years ago. I remember it because it was a lovely spring day, and the apricot tree by the front walk was covered in green shoots. Habari drove us across town in his battered old car, cautioning me that what I was going to see would be surprising, but that no matter what I saw and how it made me feel he was relying on my discretion afterward.

"Why?" I asked, amused. "Are we going to be breaking the law?"

"Only the laws of physics," he told me. "And they're not being broken, really. You're going to see what's behind them."

I was beginning to wonder about my soft-spoken friend—was he taking me to see some weeping Madonna miracle statue? Or something more modern, like a self-proclaimed UFO abductee? But Habari wouldn't tell me. Eventually we arrived at Stanford Hospital, parked, then made our way in and past the emergency desk. The reverend had one hand tucked in his coat pocket and a look of concentration on his face.

"Now, say nothing and do not move," he told me as we reached a momentarily empty corridor of the hospital, then waved his free hand in the air in front of us. Nothing happened, which did not surprise me, but the intent way Habari stared at the air, as if something really had happened, made me nervous. Then he withdrew his other hand from his pocket.

At first I thought he was holding some incredibly bright arc light, or even a magnesium flare, but this light did not spark and fountain like a flare, it simply shone with blinding brilliance so that I had to turn away.

"No," he said. "Be brave, Edward. And see!"

I felt his hand on my shoulder. The light he had held was suddenly gone, but another, lesser light hung in the air before us like a loop of blazing wire. He led me through it—I confess I cried out a little, thinking I would be burned—but there was no heat, and when we stepped through to the other side nothing had changed except perhaps a slight alteration in the quality of the light and an unusual echo to the sounds we made.

Habari asked me not to speak, to save my questions, then he led me down the corridor into a part of the hospital where we began to see other people again—nurses, patients, family members waiting—but every single one of them was completely motionless, as if they had been sealed in amber like prehistoric insects. I could not touch them directly—something like magnetic resistance kept me away—but I could get close enough to see that they were not imprisoned by anything, but rather that time had simply stopped. For them, all of them, but not for us. I was very frightened.

"Oh my God," I said to Habari. "What are you?"

He smiled. "Your friend, Edward. I promise you that."

He led me past the motionless staff members and toward the wards. There too, everything had stopped as if a switch had been thrown, the patients and visitors alike all still as statues. As we walked among them I could hardly breathe. Just outside one of the rooms a little Hispanic boy had been running up the corridor, but now hovered in mid air with only the tip of one foot touching the ground.

Then we stepped through into that room, and I was suddenly even more frightened, because people were moving there. Not everyone—a nurse and several family members stood beside the patient's bed, and they were just as motionless as anyone in the corridors outside, but others nearby were moving and talking among themselves. Even more disturbing was that the person on the bed, a man not much older than myself, although very thin and with many dark, ugly bruises on his skin, also stood beside the bed—looking down on his own body with a look of obvious astonishment!

I let out a gasp of despair and confusion. I was quite overwhelmed.

Then one of the moving figures turned and looked toward us. Not directly, as though we were as plain to see as everyone else, but as if he had heard something, or perhaps seen movement in the corner of his eye. But that eye and its twin were hideous, faceted like those of an insect, and the monster's face though more or less human was covered in scales like a lizard's, bright, coppery red and brown scales.

I confess I tried to run. Habari gripped my arm and would not let me go. "Do not fear," he said. "He can't see you, and if you stay quiet he'll go back to what he was doing."

I didn't want to stay quiet. I wanted to get out of that building, out of that nightmare, away from everything that I was seeing, but Habari's hold on me was astonishingly firm.

"You are looking at a prosecutor of souls," my guide told me. "Many would call him a demon. The woman at the end of the bed is what would be called an angel. She is there to defend the man who has just died. That's him, looking down at the body he has left behind. The dead man's name is Morton Kim, and he is a good man, a kind man. I think his afterlife will be a happy one."

The thing with the bug eyes was not looking at us any more, not even as Habari spoke in an ordinary, conversational tone. "Why don't they hear you?" I asked. "Who are you?"

Habari only shook his head. His right hand, the one that had blazed like the sun just a few moments ago, looked almost ordinary as he held it up now, although it still seemed to glow slightly. "They don't hear me because at the moment I am a servant of someone more powerful than either of them."

"You mean, like God?"

He smiled. "We're all servants of the Highest—even Fishspine there, Hell's prosecutor. But my sponsor is at least more powerful than either this angel or this demon. Now let's leave them to their business."

He led me out of the room and down the corridors again until we found the glowing hole through which we had entered. When we stepped through it, all was as it had been. A few seconds later an orderly rounded the corner, moving like every human I had ever seen before this hour. He glanced at us briefly and without interest, then continued on his way.

Habari didn't explain anything about what had happened as he drove me back. He didn't lecture or solicit or proselytize. He didn't need to. What I had seen was so far beyond anything I'd ever experienced that I was shaking like a man with a fever. He took me home, poured me a glass of wine, then made himself a cup of tea and sat with me until I was feeling a little less overcome. He left me with promises to return the next day and discuss our "adventure" as he called it.

Whoever you are, reading this, you probably already have several ideas to explain what happened to me—hypnosis, drugs, perhaps just ordinary mental illness. I had all these thoughts myself, so after a nearly sleepless night, I was quite angry by the time Habari returned. He seemed to have expected this reaction and took me on another journey, this time to an apartment building in the Ravenswood district.

"It's sad—there's been an electrocution," he said. "Faulty hair dryer."

The scene was much the same but without the doctors and nurses. The paramedics were strapping the body of a middle-aged woman to a gurney, but when we went through the shining opening her soul was out of the body, watching the ambulance workers and the heartbroken grandchild who had found her, weeping as if her heart was broken. Within moments an advocate angel and a demon prosecutor both appeared, the former a young man with luminous features, the latter another young man without a head, but with a face in the middle of his naked torso. The deceased woman looked at him with fear, but the handsome young man stepped up and spoke to her, calming her.

"Smearhawk," said Habari, nodding at the headless demon. "As a prosecutor he's a tough opponent, but I think he'll be unlucky here."

And then the judge appeared.

We once bought a toy for one of the children's birthdays, a device that attached to the hose like a sprinkler and sent showers of water up and down and around as it spun like a merry-go-round. The kids loved it and played with it that whole summer. At just the right angle the sun's rays would make a wonderful shining rainbow that hung where the water sprayed, staying in one place even though the water itself was rising and falling and spurting out in all directions as the sprinkler device revolved.

The heavenly judge was like one of those, a frozen shower of light, but awesome and frightening, too.

"We should go," Habari whispered to me. "The Powers aren't like the lower angels. He might detect us if we remain too long."

Over the next several days Dr. Habari took me on several more of these astounding journeys outside of the life we know, until even I had to admit that if I was being tricked I could not imagine how he was doing it. Once I conceded this he told me that perhaps now I was ready to hear the truth—the real truth. But he wanted more from me than simply to recruit another believer.

"What is the point, Edward," he asked me on the day he finally explained it all, "of surrendering yourself to the very same arbitrary rules and bullying use of power you fought against on Earth? You stood up for what you believed even when it was difficult—what your mind and heart told you must be true."

"But it wasn't true," I said. "That's just the point. I was wrong."

"Ah, but only as to the nature of the battlefield. The conflict is just as fierce as you perceived."

I was confused and told him so. What conflict did he mean?

What he meant, he explained to me over the course of a long afternoon and evening, was that there were dissident elements in Heaven itself—it still seems so strange to say that, so old-fashioned!—that felt the fate of man was too arbitrary, that sentences which could never be appealed made no sense for eternal entities like souls, that Heaven itself had become hidebound and dictatorial. Instead of a timeless home for weary souls it had become a place where rules strangled freedom and dogma had overcome the birthright of all humans, which was the right to question, a gift that their Creator had blessed them with. The elements of which Habari spoke, felt that it was time for a change. They were the ones behind Habari's Magian Society—a very different kind of charity organization than I had suspected!

As he detailed his complaints with the ordering of Heaven I began to look at him with more than a little fear.

"Oh, my lord!" I said. "Are you . . . a servant of the Devil?" Now that I believed in Heaven I had to believe in Hell, too. Had the leer of the great Enemy of Mankind been hidden behind Habari's kindly, philosophical mask this whole time?

He laughed. He laughed very hard. "No, no, no!" he finally managed to say. "Not me. The plight of the citizens of Hell is far worse than anything we face in Heaven. No, although there are doubtless more than a few souls trapped there who deserve better, there are far more who have done things so terrible that any ordinary Creator would have destroyed them instantly. God's mercy, and His plans, are still a mystery beyond any of our complete understanding." He shook his head. "No, my master and my colleagues and I represent something different. Do you remember some of the articles I sent you? About political philosophy?"

"Certainly," I said. "About the, what was it called? The Third Way?" But then, as the old expression goes, the penny finally dropped. "Is that what you represent? Some breakaway sect?"

"We do not wish to break away from Heaven so much as we hope to coexist," he told me. "That is where one of our names comes from—the Magians. The Wise Men brought three gifts, you see, representing three different ways. Because that is what we wish to become, Edward. A middle path. A third way."

He went on to tell me that he and his colleagues had found (or created—it was not clear) a place beyond the mortal Earth for the souls of the dead, a place that did not belong to either Heaven or Hell, and that they were founding a sort of free state for those who had done good things in life but would not be happy delivered into a rigid, rule-bound afterlife where happiness was imposed. Habari's rebels wanted free-thinkers, people who would benefit from this alternative third way.

"People like you, Edward," he told me, patting my hand. "You are a perfect candidate. You will be the first, but you will not be the only one—not for long."

I asked him if he wasn't frightened about what God would think of them—of us. For the first time in my life I had to seriously consider the jealous God of the Old Testament, and it terrified me.

"I've never seen the Highest," he said. "And there are others far, far higher in Heaven's hiearchy than me who say they've never seen the Highest either, or received any indication that He, in fact, is ruling Heaven. We're not resisting God, Edward—we're resisting heavenly inertia."

"But what if those are the same thing? Aren't you afraid?"

"I've prayed on this," Habari told me. "We all have. And one answer keeps coming, although I suspect it is only the answer of my own logic. We've made our intentions plain enough, at least to the Highest we all worship in our secret hearts. He has done nothing to stop us. Does that not suggest that He might not care—or might even approve of what we do?

I sat for a moment staring at Walker's typewritten letter. I felt, as Edward Lynes Walker himself must have felt—like a man who had been swimming near the shore and suddenly realized the current was pulling him far, far out to sea. Could this be real? Did Habari truly represent some dissident faction of Heaven or was he an agent of Eligor's? Or could he even be Eligor himself? Clearly, whatever he was, the being who called himself Moses Habari had abilities I didn't quite understand. If he had taken Walker, a living man, through a Zipper to Outside and then showed him a soul about to be judged, without either the prosecutor or the advocate knowing he was there, he was doing something so far beyond the rules I knew that it might as well have been magic. The higher angels and, presumably, the higher demons can do things we rank-and-file can't, but they are also very powerfully limited by the Conventions when they manifest on Earth, even Outside. I could believe that Habari and his lot (if he wasn't some kind of lone wolf) might be willing to break the Conventions, but how could they get away with it? The whole system was set up to make sure a Principality or a Hell-Duke couldn't just go strolling around Mortalville breaking the rules. I couldn't even imagine how anyone could get around it and still do what Habari had done.

I didn't have any answers. I felt like Woodward and Bernstein talking to Deep Throat in a Washington garage, learning that their story reached all the way to the White House. But I doubted that either of those two reporters worried that their discoveries might threaten not only their immortal souls but also the very foundations of the universe.

I really, really wanted a drink. Instead, I went back to reading the extraordinary document that had been hidden in the atheist's bible.

But even as I began, in the days and weeks ahead, to believe more and more in what Habari and his colleagues were trying to do, there was a sticking point: to be certain the experiment would work (and it was going to be an experiment, an unprecedented one, since Habari said no soul had ever before been stolen out from under the noses of Heaven and Hell) this first "extraction," as he put it, would have to be performed like a military operation, with care, precision, and perfect timing. That would not permit waiting for the first volunteer to die a natural death. Needless to say, I was not pleased to learn this.

"You are our ideal candidate, Edward," he flattered me, "but in the time we might wait for nature to take its course with you we will lose hundreds, perhaps thousands of other suitable souls to our twin rivals." Naturally I asked him if they couldn't find someone else like-minded who was already close to death, but he said no. Perhaps it could be done when they were certain it worked, he explained, but to begin with they wanted someone strong in mind and body at the end, someone prepared and fully understanding what was to happen.

"But what about my wife?" I asked. "I'll lose the chance to be reunited with her after death!" Now that I believed in life after death, I wanted nothing more than to see Molly again.

Habari looked sad. "Even if you saw her, Edward, you wouldn't know her," he said. "And she would certainly not know you. The souls of the departed do not keep their memories, or at least, that is what we understand. Those who speak for the Highest are close-mouthed about it, but we do know that the departed do not simply go on as the people that they were, at least not in Heaven. Sadly, the same is not true in Hell. This is one reason a third way was needed. But we have a greater goal, and although I can't tell you what it is, I can at least say that if we are successful in all we plan, it is possible that one day you and your Molly will be truly reunited, this time for eternity."

I mourned a long time over this, but at last, after much soul-searching (a phrase that means quite different things to me now, than it did only a short time earlier) I agreed to be the Magians' guinea pig. Habari and I began planning my death. . . .

I skimmed through the next two pages, which was about how Walker put his affairs in order but without making it obvious what he planned. I'm sure he was not the first prospective suicide to have done such a thing, but he was certainly the first to do it while planning to scam both Heaven and Hell. My admiration for Walker grew as I thought about it. What he had done took guts, real guts. Like one of the early astronauts he had been given a lonely role to play, but without the potential for glory if he succeeded. He even referred to himself as an "after-naut," a joking term he had picked up from Habari.

Disappointingly but unsurprisingly, Walker had very little to say about what was supposed happen to him after he connected the hose to the exhaust pipe of his 7 Series BMW, except that he had been assured he need do nothing, and that Habari and his "people" (a pretty dubious term, I think you'd agree) would handle all the details. I couldn't help wondering whether they had succeeded. Certainly Walker's soul had gone *somewhere*. I had been an eyewitness to that.

He closed with part of a poem by a writer whose name I didn't recognize, R. W. Raymond.

> *Life is eternal; and love is immortal; and death is only a horizon; and a horizon is nothing save the limit of our sight.*

He signed the last page,

Yours in hope,
Edward Lynes Walker

twenty-eight

going to mecca

I FEEL WEIRD admitting it, but the first person I thought of calling when I finished reading Walker's astonishing letter was not Sam, or Monica, or even my bosses upstairs (although I'd have to, of course) but Caz. Since we'd parted, I'd been carrying around the memory of what we'd done together—how we'd *been* together—and I still couldn't find a proper place for it in either my heart or my head. Thoughts of her kept drifting through my head like sun showers, and like sun showers I couldn't tell whether they were a relief to my feverish mind or precursors of bigger, darker storms to come. What the hell, literally, had I been thinking? What was I doing? How could I hope to keep something like this hidden from Heaven?

But, oh, dear God, how I missed her. It hadn't been just lust, or even simply love—as if that could ever be simple. We had felt right together. We were twin souls separated by a million years' history of war and hatred and treachery. If the whole thing hadn't been so painful, it might have been funny. I mean, was there ever a more doomed relationship?

I sure can pick 'em.

But now it was time for your friend Bobby Dollar to force himself back to the issue that was literally at hand, the pages of Edward Walker's confession-slash-suicide-note piled in my lap. Everything Habari had told Walker might be true, of course—clearly, he was no ordinary reverend doctor. But Walker still might have been duped, especially if

Habari was working for someone like Eligor—which, after hearing about the powers Habari had exhibited, seemed increasingly likely. I had already established a tenant/landlord connection between the Magians and the grand duke; not exactly a smoking gun, but in this game, I find coincidences generally pretty suspicious. Heaven moves in mysterious ways and so does Hell, but they have their fingers everywhere and seldom by accident.

Whatever my own speculations were, though, I had to make a report to my bosses and quickly. I may be a lousy angel and a grumpy, ungrateful employee, but I'm not a fool, and Walker's story could represent the thin end of the wedge for some Opposition plan to short-hop each and every human soul after death. Even if it was something less dire than that, it was still way too big for me to be coy about what I'd found. Honor, duty, and the always-popular covering of my own precious *tuchis* mandated contacting Heaven as quickly as possible.

Not because I was going to tell her any of this, but just because I had to do something about the ache I've already mentioned, I called Caz on the emergency number she'd given me. I was close to blurting out actual feelings but had a sudden, frightening image of a Heavenly court martial playing back the voicemail while they all shimmered ominously at me, so I left her a bloodless message to the effect that I wanted to speak to her, then headed across town toward the company office to make my report.

I tried Sam's phone, too, but only got his voicemail. I hoped that meant Monica and the others no longer needed to sit vigil by his bedside answering his calls. On top of all my other worries I felt like a total jerk that I couldn't visit my best friend, but there was no sense borrowing trouble. I rang The Compasses and had a brief chat with Chico. To my relief, he reported that Sam was out of danger, which meant he was not going to have to get another body. Getting a new one is an iffy thing at the best of times—lots of recuperation and a recovery pattern that, though faster, isn't that different from a stroke victim's. Of course, after Leo's death on what I thought of as the Heavenly operating table, I have a deeper distrust of the process than most of my peers.

"What about me?" Chico asked as I was trying to wrap up the call. "No, 'How's it going, buddy?' No, thanks for saving your scrawny *culo* the other night? While getting the shit kicked out of my bar by some kind of crazy old-school demonic motherfucker? *Chupa mi verga,* Dollar!" Chico thinks he's Mexican, and not just in appearance—he thinks his *soul* is Mexican. Maybe it is, but I don't know how being part of *La Raza* can survive death and angelic transformation. Still, why argue with a grumpy bastard who keeps an automatic shotgun full of silver salts within arm's reach?

"Sorry, man. What can I say? I'm in your debt. I didn't know you were that badass."

"Only when I need to be." He sounded mollified. "Anyway, it's tough out there. You take care, BD. "

"Trying my best, *hombre*."

I parked around the block in case Eligor's men were staking out our office, then slipped in over the fence from the courtyard of the office building next door. Alice's desk was next to a window. She watched me climb, cling, then awkwardly drop as if I were a very unimpressive clown performing at a child's party. "Not getting enough exercise, Dollar?" she asked after I mounted the stairs and stumbled in.

I was still puffing a little as I dropped into a chair to examine the hole I'd just torn in my pants. I was running out of jeans, and I was going to have to start wearing something sturdier, like those ugly tactical khakis. "No, it's just that visiting you always brings out the swashbuckling romantic in me, Alice."

She shook her head. "Save the bullshit. I got a lousy chimichanga from GoGo Burrito and it's backing up on me. I'm going home early. What do you want?"

"I need to send a p-mail. Private, too. I have to do it myself."

She raised an eyebrow. "Ooh, you really *are* a man of action, Dollar. I'm all aflutter . . . but that might just be that chimichanga." She gestured vaguely toward the inner office door. "You know where it is. I'm going to lock up, and you can let yourself out. Do *not* try to sleep here."

"I'm not homeless!"

"You will be if you keep gouging your expense account for fancy motels."

"Fancy? These are the kind of places that make you use the last guest's soap."

She rolled her eyes and went back to whatever she had to finish before she gave herself the rest of the day off.

Sam always calls sending a private prayer-mail "going to Mecca," not because you're surrounded by other pilgrims but because the process itself is less like one of those baroque churches full of golden clouds and plaster cherubs and more like that big block of stone that all the Islamic faithful go to see. The room is small and has no windows. The only thing in it is a standard wooden desk, and the only chair in the room is facing it instead of behind it. On top of the desk is a big black blotter like you'd see in an insurance office, and sitting unceremoniously on top of that is a cube of clear crystal about a foot and a half square. At least I always assumed it's crystal—maybe it's some cheap glass thing they bought in one of those home decorator stores. It wouldn't shock me. One thing about my bosses, at least in their operations here on Earth: they're more into making things work than making things look good.

I sat in front of the cube and composed myself. I had my eyes shut, because if they were open when the light of Heaven came I'd have been seeing a shiny green cube in front of everything for the next half hour. I mean, it really scorches your optic nerves. So I waited. I saw the first great flash against my eyelids and then the light dimmed down to a healthier level, and I opened up.

What's the light of Heaven look like on earth? Like sunlight streaming through the clouds in the tackiest garage sale painting you ever saw. Really, it's so beautiful it's embarrassing. No subtlety whatsoever.

A voice spoke. As far as I know it was only in my head, one of those sweet, indefinable angel voices that could be either male or female.

God loves you, Angel Doloriel. The question, "So why are you bothering us?" was, as always, only implied.

I spoke the formula for a secure report, then described what I had just found and read. When I was finished, I took the envelope out of my pocket and showed it to the cube, then held the pages up one after another in front of that giant paperweight full of clouds and bright sunlight. When I'd finished the sweetly androgynous voice said, *Your report has been received.*

I was just getting up to go when the voice came again. *Archangel Temuel will speak to you.* I was a little surprised.

Doloriel, I've just seen your message. My supervisor was nothing but a voice coming from the brilliant clouds. *This makes it all the more important that you attend the summit conference, which has now been officially decreed. Be my eyes and ears.*

Which was a weird thing to say. Because the summit conference was going to be as stuffed with angels as a clown car full of guys in big shoes. Did Temuel mean he wanted me to be his own private source? I could understand that, I guess—anybody who's ever worked in a bureaucracy could—but coupled with his remark about my misremembering his Clarence comment, it unsettled me a bit.

I didn't reveal that, of course. "Just give me the details."

It starts this Friday. You won't have to travel far. It will be at the Ralston Hotel, in your city.

I probably looked a little surprised. I don't know if they can actually see us through the heaven box, but I explained my reaction anyway. "Right here in Jude? Not in, I don't know, Vatican City or something? Vegas? I know those Hell guys love to convention in Vegas."

Perhaps because the . . . problem began in San Judas, our superiors and the Opposition both think it would be the best place to discuss the issues. Did he sound a little worried or was he just irritated with me for asking questions? *And as you can guess, Angel Doloriel, there are many issues, crucially important issues, and your new report only adds fuel to a fire that is already burning. Can I count on your focus and cooperation?*

The Bobby Dollar credo: When speaking with management, answer anything that could have more than one meaning as though the obvious one is the only one you noticed. "Of course, Archangel. Thank you for your confidence in me."

You're welcome. And thank you for your hard work on the Walker case. I'm sure your report will cause quite a stir in the highest circles.

And with those even more ambiguous words he was gone. The cube mellowed to a faint golden glow, then even that vanished, but not before something about the unearthly quality of the flaring light caught my attention. I couldn't help thinking about Habari's astonishing display of power, of how Edward Walker had talked about the reverend doctor's hand glowing like a magnesium flare when he opened a Zipper in that hospital. Had it been the same brilliant, ineffable light I had just closed my eyes against? Could Habari somehow be connected to Heaven after all? Or could Hell mimic that very, very recognizable radiance? I supposed it was possible—after all, that was the Devil's traditional schtick, to seem fair but be foul, or something like that. But then again, it was a living mortal who had been tricked, so maybe they hadn't needed to work all that hard. I suddenly wondered if someone like me could perform that trick, too—if any angel could do it.

I left the office doors locked behind me and clambered back over the fence into the courtyard of the little office complex next door. When my feet hit the ground, I turned and found myself about a foot away from a grinning, corpselike face. I had my new automatic from Orban out and my finger on the trigger before I realized it was my dancing acquaintance, Mr. Fox.

"Jesus!" I said, taking a step back and putting the gun in my pocket. I hate to take religious names in vain—it's frowned on for guys in my line of work—but sometimes it just jumps out. "What are you doing sneaking up on me? I almost shot you!"

"No sneaking, Dollar man! Saw you climbing over the fence and thought we must have a chitter-chat." He laughed and did a quick time step. Only then did it occur to me to look around the offices facing the courtyard. Only one employee sat at a window desk, a young black woman, but she was staring at me and the paper-white Asian guy with alarm. She was also fumbling blindly for her phone.

"Come on." I headed for the way out. "Tell your story walking. I think that lady's calling the cops."

"No fear. Foxy has friends on the police. Friends everywhere."

"I'm glad to hear you're so popular. I'm not."

We reached my car, and he hopped into the passenger seat without being asked. He looked around appreciatively, like I was his prom date and this was the limo. "You don't have your old car anymore, Mister Bobby."

"No. Where can I drop you?"

"Doesn't matter," he said, just brimming with good cheer as I put it in drive. "When we going to do some more business, Mister BD? Only two of our auction crowd shot dead—many more to choose from!"

I weighed whether there was anything to be gained from further exploration in that direction, but after seeing how quickly and savagely Eligor had jumped on our "secret auction," I didn't really want to put any more people in harm's way.

"I think I'm out of the artifact-selling business."

He gave me a look of comical sorrow. "Truly? But there are many adventures yet to be had! Are you certain? I could conduct things in a more discreet manner—only one buyer at a time, strictly vetted by yours truthfully, Foxy Foxy!"

I was beginning to wonder if this guy was going to be popping up unexpectedly for the rest of my life. "No. Seriously, no. I don't want to sell anything."

"Pull over here," he said abruptly. We were in the middle of a street a few blocks from Beeger Square. "Think it over, Dollar Bob. There are oh-so many ways to do this!"

Frustration momentarily overcame discretion. "Look, I don't *have* it. I don't have the feather. I *never* had it, but I was trying to find out what everyone thought I had. Now I know, so I don't need any more buyers." I pulled over into a bus stop in front of Survival of the Fittest. Various people on running, spinning, and rowing machines inside watched as the door swung open and Fox popped out in all his pale, pirouetting splendor. He was laughing again but his eyes were sharp, and his affect was the most serious I'd seen from him. "Ah, don't try to fool the Fox, D-man. Foxy knows better. Do you think I put my so-good reputation on the line, if I didn't know for certain you had the feather? I smelled it on you."

"What . . . ?"

He leaned back into the car, still twitching his skinny butt in front of the gym window. It must have looked to the membership like I was dropping off some hustler I'd picked up down at the waterfront. The expression on Fox's face was so odd, I briefly considered bailing out of the driver's door: he was, well, baring his upper teeth and whiffling his nostrils. Yes, I said whiffling. I don't even know what it means, but that was what he was doing.

He nodded. "I still smell it. Maybe not so strong now, but the smell of a big angel is something Foxy knows very well!" He laughed again and backed out of the car. "Let me know when you are done telling silly tales. Remember: Foxy Foxy is your actual friend, Mister Bob from Heaven. He does not take sides. He wants to help you!" He gave me the smallest hint of a jazz-hands finale, then sauntered away whistling something that sounded like a Mongolian show tune.

As I sat there wondering what the hell he had been talking about, how I could smell like something I never had, and what kind of weird thing the slippery, strange Mr. Fox might actually *be*, my phone rang. It was Caz's number.

"I'm glad you called," I said quickly. "I really want to talk to you."

She hesitated for a moment before she spoke. Her voice was strange, flat. "I'm sorry, I just wanted to let you know I won't be available until later today. I'm in an important meeting."

"You can't talk now? Okay, when? I really need—"

"Yes, thank you. I'm glad to hear that everything's going well." And then she hung up.

I had only seconds to sit wondering what *that* had all been about before the phone rang again; an even more familiar number.

"Sam?"

"So we're on a first name basis, huh? That's nice to know after you nearly got me killed and then didn't even visit me while I was lying in the hospital, a crippled wreckage."

"Sam, I wanted to! But Monica told me I shouldn't—"

"Man, get your panties unbunched—I'm just giving you shit. What's up?"

"How are you? Are you still in the hospital?"

"Broke out this morning. People with bedpans are looking for me in five states. You want to get lunch?"

It was after three in the afternoon but I hadn't eaten since breakfast. "Yeah, sure. How about someplace nobody knows us?"

He suggested a Burmese place I'd never heard of in the Mayfield district, and I said I'd meet him.

As I was tooling up Broadway I saw the beggar guy I'd met the first time I'd gone looking for Fox, and it reminded me of something I'd been wondering earlier. I pulled over in a loading zone and walked out to the traffic island where he and his GOD BLESS YOU sign sat waiting for people to drop money in his cardboard box. It didn't look like many people had bothered to contribute. I examined him carefully as I approached, but he didn't seem to be anything but what he appeared, another sad character who'd fallen through the cracks of modern life. Here in Jude we've got lot of homeless vets hanging around downtown, and he had that look, right down to the fatigue jacket that had to be a bit hot on this warm early spring day. "Tell you what," I said, taking a twenty out of my wallet and displaying it. "I'm going to show you something. If you can describe it to me, you get this."

His expression went from interested to sour. "Oh, man, you ain't going to wiggle your johnson at me, are you? I don't play that way."

"No, no. Nothing like that." I looked around to make sure nobody was nearby, then I carefully opened a Zipper (the Heavenly kind—get your mind out of the gutter) which hung in the air just at the edge of the concrete island, bright in the middle of its line but diffuse at the edges, like the arc of a marine welder. "What do you see?"

He followed my pointing finger. "Umm . . . I don't know, man. That car dealership? Or that tall place there, the one with the dude washing the windows?"

"No, not the buildings. Right here. Just in front of you."

He looked sad. "I don't know what you want me to say, man. You pointing at a car?" He squinted, facing right at the Zipper which hung only a foot or two away. "Something else?"

"Look, I'm going to take your arm. Just walk a step this direction. I know it's weird, but I'm . . . I'm checking atmospheric changes. Just tell me if you feel or see anything out of the ordinary." I took his spindly upper arm and guided him forward. He felt like he was getting ready to run. One more step and he was standing right in the Zipper—or rather, right where it would be if it existed for him. But he couldn't pass through it, even with me touching him.

"Hey, I don't . . ." He was getting nervous now. I let go.

"Never mind, man, that's exactly what I needed. Here's your money."

I left him there, looking after me as he rubbed his thumb back and forth across his new twenty. Clearly, whatever Habari could manage, an average earthbound angel like me couldn't get an ordinary mortal into a Zipper.

As I got back in my car the phone ran again. Caz this time.

"Hello? Can you talk now?"

"For a minute," she said. Her voice was still flat, which frightened me. She sounded like something had hollowed her out.

"Then I'll make this quick—I really need to see you."

"No." And for the first time I could hear something else—pain. "No, we can't. It was a mistake. All of it."

"It wasn't! Nothing that . . . nothing that good could be a mistake. Not if you felt the same."

"I can't." Her voice was ragged. "Don't you understand? It's impossible. *We're* impossible. Forget it ever happened. Forget me. Just . . . look after yourself, Bobby. Because things are going to get bad."

"Caz, wait—!"

"Don't call me any more. Pretend it was a dream, like I'm doing. Even in Hell we dream sometimes."

And then she was gone. I kept calling back, but she wouldn't pick up.

twenty-nine
sand point

SAM LOOKED rough, but anyone who wasn't an angel would have looked a lot worse. He had purple-grey bruises on his face and an impressive zigzag-shaped scar on his forehead. He also walked like he had rickets. "Try the little pancakes with dipping sauce," he said, wincing as he slid onto the bench across from me. "They're real good."

"You look like shit. I thought we were going someplace nobody knows us."

"These people have two restaurants, one down near Shoreline that I go to all the time. I've never been to this one."

I nodded, then ordered the pancakes and what appeared to be a spicy beef casserole. They didn't have any Burmese beer so I had a Singha instead, which is at least from the same part of the world. Sam had some kind of fish soup thing and a ginger ale. "And get the bread," he said. "It's like Indian bread with lots of layers, a cardiac's worth of butter in each piece."

"You look better than I thought you would," I told him. "But then it's hard to separate the new damage from all the preexisting ugly."

He laughed, then told me about his time in the hospital. Apparently the people there had heard about the gas pipe explosion at The Compasses (the official story our fixers had chosen) and he got lots of sympathy from the staff. Sam being Sam, just listening to him describe the various nurses and orderlies and their conversations kept me entertained until the food arrived.

He downed his ginger ale and called for another. The woman behind the counter looked at him as if he'd asked for the space shuttle to be summoned, but eventually brought him another bottle. "Okay," he said. "Your turn, B. Now you tell me why you look like you misplaced your dick and the replacement's going to take six weeks to get shipped here from Korea."

"That obvious, huh?" I couldn't help smiling. "I'm glad you didn't get snuffed, Sammy. I don't know anyone else who says silly shit like that."

I wasn't going to tell him about Caz, not because he would have been horrified (I don't think he would have been) but because I didn't want to put him in a position where he would have to lie to our bosses to protect me. I don't even know if it's possible to lie to Heaven, except the way I'd already been doing it, by omission. Instead I told him what he was going to hear about soon anyway, which was Edward L. Walker's last statement to the living world.

When I got to the part where Habari took Walker through to Outside, Sam paused with a look of incredulity on his face and a long noodle dangling from his fork. "No shit? He took the guy through a Zipper while he was still alive? How?"

"Just wait. It gets weirder." I gave him the rest, including Habari's claim that he was part of some kind of "third way." Sam waved a piece of *platha* bread in irritation. "I don't give a damn about the philosophy, but the rest is bullshit. You can't take a living mortal Outside. At least folks like you and me can't. Maybe Hell's winning the technology race, but I'll bet it was some kind of trick."

I doubted this because the whole thing Walker had described was too much like what we angels and our counterparts experienced when we use the Zippers, but I had to agree with Sam about it not usually working on mortals; the guy with the GOD BLESS sign was probably still wondering what I'd been trying to get him to look at.

"But what if it's not, Sam? What if this kind of shit is really going on in our own building?"

"Look, B, we all know God didn't make the world perfect. If He'd made his angels perfect there wouldn't even be a Hell, right? He must have given them all freedom of choice just like He gave all the folks down here on Earth, otherwise there wouldn't have been a rebellion in Heaven, and the losers wouldn't have all wound up down in the boiler room. So even if this is some kind of conspiracy—and we're a long way from knowing that for sure—it's still business as usual. Right?"

"I guess so." But it did make me feel a bit better. That's what I love about Sam. He's like one of those airline pilots who can get on the microphone as you're spiraling straight down at four hundred miles an hour and say, "By the way, you may have noticed we're experiencing a few difficulties, but we've got everything under control." He might be lying to you, but it beats the crap out of, *"Oh, fuck no, we're all going to die!"*

"Anyway," I said, "now there's this big conference at the Ralston about missing souls, big swinging dicks from both sides, and I'm supposed to go. I'll probably have to answer a bunch of questions about the Walker thing now, too."

"You'll be fine, it'll be neutral ground."

"Yeah, but I still don't know how I wound up in the center of this thing. Why me? What did I do?"

Sam had an odd look on his face. For half a second I thought he was going to say something truly startling, but instead he leaned forward and snagged my last two pancakes off my plate, then gulped them down.

"Hah! Fortune favors the faster eater," he said. "Look, don't sweat the summit, B. I'll be along to keep you out of trouble."

I had half-hoped he might volunteer, but I really didn't want him to get hurt again helping me. "Naw. You've got your own work to do, you poor creaky old bastard, and you're just out of the hospital."

He grinned. "Technically I'm not out of the hospital, I'm just taking a really long crap. I left a note on my pillow saying I'd be right back. Besides, you didn't hear the rest of what I was going to say. I have to go to the conference anyway, so I've already got the time off work. Young Clarence is going to take all my clients. I don't know what they're going to do about yours, though—they'll have to train a chimp or something."

"You?" This surprised me. "Why are *you* going?"

"Because the call where Walker failed to show was originally mine, remember? It only got rolled over to you when I couldn't take it. So I have an order to appear. Didn't the Mule tell you?"

I was definitely beginning to wonder about the Mule but I didn't say so. If I let myself get any more conspiracy-crazy I was going to wind up as one of those guys who call in late-night talk shows to explain how America faked the moon landing. But it did remind me of something. "By the way, how's the kid coming along? I know you're letting him work on his own now, but what do you think of him? Ever find out how he got jumped out of Records directly into a field office?"

Sam shrugged. "Nope. I asked around, but nobody at Records would cop to knowing anything. And *he* sure doesn't seem to. Maybe someone in a high position recognized him, if you know what I mean." There's a consistent strain of paranoid thinking among us earthbound angels that even though we don't remember our previous lives, our bosses almost certainly do.

"Yeah, maybe," I said.

"Maybe is the new definitely," Sam said. "Get used to it, Bobby my boy. You have to learn to embrace uncertainty."

"That's the kind of shit you used to say when you drank," I told him. I may have said it a little more sourly than I meant to: he had reminded me not just of the Mule but of my night with Caz, too. Besides, if an angel falling in love with a demon didn't count as embracing uncertainty, what would?

"Yeah, you're right." He downed his ginger ale and reached for his wallet. "And believe me, when that horn-headed whatchamacallit of yours was kicking my ass, I was definitely rethinking my choice to go straight. I mean, who wants to die sober?"

"Even worse," I said, pushing a ten and a five across the table for my share, "who wants to die sober more than once?"

I dropped Sam off at his apartment in Southport and drove slowly back up the Bayshore, not by choice but because the rush hour had begun, and the traffic was moving at walking speed. Normally I'd take surface streets but Orban's Benz had decent air conditioning, and I was in no hurry. I had nowhere to go, after all—I hadn't picked a motel for the night yet, and I'd just finished eating. When I finally got tired of staring at other people's brake lights I got off the freeway and followed Bay Avenue east from the Palo Alto district, headed out toward the Ralston Hotel. The office complexes and condos along the bay front had all been full just a few years back, during the last internet boom, but harder times had driven a lot of the new tenants back into cheaper parts of town or out of the area entirely. I could see a lot of "For Lease" signs and a lot of untended grounds. It was kind of depressing, but I wasn't on a sightseeing tour, so I followed the curving road past offices and warehouses, through East Bayshore all the way out to Sand Point, a jutting finger of land which had long, long ago been the site of an important lighthouse. The antique lighthouse tower still stood just beyond the hotel at the end of the point like a younger brother waiting for an older sibling before going in to swim, and I knew they kept the light shining picturesquely out over the water at night, but I doubted it was any use now except as a post card item.

The Ralston was one of those big old places built in the earliest years of the twentieth century, and although it had been kept up very nicely and had even undergone an extensive renovation in the late 1990s, it still looked strangely out of place, looming up all by itself in front of the sullen green bay. It seemed like it should be the centerpiece of a city block, like the Mark Hopkins in San Francisco or the Waldorf in New York, but there was no city block around it, just a few smaller office complexes perched a respectful distance away on either side. Despite the big flag snapping in the stiff bay breeze atop the green copper roof and all the cars in the parking lot down below, the hotel seemed strangely solitary, like the statue of Ozymandias Shelley describes standing forgotten in the middle of the desert.

The words of the poem came back to me, but from what part of my memory I couldn't tell; I couldn't remember actually reading it during my angel years. Seepage from my past life, maybe. Our bosses claim it doesn't happen, but most of us don't believe them.

Round the decay of that colossal wreck, boundless and bare,
The lone and level sands stretch far away . . .

No matter how I tried to concentrate on the banks of flowers in vast planters outside or the bright striped awning that fluttered over the front entrance like a king's coronation train, I couldn't make myself like the look of the place. After another couple of minutes I turned my car around and headed back, westward into the setting sun.

As I got back on the freeway I tried Caz again, but she still wasn't picking up, and I couldn't think of anything I hadn't already said in the previous three messages. The traffic was still bad, so I peeled off a few exits before I'd planned and headed up the Woodside Highway. On a sudden whim I picked a place just at the edge of Spanishtown called the Mission Rancho Motor Lodge and checked in, taking a room at the far end of the top floor overlooking the local park. I wasn't exactly certain why the place called to me but it did, and I've learned to trust my instincts.

I didn't figure it out until I got back from a late dinner of *tacos al pastor* at a little place in the neighborhood and dragged a chair out onto the balcony to watch the lights come on. Not too far away, at the edge of the park and almost hidden by the apartment buildings and commercial buildings that had sprung up on all sides of it, stood the hacienda silhouette of Mission San Judas Tadeo, the place where the whole crazy, haunted city had got its start. The mission building was dark except for a light over the front door, and the streetlights in the park barely bounced back off the adobe facade; even so, the low building looked welcoming, like a campfire would to someone wandering lost in the woods. As I sat staring at the mission, thinking about the poor Indian bastards who had been shanghaied into building it for the Spanish priests, something clicked into place—not about the big questions I was grappling with but about why I was there at that moment, and why I'd had that reaction to the Ralston Hotel. All that gilt and carved stone, the sheer size of the place, had reminded me of the Vatican, something I'd seen only on television but which, to be honest, had always made me a bit queasy. Because as far as I'm concerned, when you pile up that much treasure in one place you're not glorifying Heaven any more, you're showing off how much power you wield right here on Earth. The padres who convinced or browbeat those Ohlone Indians to build the mission (the select few of them who'd already survived the plagues of European diseases) might not have been much different than their buddies back in Rome, but in their own way they had been trying to make a place where they and their charges could talk to God and feel His presence—a house that was just big enough for Him and a few followers, not a giant "screw you" to the rest of the world like St. Peter's. Maybe the Vatican had once been that way too, but it sure wasn't anymore. I could still see what the mission had been, however—a spot that for a hundred years and more had served as the heart of a community, offering real comfort instead of threat and spectacle.

I don't know, maybe all that was just more of my sour mood. I had a lot of reasons besides the gaudiness of its appearance to dread going to the Ralston, and I was probably over-sentimentalizing San Judas's homey little mission, but as I sat there on my motel balcony watching the nighttime traffic eddy past, listening to the sound of other people's televisions and conversations and music echoing out over the park, motel sounds and neighborhood sounds mingling together, I felt as if I had found something important in the middle of everything—a reason to keep on doing the strange and frustrating things I do.

thirty
sat on a panda

FOR MOST people, packing for a conference means throwing clothes and toiletries in a suitcase, calling someone to feed the pets, and maybe asking the post office to hold the mail. In the current life of B. Dollar, Angelic Vagabond, the list was more like: Clean gun. Pack gun. Pack extra silver bullets. Consider obtaining second gun.

I did have to choose clothing suitable both for official functions and for being chased by a monstrous soul-sucking creature whose only weakness was a mild dislike of water, which made me wish I had a rubber tuxedo. I settled for my one suit. In my line of work, and with my particular sorts of friends, I don't go to many funerals (or weddings) so it was fairly clean.

I also decided against getting a second gun because the weekend ahead looked to have one upside—I was not all that likely to be attacked by the *ghallu*, or even Howlingfell or Eligor, although the last two might well be in attendance. See, one thing about a summit conference in our business; everybody's walking on eggshells. Nobody wants to spark off the apocalypse so everyone would be cautious. If Eligor was behind the horned monster, as I was pretty certain he was, he wasn't likely to set it rampaging through the Edwardian decor of the Ralston, especially with infernal royalty like Prince Sitri in attendance, folks even higher up the food chain than the grand duke himself.

I called young Clarence and caught him between clients. He seemed to be in a good mood. What was the deal with him? Why had Temuel asked me to keep an eye on him, then denied it? Could the kid somehow be involved with the heavenly insiders Habari had talked about? Some kind of agent for these mysterious Third Way guys? And was my supervisor in on it too? But if so, why hadn't the kid been on the scene the day of the first soul-napping? Since it had been Sam's case it would have been easy for him to be there. It only rolled to me because they were tied up when it went down. If having him present for the Great Walker Extraction was the reason someone had dropped Clarence in our midst, the kid had blown it pretty thoroughly, so why was he still here? Maybe he and his Magian masters were playing some longer, deeper game. But it sure was hard to believe any of that about Clarence while I was talking to him. If his dorky-kid-brother act *was* an act, it was a brilliant piece of method theater.

"So I hear you're going to the summit conference," he said to me, in the exact same awestruck tone as an eleven-year-old talking about the All-Star game. "That's going to be amazing! Are you excited?"

"Oh, yeah, there's nothing like standing at a public urinal next to some guy from the other team whose entire mission in the universe is to spread venereal diseases."

"That's funny," he said. "You're really funny sometimes, Bobby. I heard some of the biggest guys from our side are going to be there. Karael and the warrior angels. I even heard that Eremiel is going to be there! I've never seen him but I've heard he's awesome."

I confess I rolled my eyes. On Heaven as on Earth, fanboys are fanboys. "Yeah, Eremiel's one of the guys who knows Hell really well, so of course he'll be there. Angel of the Abyss. I think he's leading the delegation."

Clarence started to say something and then laughed. To his credit he sounded embarrassed. "I almost asked you to take pictures."

"Yeah, that's not going to happen."

"But it is pretty amazing. Even you have to admit it, Bobby. How often do you get all those angels and demons in one place?"

"It ain't easy. They manage it just frequently enough for the occasional world war."

"Sam says he's going to be there, too."

"So he told me. I suggest you don't ask him to bring back you back a souvenir ashtray. How's he treating you, by the way? Letting you all the way off the leash now?"

"Oh, he stays in touch." Clarence went a little vague. "He's been fine," he added a second later. "He's not the most soft-spoken kind of guy, but he's showed me the ropes and answered all my questions."

"Barked at you a couple of times, I'm sure. But that's Sam. He's old school." I was feeling the press of time. "I'll see you around. If I can get you Karael's autograph, I will."

"Now you're just making fun of me."

"Don't be so sure, Junior. Everyone knows I have no shame."

All the way out to Sand Point I kept trying to call Caz, but she still wasn't picking up. It was crazy, I knew. I should have been pretending it never happened, praying no one would ever find out, but instead I was desperate to talk to her. What had she done to me? Or, to be more accurate, what had I done to myself? I couldn't stop thinking about her. I've been with more than a few women, angelic and mortal, but I never had a problem moving on. Rather the reverse, as Monica kept pointing out to me: I'm not exactly Mr. Relationship. Too many lone-wolf detective movies, too many crime novels where the woman turns out to be faithless, or maybe I'm just a selfish bastard. Any way you sliced it, though, whenever I stopped actively forcing myself to think of something else, my memory filled up with images of the Countess's pale body, her fiercely solemn face, the unforgettable feeling of her cold, smooth skin.

It couldn't be love, though. Who but a teenage metal-head could actually fall in love with a demon? Certainly not a guy whose life work was to thwart and even destroy such creatures whenever possible, right? But every time I listened to her message machine come on, her crisp accent as she repeated the number, followed by the message beep that meant nobody was picking up, I died a little bit inside.

The front walkway of the Ralston was crowded with new arrivals, their luggage, and hurrying bell staff. The parking lot was just as busy. I spent fifteen minutes driving around until I found an empty space on the outskirts of the lot. See, I was already thinking quick getaway, even though it was very unlikely anybody was going to make a serious move at me on neutral ground, especially neutral ground crammed to the rafters with major figures from both sides of our particular struggle. But the idea of trying to dodge the *ghallu* or his Lordship Eligor while waiting for the valet parking boys to find my car was enough to make sure I left Orban's Benz out in the open. I only wished I could have parked it closer to one of the exits.

If you had walked into the Ralston's lobby beside me, no matter how obtuse you might be about things supernatural, I'm pretty sure you'd still have noticed something was strange. For one thing, the guests milling beneath the high, decorated ceilings and the huge, ornate chandeliers all seemed to be either strikingly beautiful or so ugly it made your eyes sting. See, when the higher angels take human bodies, they almost always look gorgeous—androgynous, some of them, but still Hollywood handsome. They may dress like Mormons on Sunday (and most of them do) but it's hard not to notice that little something extra they all have, the grace of movement and perfection of figure, even under a boring off-the-rack suit. And most of the demon lords like to cut an impressive figure, too . . . it's just that among Hell's officer corps that can go either way. Some of them are as gorgeous as the prettiest angels, so fine to look at that it could make you weep, and the only way you can tell that they *aren't* Heaven's is that they dress better, or at least more extravagantly. Their suits come in colors not found in nature (outside of a tropical orchid forest) and their hair is so fabulous that the coolest club kid would immediately give up, shave their heads, and get a job at Kentucky Fried Chicken. Rock star glamorous. But the *rest* of Hell's representatives seemed to take a fierce pleasure in presenting the most disturbing façade imaginable, as long as it was (barely) within the bounds of human possibility.

Within seconds of stepping into the lobby, I saw a man as white as Foxy Foxy, but seven feet tall, and with abnormally long fingers, drinking from a glass that looked like a thimble in his hand; a burn victim (or at least someone who *looked* like a burn victim) swathed in bandages like Boris Karloff's mummy; and a trio of starvation-slender women with smeared mascara and too-bright eyes. These last were the infamous Weeping Daughters, and I'd encountered them before in extremely weird circumstances. I'll tell you about it someday, but I immediately changed direction so I wouldn't have to walk too near them on my way to the registration desk.

The tall guy, the mummy, and the Daughters weren't the only freaky ones by any means: about a third of the people in the lobby were so unusual that I wondered how management explained it to the staff. The Ralston lobby looked like someone was throwing a really dangerous Hallowe'en party right in the middle of a convention of FBI agents.

As I was checking in, relieved that my reservation was in order, so I wouldn't have to spend too much time in the open where I was liable to be recognized by anyone I wanted to avoid, I saw a flurry of activity at the huge front door, bellboys and porters leaping into action like lifeguards who have just noticed a rich man drowning. They swung both glass doors open at the same time, then half a dozen stout fellows in Ralston's grey livery began a strange charade of struggle. At first I thought they were trying to wrestle the world's biggest bundle of luggage into the lobby and I wondered what kind of guest could possibly need so much stuff. But as they laboriously tugged and maneuvered the immense wheeled cart through the doors I suddenly realized that the world's biggest bundle of luggage was actually the guest. He was *huge*—five-hundred-pounds-plus huge—and if he had a neck, the weight of his immense bald head had shoved it well down into his torso. He looked like nothing so much as the world's largest bullfrog wrapped in a beige silk suit the size of a Mini Cooper.

A high-ranking hotel functionary, almost certainly the manager, hurried across the lobby toward the front entrance, managing to make a flat-out sprint look like Astaire easing onto a Rio dance floor. As he approached the monstrous pile of flesh, its dome-shaped head swiveled ever so slightly toward him, turret-like, and the tiny eyes glittered deep within the folds between brow and cheeks. I feared the hotel manager was going to be speared by a huge sticky tongue and swallowed, but instead the manager smiled like seeing this hideous goiter with a face was the nicest thing that had happened to him all month.

"Your Highness!" he cried. "It has been too long! Such an honor to have you with us again!" He clapped his hands and waved at the sweating bellboys who had just dragged this chariot of flabby filth into the lobby. "Please take the prince to the Roosevelt Suite!"

Prince, yes. Of Hell. That must be Sitri, I realized—the one who outranked even Eligor. The one Grasswax had gambled with and lost. And now that I'd seen him in the temporary but generous flesh, he looked even less like someone who'd enjoy being welched upon. Could he be a player in the whole golden feather thing, somehow? I wanted to know. Hell, I *needed* to know.

I intercepted the prince and his entourage just as they reached the freight elevator, the only thing big enough to carry him and the industrial-grade golf cart that trundled his bulk around. His fleshy fingers were as big as kielbasas, with several shimmering gold rings nestled deep in the folds of each digit. So much light bounced off them that if he had moved his hands around a little more they would have looked like troop transport planes coming in for a night landing, but they stayed folded across the immensity of his belly. Now, bear in mind that since this was only a temporary body, he could have looked like anyone he wanted to: Brad Pitt, Nijinsky, even the Reverend Billy Graham. But he chose to look like that. *Chose.* If that doesn't give you a little insight into the monarchs of Hell, I don't know what will.

Anyway, Sitri was one of the very highest of Hell's high rollers, and if I'd had any sense I wouldn't have even gone near him, but you already know I'm a bit deficient in that category. I figured I might never see the guy again outside of the conference room, and I wanted to see if I could shake loose any interesting information. Sometimes a surprise attack is the best way to do that.

"Excuse me!" I shouted, hurrying toward him. "Your Highness!" The bell staff were trying to angle him into the elevator, which required a great deal of stopping and starting of his cart, which someone other than Sitri himself must have been operating, since I never saw him move a single gelid muscle below the topmost of his chins. "Prince Sitri, I'd like a word with you."

The eyes rolled toward me. They were black, all black, and shiny.

"Bobby Dollar," the prince said, his voice like a cement mixer full of bowling balls and crude oil, so low that just listening to it made me feel like I was biting down on a manhole cover. "I know you, tiny fellow. But you have my name wrong." His wide mouth frowned just a little, a downward feint in the center of a rubbery front nearly a foot wide. "I am Prince Sajatapandra."

I really hated that he knew who I was. "Hey, fine," I said. "Sat On A Panda, whatever name you want. To be honest, I don't care if you call yourself Princess Grace of Monaco, I just want to talk to you for a moment . . ."

"Who are *you*?" the manager squeaked at me. He looked like he was having a minor coronary. "You cannot bother his Highness!" Two more huge but not at all flabby shapes stepped out of the elevator, luggage-laden bellhops scuttling out of their way like spooked mice, but Sitri only glanced at his bodyguards and they stopped just inside the door of the huge elevator, staring down at me with faces that wouldn't have looked out of place on Easter Island. Either one of them could have torn me into bite-size pieces with his fingers alone.

"Go ahead, Dollar," the fat thing said. "You have my attention. Of course, you may regret that at some later point." Prince Sitri made a noise like a medium-sized brick wall collapsing into the mud; a laugh of sorts. He'd amused himself.

"Just wanted to ask you about a prosecutor named Grazuvac. The extremely late Darko Grazuvac. Or you may have known him better as Grasswax."

At the sound of that name Sitri rolled his flinty little eyes toward the hotel manager, who was still as pink as a boiled crab. "You. Go away."

The manager didn't say a word, but obediently scuttled out of hearing distance and busied himself rearranging a perfect flower arrangement on one of the hall tables. Sitri rolled those gleaming shark-orbs back toward me. "Grasswax is dead. Seriously and thoroughly dead. But you probably knew that. So what about him, little angel?"

I didn't see a flash of concern or guilt or anything in those eyes, but then I probably wouldn't have even if he'd squeezed the life out of Grasswax with his own fat hands. You don't get to be a prince of Hell without having a pretty damn good poker face. "I heard he owed you money, Prince. Or at least owed you something. Gambling debts."

Again the doughy smile, and this time it was big enough for me to see the teeth behind it, each one filed into a perfect little point. If you ever crossed a piranha and a giant salamander and bombarded it with Gamma rays, Prince Sitri would probably be your first result. And your last. "Grasswax . . . gambling. Yes, I seem to remember he had a weakness for a flutter. He may even have lost to me a few times at the races. Are you suggesting that I would have him killed over such small change?" Again that titanic, stony chuckle; his chins didn't stop moving for several seconds afterward. "Oh, my dear fellow, what an idea!" Then the smile vanished. The voice still sounded like a tank idling, but suddenly I could hear the full depth of the hatred his kind feel for my kind. It wasn't a good feeling—just meeting his eyes made my stomach squirm. Sitri was a very, very old and very powerful demon. "And even if I had, little angel," he said, the rumbling a notch louder than before, "what business of yours could it possibly be?"

For the first time, I really felt the breadth and depth of my own impulsive stupidity. Even though we were a little way from the main lobby down a hall, there was still plenty of traffic, most of the folk looking as though they belonged to one side in the great struggle or another. Every single one of them was now staring at us, most with the kind of expression zoo-goers wear when some crazy sonofabitch climbs over the rail into the grizzly bear enclosure. Still, it was too late to pretend I'd fallen in by accident.

"I heard that Grasswax had something of Eligor's. Something special. You know Eligor, right? Tall fellow? Owns about three-quarters of this city?"

"Our host, you mean? Mr. Vald?" Fat Boy was suddenly smiling again. "Of course I know him. He owns this hotel, too." My expression must have amused him, because he laughed again. "Oh, did you not know that?"

Eligor, the guy who wanted to murder me—if I was lucky—owned the Ralston? Now I felt like the grizzly bear was putting on his Kiss the Cook apron and firing up the barbecue, but I soldiered on. "Yeah, that guy. I wondered if you might be able to tell me whether Grasswax might have stolen that something from Eligor with the hope of paying his debt to you."

"Ah." He nodded, or at least compressed some of his chins. "So you're not asking me whether *I* killed that punk Grasswax, you're asking me whether my dear friend and colleague Grand Duke Eligor might have killed him?"

The manager was looking at his watch. He'd arranged the bejesus out of those flowers, and now he was getting nervously impatient again. I decided I'd already drawn enough potentially fatal attention to myself for one afternoon. "Yeah. I guess so. And?"

Sitri's lips writhed in distaste like a pair of mating eels. "Grasswax was a fool who didn't know his limitations." A large gray-blue tongue crawled out from between the sharp little white pickets and moistened those lips, making the long, rubbery things look even more like sea creatures. "Anything that happened to him was richly deserved. He is not mourned or missed. And neither will you be, little angel."

"Come along, your Highness." It was the manager, bustling back into the midst of things as if invisibly signaled.

I couldn't think of any way to dig myself in deeper so I gave him my best jaunty salute. "Right, then. Enjoy your stay." As I turned away I could hear the freight elevator groan, indicating they had finally managed to maneuver Sitri into it.

So now I had a few more pieces to play with. Sitri knew Grasswax and I was sure he knew damn well why Grasswax had been so thoroughly dispatched, that was obvious. Now, demons lie constantly, but they also speak the truth if it suits them. His Flabbiness hadn't minded talking about Grasswax, which meant he either enjoyed the fact that Eligor's troubles were so well known, even if they reflected ever so slightly on himself, or he was as innocent of wrongdoing as a demon prince can ever be—at least, in the case of Grasswax's messy and extremely painful death.

Or he might have felt certain he was talking to a dead man, so he didn't need to be too coy. I couldn't find much to cheer about in any of those possibilities, and the whole thing hadn't got me closer to anything important, just guaranteed that yet one more of the nastiest bastards in this or any other universe was now thinking about me and my nosy nature.

Good one, Bobby.

thirty-one

something to my advantage

I HADN'T EVEN made it back across the lobby to the guest elevators when a hand full of steely fingers closed on my arm. Startled, I clawed in my pocket for my concealed automatic even as I turned. Reflexes aside, I knew nobody was likely to attack me in the middle of the biggest summit for decades, but I was still relieved (slightly) to see that the person who'd stopped me was from my side. At least as far as I knew.

The angel holding my arm had the tanned, fit look of a mid-career military aviator. In fact, everything about him looked military, the creases in his expensive charcoal gray suit so sharp that it might as well have been a dress uniform.

"Slow down, son," he said, and the iron grasp of his fingers made certain I did what he suggested.

I had never seen him wearing flesh and, in fact, had only seen him once in any form, but I hazarded a guess. "Karael?"

He didn't bother to acknowledge it. "I saw your report. You're testifying tomorrow, but I want a chat with you ahead of time." The way he said "chat" made me think of rubber truncheons and other painful methods of ensuring team play, but I think that was just his style. "Now you've seen how hard these bastards will work to cover their tracks, to make it look like the breakdown is on our side."

I looked around, worried about eavesdroppers, but if Karael wasn't worried I decided I shouldn't be either. This guy had been fighting the

Opposition since before the Seventh Day; he must know what he was doing. In fact, that was what was worrying me more than any demons listening in. Still, I lowered my voice. "Hold on. You're saying that this whole Third Way thing is a front? That the other side have been pilfering the souls, and that's their cover?"

He frowned like I was a school kid who'd just spelled *C-A-T-T.* "I'm saying that we give them *nothing* for free, and that includes this conference. Tell the truth about what you saw when the first soul went missing, but don't go overboard. Don't give them anything else. Unless you have to."

Nothing like directions from the top so vague that no matter what happened, it was still going to be my fault. I'm not an idiot, though, at least not most of the time, and I wasn't going to argue with him about it in the middle of the Ralston lobby. In fact, I wasn't going to argue with him at all. That's one of the more pointless ways to spend your time with a higher angel. "Of course," was what I said. "Can we go over it before I have to stand up in front of everybody?"

He nodded. "Excellent. Breakfast at 0800 local time. In that restaurant there. Are you paying attention, son?"

I had to tear my eyes away from his shoes, which were so shiny and deep black I thought I could actually see gravity bending inward around them. "0800." I checked the sign. "Café Belmont."

He looked my civilian clothes up and down. After the week I'd had, there might have been a few stains. "You're not going to wear that, are you? We represent Heaven, son. The Highest."

"I have a suit."

"Good." He paused as if considering what to say next. After the sniper-like efficiency and speed of his previous conversation it almost seemed out of character. "I've been checking up on you, Angel Doloriel."

How many ways could I dislike that? Several, just off the top of my head. "Oh?"

"I hear that you were trained by Archangel Leo Lochagos. Out at Camp Zion. If you're one of Leo's boys, that's a heck of a pedigree."

"Uh . . . yes." This paragon, this uber-leader of the angelic hosts, had known Leo? My Leo?

"He was a good one." Significant pause. "I worked with him more than once." Karael made *work*, which in his case almost certainly meant *war*, sound like the most glorious thing an angel could do—which, I suppose for him, it was. "We should never have lost him that way." He finally let go of my arm. "See you at 0800. Remember, you're not just an angel, you were a Harp. That *means* something. Don't let me see you wearing that piece of shit."

I stared after him as he walked away, measured and straight as an architect's tools. He was by no means one of the biggest bodies in the room, and certainly there were quite a few who were way uglier, but I wouldn't have wanted him angry with me for any money. But what the hell had that been about Leo, long dead now and beyond resurrection? A hint? A warning? In either case, my arm still tingled where Karael, Master of Demons, had no doubt crushed several thousand capillaries beneath his righteous fingers.

Although Karael's mortal body had looked pretty much like I'd have guessed it would, it was still a strange sensation to see him and so many other important angels wearing flesh. They don't show up down here very often—almost never. The lords of Hell love to spend time on Earth, of course. If your home decor prominently featured rivers of lava, pits of molten human feces, and the constant shrieks of the tormented, you'd probably spend most of your time at the office, too. But the big angels were usually, excuse the pun, above such things. You saw them on the other side of the Zippers, of course, but they didn't have to embody themselves there.

I glanced around the lobby as I hurried to the elevator, anxious to avoid any more meetings, but I didn't recognize any of the faces around me. This did not break my heart.

My room was reasonably nice, although someone seemed to have gone out of their way to push the walls closer together than in a normal hotel room. It was hard to squeeze between the end of the bed and the cabinet that the television sat on without turning sideways, but I was so happy I was going to be in the same place for two nights in a row that it didn't bother me. The Ralston's decor was Gilded Age: molded ceilings, ornate, overstuffed furniture, and a headboard on the bed so lumpy with carved roses that I had to pile all the pillows against it just so I could sit up comfortably.

I wanted to go back down to that lobby about as much as Dante probably wanted to go back to the Inferno, but it was almost dinner time and I was beginning to get hungry. I ordered some nachos from room service, then turned on the television and watched the news. Sometimes it's oddly relaxing to watch shit happening to other people, not to mention that when you know there's life after death, you don't feel like such a jerk about doing it.

About the time the nachos should have arrived somebody knocked on the door. Your friend Bobby Dollar is no fool. I put it on the chain before I opened. It was Sam. I was actually a bit surprised to see him.

"I was hoping to come in and get out of the decor," he said, "but I see you've got it in here, too."

"How did you find my room? I would have thought the security would be pretty fierce around here, considering what's going on this weekend."

He gave me a look. "Suspicious much? Don't moisten your pants. Alice told me."

"Great. She'd probably do the same if Hell's Horned Avenger asked, too." But I was at least a little relieved. Obviously if I was in Eligor's hotel I wasn't going to be able to hide from him, but I was hoping any casual acquaintances with a grudge might have to work a little to find out where exactly I was. "I should have hung a soap on a rope over the doorway to keep creatures like you at bay." I was joking, of course, but I also couldn't help noticing that Sam looked a little rough. His suit was badly wrinkled, his bruises and scars were still painfully apparent, and his shoulders had a slumped angle I wasn't used to seeing.

He made his way in and rifled the minibar, coming away with a can of ginger ale. He took the room's one chair and put his feet up on the desk. "So what's the good word, B? Did you clock all the horns down in the lobby? It's like a metal band's wet dream down there."

My nachos came and Sam helped me eat some of them, but without his usual gusto. We talked about my conversation with Sitri and the unwelcome news that the hotel belonged to Eligor the Horseman, Grand Duke of Hell, a name not exactly synonymous with hospitality.

"The big guys have to know that the hotel belongs to him," Sam said, sucking the guacamole off a chip before putting it in his mouth. "Maybe they rotate—this conference at Eligor's place, next one at the Vatican or Dollywood."

I wasn't going to be distracted by jokes. "No offense, Sam, but you look like shit. I'm worried about you." I almost asked him if he'd fallen off the wagon, ginger ale notwithstanding, but that's not the kind of thing I'd feel comfortable asking even Sam. Still, he had an air of defeat about him that I hadn't seen lately, maybe ever, and at a time like this it really worried me. "Anything you want to talk about? Seriously?"

I could see him halfway to brushing me off, but then he stopped and gave me a long look. "What do you mean, worried about me?"

"You haven't been your old self since they saddled you with Clarence. Like something's bugging you." It was hard to confront him. I was basically accusing my best friend of lying to me. "We're deep into some scary shit, Sam—worse than in the old days. If you know something that I don't, it's time to tell me."

Sam sighed. That was odd. I don't think I'd ever heard him do that before. "Yeah. Yeah, there *is* something bugging me, Bobby. And you're right—I haven't been all the way square with you."

If you've ever demanded to know whether your significant other was sleeping with someone else, you'll understand the ambivalence I was feeling now. I had really hoped Sam would deny it and make me believe it. I didn't say anything, just looked at him, waiting, my stomach heavy as a rock.

"You were right about the kid," he said at last. "I don't know the details—what I said about asking around in Records is true—but he's definitely working for somebody on the sly. And he's interested in *you*."

"In me? Why?" I let it filter for a moment. "Hold on. You mean the kid was sent to spy on me . . . and you went along with it? You were the one who asked me to take him off your hands!"

"Hold on, B, hold on—I didn't know it then. I thought he was sent to keep tabs on *me*. I asked you to take him because I wanted to find out what he'd do when I wasn't around, what kind of questions he'd ask. I only found out later that you were the one he was after."

I couldn't make any sense out of it. In fact, the whole conversation seemed a bit like a dream, full of twists and turns and non-logic. "Why should the kid be watching me? And what do you mean, you found out?"

Sam looked embarrassed. "Well, actually, Temuel told me. Apparently he made some inquiries of his own and then got told to lay off, that it was you the higher-ups were interested in and the Mule shouldn't interfere. As to why they're interested in you . . . hell, I don't know."

I sat back in my chair. I felt like I had been punched. "So our bosses sent Clarence to get the dirt on me?" I wanted to go find the kid and give his Dockers-clad ass a good kicking. "Shit! What did *I* do?"

"You're a nice man, Dollar, but a lousy angel." Sam stood up. "Think about it. You said yourself, this is a conspiracy, so maybe this little inquiry isn't official. Maybe whoever put the kid onto you is trying to cover his own angelic ass for something. It could even be Temuel pulling a fast one on both of us."

"Or maybe whoever engineered this missing-souls thing is looking for a fall-guy, and I've been elected," I said. "After all, it wouldn't take much to make Karael and the rest believe I'd gone rogue." I had a sudden urge to hole up somewhere, maybe not even in San Judas, and just stay that way until Judgement Day—maybe longer. I was that sick of all this spy-caper bullshit.

"Nah, you'll be okay." Sam downed the rest of his ginger ale. "I'm pretty sure this crap is going on all the time in Heaven, Bobby, whether you and I know about it or not. You try to figure out what's going on over our heads, you'll go crazy."

I couldn't process it all yet. I'd need time to figure out how this new information fit in, but time was the one thing I didn't have much of. "And you're sure you want to stick around while I'm being fitted for a frame-up, not to mention that I'm Eligor's target of choice? Are you even up to it? Because I wasn't joking earlier—you look terrible, Sam."

He waved his hand as he got up. "Hey, I'm fine, fit, and sober. Okay, not fit. The thrashing from that red-hot bruiser of yours makes me feel like I'm about two hundred years old. I think after the Inquisition—oops, the *summit conference*—is over I'm going to take a couple of weeks off and get better before I go back to the grind."

Sam was one of those guys who'd respond to losing a finger in a chainsaw accident with, "Well, at least I can hock one of my rings," so I knew he must really be hurting. "Look," I told him, "I'm not going downstairs tonight, and I know you don't like to hang out in bars anyway, so why don't you just stick around? We'll watch some porn and charge it to the office."

He smiled, the first time he'd looked like his regular ugly self in a while. "Nice idea, but I've got a room of my own and I get dirty movies there too. Phone me if you need me. I'm going to crash." He paused in the doorway. "*Breast In Show* looked good. I think it's even in 3D. Don't get your eye poked out."

After Sam had gone I put the chain back on the door and prepared for a night in. Unlike my best friend, I have no wagon upon which I have to remain, so I found a couple of little bottles of vodka in the minibar and some orange juice and retired to my bed and its bumpy headboard. My brain was too full of weirdness to watch anything in a serious way. I channel surfed, drank iceless Screwdrivers, and tried to figure out how I'd landed myself in so much trouble.

Latest information piled now on top of earlier unanswered questions, I did my best to find the disinterested, calm state where thinking happened without me trying to make it so. I sort of got there, but things swirled in my head like one of those money-tube game shows, every idea a dollar bill, and for all my grabbing, I felt sure I was still going home broke.

The Clarence stuff made no sense at all: the kid had been dropped on us before the souls even started vanishing. Before I met Caz, too. But if Edward Walker and the rest of the MIAs wasn't the issue, and Clarence's arrival predated my relationship with the Countess, why had anyone Upstairs suddenly become interested in me? It wasn't like I had just started slacking, complaining, and taking the Lord's name in vain last week. No, I just wasn't ready to make any guesses about that stuff yet.

Sam's revelations about the kid hadn't answered any of my other questions, either, and I still had a ton. Where had Eligor's feather gone? How was I going to stay ahead of the *ghallu*? And did my new chum Prince Sitri fit into this mess somewhere? Clearly the fat bastard didn't mind talking, but as with any demon, believing anything he said was like wearing an "I'm With Stupid" t-shirt with the arrow pointing straight up at your own stupid face. Still, the one thing about demon lords is they hate each other almost as much as they hate us—more, sometimes—and Sitri didn't seem to have much of a problem about getting into Eligor's shit. I was sure he was telling the truth about the ownership of the hotel—why lie?—but everything else had to be checked, or at least carefully considered.

So, where did that leave me on the big questions? What did I know for certain?

According to Caz, Eligor had made a deal with someone in Heaven, with the marker of that deal being a golden feather. That deal hadn't necessarily been about the missing souls and the Third Way, but it was an awfully big coincidence timewise if it wasn't.

Caz's story (which I wanted to believe, of course, but not being a suicidal idiot had to take with a few grains of salt) was that she had stolen the feather from Eligor as protection and then passed it on to Grasswax when things got hot. Howlingfell said Eligor had sent him to be Grasswax's bodyguard, which must have alarmed Grasswax quite a bit; Eligor was as much as telling him, "I know you've got it." The deal with Edward Walker's soul or lack thereof then went down, and by later that same day Grasswax was dead in a very ugly manner that suggested he'd pissed someone off pretty thoroughly or else that they'd wanted information badly, which supported Caz's story. A short time later, I was entertaining visits from the *ghallu*, which Caz and Howlingfell had both confirmed was Eligor's fetch, and that suggested that Grasswax really had told the Grand Duke—probably while vomiting blood—that he gave the feather to me.

Why me? Sure, Grasswax hadn't seemed to like me much, but pinning it on me still seemed pretty extreme when he must have known he wasn't going to survive being questioned by Eligor and his minions. I didn't have the feather, so who had he been protecting? Caz? Didn't seem in character from a nasty piece of work like Prosecutor Grasswax.

And now I had to fit our young friend Clarence into all this, too. My bosses were spying on me for some reason. Why? Had one of them known that Walker's soul wasn't going to turn up, and also knew I'd be on the case? That still didn't explain much.

A sudden thought from earlier reoccurred to me: what if Eligor wasn't the only player? What if someone like Sitri wanted the feather too, to blackmail Eligor or whoever the feather belonged to? Could the fat prince have been the one who actually tortured Grasswax, trying to get in on the Great Plumage Hunt? If so, Caz was mistaken . . . or was lying to me, and so was Howlingfell. But it still didn't explain where the golden feather was now, or the weird thing my albino buddy Fox had told me about Eligor's prize: "I smelled it on you."

You can go crazy with this stuff—wheels within wheels, as Sam put it. Is it any wonder every now and then I have to stop thinking and just *do* something?

And just to round it all out, I had found a connection between Eligor and Reverend Doctor Habari, the front man for the Magian Society. So what if this whole Third Way mess was some kind of massive, deep-cover fraud Hell was putting over on us to disguise the fact that they'd found a way to shanghai souls before they ever reached judgement? Or a private play for infernal power by Eligor (or Sitri, for that matter)? Either way, the stakes were clearly high, because if Eligor was willing to let his hired demon smash up The Compasses he was obviously more worried about finding the feather than being discreet.

And of course I had to deal with the possibility that the answer was *None of the above* and that the Magians really did represent some fifth column in Heaven, maybe even the first stages of an attempted coup. We hadn't had one of those get even close to success since the Light-bringer first tried to snatch the car keys and Daddy took the T-Bird away. Another such revolution from within would be way out of my league, and yet I was right in the middle of it and getting very little support or information from my bosses. As you can imagine, the word "scapegoat" kept coming back to me. It wasn't a word I liked.

Caz drifted through all these thoughts like a trail of smoke or a hint of some exotic perfume. Had she been using me to get herself off the hook or to push some agenda I couldn't yet see? That was certainly within the character of her calling. But asking me to believe she had fooled me so completely was asking me to believe that I had learned nothing in all the eventful years of my angelic life, that I was as gullible as the newest halo fresh off the heavenly bus and had fallen in love with an unrepentant hell creature after we spent one night together.

All these possibilities jostled around in my brain like cranky kids kept up too late. At last I gave up trying to figure it all out in one night and called the office to check my conference schedule for Saturday and Sunday: I did not want to be asking Karael rookie questions over our shared breakfast. The very thought of his handsome mouth curling in a little Clint Eastwood smirk of contempt at my helplessness made my scrotum climb to higher ground. Once Alice finished complaining about me (which took several minutes) I got what I needed, plus some information that surprised me a bit and which I put aside to chew over later. Then I called Fatback and left a message on his answering machine (since at this time of day he would still be on the Last Train To Porksville) asking for whatever he could find about the Ralston Hotel, emphasis on escape routes, and also for some info about a few other things that had been troubling me. Since I'd finished the vodka and didn't want to wait for room service, I took two tiny bottles of Bacardi out of the minibar and began working on them. I still had some orange juice, after all, and any sailor knows that when the weather ahead looks foul, it's time to break out the rum.

I had been brooding and flipping channels for hours, letting bits of images and sound wash over me—half an inning of a baseball game, some incomprehensible cop drama featuring corpses and forensic labs staffed by improbably good-looking scientists, a local weatherman doing his best to seem responsibly worried as he reported a tiny bit of incoming rain that might force a few folks to roll up their car windows, plus old movies, infomercials, children's cartoons that seemed to consist mainly of primary colors and loud shrieking—anything that would hold my attention for a few seconds. I finally found a program about soldier ants and even settled into it a little. I confess I might have dozed, or been about to; either way, the knock on the door startled me badly.

One of Prince Sitri's Easter Island statues blocked the space beyond the chain. For an instant I could only wonder if the modest metal links would keep him out during the second or two it would take me to get to my coat where it hung over the chair and the automatic full of silver bullets in the pocket, but he only made a grunting noise and pushed something through the space between door and jamb—an envelope. When I took it, he turned and walked away, surprisingly quietly for a man (or at least a male human body) big enough to have his own zip code.

The envelope contained a note written on impossibly dainty, almost transparent paper in a finicky little hand that it was hard to feature as the product of Sitri's immense, pudgy paws.

"If you come down to the lobby bar at midnight you will learn something to your advantage," it read. At the bottom was a single florid letter "S".

I wondered why he hadn't just invited me to the Roosevelt Suite. It didn't seem likely that Prince Jabba the Hutt and I would be able to have a surreptitious meeting in the crowded lobby, even after midnight, but on the other hand there'd be enough people around that it didn't seem likely he was going to bump me off, either. I was already in the game and had pretty much bet my house, so I couldn't afford to ignore the summons. I pulled on my coat, but not before putting on my shoulder holster and making sure that I had a round chambered in my new FN automatic. Nobody wants to be the guy they say, "He forgot to load his gun," about while shaking their heads grimly.

I didn't encounter anything in the halls, but I heard enough weird sounds from behind doors to make me hope some local channel was showing slasher movies. The elevator was empty too, although I swear somebody had cranked up the air conditioning way beyond what was reasonable, and I had to suffer what felt like cold breath on the back of my neck all the way down to "L." Signs and portents. Unfortunately, when you live in my world they're as ubiquitous as advertising and even harder to sort through for truth.

The lobby was still a busy place, with all kinds of folks from my side and not-my-side going in and out, grouped in chatty little bunches. Looking at a troop of obvious Hellspawn laughing and smoking outside the front door, I wondered how many crimes under investigation by Interpol could have been solved merely by listening in on their cheerful conversation.

The bar was full but not crazy full. I stood for a moment in the doorway looking around for either Sitri or his bodyguards, but even with all the weird looking people in the room I didn't see any as weird as the prince. Then, at the corner of my eye, something bright caught my attention.

She was sitting at the bar by herself with her back to me, but even without the fall of pale gold hair down her shoulders and back, I would have known that slender shape anywhere, anytime. She wore a black skirt that showed her fine, pale legs and a red cashmere sweater that clung to her like a second skin, displaying the delicate bumps of her spine like a topo map in scarlet. Before I could get a chance to tell myself it might be someone else, fruitlessly denying the knowledge that was throbbing in every nerve of my Earthly body, she turned to the bartender, and I saw her face in silhouette. It was indeed the Countess of Cold Hands, her very own self, just as I had known from the first moment I spotted her. It was Caz, and she was all alone as if waiting for someone. As if waiting for me.

thirty-two

saddest sound i ever heard

THAT WAS an intense couple of seconds, let me tell you. There she sat, staring at the mirror behind the bar, and it was like one of those movies where the single spotlight comes on and everything else goes dark: I couldn't see anything but her. I had been smothering my feelings so strenuously for the last forty-eight hours or so that the intense wave of longing that rolled through me almost made my knees buckle. She was so beautiful. Her face was perfect.

No, not quite, I realized; that kind of perfection only exists after someone's used an airbrush on a photo, but Caz came very close. Her only flaw—and it didn't seem like a flaw to me—was that her high-bridged, slender nose and her fine bones gave her a look of fragility, of something fierce that had known a cage, that knew it could be broken and feared that beyond all else.

She looked young, but also like she might not age well. She looked like she could be damaged and probably would be. But still, my God, she was beautiful.

And in fact she would *never* age, I suddenly realized. She would appear this way forever, or at least as long as it suited her. Casimira of the Cold Hands would never get any older than this. But that didn't mean much to me anyway. Chances were good that, one way or another, I wasn't going to get any older either.

As I moved toward her she seemed to sense my presence, or at least that she was being watched. I wasn't surprised—it seemed like I'd never stared at anything so intently in my short angelic life. I was so surprised to see her in the Ralston that for a moment I literally couldn't think of what to say.

She turned and her eyes went wide.

"Hello, Caz," I managed to say. Clever, huh? I'd like to see you have come up with something better under the circumstances.

The look on her face seemed close to panic. "Bobby, what are you doing here?"

"What am I doing here? What are you doing here?" I suddenly felt conspicuous, but if anyone in the bar was watching us they were being cagey about it. "Why didn't you call me back?" Now that I stood in front of her I was more than a little angry, but that was only part of the storm that was blowing my emotions this way and that. For those who don't know anything else, let me just tell you, it's really weird to live in a human body. You can feel the hormones pumping, feel the hide bristling, skin stretching and shrinking, feel yourself being tugged by fight-or-flight impulses like the animal that you are. Or were. I wanted to grab her, kiss her, drag her to my room, but just as powerfully I wanted to shake her until tears came to those robin's-egg-blue eyes, make her feel how much I was hurting. Yet another part of me was terrified that one of Eligor's minions would spot her, and I'd have to decide between some kind of fatal standoff or else stand helplessly and watch them drag her back to the beast she had cheated, a creature that I already knew did not take losing well.

"You can't be here, Bobby!" She grabbed her drink and downed it and began fumbling in her purse for money to leave on the bar. "He'll kill you!"

"Who, Eligor?" I was confused. Why was she worried about me instead of herself? Everything seemed to have gone topsy-turvy. "No, this is a summit conference, there's an official truce. I've been ordered to be here and the place is packed with angels. I'm in no danger at all." Okay, not completely true, but I had bigger worries at the moment. Just seeing her again had me terrified that something might happen to her. Even if she'd lied to me, tricked me. Even if she didn't care about me at all. "You're the one who shouldn't be here, Caz. Your ex owns this whole fucking hotel . . . ." I was startled by something that flickered across her face—something like shame. "Wait," I said. "You knew that already. You must have. Caz, what are you doing here?"

"Oh, Bobby . . ." But she was looking over my shoulder now, and the shame was replaced by something else entirely.

"Well, well, well!" said a voice I knew. It lifted the hairs on my neck, which were just starting to relax, right back up again. "Two of the most interesting people I know!"

I spun. The Grand Duke was only a couple of yards away, leaning on the bar, dressed in his Kenneth Vald best, a linen suit and expensive moccasins that made him look like a rich colonial—which, in a sense, he was. Eligor wasn't from here, but he definitely owned a lot of it.

I wasn't in any condition to play his game. I didn't reply, but I didn't reach for my gun, either. Once I found out he owned the place, I had decided there was a good chance I would bump into him. I had just hoped it would be somewhere I felt safer, like when I was sitting next to General Hard-Ass Karael, Scourge of All Hellspawn.

"Oh, sorry, am I interrupting?" The Horseman was the very soul of graciousness, that blond lord of Hell, cheerful and charming. Now the people in the bar were definitely watching. Eligor swung a lot of weight and not just in San Judas. "Oh, that's right, I forgot—you two already know each other." His smile was cold and clean as a surgical blade. "I'm not surprised. You're both very . . . enterprising." He turned to Caz, whose face had gone dead as a doll's. "But I'm afraid I really do have to interrupt. We have a meeting, Countess. People are waiting for us." He didn't beckon or even raise his hand, but she rose from her bar stool and went to stand beside him, obedient as a dog. I met her eyes again, but there was nothing there for me, her expression so empty that I began to wonder if everything else I had seen on her face tonight and those other, more intimate times had just been more of her masks.

"A pleasure to see you, Mr. Dollar, even briefly," Eligor said. "I hope you're enjoying your stay."

"It's a very nice hotel." I was determined not to spend the entire conversation in stunned silence. "But, honestly, Vald, some of the people you let in here . . . !"

Again the smile, meaningless as the grin on a great white shark. "Ah, but the duty of a host is to find a way to accommodate every guest. That's why I'm so happy to have the Countess back. She is very good at finding what people need and giving it to them." He started to turn, then paused. "Please, don't let me rush you off, Mr. Dollar. The lady and I have to go, but I hope you'll stay and have a drink on me." He looked up, made eye contact with the bartender. "I'm sure you have lots of old friends who'd love to find you here and catch up on old times."

He walked away then, graceful and self-assured as a cat, with Caz at his side. I half thought she might turn to look back at me but of course she didn't.

I sort of collapsed onto the stool Caz had occupied, because at the moment I didn't trust my legs to carry me across the room. I had been shot in the heart without anybody even pointing a gun at me.

The bartender came to take an order, but after the eye contact between him and his boss, I couldn't imagine letting him pour me anything so I shook my head. I felt like someone was waving a big magnet around near my internal compass: I suddenly didn't know where to go next, what to do. Why was Caz here? Why had she gone back to him? And why had Sitri wanted to send me down here, unless it was just to provoke his rival, the grand duke. Caz had told me she'd stolen the feather and that Grasswax had done something with it, so why would Eligor take her back? Did she have it all along and now had used it to buy her way back into safety? Or was the truth something worse? Had I been played like a sucker from the start?

A heavy hand fell on my shoulder. "Fancy meeting you here," said another voice I recognized and wished I didn't. Just the thought of having to go through something like this now made me so tired I almost didn't answer, but I forced myself to turn and face the unibrow and the nasty little eyes beneath it.

"Howlingfell," I said. "It's so nice to see you that I'm even going to say please when I tell you to take your hand off me."

He smirked and stepped back. He was wearing a shiny new suit that made him look every inch the jumped-up punk he was. That didn't mean he couldn't kill me, of course. I know lots of people who were killed by punks. In fact, punks with a grudge are probably the most dangerous type to deal with. Give me a crazy-ass, violent drunk any day.

"You look a little depressed, Dollar," he said. "Found out your girlfriend went back to the guy with the power and the money, huh? Isn't that too bad."

"Howly, do me a favor and fuck off, will you?" I stood. "I don't need you, and since we're under truce I can't do anything useful to you, so why don't you go back to pissing around the edge of your tiny little territory and leave everything else to the grown-ups?"

His lip twitched back. He was in a mortal body, of course, but he still looked like his first impulse was to go for my throat with his teeth. "You think you're something special, Dollar, but you're not. You're just dog shit to someone like Eligor."

"And that's *your* job, huh? Cleaning up the shit? Nice resumé-builder."

He stared at me. His eyes, which at first had looked brown, now caught the light and gleamed deep red like a Sangiovese Grosso. "You wait, you little snot," he said, just quietly enough to make sure everyone in the bar was trying to hear. "As soon as this conference ends, you're mine. I'm going to eat your liver. And even your fancy girlfriend will forget you. She probably already has."

It took every bit of self-control I had not to shove my fist right into his bushy-browed face. "Glad to hear you're getting serious about your diet, Howly. But there's no organ meat in the world with enough vitamins to wipe away all that ugly."

I thought he might jump me as I walked off, and I almost wouldn't have minded. There's a certain therapeutic value in getting bloody (as long as you make sure the other guy gets bloodier). But all Howlingfell did was let out a snarling breath that sounded like a lion imagining the day the keeper would forget to lock the cage door.

By the time I got back to my room my phone was vibrating. All I really wanted to do was find out what would happen if I mixed all the little bottles left in the minibar together and downed the results, but out of long habit I dragged it out of my pocket to check the number, then answered.

"George, what's up?" I'd almost forgotten I'd called Fatback. After seeing Caz I barely cared.

"Well, my fees, for one thing, if you keep leaving me these hurry-hurry-need-it-now messages."

"George my friend, after Porky and the one in *Lord of the Flies*, you are the funniest pig ever."

"I'm calling because you said you needed help." He sounded hurt. Why is it that every time I feel like I've been gutshot by life, everybody else suddenly decides to get sensitive?

"Sorry. Rough evening. Thanks for calling back. Find anything yet?"

"I'm sending you specs on the Ralston. Yes, it's another Vald Credit property. At least there are plenty of fire escapes."

"That's good, because right about now I wouldn't mind burning the place down." I flicked through the files just to make sure they'd all arrived. Schematics, emergency information that looked like it had been lifted straight out of the San Judas FD main server, all kinds of goodies. "Seriously, great work, George. That's just what I needed."

"You're welcome, Mr. D." He sounded cheerful again. "Any time." Sometimes George seemed almost pathetically grateful for any kindness. I guess when you spend your entire thinking life in the body of a Majestic Large Black boar hog you're going to have a bit of an inferiority complex. But even though Fatback was a good guy, I didn't want to be talking to him or anyone just then, I wanted to be drinking myself unconscious.

"Anything else?" I prompted him. "About Leo, maybe?"

"Nothing other than what you already know, Bobby. There was a big stink at the time, in your circles, when he died, if you know what I mean. Lot of scuttlebutt, loose talk, folks who thought he'd been bumped off for asking too many questions or knowing things he wasn't supposed to know. But I can't find anything new. Oh, but speaking of dead guys . . . ?"

I could almost hear the minibar calling to me—*Oblivion, Doloriel, sweet oblivion*—but I did my best to pretend patience. "Yeah?"

"That Habari guy you asked about? The one with the what's-it-called society?"

I immediately became more focused. "Magians. Yeah? What do you mean, speaking of dead guys? Did he turn up in a morgue or something?"

"In a manner of speaking. But not recently."

"Stop confusing me, George. I'm fucking exhausted."

To his credit, Fatback didn't sound offended this time. "Well, it's not the same guy, obviously, but how many times do you run across a name like that? And a reverend, too?"

"Just tell me."

"I found a guy who had the same name, first, middle, and last. And he was even a reverend. But he died seven years ago, almost eight, and he didn't have anything to do with any Magian Society." He gave me the details, which upset me considerably, because if I was going to figure out what all this new stuff meant I'd have to put off the drinking binge that had seemed like the only thing alluring enough to keep me alive until tomorrow.

I thanked him again and then called Clarence the Boy Angel. Although by my standards it wasn't particularly late, I obviously woke the kid up. I wondered if the little company spy had gone to bed in his footie pajamas with his nice landlady reading him stories or something.

"Bobby?" He groaned. "What time is it?"

"Too late for you to be awake, obviously, so I'll make it short." If Sam was right I couldn't trust him an inch, so I paused to figure out how best to phrase my question. "Look, when we went Upstairs and I had you look up all those names, did you only check the rolls of the living or whatever they call that stuff at Records?"

"Do you mean did I check dead people?" He sounded a little more awake now and cranky. "Of course I did. And I told you, I couldn't find anybody by any of those names except that one guy, Jose Patrillo."

Who was the ringer I'd put in to test him. So Habari was dead, but he wasn't in Heaven's records? What in the name of the Highest was going on around here? But just before I hung up, I thought of another question. "How far back did you look?"

"You mean how long in the past?"

"To see if any of them had died, yeah."

He snorted. "Well, considering you told me that you'd just seen the guy in the flesh, I only went back a little way. I think I checked the deaths for the last couple of years in case he'd passed fairly recently but had been misfiled."

So Fatback's information was probably right, and the kid might even be telling the truth—about this, anyway. No matter what, though, things were getting very deep now, very deep indeed. "So you only went back maybe two years? If I told you somebody with that same name had died seven years ago right here in San Judas, that wouldn't surprise you?"

"Somebody dies every few seconds, and lots of people share names, Bobby." It sounded like he was getting impatient with me. It made an interesting contrast. "No, that wouldn't surprise me very much at all."

"Okay. Thanks, kid." I almost asked him why our bosses had set him to snoop on me, but I also knew it was a bad idea to show him my hand. Never give up anything for free. "Go back to bed."

"You sound like shit, Bobby." He actually sounded concerned—an actor to the end. "I think you're the one who needs to get some rest."

"Oh, yeah. Soon as I can find some quarters for the vibrating bed."

But I knew now that despite having to meet the scary soldier angel for breakfast at eight o'clock sharp (not an hour of the day I particularly enjoy even at the best of times) I wasn't going to get a lot of sleep because there was too damn much to think about. The world I'd thought I knew was proving to be an even more dubious proposition than I'd figured, and I'd always thought of myself as a cynic. Plus, just to make my happiness complete, after breakfast I was going to be interrogated by the biggest powers on both sides of our permanent war—a great chance to make new enemies.

I locked the minibar to force temptation to work harder, since I could no longer afford to get slaughterously drunk. The sound of that key turning in its tiny little lock seemed like one of the saddest sounds I'd ever heard.

thirty-three

the odor of violent subtext

SEVEN MINUTES after eight in the morning is not my favorite time of day, and adding lukewarm scrambled eggs and the hard face of Karael only a cup of coffee and a grapefruit away didn't do much to improve it.

"Sit up, Angel Doloriel. This restaurant is full of creatures who spend their entire miserable existence looking for any sign of weakness on our side, and you're slouching like a school child who forgot to bring in his homework."

My problem was that I *had* brought my homework to the summit conference, and it had kept me up half the night. The alternative had been to spend the wee hours of the morning cursing Fate and wondering what Caz was doing back with her ex, a monster who didn't even have Hitler's fondness for dogs. But I couldn't tell that to the general, of course, so I just nodded. "Sorry. Up late. Working."

"This *is* your work, Angel Doloriel. In a little over twenty minutes you're going to be in there with the big boys, and so far, I'm underwhelmed by your effort." His mouth tightened into a very thin line. "There's egg on your lapel."

I brushed it off and did my best to transfer the rest of it from plate to mouth more carefully as Karael explained again, for the third time since I'd stepped out of the elevator, what I was supposed to say and not say.

"The report you sent about this Third Way nonsense does not officially exist, Advocate," he explained again. "It's being held back until after the conference is over. We don't want to start something before we know all the facts."

"But why are we having a summit, then?" I noticed that thinning line again and wiped my mouth with my napkin. "Isn't the Third Way exactly the sort of thing that should be . . . um . . . discussed with the Opposition?"

The line quirked up on one end. "You think so? That this is all about getting to the truth? Son, if we always let actual truth turn into official truth this cold war of ours would have turned hot a long time ago. You remember Sodom and Gomorrah? Or at least heard of them? Well, just change the names to Rio or Berlin or Shanghai, imagine those burned to the ground tomorrow with millions of casualties just for starters, and you'll have some idea of why you're going to do what you're told."

Ten minutes later, I was marched into the Ralston's Elysium Ballroom, sometimes known as the Cloud Room because of the billowing, cloudy sky painted across the high ceiling. Packing his demon cohorts and angelic enemies into such a room must have amused Grand Duke Eligor to no end, and it was packed. A few hundred were grouped around the various tables, although most of their chairs had already been turned for a better view of the stage, where the main business would take place at a long table set with microphones. Other than Karael beside me, the main movers for both sides were already in place: Eremiel, our Heavenly expert on Hell, whose rawboned face and longish hair gave him the look of a nineteenth-century abolitionist preacher, very much in tune with the Gilded Age setting. The third of the important angels had to be Phanuel, the famous Angel of Exorcism, but by the standards of the Elysium Ballroom he was not very interesting to look at, just another Hollywood male lead in a sober suit.

As expected, the Opposition was visually a bit more interesting. Once you could stop staring at the jellied mass of Prince Sitri you noticed Adramelech, one of the old, bad ones, who had done less than the rest to pass as human. From a distance he looked okay, just an old man in a black suit with a skin color that suggested lots of sunlamp time. Only when you got a little closer could you see that what covered his face looked less like skin and more like a mask of sandstone, yellow and granular. The only things that moved in that stony mask were the eyes, black and liquid as tar. Just seeing the stillness with which he waited for things to start made it clear how big this all was. Adramelech scared me. Badly.

The last of the satanic negotiators was also the most ordinary looking, dressed in a sharp bespoke suit and wearing a pair of black-rimmed hipster glasses like an entertainment industry lawyer. This was Caym, another heavy hitter, president of the main Council of Hell and one of the smartest in the Opposition's stable. What interested me, though, was that according to Fatback's grapevine he was also Eligor's mouthpiece, pushing the Grand Duke's agenda in the deadly arena of infernal politics. I decided I needed to keep a close eye on him for clues to what Eligor had in mind.

Many others were on the stage with them, the great and good (or nasty and bad) of both sides. Terentia and Chamuel, both part of the Ephorate that had grilled me in Heaven, were there in human form, as were many other angels and demons I didn't immediately recognize.

"Don't gawk," Karael said sharply into my ear. "I'm going up there now. There's a seat for you in the second row with your name on it. Sit there, keep your mouth shut, and remember everything I told you."

As the Angel Militant climbed the steps to the stage, his back straight as the shortest distance between two points, I found the chair marked "Dollar" and slipped into it. Like a wedding between the Hatfields and McCoys the audience had been seated by affiliation, and I was happier than I'd been in a while to be surrounded by fellow employees of the Highest.

With Karael in place the conference finally lurched into life. Adramelech—acting as chairman because we were on the Opposition's home ground—gave the opening remarks, a blur of verbiage that managed to be both dryly politic and yet clearly menacing, with several comments about "temporarily putting aside our very real differences to address the mutual problem." Eremiel spoke for our side and managed to be succinct and even occasionally funny, as when he referred to the chairman as the "honorable Adramelech—which must be the first time those words have been spoken together." Even a couple of the Hellspawn grinned at that.

And of course before they could depose anybody there were more speeches, about an hour-and-a-half's worth. It seemed like everybody who'd ever been fitted for a halo or issued a pitchfork had to have their say. The delegates from Hell seemed to range along a continuum from the noisily nasty ones, who were like professional bigots, complaining about how really it was *their* side that was misunderstood and stigmatized, to your basic politburo thugs, the sort of bureaucrats who signed orders for torture and execution and then paused for a catered lunch before going back to work. Their basic stance on the entire Heaven/Hell conflict was "Lies, lies, all lies. We will bury you someday."

My side had its own version of this kind of crap, of course, but the range was more like militant Christian war hawks at one extreme, and gray little European Union bureaucrats at the other. Either way, by the time the preliminaries ended a whole lot of nothing had been said, but the massive ballroom stank with the odor of violent subtext. The only thing that had been made definitively clear was that neither side was taking the blame for the missing souls. Then the parade of witnesses began.

I tried to stay focused—you never knew when some little slip would turn out to be important—but with pride of their hosting privileges, the other guys went first and called up a numbing stream of minor infernal bureaucrats to explain all the ways they had noticed something amiss without in any way conceding that they might have made an error and without giving away anything substantial about Hell's internal procedures. In short, a snore-fest. No doubt following the official party line, most of Hell's deponents hinted darkly that only the Highest, who liked to make His own rules, could pull off such a thing. The only one that really caught my attention was a scrawny underdevil who even in human form looked like he'd lose an arm-wrestling match to Olive Oyl. He said that some nameless archdemonic supervisor had assured him that the souls must be hidden in some Heavenly safe house right here on Earth, like high-value defectors, because other than Upstairs or Downstairs there was nowhere else to go.

"The Tartarean Convention specifically states that no new territory can be opened without the consent of both Heaven and Hell," he said piously. "And such a thing has never happened. I looked it up."

While a few of the audience on the other side of the ballroom chuckled at this wet-behind-the-horns simpleton, I sat forward in my chair. A puzzle piece that had been sitting prominently to the side of my unfinished mental jigsaw, a piece labeled "Why the feather?" suddenly seemed to have found its place. I snuck a look up at Eligor, who sat at the back of the stage with other infernal dignitaries, but his calm smirk was unchanged. Nevertheless, his friend Caym quickly ended the skinny demon's testimony and sent him back to sit with his catcalling comrades. I wondered if Eligor was even now imagining how that gawky, talkative underling would look as demonic macrame, á la the late Grasswax.

Soon it was Heaven's turn to bore everyone in the room to death, although Sam's testimony provided a few entertaining moments when he followed a bunch of Heaven's least forthcoming pencil-pushers into the witness chair. Adramelech seemed interested in hearing what he had to say, but Caym just looked focused and blank, while Prince Sitri, who had barely spoken, continued his imitation of the world's largest melted candle.

"You were the first of your cohorts to receive the summons to the death scene of Edward Walker, were you not?" Adramelech asked Sam.

"I certainly was," Sam drawled.

"Why didn't you obey?"

"Other than my documented allergy to work?" Sam paused to let the quiet laugh die away on both sides. "Because I was busy training a new recruit, and he was very eager to learn the ropes." He nodded as if remembering a sunny day on the river when the fish were biting. "Yes, sir, these young fellows, they're much more aggressive and impatient than we were. Wild young guys. I'd hate to be in the Opposition's shoes when they get the reins in their hands . . ." He broke off as if he'd said too much, but his grin said, *We're having fun now, huh?*

Adramelech was not intimidated and certainly not amused. His wet black eyes were like puddles of tar on a beach. "Stick to the questions, little angel." His voice was as dry as Thirst itself. "Did you answer the summons?"

Sam smiled. "You know that I didn't, Senator." Adramelech was famously the president of the Great Senate of Demons, so this was a bit of a swipe, but the stony face didn't show even the tiniest crack.

"Then we need hear no more from this honorable gentleman," said Caym, blinking and pushing his glasses back up his nose. "It's almost noon and we have many more witnesses to depose. Unless his Honor objects . . . ?"

Adramelech made a noise of contained disgust and shook his head.

Sam gave me a little thumbs-up as he passed me on his way out of the ballroom. I half wished he would have stayed, just so I could have seen at least one friendly face.

They broke for lunch but I didn't feel like eating. I went back to my room to see if it had been searched—it had, of course—and then got a soft drink from the machine before returning to the ballroom. The atmosphere seemed to have become even more tense, frustration setting in as both sides realized nothing was going to be accomplished, and nothing was going to be said that everyone didn't already know.

Shortly after the proceedings resumed I got my call to the stage. As I climbed the stairs I thought I was being stared at a little more intently than I had expected, and not just from the Opposition side of the room. I couldn't help wondering whether the Heavenly bastard or bastards who had set Clarence on me might be watching me even now, in this very room.

No matter where some handicappers may rank me, I'm not the dumbest guy ever to wear a halo. I did exactly what Karael had told me, answering the questions as truthfully as I could while staying resolutely clear of anything controversial. At least I did until Prince Sitri sideswiped me with a surprise inquiry. His soggy, wheezing voice made me want to clean each of the words thoroughly before I allowed them into my brain.

"Isn't it true that you've been following up on the case since the disappearance of Edward Walker, Mr. Dollar? That you have been investigating various unusual acquaintances of Mr. Walker's?"

Karael, bless him, bristled and half-rose from his chair. "What our people do and what our internal policies are in an unprecedented case like this are none of your business!"

One of Sitri's eyebrows rose like a caterpillar climbing a glob of suet. "Pardon me, but aren't missing souls all of our business? Is that not the reason we are gathered here in this lovely hotel? Surely only someone with something to hide would object to my question?"

I could see dozens of laptops and phones around the room suddenly being assaulted by ten times that many fingers (in most cases) as heavenly and infernal bureaucrats took note of this interesting little *contretemps*. The flurry of typing and texting brought home to me the strangeness of the whole conference in a way nothing else had. All these creatures of light and darkness, immortal and immensely powerful, with abilities humans could only guess at, and yet by mutual consent they were meeting here on Earth where they had to make do with the stumbling artifacts of mortal technology to do their jobs. It was like the UN deliberately holding their deliberations by candlelight in Dark Ages France.

In Caym, Karael had an unexpected ally in trying to cut off this line of inquiry. The bespoke demon suggested that perhaps a Rules Committee meeting should be convened to decide on whether Sitri's question was permissible under the agreed format. Many in the audience groaned at this time-wasting idea, but a few demanded it be implemented. A couple of spectators cried "cover-up!" from the infernal side of the room. The argument became general and rather shouty.

Adramelech, perhaps because he was also playing Eligor's game, or maybe just because he was a million years old and needed to piss, finally slammed his gavel hard against the tabletop and rasped for silence. In the ensuing hush he turned from side to side, stiff as a tortoise who had just woken from hibernation, then said, "We do not have time to do this today. We have only today for all the witnesses. These points can be resolved before the deliberative phase tomorrow, time permitting." Which effectively closed off Prince Sitri's question and anything like it. I saw no disappointment in the glittering eyes that peeped out of the prince's drooping facial flesh, and I wondered if the whole thing had just been Sitri's way of poking at his rival Eligor, like the little confrontation he had arranged between Caz, me, and the Horseman in the hotel bar the night before.

I answered a few more procedural questions and was interested to note that nobody on either side seemed willing to bring up the strange coincidence of Grasswax getting snuffed at the same site only a few hours later. In fact, the whole subject of what really happened around the Walker disappearance seemed to be surrounded with an invisible fence like the kind people use to keep wayward dogs in the yard. But how did they get all those demons *and* angels fitted with shock collars? How could a supposed inquiry work so hard not to inquire? How high did this Third Way thing go—and did it reach that high on both sides?

After I was released from the stage, a number of other angels were interviewed about the souls who had disappeared after Edward Walker, but none of it gave me anything to work with or pushed the discussion forward much at all. Already any pretense of fact-finding had disappeared into partisan bickering. If you think watching Congress make laws is unappealing, you should see the sausage-factory of the eternal powers at work. Gosh, you would think they didn't like each other or something.

Five o'clock was approaching. I was hungry and depressed, two things that don't usually go together for me, and I was just contemplating sneaking out as soon as Karael looked away for a moment, when Adramelech abruptly gaveled the whole thing to a close.

"We will resume tomorrow morning," he said, his words like wind over dry hills. "I suggest that all participants consider ways to make our next session more productive. I am not impressed with our progress today, nor does it make me hopeful of any real joint solution to our problem."

He walked from the stage as slowly as a tin toy overdue for a winding. Caym followed him while Sitri waited patiently for the hydraulic lifter that would move him into his cushioned golf cart. The prince's pudgy fingers were tented on his chest, and to my untrained eye he looked rather pleased with his day's work, which as far as I could tell seemed to have consisted of nothing more useful than taunting Eligor with hints about the Magian Society. Should I try to question Sitri again? I wasn't kidding myself he would do me any favors, but I wondered how deep his rivalry with Eligor went. Enough that he might throw me a bone, if only to help bury the Grand Duke? But he was rolling toward the freight elevator, and I didn't have the strength of will to chase him just now.

I checked in with Sam but the ache of my buddy's injuries hadn't been improved by a long day in a ballroom chair. He was going to take a nap but promised to catch up with me later, so I went upstairs and called in a room service strike on my position, then took my coat and tie and shoes off. I'm not a suit person by nature, as you've probably guessed. When forced to wear one, I always have to fight the urge to find a jagged rock and rub it off me like an itchy old snakeskin.

I've always found hanging out for long stretches in a hotel room a strangely mixed experience. The sense of *other*ness never goes away, the knowledge that you're not in your own place, although the anonymity of the situation is appealing. It's like being the last undiscovered guy in a game of hide and seek. You just settle into being on your own, and if it lasts long enough you even stop thinking about anyone looking for you. That is, until someone finds you.

I had been mindlessly flipping channels for so long that the sky beyond the room's flimsy muslin curtains had gone from pale blue to black, and the baseball games and prime-time dramas were winding down. In fact, I was winding down too after my long night and early start, my eyes starting to droop, when someone knocked on the door.

I'd called Sam an hour earlier and he'd said he was taking Advil and staying in bed, so the chances were good my late visitor was someone I didn't want to see. In this situation, that meant "someone I might have to shoot." My dwindling supplies of adrenaline were enough to get me off the bed quickly and over to my coat and shoulder holster. I still had the extended magazine on the Five-Seven automatic. I wanted it loose and in my hand from the start so it wouldn't snag on anything, so I hid it behind my back as I cracked the door, stepping back in case somebody strong was planning to kick it hard enough to break the chain. My heart was beating fast, and I was ready for anything Hell might send through the door.

Well, almost anything.

"Let me in," Caz said in a cold, flat voice. "This hotel is crawling with busybodies and spies. You can call me a whore when I'm inside and the door's locked."

She came in with her head up, looking defiant, ready to be slapped or cursed. I closed and locked the door and put the chain on, wondering just for a moment if I might have dozed off, if this could all be some kind of dream. She stared at me, waiting for me to do whatever I was going to do next, and to be honest, at that exact moment I didn't really know. The less angelic parts of me ended that confusion by grabbing her shoulders and pulling her toward me, then I used my mouth to silence the question she started to ask and dragged her down onto the bed. At first she seemed to be struggling, but it was only to get her clothes off. I didn't even bother with most of mine. We rolled, grabbed, scratched at each other. She was weeping and cursing as I entered her. I might have been doing the same.

thirty-four
breathing together

IT WASN'T love, and it wasn't just lust—it was *hunger*. I don't know what I wanted at that moment, but I wanted it so badly I couldn't think. I finished quickly and collapsed gasping on top of her, and only then felt the sweat that was gluing our bodies together and dripping from my forehead into her hair. I couldn't speak. Words were the last thing on my mind. She lay panting, her face turned away from me, her clothes half-on, half-off except for what was scattered around us on the bed and the floor. For long moments we just lay there, breathing into each other's ears as if everything else didn't exist. Did you know that was the real meaning of the word "conspire"? To breathe together. But what kind of conspiracy was this?

"Caz." I said. "Just . . . I don't understand any . . ."

Her hand shot up, pushing my chin back, forcing me up and away from her. For half a moment I thought she might go for my unprotected throat. Then, as she wriggled out from beneath me, skin sliding on damp skin, I was terrified that she was going to leave me. She got a knee into my gut and pushed me farther up and to the side until I had to roll off her, my naked belly and groin exposed, helpless as an animal ready for slaughter. But instead of killing me she clambered on top of me and reached down to yank and squeeze me until I was hard again, then she gripped my ribs with her knees and sank down on my cock, a look of such obsessive concentration on her face that for a moment I wondered if I was in her mind at all.

She rode me like a Valkyrie swooping down through the lightning to the last battle, late for the Twilight of the Gods. When I reached up for her pale breasts bobbing and shuddering just above me she clamped my wrists with her hands instead and forced my arms back down, pinning me with the fierceness of her need, rubbing and grinding on me until we both came together in a moment that seemed more heart attack than heart's desire. But that wasn't enough for Caz. She stayed on me, squeezing me inside her, and continued to ride me, until I felt another shudder build up inside her, a tremor that seemed to run up and down her spine until she quivered and then went rigid, then shook again for some seconds before sliding off to lie beside me, arms above her head, still twitching like the victim of an electrical shock.

"Oh, God," she said in a ragged whisper.

". . . But how can the Robo-Chop do all these things?" somebody squealed on the television, which was still on. *"Don't the blades get dull?"*

"If they do," answered some shouting Australian, *"then we'll replace 'em! Absolutely free!"*

A great gust of cheers and applause greeted this announcement. I rolled onto my side and reached for Caz, who was facing away from me, slender back and buttocks as vulnerable as a child's, but when I touched her she pushed my hand away.

"Don't."

"Just . . . Caz, talk to me."

She shuddered a little. "Don't. I'm serious. You know you're going to wind up telling me what a whore I am and how I broke your little heart. Let's just skip the preliminaries."

This time I grabbed her arm hard enough that she couldn't throw me off, and before she could really start struggling, I pulled her around to face me. For a moment she still kept her face turned away, the face that had haunted me for days, but then she gave up. Drops of sweat clung to her forehead and cheeks but her eyes were dry as they met mine.

"Don't ask the questions because there are no answers," she said. "You and I, we had a moment, okay, but we can never be together in a million years. Just forget about it. I only came here to tell you something."

"The hell with that." I sat up. She stayed on her back, delicate and damaged, putting me even farther in the wrong. She was lying right there in front of me, telling me I couldn't have her. I fought against a cloud of red fury that could deliver nothing but disaster. "No! I don't believe this is nothing. I know nothing, and this isn't it."

"Okay, so call it lust." She slid farther up the bed so she could lay her damp, white-gold head against a pillow. The ivory length of her from navel to feet stretched beside me, distracting me, especially the abbreviated triangle between her thighs that gleamed like straw spun into gold. "We have that on my side, too. It's nothing unusual."

"Damn it, Caz, what do you want from me? If you're going to dump me, what are you doing here?"

"Dump you?" She pushed herself back against the bumpy headboard but didn't seem to notice how uncomfortable it was. "You have an inflated sense of yourself as a lover if you think a one-night stand means happily ever after, Dollar. Especially between you and me."

"Are you telling me you don't feel the same way?" I wanted to hit something. I wanted to rip the covers off the bed, spilling her and everything we'd done like a magician's tablecloth trick gone embarrassingly wrong. "Go ahead, then. Tell me. Let me hear you say it."

She looked at me then, really looked at me for the first time since she'd come through the door, eyes somber and serious. "I don't feel the same way you do, Bobby."

It was like being knifed in the gut. I've had that happen, so I know. The air pushed out of the belly, the cold, hard ache of something that shouldn't be there, shouldn't *ever* be there—it was almost exactly the same. "You're lying."

"Lying is what I do," she said quietly. "It's my job. But I'm trying to do you a favor and tell the truth for once."

I got up and walked to the minibar, but taking a drink, especially out of one of those puny little bottles seemed like such a weak thing to do, such a *human* thing, that I turned around again and walked back to the bed. My entire life, the Highest's grand plan for Doloriel, had shrunk to the dimensions of this little hotel room . . . or even smaller. To the size of a mattress covered with damp sheets. I have never wanted so badly to hit someone, to hurt someone the way I was hurting but I have also never wanted so badly to grab that same person and carry her away, to flee the wicked, wearisome world and spend the rest of whatever life I had trying to make her happy. "Torn" is not the word. "Confused" is not the word. I don't think there is a word. "So, why did you come here?" I managed at last. "Why, Caz?"

"To warn you," she said. "To try to save your life."

I laughed, I'm sure rather bitterly. The life in question didn't seem like an important commodity at that moment. "Some demon you are."

"I didn't say I don't care about you at all." For a moment she had to look away, and I had a stupid hope that I had broken through somehow, that she was going to tell me that all the rest of what she'd said had been another lie. But when she turned back to me her face was horribly, horribly composed again. "Of course I do, in my own way. And I don't want anything to happen to you—at least, not because of me." She sat up and gathered her clothes, then slid off the bed and began to pick up her shoes and the rest of what had fallen, rewinding the spool of our sex, making it as though it had never happened. She was still half-naked, and despite my guts roiling and my head pounding, the sight of her bending over to get her coat was too much for me. I tried to put my arms around her but she violently yanked herself away from me.

"No! Don't! I can't! I can't do that again." She backed away, then after staring me down for a moment, stepped into her panties and began slowly putting herself back together. Every glimpse of flesh made my chest ache, especially when she buttoned up her shirt and the main expanse of her pale skin disappeared like the sun going behind clouds.

"Now," she said when she was dressed, "we can argue some more or you can listen to me." She looked at her watch. "We don't have much time before I have to go."

"With him?"

"Argue or listen?"

I closed my mouth.

"Eligor's ending the conference early," she said. "I heard him talking to one of his subordinates. Tonight, at midnight."

"What are you talking about? He doesn't have the power to do that even if it *is* his hotel This is a goddamn summit conference! He's outranked by a bunch of guys on his own side, let alone what *my* side would think about it. You're wrong, Caz. It's not going to happen."

"I heard what I heard," she said, cool as a marble fountain. "And if he's doing it, it's probably to catch you by surprise, Bobby. He told me he wouldn't . . . he said he wasn't interested in you anymore, but we all know what his word's worth."

"Hold on. He told you he wouldn't go after me anymore? Is that what you were going to say? Why would he say that? What did you tell him? Or what did you *give* him . . . ?"

"Now you're arguing," she said.

"Fuck it, that's not fair . . ." I began.

"But there's more!" shouted the audience along with the Australian television huckster. He continued on, whipping them into a frenzy. *"That's right! For this one low price you can get two Robo-Chops, plus two shredder blades, two deli slicers, and this beautiful serving plate!"* The infomercial audience sounded like they were nearing the climax of a particularly noisy orgy, or else, perhaps, watching the Christians being delivered to the arena sand to meet the maneaters. I stalked to the television to turn it off, then began looking around on the floor next to the bed for the remote.

The door thumped closed.

I ran after her, snagging myself on some trailing bedclothes. When I had untangled my legs and got the door open, Caz had already vanished around the corner of the corridor, no doubt heading for the elevator. I could hear other voices in the hall and hesitated, balancing my need to catch her with my desire not to be running around Eligor's hotel with my dick dangling and no gun. Caution won out, but only barely. I threw on my pants and pulled my jacket on over my bare chest, shoved the automatic into my pocket, and pushed my feet into my shoes without untying them before I hurried down the hall.

Three minor angels were having a rare old time trying to open the door to their room. They had clearly been tasting the unfamiliar freedoms of mortal bodies, especially the sort that came from fermented grain, but I still didn't want to make a spectacle of myself chasing down the corridor after a female demon who had probably just passed them—something that might pierce the haze enough to be remembered tomorrow. I manufactured a little you-ought-to-know-better smile as I walked by, sending them into gusts of embarrassed laughter, then I moved briskly toward the elevator.

Could she be right somehow? Did Eligor, maybe with Caym's help, have the clout to shut down the conference? And would he really do it just to get a crack at me?

He thinks I tricked him, I realized. *He thinks I tricked him about the feather, not to mention he obviously knows there's something between me and Caz, whether she told him about us or not.* A grand duke of Hell might or might not have ordinary kinds of sexual jealousy, but they all had a very keen sense of possession, and I'm not talking about *The Exorcist* variety. Yeah, he might just be that unhappy with me.

But whatever Caz thought, there was no way Eligor could manage to end the summit in the middle of the night as far as I could see. It was past eleven. What was he going to do, call up Karael and suggest sending everybody home and postponing the rest of the joint powers' little circle jerk? The higher angels hate putting on human form in the first place, hate leaving Heaven; I could just imagine how that proposal would go over with Karael.

When I reached the elevators I could see that the one Caz must be in had already reached the second floor. I jumped into one of the others, gambling that she was going all the way down, figuring that if she didn't I could come back up from the lobby and search the lower floors. When the door pinged open, I pushed out past a group of snickering, drunken demons and hurried across the lobby but saw no sign of her anywhere, so I headed for the main entrance. I almost smashed through the nearest glass door when it didn't open fast enough because I'd spotted her long legs walking away from valet parking along the front of the hotel, toward the parking lot. None of the valets or visitors seemed to be paying much attention, so I sprinted after her.

I caught her just at the edge of the building where she had stopped as if to wait for someone. I was pretty sure that someone wasn't me. The smell of the bay was strong, and I could hear seagulls keening. I hadn't been outside since I'd checked in. I'd almost forgotten we were out at Sand Point.

When she saw it was me, her whole body slumped like she'd been shot, but she straightened up again and stepped away from me as I approached. My coat was half-buttoned over my shirtless chest, my shoes only barely on my feet. I must have looked like a lovesick hobo.

"Now what?" There was enough chill in her words to make goose bumps.

"I don't believe you're doing what you want to do," I said.

"You don't know anything about what I want, Bobby. You only think you know. I'm not who you think I am." She said it with the patience of a weary parent dealing with her spoiled child. "I'm a million times worse than you can imagine. I've been in Hell for centuries." She laughed. It was painful to hear. "They broke me a long time ago. I'm a lifer."

"Bullshit. You wouldn't have—"

"Wouldn't have what? Fucked you? Do you think that makes you unique? Grow up, Dollar!" She looked over her shoulder as a big, black car came sliding up from the front of the hotel. "Oh, shit."

She grabbed me then and pushed me back into the shadows of the building, but the car just eased up and settled to a stop at the edge of the sidewalk less than ten yards away. I could see a pale-haired silhouette in the front seat that had to be Eligor.

"You're going away with him, huh?" I was beginning to wonder how much of her visit had been her idea, and how much might have been Eligor setting her on me just to soften me up for the killing blow. At the moment, though, I didn't care if he shot me through the heart. Wouldn't have been the first time. Wouldn't even have been the first time tonight. It never even occurred to me that I was carrying a gun too.

"Yes, of course I'm going away with him. Don't you understand? *I don't have any other choice.*"

"Does he have the feather?"

She shook her head, but she still had me pinned back against the concrete wall. "Wake up, Bobby! This isn't a detective novel. No, he doesn't have it. I don't have it either, and I don't know where it is. I told you what happened."

"Then why did he take you back?"

She stepped back again so that half of her was bathed in the light from the hotel's grand front entrance. Behind her I saw Eligor lean forward a little as if he was watching. For just a moment his eyes gleamed red in the darkness of the front seat, as if he was his own anti-theft system.

Fucking show-off, I thought.

"He let me come back . . . because he wanted to know about you. All about you. And I told him everything. There? Are you happy? I sold you out, Bobby, just like any good demon. Just like you should have expected."

"But everything else—"

"Everything else was a lie!" She lowered her head for a moment. When she lifted it she wore an expression of rage and misery like I'd never seen. "I thought we might have something, sure. I like students. I told you that. I thought we might study things together. I thought we might even learn from each other. But I was wrong. You've been wearing a body too long, Dollar. You're just like any other angel or demon who's gone native. You're letting your human disguise convince you of things that aren't so—that can't be so." She stepped all the way out into the light. "Goodbye, Bobby."

She turned toward the long, black car.

"But damn it, I love you," I said, loud enough that even the monster waiting for her behind his tinted windows must have heard. "I don't care about Heaven or Hell, Caz. I just want you."

She hesitated for such a long moment I thought time itself might have ground to a halt. Then she came back toward me and grabbed my lapels as if she wanted to shake me the way I'd wanted to shake her since she first walked into my room. She pulled at my coat so hard I thought she'd rip it, then stood on tiptoes and put her face close to mine so I could feel the chill of her skin, the heat of her breath. She stared at me. I could not have told you for all the glory of Heaven what she was thinking.

"I love you," I said again.

She turned away, empty, hopeless. "Then you're a fool."

She let me go and walked toward the car. The door opened as if by magic and she slid inside, then the black sedan pulled away from the sidewalk and slipped off into the night.

I must have stood there for several minutes watching the taillights dwindle and then disappear in the fog off the bay, wondering why they spent all that money on an expensive replica lighthouse if they weren't going to turn on the goddamn light, before I realized that something felt funny on the front of my jacket. Only half paying attention I rubbed my chest, looking for wounds Caz's fingernails might have left, thinking at least I would have a few days before those last traces were gone, too, but something hard and heavy was making a lump in my kerchief pocket. I took it out and let it slink into my palm, then took a few steps out into the light so I could see what I had.

It was a heavy, shiny little oval sitting on a snaky pile of chain like the last little serpent's egg in the nest waiting to hatch. As I turned it back and forth I finally realized through my haze of blasted thoughts what I was looking at: the locket Caz wore around her neck, the gift her husband the Polish count had given her (if any of her story was true) on the night she'd killed him.

What did it mean? An apology? A curse? Maybe even—and for a moment I almost let my useless human heart get the better of my sense—a promise of sorts? Or was she just telling me that she was done with all obligations, obligations to the dead and to the living as well?

I flicked it open. Inside two curls of hair lay twisted together like the DNA of some unknown species, one brown, which must have come from her little maid, the other a gold so pale it almost looked like platinum, which could only have come from the Countess of Cold Hands. I closed it and walked back to the hotel entrance.

I was standing in the elevator watching the lights flick slowly upward toward my floor, feeling empty and cold as an abandoned house, when the bomb went off in the ballroom downstairs.

thirty-five

boom boom

THERE'S AN evil old song by Little Walter called, "Boom Boom, Out Go the Lights," and that's pretty much how it happened. The explosion down in the Grand Ballroom rocked the entire building, most definitely including the elevator shaft. The car lurched up and down and even a little bit sideways, knocking me around like a pinball, and then suddenly everything went dark.

How do I know the explosion was down in the ballroom? Because if you were going to make sure the summit conference didn't continue, where else would you put a bomb except in the room where it was happening, the only room big enough in the hotel? Eligor's own hotel.

He blew up his own fucking hotel! I remember thinking as I stood very still, trying to figure out if there was structural damage to the elevator and shaft or if it had only stopped because the power went out. But I came as close to admiring a murderous bastard of a demon-lord as I can get. Eligor the Horseman had *cojones*, I had to give him that. There was a lesson in this for me, too; I'd been trying to imagine how he'd get it done and hadn't even considered that he might just blow the shit out of his own joint and kill a few dozen people at the very least, not to mention seriously inconveniencing hundreds of his closest allies. I'd seen how crowded that lobby was and couldn't even imagine the scene now. I would never underestimate him again.

Eventually, I pushed up the emergency hatch on the top of the elevator and climbed out, then reached up in the dark. I seemed to be only a short distance under the next floor, so I braced myself against the walls of the shaft and worked my way upward until I could perch close enough to the door to work on it. It was hard to find leverage, but at last I got my fingers into the crevice and pulled it far enough apart to risk scrambling over and out. The escape was a lot hairier than I would have liked—it was pitch black, and even though the elevator was blocking the shaft, that was only in the spot just beneath me. If I didn't manage to stay on top of my particular elevator I could have a straight drop to the basement. Anyway, I managed at last to clamber out onto the floor, covered with greasy carbon stains, the muzzle of my gun causing a permanent groin bruise through the inside of the pocket.

Some emergency lights came on now, casting a dull red—dare I say hellish?—glow over everything, so that even with my better-than-average sight I had to get real close before I could be certain I was on the third floor. Sam's room was on the next floor up so I headed for the stairs. The stairwell was crowded with overstimulated people, most of them hurrying down toward the lobby before the hotel fell over or something, others in just as much of a hurry to get away from the lower floors where the explosion had happened. I smelled smoke but hadn't yet seen any sign of fire, though the other guests looked and acted like terrified animals. There's nothing like sudden disaster to deliver humans back to their original state of being, and even if you're a demon or an angel vacationing in a human body, it works pretty much the same way.

I found Sam sitting in the open doorway of his room pulling his loafers on. I dropped down beside him because I wanted to tie my own shoes properly. I had a gun, yes, but no socks, no flashlight, no shirt, and no wallet. It's hard to be prepared for a major explosion in your hotel, but I'd definitely dropped the ball.

"So, you don't need a new body yet?" Sam asked.

"Not yet, but give me another ten minutes. Eligor's men are going to be looking for me and I'm sure they'd like to change that." Actually, I thought they were more likely to want to capture me if Caz had been telling the truth, and their boss still didn't have the feather, but I didn't want to waste time explaining everything.

Sam had the good grace not to ask any difficult questions, just climbed to his feet and slapped the place under his coat to let me know he was armed. "They might get an argument, then."

I felt ten times better just knowing he and I were together. Not only wouldn't I be worrying about what had happened to him, I knew from long, firsthand experience that he was exactly the right kind of guy to get into and out of trouble with—good thinker, good shot, good liar.

"So I'm guessing we want to go down where the other people are, if someone's after you," he said.

It took me a second to answer. "Yeah, sort of. Follow me to the stairs . . ."

Flashlight beams were now sweeping the wall at the far end of the corridor. The hallway had cleared in the half a minute since I'd gotten there, so whoever was coming with all those lights had deliberately forced their way upstream against the fleeing guests. In other words, they were almost certainly bad news.

Even as I yanked at Sam's sleeve they appeared around the corner at the end of the hall; big, hunched figures wearing heavy gear and some kind of night-vision goggles that protruded from their faces like the eyestalks on a snail. Sam and I legged it the opposite direction, back to the stairwell I had used to get there. We opened the door as quietly as we could, but Eligor's men must have been using amplification devices, or else they just had extra-good hearing. Muzzles flashed in our direction and we heard the stuttering, ripsaw noise of automatic fire as we dove through the door and slammed it behind us.

"Hold on a second," I said.

"Not a good idea," Sam replied.

"Just let me . . ." I finally got the extended magazine out of my gun and thumbed the silver slugs out of it, back into my pocket. Then I leaned out into the stairwell and tossed the empty magazine onto one of the steps above us "They've got infrared goggles—they'll spot it. Maybe they'll think we went that way." And they would also take note that I had a large hand gun, which couldn't do anything worse for us than make our pursuers a bit more cautious.

As we sprinted down the stairs past the third floor and heading for the second, I said, "We need to get out of this building fast. The next floor down's the mezzanine, right over the ballroom, and if it's even still standing it'll be full of firemen, and who knows what else."

"So why do you want to go that way?"

"Because we're going to sneak out the back." I fought to get my breath. "Out to the marina." The hotel had its own little harbor, because more than a few of the Ralston's guests liked to arrive in expensive watercraft.

"Why?" Sam was panting, too. Our conversation sounded a bit like we were both being strenuously massaged. "We going to steal a yacht?"

"Better. Now shut up. I'm trying to read my phone."

We dashed out onto the second floor, which was empty but full of hanging dust and the smell of burning. I hoped it was all from downstairs and that we wouldn't suddenly find ourselves caught between Eligor's security goons and a wall of fire. The only good thing was that the group chasing us had been comparatively small, no more than half a dozen men. Twice that number had probably gone to my floor but they would find out pretty quickly I wasn't there. If the Grand Duke hadn't been so busy making a point, watching Caz tell me off without even bothering to intervene, he might have called his men and told them I was out in front of the hotel. At least, that was the only reason I could see that he'd let me walk away when I was right there for the taking.

We sprinted through the second floor's wide hallways past various meeting rooms and got to the end and the other fire stairs just as someone kicked open the stairwell door we'd exited. A spray of gunfire spattered the wall just to our right and petered out across the ceiling.

"Stop!" someone shouted. "This is the police! You can't escape! Drop your weapons and lie down."

"If that's the police," Sam grunted as we wrestled open the door to the stairs, "then I'm the Little Drummer Boy."

I plunged down the stairs with my big buddy right behind me. "We have to find a way out to the marina without going near the lobby, 'cause everything there's blown to shit."

"There's an escalator on this floor that leads to the pool," Sam said. "We can get to the boats without having to go near the lobby end."

I heard the stairwell door open above us, a spatter of gunfire, then curses. The shots must have been accidental. One of the bullets actually pinged down the walls past us, kicking up gouts of plaster, shredding the wall hangings.

The first floor wasn't damaged at this end, but the smoke and dust were even thicker, and the far end at the front of the hotel was clearly on fire, flames gleaming through the gray haze. I could hear screams now, and not just the agitated voices of rescue crews, but honest to God screams of pain and terror. I did my best to pretend that it wasn't my fault—all this destruction and carnage just so Eligor could catch me.

But had Eligor really set off a bomb just so he could catch me off guard? Surely there were easier ways he could have done it—waited until tomorrow then thrown a cordon around the hotel being one obvious way. Why blow up the place?

Because he wants the conference stopped, I realized as we hurried toward the escalator. Bobby Dollar was only part of what was bugging the Grand Duke. The whole discussion was getting too close to things he didn't want discovered—*especially* if he had made a deal with someone in the heavenly hierarchy. His fellow demon lords would forgive any kind of murder or treachery but they would never forgive a deal with the enemy.

"Shit," said Sam, staring down at the long, unmoving escalator. "Of course. Power's off."

"Then we do it the old-fashioned way," I said. "Don't trip."

When we were halfway down the bad guys came out of the smoke and dust behind us like armed ghosts. They were shouting for us to stop, but they weren't pretending to be police any more, and if they didn't really want to kill me they were doing a good job of acting like they did. A stream of automatic fire took the rubber handrail off just behind Sam, so that it flew through the air like a dying mamba. The next burst laid a trail of holes down the aluminum escalator wall in front of me. Another *pak-pak-pak* blew the crystal chandelier hanging over our heads into glittering splinters, raining sharp fragments down on us.

We ran with our heads down as the floor-to-ceiling glass windows exploded into shards behind us. We ducked out through one of the automatic doors our pursuers had just conveniently blown into powder and then sprinted along the edge of the pool, both bent over like Quasimodo searching desperately for a bathroom. Out in the comparatively clean, cold bay air I realized for the first time how much smoke and particulate I'd been breathing and silently thanked my bosses for lending me a good, sturdy body in which to run for my life.

"We need to buy some time," I gasped.

When the men in combat gear burst out of the hotel after us, Sam and I both turned and began firing. They dropped back into the cover of the doorway and returned a few volleys, but they were shooting wildly.

I had squeezed the trigger several times before I realized that I'd only had twenty shots to start, and unless I found the time somewhere to hand-load the shells jingling in my pocket, fifteen or sixteen shots was all I was going to have for a while. I would need to be careful.

We fired as we ran, just like Butch and Sundance, and because Sam was a better shot than me, and because he wasn't wasting silver, I let him do most of the shooting. We skirted the pool, ran down a tanbark-covered embankment (ripping the hell out of a bunch of inoffensive plants some hotel gardener had probably spent several days placing just *so)* and then hurried along the jetty beside the boats with their furled sails. The bigger ships had their own part of the marina, but I doubted that was where we'd find what I was looking for.

"It'll be over here," I told Sam. "By the harbor master's office."

"And 'it' is what, exactly?"

"Excursion boat," I said. "The hotel does their own fishing tours. Cabin cruiser." Fatback's hotel maps and information were going to keep us alive, I was almost certain. "I know you can pilot one, but can you hotwire one?"

Fire engines were screaming up to the hotel behind us, and the sky was beginning to turn scarlet, which made us better targets. The bullets started to chop along the dock behind us, and I reflected that even if Eligor had other, better reasons for derailing the conference, his men still seemed very willing to shoot lots of bullets into his friends' expensive boats to try to keep me from leaving it.

We found the hotel's twenty-five foot cruiser whose stern proclaimed it the *John P. Gaynor*, whoever that was. To my very cursory inspection it looked like a reasonable little craft. I turned and ducked behind the gunwale and made an old word literal by sheltering behind it as I fired several rounds at our pursuers, forcing them to take cover behind a shed. Sam was already in the cabin, on his back, fumbling in the dark. I found a flashlight clamped to the wall and tossed it down to him, then went back and fired off a shot every time I saw something move behind the shed. I think I hit one of them; I certainly heard the sound of someone made profoundly unhappy by something. Whether it was the same guy, enraged by his wound, or some buddy of his making a heroic play, one of the guards then charged out from behind the shed and right toward us, automatic rattling, the flashes on the masts between us throwing long, quick shadows. He was wearing a black riot helmet, and it was hard to see him clearly with the fire and smoke billowing out of the building behind him, but I remembered Leo telling us that shooting last was often more important than shooting first. I hunkered back down behind the gunwale until only my eyes and the top of my head were sticking up—parts of me that I would have hated to lose but which I would need to make the shot. I let him get to within twenty yards, his bullets stitching their way along the cabin behind me, shattering glass and smashing expensive wood, before I pulled the trigger. His plexiglas mask spiderwebbed, and he tumbled forward and slid a couple of feet then lay still, but his helmet came off and kept rolling, its progress as uneven as a fumbled football. I hoped I'd just shot a demon, not some poor bastard of a security guard, but I didn't have time for a forensic exam. Behind me the boat's engine coughed and then caught, and Sam yelled, "Get your ass in here!"

Sam steered us out of the berth while I was still trying to find my footing to get down to the cabin. A few more shots hissed past, and one cracked against the wall behind me, but already the muzzle flashes were dim as birthday candles. The shooting stopped as I leaned into the cabin, feeling for the first time as if I really might survive this fiasco.

"Where?" Sam shouted.

"I don't know! What do I look like, Mr. Bay Cruise Expert? The hell away from here."

"There's a landing not too far from my place," he said. "We can make it in ten minutes."

I hadn't thought of heading down toward Southport, but it made sense. I crouched beside Sam as he piloted the cabin cruiser out of the estuary and into the dark waters of the slough. The boat began to pitch as we got out into the bay proper, and the wind kicked up. My stomach protested, but I was just glad not to be shot at and not to be in that hotel, which now looked like something out of *Gone With The Wind*, hungry flames leaping on both the first and second floors as fire engines, ambulances, and police cruisers screamed toward it from several directions.

"You want to tell me what any of this is about?" Sam asked, squinting through the cracked windshield.

I weighed how much truthiness would feel comfortable. I still didn't want to put Sam in a bad position, and just because we had got away didn't mean this was the end. Eligor had a long reach, and for all I knew they'd reconvene the conference next week and start asking questions again. "I seem to have pissed off the hotel owner," was all I admitted. "Guess I left too many wet towels on the floor."

Sam gave me a look and went back to squinting at the dark water. I was glad he was being careful. The public wetlands start just south of Sand Point, and there aren't many lights out here, because what do sandpipers and curlews need with streetlights, anyway? More than a few ancient piers and even some abandoned boats lay half-buried in silt up and down the shore, and most of them could punch a pretty good hole in anything smaller than a tanker.

I clambered back up the cabin steps, so I could hunker down in the clean, nippy bay air and try to get my bearings. I had about nineteen seconds to think about what I was going to do next, which I wasted on several lurid fantasies of me single-handledly yanking the head off one of Hell's most prominent nobles. Then something buzzed past me and smashed into the gunwale, showering me with chips of mahogany. The actual crack of the gun followed an instant later.

"Sam! Those fuckers are still after us!" I slid toward the rail on my belly, then cautiously lifted my head. They were at least a couple of hundred yards back, but their craft looked wider and faster than ours, and its full complement of running lights made it burn like a star. "And they have a better ride than we do!" I cursed myself for relaxing too soon: I should have realized Eligor would have more boats. I steadied the Five-Seven on the railing and squeezed off a shot, just to let them know there was a downside to all that light they were showing, but I don't think I hit anything. I was now down to about half a dozen rounds in the mag and the loose ones rattling in my pocket, depending on how many had fallen out. "Sam! Fucking do something!"

"Do you really think there's anything more useful I can do than keep the throttle all the way open and try to avoid running into anything?"

"Point taken." I inched toward the stern railing, feeling very strongly that I didn't want to get my head blown off. "Cabin cruisers don't have torpedoes or anything, do they?" I called.

"Oh, yeah, thanks for reminding me. There's a Polaris missile down here under the cooler."

"You don't have to be sarcastic just because I don't know shit about boats." A few more shots, or at least their hissing ghosts, snapped past. I chanced a quick look. "They're gaining on us!"

"Fuck me." Sam went silent for a moment, long enough to worry me, then said, "Keep your head down. There's a nearer place I can land, but it's probably going to be rough."

"What does that mean?"

"Don't ask."

I popped up and squeezed another shot into the center of the constellation of lights. Their boat was higher than ours, and I couldn't see anyone on it, so I aimed for the cabin windows but again didn't seem to hit anything. *You* try shooting a pistol at a pitching boat from another pitching boat two hundred yards away, then you can criticize.

Our cabin cruiser's engine was whining like a wood-chipper with a stump caught in it, and I began to wonder if we were even going to make shore. We took a sharp, deck-swamping turn toward the nearest bank and began slaloming through an inlet where reeds grew high on either side, hiding us for the moment. I crawled to the cabin stairs. "They can't see us."

"Stay the hell down," my friend suggested. "You're not that much fun, but I still don't want to lose you." As if to prove the opposite he suddenly swung the wheel wildly to one side, sending me tumbling. "Old dock," he called as I picked my bruised body up from where I'd slammed against the outside of the cabin wall. "Now, shut up."

I wanted to point out that he'd been doing most of the talking, but I was too busy clinging to the slippery deck with my fingernails. Try it some time, it's fun! A moment later I saw a searchlight beam sweeping the reeds just to one side. Eligor's men were much closer. The narrow, shallow estuary didn't seem to be slowing them down much at all.

In fact, it slowed them down so little that a moment later the light fell directly on us and made the cabin glow like a Nativity scene in the town square as shots began to ring out again. This time they were definitely hitting things. Bits of wood and aluminum and fiberglass, and whatever else held the cabin cruiser together, were flying everywhere like razor-sharp pinwheels. One splinter about the size of my hand stuck into the cabin wall near my head and quivered as each new bullet slapped the boat. I scrambled on my belly until I could slide headfirst down the steps into the cabin. "Where's this landing?"

"What are you doing down here?" Sam asked, risking a look back at me. "Get the hell up there and shoot something!"

Turning around in that narrow space wasn't easy. I had just reached the top again when somebody or something squared up our cabin cruiser like a hanging curveball, bringing us to a surprisingly immediate, noisy, violent halt. I pitched backward, managing to keep my feet on the steps but smashing the base of my head against the low doorway. My gun flew away, bouncing then sliding along the darkness of the deck. I tried to crawl after it, but my body abruptly decided that my muscles should stop working for a few moments, and I collapsed onto the wet boards.

Even as I lay with a skull full of sparks, trying to remember which of me was the top part and which the bottom and how to make either of those work, everything around me, gunwales, bullet holes, shattered cabin windows, suddenly leaped into brilliance as a cruelly bright light set it all ablaze. A moment later I heard another loud crunch, this one farther away, and angry voices shouting, but I was still trying to find the correct sequence that would make my rubbery body function again so I could get up onto my hands and knees and look for my gun. I heard nothing but ominous silence from the cabin where Sam was.

I had just begun to crawl when shadows started clambering over the railing of our boat, dark, shouting shapes. I tried to stand but it didn't work. Something cold and hard pressed against the back of my neck.

"Got you, you little shit," said Howlingfell. "Fucked up the boss's boat, but it was worth it."

The pressure increased, the barrel of the gun pushing brutally hard against the base of my skull until I gave in and let him force me onto my belly. He slid the gun down to rest against the highest knob of my backbone.

"You think you'll get lucky and make me kill you, Dollar." He was breathing hard, but not that hard—it sounded more like hunger than pain. "But I'll just put one in your spine. We can do everything we need to do with just the nerves of your head working—eyeballs, teeth . . . oh, there's plenty to work with. You'll scream out everything you know, Dollar, but it still won't end. Not for days. I promise."

thirty-six
departed this earth

SO THERE I was doing what comes naturally, dripping wet on my hands and knees with a gun against my neck, surrounded by the lights of Howlingfell's nearby boat and the worried shouts of his men, who seemed to be dealing with a fairly large hull breach of their own. Even though my head had slammed into the wall thingy above the steps leading down to the cabin, and now felt like a beachball full of sand and broken glass, I still couldn't help noticing a weird noise close behind me. Howlingfell noticed it too, and though he still held the gun against the knob of my spine, I felt the pressure ease just a little as he turned to look behind him. I know I should have heroically leaped to my feet and punched his lights out in his moment of distraction, but to be honest, I wasn't exactly sure where my feet were. But I did crane my neck so I could look, too.

A big shape came trudging up the steps from the cabin below, and for a brief, happy moment I thought it was Sam. It wasn't—it was one of Howlingfell's men, but he was making a strange gargling sound that didn't quite form words. As he rose into the light I could see he was struggling with something; one more wobbly step, and I saw the gaff hook through his throat, the long handle banging against his chest as he struggled to pull the barbed metal out of his neck.

"Shit!" was the only comment Howlingfell had time for, then Sam came up the steps behind the gaffed guard and shoved him out onto the deck where he fell beside me and lay twitching, still trying to get that hook out of his neck. It would all have been great, except Sam's hands were up, and they were both empty of firearms.

Howlingfell swung the gun away from me and pointed it at Sam. Eligor's men may have wanted me alive, but I was pretty sure that wasn't true for my buddy, so I did the only thing I could manage while down on my hands and knees—I slammed my thick, useless head right into Howlingfell's gut. He stumbled back against the rail and the gun flew up as he squeezed the trigger, the bang so close to my face that for a second I thought he'd blown my head off, but the shot hadn't hit anything. Sam took a step over the dying guy and, because he couldn't get close enough to do anything else, gave Howlingfell a hard shove in the chest that sent him over the rail and into the estuary.

Sam dragged me to my feet. I spotted my gun and lunged for it just before my buddy climbed over the rail and jumped into the dark water. I could hear Howlingfell thrashing nearby but couldn't see him. I squeezed a shot off in his direction anyway, and then, just for good measure, shot one of the nearest moving shapes on the brightly lit boat, sending it spinning down to the deck.

"Tell the boss we need *back-up*!" I heard Howlingfell screech past a mouthful of dirty water and weeds, then I followed Sam over the side toward the shore. How many shots did I have left? Probably two or three, and that was going to be it. My pockets were empty, the loose shells gone now, just so many expensive, shiny pebbles sinking to the estuary mud or rolling across the deck of the ruined cabin cruiser. I hoped that at least one of Howly's men might step on one and slip and break his neck.

The water was cold and muddy and just disgusting, but in that moment of unexpected freedom it felt like the finest spa treatment ever as we swam and sloshed and splashed toward the bank and its thicket of reeds. We had slipped beyond the glare of their lights, and I could hear the shouts behind us turning to panicky rage as the guards realized their leader was in the water and we were gone. The footing was terrible, slippery mud and tangles of roots, but we pushed and shoved and dug our way forward through the close-packed reeds like we were still swimming. A couple of shots snapped past us, and I realized we were probably creating a visible trail of thrashing stems, so I grabbed at Sam's collar and whispered for him to slow down. A few more shots cracked the night but none of them came close enough to make me nervous. We hunkered down until only our heads were above the water and kept going.

Something close to half an hour later we abandoned the reeds at last and collapsed in exhaustion on a bare, muddy lump of exposed ground. The moon looked down with its usual magnificent unconcern as we coughed and spat out water and only the Highest knew what other muck, then spent several more minutes just trying to get air back into our lungs. At last I sat up and made a quick inventory. Wet shoes, wet pants, wet jacket. One gun with three bullets in the pipe and a few more that had stuck in my pockets. The rest had fallen out into the ooze during our escape. It took me long moments to make my cold, slippery fingers work well enough to hand-load these extras, but I now had half a dozen fifteen-dollar silver rounds in my gun (it would have been cheaper to throw bottles of Chivas Regal at them) no other weapons and no cellphone—mine had tumbled out of my pocket with the extra bullets. I turned to Sam. "Do you still have your phone?"

He spat. It didn't make it off his chin. He finally rubbed it away with his muddy arm, which left him looking like a war-painted otter. "No. Fucking thing popped out somewhere along the parade route. My gun, too. You still have that plastic piece of shit you got from Orban?"

I showed him the Five-Seven.

"Well, that's something, anyway," he said. "I got nothing but a flashlight and a headache."

"Then we'd better start walking. Which way?"

He climbed to his knees, then cautiously lifted himself enough to look around. Other than massive power pylons looming on either side of us and the dark wires that sagged between them like scratches across the face of the moon, there were no landmarks I recognized except the faint, dark outline of Shoreline Park looming out of the bay a short distance south of us. "We're only a couple of miles from my place," Sam said. "We can probably get there from here without being spotted, and I've got a fuckin' armory hidden under the floorboards for just this kind of evening's entertainment."

"Go." I didn't have the energy to wait any longer. I knew if I didn't get moving soon I'd forget how it all worked. I hadn't been hit by any bullets, but I felt like someone had taken a piece of pipe to me and shifted a few things around in my torso and head pretty good. "Liked the gaff hook, by the way."

"I guess the Ralston does fishing charters. Darn nice hotel."

"Yeah. Well, they won't be doing any for a while because we just sank both their boats."

It was a long, slow trek by moonlight over the squelching ground and watery ruts, through pickleweed and salt grass and all kinds of other stuff that naturalists love but which is pure hell to wade through when your body's covered in bloody scrapes. As we got closer to the end of the nature preserve, I could see a few fluorescents burning in an office complex that backed onto the slough we were currently following. This tiny hint of civilization cheered me, but there was no way I wanted to go near that much light until we were almost at Sam's front door.

He finally led us over a little bridge that crossed the slough and into a tidy little park. The moonlight picked out picnic tables and a kiddie area with a slide and some swings. "Garcia Park," Sam said. "We're close—we won't even have to go near a main road. There's a cemetery on the far side of this, then it's only a hop and a skip across the fields to my place."

"Do you see me hopping or skipping?" I asked, tired and sore beyond belief, but his mention of the cemetery had reminded me of one of the odder things Fatback had told me about the real Reverend Habari he'd found, and that made me quiet again.

The park was a small one, and before too long we were laboriously climbing over the iron pickets that fenced the cemetery. "I remember this place," I said as we made our way between the monuments. The graveyard had gone more than a little to seed—it looked like the last time anyone had mowed the grass might have been last fall, and the only flowers were plastic, fake as tinsel, even by moonlight. "You used to hang out here a lot," I said. "I even came with you a couple of times."

Sam was silent for a few steps. "Drinking days," he said at last. "Yeah, I killed a few bottles out here. Helps a man keep things in perspective."

"Cemeteries or empty bottles?"

"Both."

I didn't point out to my buddy that he wasn't actually a man and hadn't been one for some time, if ever—none of us earthbound angels likes being reminded. Instead, I was trying to recall exactly what Fatback had told me—southeast corner? As best as I could tell, that seemed to be where we were headed, but it was another reason to miss my phone and all my notes. "Hey, let me have the flashlight, will you?"

Sam gave me a strange look. "What the hell do you want it for? We're trying to keep a low profile out here."

"Just something I was thinking about. C'mon, we haven't heard a whisper of those guys in an hour."

He reluctantly handed it over. It was a small light and not likely to give us away, but I kept it pointed near the ground anyway, sliding the dim beam across the headstones as we made our way over the untended lawn, much of which was more dirt than grass, a few yellowing strands still holding onto the edges of the bald patches like columns of retreating troops.

"Bobby, the light . . . you're worrying me."

I started to respond but something had caught my eye. I cut left and began walking toward it. Sam called that I was going in the wrong direction, but I wasn't listening.

He trotted after me. "Bobby? What the hell?"

"Hell is not the location I'm interested in right now."

"What are you talking about?" he said, but he didn't sound good. "What—?"

He didn't get a chance to finish his question because the distant noise that had been building for the last few seconds was now too loud to ignore. "Helicopter!" he said in precisely the way Captain Hook would have said, "Crocodile!" I killed the light, and we both threw ourselves to the ground, huddling face down and hoping, I suppose, that we would look like loose boulders in the middle of the churchyard. The stick-in-the-spokes noise got louder until the thing seemed to be right above our heads. A light stabbed down from it and swept one way across the cemetery grounds, then the other, but it didn't touch us. I know because I peeked. The helicopter continued on past, and I could see the beam reaching down here and there but farther away each time.

I got up when I couldn't hear the chopper blades any more and turned the light back on, then found what had caught my eye. After I had been standing there looking at it for long moments without saying anything, Sam clambered to his feet and limped over to stand beside me. "What's up, Bobby?" he asked, but he sounded like he knew. He sounded like the guy who says, "How long do I have, Doc?" when he already knows the answer is "Not long."

I let the beam play up and down the headstone. There really wasn't any need to say anything, or at least I didn't think so. The words were old and weatherworn but still quite legible, even by the weak beam of Sam's flashlight.

Moses Isaac Habari
Born January 14, 1928—Departed this earth May 20, 2004
Father, Brother, Pastor, Man of Peace

I turned and looked at Sam, but he just stared at the tombstone. "How did you know?" was all he said.

The sound was faint as a whisper, but because it came in the silence after Sam spoke—a silence in which a hundred different things I might say were swirling in my head—it was loud enough to startle. I turned just in time to see a half dozen figures loping toward us from about a hundred yards away across the cemetery.

Discussion time over.

We ran but we were already exhausted, wet, beaten, and bruised; before we had gone ten steps shots were whipcracking all around us. Our pursuers had lights on their guns this time, and every time I swerved at least a couple of them tracked me. I followed Sam, hoping he knew this place well enough to find us an escape route, or at least a place to make a stand, but although we crested a rise and saw we had almost reached the end of the cemetery, this part didn't have an iron fence but a high memorial wall made of stone. It looked big and strong enough to stop anything short of a grenade launcher, but we were on the wrong side of it for a standoff. In fact it looked a lot more like the kind of place a firing squad takes you just before they offer you the cigarette.

"What the hell . . . ?" I gasped.

"Sorry," was all Sam said, but we were already stumbling downhill, the wall looming in front of us, and I had to slow down so suddenly I almost ran into the list of carved names of dozens of folk, probably soldiers, who might have faced last moments much like this one. I spun and squeezed off a round—five left—but the men chasing us had already taken protected positions behind the headstones. None of them was more than a dozen yards away, and four or five beams converged on us like the end of a failed prison break from some old comedy film.

"There's nowhere to go, Dollar!"

"Drop dead, Howly," I shouted, "you probably said that last time, too." But I couldn't muster much bravado while we were making such an attractive, easy target.

"Throw down your gun or I'll blow the shit out of your friend Sammariel, and you'll still be in as much trouble as you already were."

"Don't do it," Sam said quietly.

"Not many alternatives as far as I can see." I held the gun up and showed it to him, then dropped it into the grass. At Howlingfell's urging I kicked it several yards away. Once he was satisfied he shouted for us to get down with our hands behind our heads and stay that way. I was flat out of ideas so I did what he said, wondering if I would at least get a chance to stick a finger in one of his squinty little eyes before Eligor's crew started working on me for real. Sam let himself down beside me, heavy and slow.

"You got another gaff hook in that coat?" I whispered.

"Not even a safety pin," he said. "You shouldn't have given up your gun, Bobby."

"Yeah, well, you seriously owe me a bunch of explanations." I kept it quiet because Howlingfell was moving toward us. "And I'm not going to let anyone shoot you until I get 'em." But it was all bullshit, of course. We'd managed to catch Howly and his men by surprise once, maybe even twice if you counted going for the boat in the first place, but although we'd proved Eligor's enforcer could be tricked, he wouldn't fall for the same trick twice and I was fresh out of new ones. As if to demonstrate his newfound caution Howlingfell came toward us almost crabwise with his gun pointing right at me, and stopped when he was still six feet away. A man's height. The depth of a grave.

"No more bullshit from you," he said. "No more smart talk. Thought it was funny shooting me in the nuts that time, did you?"

"Subtle," I said. "But hilarious, yes."

"Fuck you, little man. You won't be laughing much longer. Do you know what Grasswax said, even after we'd cut out half the shit in his body and showed it to him?" Howlingfell made his voice whiny. "*'I can still feel it!'* That's what he said. Talk about hilarious! *'Don't squeeze—it still hurts!'* And those guts weren't even connected to him anymore! That's what Eligor's special doctors can do." He smirked, the gun still pointed at my throat. "The boss promised I could have a front-row seat for your show, and I'm going to enjoy every moment." He reached into his pocket and pulled out a phone, but the gun never moved, and he was out of my reach anyway. He flipped it open like it was some kind of Star Trek communicator and thumbed a button. While he was waiting, he turned to his men behind the tombstones, who were still pinning us with their lights. "When I'm out of the way you can blow the big one to ribbons," he called. "Use the darts on the smaller one." Someone must have picked up on the other end of the call, because he suddenly dropped his voice to something several shades more submissive. "Boss?" he said to the phone. "Yeah, it's me. Mission accomplished."

We don't always get a chance to pick our last words wisely, but I hope when my time comes I'll have better luck than that. No sooner had Howly snapped the phone shut and begun to back out of the way when something came over the wall from behind us and hopped down like a monstrous black toad, landing in a crouch just in front of me and Sam. I could feel the heat radiating from it immediately, but I had only an instant to see the horribly familiar spreading black horns and the black, alien shagginess of its face as it looked around, blue flames pluming from its nostrils, then someone behind one of the headstones opened fire. I threw myself to the side and hugged the earth as bullets spattered off the memorial wall. Some of them must have hit the *ghallu*, but I knew already it didn't give a toss about anything but silver, and it didn't mind silver much more than I would an uncomfortable sunburn.

To his credit, Howlingfell was not going to lose his prize without a fight. He stepped toward the thing with his gun raised and started squeezing off shots in quick succession, half a dozen, a dozen, the ejected shells winking in the moonlight as they spun through the air and fell to the sparse grass. Then he took one step too many and, despite all the rounds he had fired at it, the horned thing seemed to notice him for the first time.

Two steaming, slate-black hands big as shovels snapped out and folded around his arms, then jerked him off the ground. For a moment Howlingfell fought back, thrashing and shouting in the creature's grasp as smoke rose where it clutched him. Then the *ghallu*'s jaws *unhinged*—there's no other word—gaping impossibly, hideously wide, exposing flames like a crematory oven. I only had time for one horrified look before it shoved Howlingfell's screeching head and then his shoulders into that dreadful fire. His legs kicked pointlessly as the monster sucked the round bit with a face on it right off the end of his spine, then spit the charred lump onto the ground before flinging Howlingfell's slack, boneless body out into the darkness beyond the lights.

Guns were flashing and cracking now, automatic fire, and even as I scrabbled wildly on the ground for my automatic I saw the *ghallu* lunge toward the place where all the guns were blazing. My hand closed on something hard, but it was only Howlingfell's phone. I held onto it and kept groping desperately until I finally found my gun.

Howly's men probably shouldn't have fired at the *ghallu*: apparently it was prone to distraction. The demon-thing was among them in a second, tearing Howlingfell's enforcers into pieces and flinging those pieces so violently in all directions that I could feel spatters of warm blood even as I smelled burning flesh. I stuck the phone in my pocket so I could hold my gun in both hands, which was necessary because I was shaking like a Chihuahua in the snow. But I didn't fire. No way was I going to stand and try to shoot it out again with this thing that swallowed even silver bullets like Tic-Tacs. But I couldn't really think of anything else to do, either.

"Bobby! Here!" Sam was waving frantically from the far end of the wall. I put my head down and ran toward him, more worried about getting hit by a stray shot than by design, because the Terminator from the Tigris was shredding the guards he'd reached, and though the rest were still firing at the monster as they ran away, it was with a distinct lack of conviction, let alone careful aim.

"This way," Sam called, already in a flat-out sprint and making pretty damn good time if he was as exhausted as I was. "That big fucker doesn't know what side it's on, does it? I guess your headless friend didn't get exactly the kind of back-up he was hoping for."

"As far as Eligor's concerned, they're all disposable," I panted. "As for Howlingfell, I hope he's back home roasting on the tiles of hell right now, but he's no longer our problem. That thing . . . it isn't going to stop until it catches me, and once it finishes barbecuing Howly's men, it's going to be right behind us." I wheezed and coughed, staggered and almost fell. Too much talking.

"Yeah, I remember that thing from before. Faster than your fucking car, wasn't it?"

This deserved no answer, so I continued saving my breath as we sprinted out the memorial park gate and across a winding road. I hadn't run this much in years, and I hadn't been to the gym much either. I was in bad shape (for an angel, anyway) and I hoped I'd live to start taking better care of myself. We also seemed to be heading out toward the bay again. From the cemetery I heard one last scream of despair, a ragged sound that might have been someone beating a set of bagpipes to death with a spiked club. "Where . . . ?" I managed to gasp at Sam.

"The only place we have a chance," he said between breaths, now sparing with the oxygen himself. "Footbridge out to Shoreline Park." He looked back. I didn't, but whatever he saw there made him find a new gear he may not even have known he had. I did my best to stay right behind him.

But who was I behind, exactly? The Sam I'd thought I knew, my best friend, would never have kept anything really big from me—and this Habari stuff was bigger than big. Could I even trust him again? More important, could I stay ahead of that smoldering hell-thing long enough to find out?

We reached the footbridge, a narrow span with chest-high railings made for bicyclists and day-hikers that stretched over the marshlands like a yardstick balanced between the island and the shore. Our footsteps made it rumble and quiver. Then something howled in the distance behind us, loud enough to shake down the moon. I suspected my nemesis had just discovered that its quarry had skipped out again. The *ghallu* bayed once more, a sound that made the air pop in my ears, then I almost lost my footing as the sturdy little bridge began to groan and shake like seven on the Richter scale. The hot thing with horns was coming after us, thundering down the bouncing footbridge like a real freight train on a toy track. The only real question was how far across we'd get before it caught us.

thirty-seven
faith

HALFWAY ACROSS the bridge and I could already feel the heat of the thing against my back despite the chilly bay breeze. Sam was a couple of steps ahead of me but I'm sure he could feel it too. The *ghallu* was maybe forty or fifty feet back and closing fast, hindered only by the narrowness of the footbridge. It would catch us long before we got to the island side. Time for Plan B. Only problem was, I didn't have one.

But the thing didn't like water, right? And here we were running a few feet above San Francisco Bay. I seriously considered just diving over the railing into the shallow tidal inlet in the hope we could save ourselves that way, but I had no idea how deep the water was—perhaps only a few feet—and how much the creature actually disliked H_2O, and I wasn't keen on finding out both things when it was too late to try anything else.

I put on a burst of speed and caught up with Sam. "I'm going to try something," I said or tried to, through my gasps for breath. "Whatever you do, don't stop running."

To his credit (or as evidence of how fucked we were) Sam didn't even argue but only lowered his head and tried to coax another few mph out of his legs. I snuck a glance back over my shoulder and saw that the monster was far enough behind us for me to turn and drop into a shooter's crouch, which I did. The Five-Seven is a light gun, but I took a shooter's stance and braced it with my other hand, because I was trembling so damn hard, then did my best to draw a bead on one of those two fiery red eyes coming toward me like the headlights of some hell-truck. Silver might not kill it, but I was wondering what it might think about getting a bullet-sized chunk of the stuff right in the eye—and maybe, if I was lucky, right through and into whatever served it as a brain.

But I wasn't lucky. The thing didn't slow down, and its footsteps made the slats of the old bridge jump and shake beneath me as I squeezed the trigger. The *ghallu* straightened up as I fired, my gun jounced low, and instead of giving it one in the eyeball I saw a fiery gout of something burst out near its knee.

The *ghallu* lurched and lost its rhythm for a second, throwing back its head as it staggered and letting loose a rumbling sound of fury (and pain, I devoutly hoped) as loud as an avalanche of scrap metal. I fired again and hit it in the chest, and it slapped at the molten wound, not mortally hurt but pained and distracted. Then it stumbled and crashed into the railing, shattering the redwood two-by-fours into splinters as it toppled flailing into the water. As it cannonballed into the bay a hissing cloud billowed up toward the moon and blotted my view.

I stood staring for a long second, wondering if I might actually have killed it, but then the great beast staggered upright, water bubbling violently off its skin and fizzing into steam. The brackish water barely reached the *ghallu*'s knees, and it was already wading back toward the footbridge like a ground-hugging cloud. It roared again. This time it sounded like it was spitting out bay water, but that didn't make the noise any prettier.

I was already sprinting after Sam as the horned cloud began to climb back onto the flimsy bridge where it had broken through. When I looked back, the broken boards were smoldering in its clawed hands, then a moment later a long section of the railing simply broke away and the creature slipped back into the shallow water. It hissed and slashed at the unresisting tide with its hands and horns, then waded sullenly forward, looking for a better place to climb out so it could catch us and shred us.

So much for killing it with the San Francisco Bay.

Still, the beast clearly didn't like water, and enough of the stuff might at least take away much of its heat—any pain it caused the *ghallu* would be a bonus. Maybe it would even make the monster more vulnerable to silver.

Yeah, I thought, *and maybe astronauts and cowboys will appear and save me.*

I had two, maybe three of my expensive bullets left, so all I could do was try to think of some way to improve the odds a little and hope that Fate was done rubbing little Bobby Dollar's face in his own stupidity.

A few moments later, with the steaming horror still dragging its bulk back onto the bridge, we were off the walkway and into the ruins of Shoreline Park. We dashed up the Little Promenade between the dilapidated shells of what had once been restaurants and shops meant to lure the park's customers before they even reached the main events.

Some abandoned amusement parks have an eerie, haunted charm as nature in the form of trees and vines reclaims them, climbing over the skeletal rides, transforming them into a modern version of a Victorian folly, an artistic comment on the frailty of Man's works. The commentary on Shoreline Park was a little less subtle. In the years since the park closed down for good it had become a wasteland in every sense of the word; a haven for seabirds, crackheads, and any homeless folk who could manage the hike from the mainland and didn't mind living with broken glass and sharp rusted things underfoot. The walls that still stood were splashed with graffiti, both the formal tags of local gangs and others so crude and desperate that they looked more like the markings of animals, spray paint splattered mindlessly like blood and vomit—both of which were also splattered here, as my senses forcefully told me. A little patch of Hell on earth. Nice place to make a last stand.

Sam had slowed, and I joined him in a heavy, painful trot. Even our angelic bodies were pretty nearly tapped out. "Which way?" I gasped.

"I don't know. I can't take you where I was going to—that thing's too close." He looked blank and strange; I couldn't even guess at what he was thinking. We had been like brothers, Sam and I, or at least I had thought so. Now I realized I scarcely knew him. How had we come to this?

Sam pointed off to the right. "The woods are over there," he said, meaning the southern part of the island, the original turn-of-the-century park before the amusements were built, once a spot for picnics and family outings. "And the parking lot," he said absently, as if trying to remember where we had left our car.

"Two good places to get slaughtered," I said between ragged breaths. "But not what I was hoping for." I wiped sweat out of my eyes and looked ahead to the amusement park section—"Merryland," as it had been officially named, although no one had called it that for a long time before Shoreline Park actually closed. All I could see of it from here was the top of the Whirlaway and the wheel, but that was enough. The idea of trying to hide from a murderous Sumerian demon amidst that wreckage might have thrilled a movie's art director, but it left me cold. Not to mention it would take us another five minutes or more to reach it—time I didn't think we could afford. I pointed to our left beyond the row of ruined storefronts. "Are the baths still over there on the north side?" The howl of the demonic thing pursuing us rose into the darkness behind us once more. Even after all this time that sound grabbed me by my primordial shorthairs, and I could almost feel the last drops of my courage leaking out. *"Sam?"*

"Yeah. But I don't know if there's any water in them."

"Then start praying." I darted down a narrow alley full of broken, rusted chairs and bits of fallen masonry that the bay air had spent busy years covering in mold. I ran as fast as I could manage for the Kingsport Plunge, the abandoned swimming complex where flappers and their straw-hatted swains had once come to sun and swim beside the bay. We emerged from the shelter of the ruined buildings, and the moon dripped enough light for us to make our way between the long-abandoned spa pools, just so many empty cups now with scummy water and debris littering their bottoms like tea leaves waiting to be read. A few more steps and I could make out the shadowy lip of the outdoor pool, a concrete pit the size of a football field. Once diving towers, lifeguard stations, and refreshment stands had stood around it like Renaissance towns around a lake, but time and weather had swept them all away. Now only the outdoor Plunge itself remained, a Bauhaus Grand Canyon made of cement, but as we reached the side I could see that there was nothing in the bottom of it but a foot and a half of rainwater and a graveyard of rusted poolside recliners.

Well, that was just wonderful. Maybe the *ghallu* would step on something nasty while it was eating us and get tetanus.

"The indoor pools," Sam panted. "If you want water, I think they're still fed from the bay. Maybe someone left the sluices open."

Just then I heard a sound like bombs going off and turned. The monster had climbed onto one of the shops behind us, smashing the remnants of its roof as it scrambled toward the edge. It saw us then and leaped down as quickly as a cat (if cats came in combine-harvester size) then began to close the ground between us, leaping over the cement pits of the empty therapy pools.

Nobody had bothered to put a lock on the indoor pool, and we slammed through the door and into the echoing space. The reason it was open quickly became apparent. It might have been an indoor pool once, but the roof had been made of something less permanent than the walls and had long since rotted away. The ceiling was nothing but a basket of rusted metal spars, completely open to the sky, but even so the place still stank of urine and human feces and rotting dead things.

Even as we ran across the slippery tiles, I saw that for once Fate had smiled on me, or at least not simply flipped me the bird: as Sam had guessed, there was water in the indoor pool, gleaming darkly where the moon touched it through the tangle of rusted struts. In fact, the pool was nearly full.

But the moon wasn't the only thing above us. A large shadow appeared at the edge of the roof and sprang down, less like a cat or a toad this time than like something with lots of legs dropping onto its prey. It crouched in the shadows, temporarily shapeless, but I could see the burning eyes, and it could just as obviously see me.

Then Sam slipped and fell, cracking his head hard against the floor, and before I could slide to a stop, struggling to keep my balance on the filthy, muddy tiles, I was a dozen feet past him. Sam lay on the ground, not moving. The *ghallu* came toward us with horns down and arms spread. I wasn't sure how many shells I might have left in my gun—two, maybe three if I was lucky—but I stepped toward the thing.

"Hey, you—*ugly!*" I shouted. "You don't want him, you want me!"

It actually stopped, tipping its wide-pronged head like a dog.

"Come on and try me, you ancient bastard! Come and taste the twenty-first century!"

It sprang over Sam as if it had meant to do that in the first place. Something that big should never be that fast—*never*. I realized it was going to be on me before I could even get traction again, so I fired. With no time for careful placement I just aimed for the shadowy center of it and pulled the trigger, then squeezed off another for good measure. I saw both bullets hit and the thing shuddered as the silver pierced it, slowing its loping progress to a stumble. Sprays of molten orange leaped like sunspots from its torso, but the bullets didn't kill it any more than meteors would kill the sun. All that those shots did for me was allow me time to get my feet under me again, so I could scramble toward the dark indoor plunge and leap in.

Sam had been right about another thing: the pool was full of salt water from the bay—but that wasn't all. Left open to the elements and only the Highest could guess what other kind of filth, the water smelled like sewage and clung like oil. Floating branches and other debris tangled my arms as I swam. I wasted no time on the aesthetics, but paddled as fast as I could to the deep end where the chipped tiles still faintly read "12"—twelve feet, I hoped, not "Lane 12" or something equally useless. When I got there I turned, treading water, trying to keep my gun out of the muck, and waited.

I didn't wait long. Growling and rumbling, the huge thing scrabbled along the side of the pool for a moment as if gauging whether it could reach me from there, then leaped into the murky water. A geyser of steam vomited into the air.

It was fast in the water, too. It came toward me like a shark, just a dark bulge beneath the water's surface. To my horror, I learned that simply because something hates water doesn't mean it can't swim. Instead of staying and waiting for it, I dove down and felt the creature pass just above me in a wave of scalding heat and furiously bubbling froth, its flames doused but its skin still hot as a branding iron.

The *ghallu* turned then and dug back toward me, too far up for me to slip past it to the surface. I did my best to ignore the foul water burning my eyes as I tried to kick out of the monster's way, but I wasn't fast enough and a moment later it was right over me.

I am no Olympic swimmer. My superiors gave me a good body, but not Superman's. The *ghallu* had speed and strength far beyond any human frame, even one on loan to an angel. As I tried to dart away again it reached out and caught me—I could feel the skin of my ankle blistering. I did my best to turn and shoot at it, hoping I had one round left and that the Five-Seven would fire underwater, but some garbage floating in the pool had tangled itself with my trigger finger, and before I could get it untangled the monster yanked me toward it and dragged me upward.

It was dangling me upside down by one leg as it surfaced and thrashed its way toward the shallower end where it could stand up. The demon-beast's skin was black, smooth as a dolphin's, and smelled like melting rubber and sulfur. Even soaking wet the thing was painfully hot, and as it stood there dripping, up to its belly in the water, little flames began to run along its head and shoulders as the remaining moisture steamed away. I fought with my remaining strength but couldn't wriggle loose. The pain of my ankle was so intense that I could only pray that there really was one bullet left so I could put it into my own skull and end the agony. The *ghallu* had dived into a full pool and swallowed a pound of silver and still barely broke stride. I had nothing else to try.

Helpless. That's the word.

But instead of ripping my head off or burning me to ashes, the *ghallu* lifted me up and began to open its mouth, which kept opening and opening until it was a gaping hole, its distended lower jaw almost touching its chest. This time, instead of flames, I saw nothing inside it—*nothing*. Not the emptiness of an open gullet, but the void itself, belching out empty, freezing cold despite the heat of the *ghallu*'s body, a bottomless pit stinking of oblivion. And then I realized that this demon wasn't going to carry me back to Eligor, it was going to *send* me back. It was going to swallow me right down that horrible throat into Hell.

I struggled to get my gun up, but the thing was clutching me against its chest and I couldn't lift my arms above my shoulders. The tangling object wrapped around my trigger finger slid into the palm of my gun hand. It was Caz's silver locket, hard and smooth against my skin. Her parting gift . . . or her last lie. It seemed appropriate that it had kept me from firing. Then I suddenly realized what it was made from.

When Orban warned me how tough the *ghallu* was, how hard it would be to kill even with the bullets he'd just sold me, he'd said I'd need something more: "Not just ordinary silver. Special." What else did I have with even a chance of fitting that bill? But Caz's locket was only special if it meant something—if I *let it* mean something. I had to believe there was a reason it was in my hand in that moment, not lying in the debris at the bottom of the pool. Which meant . . . what? Faith?

All this flashed through my head in an instant as the thing began lifting me toward its cold-steaming maw. As the stink washed over me, I could feel the monster's fingers cracking my ribs even as they roasted my skin like a Christmas goose. In between screams of pain I kicked the monster as hard as I could but it was like kicking a steam shovel. Still, I somehow managed to work my other hand loose and grabbed the little silver locket, then pressed it against the hot, rubbery expanse of the *ghallu*'s chest, right where its heart should be if it had one. I rammed the barrel of the automatic against the locket, said a prayer that didn't really have any words—mostly that I still had a bullet in the chamber—and pulled the trigger.

The blast rocked me as if I'd been struck by lightning. I felt the pit-spawn's molten blood spurt burning onto my chest as the creature roared and thrashed, then it flailed through the scummy water toward the side of the pool, flinging me away as if I no longer mattered. I narrowly missed the concrete lip, landed hard against the tiles, and slid to within a few yards of the place where Sam lay. The *ghallu* was making terrible sounds, bending where no living thing should bend, writhing as though it was tearing itself apart inside, but it managed to pull itself out and crawl close enough to us that its huge, twitching black fingers nearly closed on me before it finally stopped moving.

I watched it long enough to make certain it was dead, or whatever happened to things like that when you shot them in whatever passed for their important organs, then I fell back and stared up at the broken ribs of the roof, gasping and shivering uncontrollably. My sides were on fire and my ribs stabbed at me every time I breathed. The gun was still clutched in my hand like a wrecked ship's spar in the grip of a drowned man. I may even have cried for a moment before I rolled onto my side and puked up a belly's worth of whatever had been in that horrible pool, then I surrendered to the darkness growing in my head.

Sam was stirring beside me when my brain began to work again. He didn't ask any questions, but his eyes got appropriately wide when he saw the immense black shape of the dead *ghallu*, the last thin wisps of steam rising from its skin as its internal furnaces shut down.

"Somebody gave me a gift," I offered by way of explanation. I couldn't think of anything else to say.

Sam rolled over and sat up, holding his head as though his hands were all that was keeping it attached. "I know we need to talk, Bobby," he said at last. "Let's get out of here. My place. We can clean up, get something on those burns, then I'll tell you everything."

We both heard the telltale sound of a gun being cocked. It echoed from the walls of the roofless hall as if someone had banged on them with a stick.

"No, I think you'd better talk right here, Sammariel," a voice said. "Because I really want to hear this. Oh, and by the way, I've got a gun. And I'm pretty sure I've also got the only bullets in the room."

thirty-eight

the third way

"YOU?" I said. "Really?"

Clarence looked at me but he kept the strange little gun pointed at Sam, which didn't really make sense. "Surprised? Or disappointed?" He was playing it very tough, but there was a telltale tremor in his gun hand.

"Depends, I guess. How did you find us out here?"

"Hold on," he said. "Before anybody does any more talking, I just want to mention that this is a needle gun full of some kind of South American plant toxin, Sam, so if you try do something dramatic like kill yourself, I'll drop you with it, and you'll be paralyzed for hours. And I can make the shot, too—I've been practicing." He looked down at the titan corpse of the *ghallu*. "Wow. Did you do that, Bobby? That must have been tough."

"Hold on, why would Sam want to kill himself?" I demanded.

"Because he's got access to at least one other body," Clarence said. "Habari's."

Startled, I looked at Sam, who shrugged. "Wait a minute," I said. "Habari was *you*?"

"Who did you think it was?" he asked me. "I thought you knew. Fuck's sake, I thought that's why you took me to that headstone."

"I knew you had something to do with all this Magian Society stuff, but I thought Habari might be . . . well, Leo. Because they both died about the same time."

"You're talking about our Leo? From the Harps?" Sam shook his head. "As far as I know, he's dead and we're not getting him back. And Habari died a year or so after Leo. But Leo *was* involved, indirectly. . . ."

"Wait a minute." I turned back to Junior, who was still trying to perfect his I'm-in-control stance. "This is going too fast for me. How did you find us here?"

Clarence had the grace to look a little embarrassed. "Sam's phone is hacked. I can always find out where he is. I had some help from Upstairs on that."

"You were tracking Sam all this time, not me?" I looked at Sam. "So you lied to me. It wasn't me he was spying on."

"Shit, B," he said, "I lied to you about a lot of things. Yeah, the kid's been keeping an eye on me all along. Some of our bosses were getting suspicous."

Then something else occurred to me, and I turned back to Clarence. "But Sam lost his phone earlier tonight, long before we got here. So how did you track us to Shoreline Park?"

Clarence stared back, but he was hesitating. "I bugged your phone, too," he admitted at last. "After I got here, I followed the noise."

If he'd had access to my phone he might know everything, even about Caz. This wasn't good at all. "So Temuel was just double-bluffing me? You've been working for our bosses all this time? That still doesn't explain how you got here, kid—you can't drive. Or did you lie about that too?"

Now Clarence looked *really* guilty. "I . . . found a ride."

I laughed despite myself. "And is what's-her-name, your nice old landlady, sitting out there in her Continental keeping the heater running 'til you get back?"

He scowled. "You don't know everything, Bobby. I've been renting from them because Burt has an indoor shooting range in his basement. They let me practice down there." He turned to Sam. "Now it's your turn, Angel Sammariel. Start talking, because once I turn you over to our superiors they'll clamp down on all this and I'll never find out what happened. How did the Third Way approach you? What did they offer you?"

"Not they," Sam said after a moment. "Kephas."

The other name Temuel had given me, along with the Magians.

"Never heard of him," said Clarence.

Sam shook his head. "Not a him, necessarily. Just a disguised presence, not male, not female. A high-up angel, though, that's for sure. Kephas offered me a deal."

"Kephas means 'rock,'" I said, remembering what Fatback had told me. "As in, 'On this rock I will build My church . . .'"

Sam nodded. "The higher angels, they like that old school stuff."

Clarence snorted at this. "Betraying Heaven is old school?"

Sam gave the kid a cold look. "You wouldn't know about it, Junior, but me and Bobby saw a lot of ugly stuff when we were in the Harps. Stuff they don't teach you in the Records department—"

"Yeah, yeah, it was hell out there," Clarence interrupted. "Spare me the justifications, Sam. You didn't like what our superiors gave you to do, so you decided to find some nicer bosses."

Sam shook his head again, not in negation but in something more like resignation. "It was our old top-kicker Leo who first got me thinking, actually. He was always talking about the politics, the stuff going on behind the scenes, wondering who was really in charge."

"Another paranoid." But Clarence sounded like he might be trying to convince himself more than us.

"Said the undercover spy to his ex-partner." Sam forced a sour grin. "After awhile, what Leo said began to make sense; whoever's really in charge, they don't seem to have our interests at the top of their priority list. I couldn't ignore that any longer. And then Leo died—the real death, the final kind. I didn't think it was an accident. Still don't. Maybe I said a few things afterward that drifted around Upstairs, I don't know. Whatever tipped them off, the Third Way group found me. Kephas was their representative, and he, she, whatever it is, asked me if I wanted to do something to make Heaven better." Sam then repeated most of the stuff I'd already heard in Walker's quasi-suicide letter about the Third Way, their belief in the need for an alternative to Heaven and Hell, their willingness to try to do something about it. "They weren't ready to move yet—this was years ago—but I couldn't take being in the Harps any longer." He turned to me. "It was beginning to feel like a lie, Bobby—all that talk about how we were the only bulwark against Hell's evil on Earth, but there we were doing all that awful shit."

"Don't apologize," I said. "I might have listened, too." But I wasn't certain about that. I don't like chaos. I don't like secrets. And I sure as hell didn't like the idea of people as powerful as Karael and his friends being angry at me.

"So I quit the Harps," Sam went on, "took an informal leave of absence, and for a while I just . . . well, sort of bummed around. Settled here in San Judas and tried to figure out what I was doing. Made friends—mortal friends, even. One of them was Reverend Habari." The tone of Sam's voice said this was important to him. "I really wish you'd known him, Bobby. He was a good man. Truly good. He wasn't just a community political activist, he would take in homeless folk and feed them and let them stay until he could get them into a shelter. He marched in all the marches, but he also stayed up late supervising the night basketball league in Sierra Park. Visited shut-ins. Read to sick folks. And then he got cancer and died. And all I could think was, 'And that's the end of a good man. He's gone.'"

"What do you mean?" Clarence sounded outraged. "He died. If he was as good as you say, then he went straight to Heaven!"

Sam's voice rose. "For what? To become what? Our masters have made certain we don't know *anything* for sure, kid. The only angels we know are like us—ciphers with their memories wiped, working for the Man down here on Earth or our bosses in Heaven. Is that what happened to Moses Habari? They just erased everything and started him over, like us? Or is he one of those poor fools square-dancing in the Fields of the Blessed with about as much of his personality left as a psychiatric patient pumped full of happy drugs?"

"It's not like that!" The barrel of Clarence's needle gun wavered, but he kept it on Sam. "We're *angels*! We work for God!"

"Well, see, that's something I'm not as sure about as you, son. All that stuff you used to ask me, 'Why this, why that . . . ?' Well, I asked those questions for real. In fact, I'm not sure if we're working for God the Highest or for somebody else entirely."

"That's enough," Clarence said. "I don't need to hear any more blasphemy, Sam. I'm sorry—you're a good man, I really believe that, but you're no angel. Not anymore. It's time for you to come back to Heaven. Maybe you can get some help . . ."

I had distanced myself from Sam, in part just to make it harder for Clarence to shoot both of us, and as I moved closer to the kid I said,

"Not yet, please. Not until I find out what happened to the souls they took. Did it work, Sam? Did you find a place to hide them where they'd be safe?"

"That was the hard part," he admitted. "We couldn't stash souls on Earth without somebody noticing, but the Tartarean Convention set things up so that at the very least, a high-ranking angel *and* an equally high-ranking demon had to agree on making any new territory outside the Earthly bounds, no matter how small. My Third Way bosses had other recruits like me, and they were ready to fit us all out with fake identities and fake bodies. I probably should have just invented a name, but I wanted to pay back Dr. Habari, at least in a small way . . ." He trailed off. "Anyway, apparently the Third Way folk got a tip that Grand Duke Eligor might make a deal—for reasons of his own that I don't know. And he did."

As Sam had been talking, I moved a little closer to Clarence, and now I quietly slipped my empty gun out of my belt.

". . . so because of that deal, we had our site," Sam finished. "It exists. It's real!"

I punctuated this fascinating revelation by hitting Clarence hard on the base of the skull with my gun butt. The kid didn't even make a noise, just dropped like a sack of apples. I didn't want to kill him, although I had no doubt that if I did he'd be resurrected again post-haste by our bosses, but I wasn't going to stand there and see Sam get dragged off either. At least not until I'd heard the rest of the story. I took the smooth little needle gun out of Clarence's hand, then turned back to my oldest friend.

"Okay, Sammy," I said. "It's just the two of us now. Convince me."

"Convince you of what? That it works? That's easy. Follow me."

I stopped to check Clarence's breathing, then turned him onto his side so if he puked he wouldn't choke on it. Not a good way to go, even if you're getting shunted into another body afterward.

"How hard did you hit him?" Sam asked as we made our way out past the outdoor pools.

"He'll be out for awhile, but I don't think the damage will be permanent."

"Glad to hear it. I kind of liked him. At first I thought he was too obvious an outsider to really be a plant."

"They double-bluffed you," I said. "Temuel got me that way, too. Does that mean he was in on Clarence?"

"Maybe. Or maybe the Mule didn't find out that Clarence was actually working for some of the higher-ups until after he asked you to keep an eye on the kid. It's always wheels within wheels, B."

"Heaven is one sneaky bastard, all right."

We fell silent as we made our way up the Grand Promenade toward Merryland and its ruined attractions, as if we were two souls traveling not to some new third destination but floating through good old Limbo, out of time, out of space. I wondered if Sam and I would ever walk side by side this way again. And no more meals at Boxer Rebellion? Really?

I had no idea what I was going to do next. I didn't really want to think about it.

The moon was still hanging around, silvering the rusted remains of the coiling Super Snake and the collapsed stalls of various attractions. This time, with nothing trying to suck my head off, I was able to appreciate the weirdness of the place. You notice I didn't say, "the weird *beauty* of the place." Shoreline Park might be many things, but beautiful is not one of them. But it smelled better out here at the north end, so either the sea breezes kept the air cleaner on this side of the island or the derelicts couldn't be bothered to come all this way just to take a dump. Either way it made a pleasant change.

The peeling facade of some kind of game booth grinned as we passed. It might have been a clown's head once, but now it was only two smears for eyes and a rictus smile of which only lipless teeth remained.

"So if you didn't know it was me posing as Habari," Sam said abruptly, "how did you know about the cemetery?"

"I got some help from Fatback. He told me that Habari had died, and when he told me Habari was buried in the very graveyard you used to take me to all the time—well, it seemed like a pretty long coincidence. Plus, I'd already picked up on at least one of the lies you told me."

"There were a bunch. Which one?"

That made me feel sadder than I would have expected. "When you came to my room at the Ralston last night. You said you called Alice, and she told you the room number."

"But I *did* call her. I'm not stupid, Bobby."

"Yeah, but she gave you the wrong room number. She told me about it. She was feeling bad because she assumed you wouldn't be able to find me. But of course, you only asked her for show. Kephas or whoever told you where I was, right?"

He only nodded, looking ahead now.

I was putting things together now. I had guessed that the angelic powers Habari had demonstrated to Edward Walker meant that one of the key players in the whole thing was probably local, since Habari the Magian worked out of the storefront on East Charleston. There just aren't that many folks with haloes in San Judas, so I had begun to think it almost had to be someone I knew, as proved by the way Habari had reacted when we'd passed each other in our cars. He had recognized me immediately, even through my cuts, bruises, and bandages. But I'd gotten too fancy and instead of looking right next to me for Habari's identity I'd made the leap to wondering whether Leo the Loke might have faked his own death.

"What about the bodies, Sam?"

He turned, startled. "What bodies?"

"The ones you and the other Magians must have worn. After all, you couldn't ordinarily pass for an African clergyman, Sam."

"The Third Way gave us those—they're a little less functional, but a lot easier to enter and leave than the regular, earthbound bodies Heaven hands out. I've got the Habari body stashed away in a safehouse, but I can't give you the location, Bobby, or the body. I'll need everything I can trade to plead down my sentence with the bosses. Hey, maybe I'll get off with a couple of million years in the fiery pit."

Now I felt queasy. He knew as well as I did that it wouldn't be anything like that simple. How could I have been so badly fooled by my best friend? And what was I going to do about him? "So now, after landing *me* in the shit, you're going to sell out the Third Way too?"

"Shit, Bobby, that was supposed to be a joke. No, the truth is, I'm not giving you the safehouse and the Habari body because I want the Third Way to have a chance to clean it up and hide their tracks from the Upstairs boys. I never wanted this to happen to you, but I believe in what they're doing. I'm not giving the Ephorate anything."

"What did you think that day you bumped into me in front of the Magian Society office?"

Sam didn't look around. "Startled the crap out of me."

"I should have recognized you by your ride."

Now he did turn. "What are you talking about? I wasn't driving my own car."

"Yeah, but no other angel would be seen dead in an old beater like that. You never cared about cars, Sam."

Crazy Town, the funhouse, stood just in front of us. It actually still had a roof and most of its walls, but that was about it. The plaster of Paris spooks and clowns had eroded from the walls, leaving only spectral outlines and the occasional disembodied foot or hand or ear. What remained had been decorated with Day-Glo spray paints in a variety of runic designs that meant something only to the taggers themselves, but now even the graffiti was fading, rapidly becoming another piece of the past. As we crunched toward the building over a litter of broken bottles, I was glad I hadn't managed to kick my shoes off while I was in the water with the *ghallu*. The wounds the creature had given me were beginning to heal thanks to my angelic constitution, but I was still injured, aching, bloody, and very, very depressed.

"It's in here," he said. "The door to the Third Way."

I frowned. "There's only one door? You have to come out here each time?"

He shook his head. "Nah, the physics of the thing—if it even *is* physics and not just some crazy Heaven magic—is weird. There's not that many spots you can get into this new place we've made. One of those spots is here, but it's not the only one. There used to be another door or whatever you'd call it in the Magian Society office, which is one of the reasons I had to go back that time you saw me. I had to shut it down before you or anyone else found it."

"And if Clarence was tracking your movements, that's probably how he figured out about you and Habari," I said. "I talked to you both about who I'd seen, and if he knew you had gone there about the same time I did—well, if he or his superiors had any suspicions, that would have sure helped confirm them."

He hesitated. "Do you really want to see this, B? It might . . . change things for you."

I stood, trying to figure out what he was really saying. "It might," I said at last. "But then again, it might not."

He smiled, and I saw once more the familiar Sam, the Sam I'd known for so long. "Look, I just want to say that it really felt like shit having to lie to you all this time, Bobby. But except for the Third Way stuff, everything else I've ever told you—everything else we've been through—was real. The truth."

"I know that, Sam. Or at least I'm willing to believe it." I gestured with the needle gun. "Now show me your secret. And please don't do anything stupid."

He turned on his flashlight and led me into the abandoned funhouse. We didn't go far, just down some steps to the hall of mirrors. Because they were metal, not glass, most of the mirrors were still in their frames, but the distorted images that had amused so many generations of park visitors were almost completely obliterated by rust and scratches.

"Third mirror from the left," Sam said.

"And straight on 'til morning. Show me."

"I'm going to reach into my pocket. Do me a favor and don't dart me, okay?" He produced a faint shimmer of something. It could have been a tangle of spiderwebs glistening in the moon's misty glow, but the only light was the dim flashlight in Sam's other hand. He opened his palm and the shimmer spread over it, then kindled into a light so bright that I blinked and stepped back.

"Don't!" I said, pointing with the gun.

"No worries." Sam held up his blazing hand and drew a line with his index finger down the air in front of the mirror. A Zipper appeared, or something that would have been a Zipper had it been more sharply defined; a cloud of radiance, a miniature nebula appearing three feet off the ground in the middle of Crazy Town. "Kephas gave this gauntlet to me," he explained. "It's how I could take a living mortal like Edward Walker Outside, through a Zipper, and manage a lot of other stuff. Duplicates the powers of the higher angels, I guess. I don't know what it is or how it works—I just call it the God Glove." Sam gestured again, and the misty light dispersed, leaving a soft-focus hole in the center of the mirror. I could see objects and colors there, like one of those little scenes inside a sugary Easter egg. "I'll step back," he said. "I swear I won't try anything. Just look."

I trusted him, but of course I also didn't trust him, so as I leaned forward I kept the dart gun pointing in Sam's general direction. It wasn't like looking at an image. What I saw had depth, another entire world beyond the scuffed, rusted mirror. I saw oak and willow trees and a stream and, when I bent a little closer, a ramshackle Victorian house perched on a hill in the distance, at the end of a long dirt road. I fancied I could even see a couple of tiny figures standing on the porch, perhaps looking back at me. I wondered if one of them was Edward Lynes Walker. "Is that it?" I said, unexpectedly touched by the modesty of the rustic scene. "That's your great alternative to Heaven and Hell? The *Little House on the Prairie*?"

"That's the beginning," Sam said. "But it'll get bigger. It will get more real. There's only a few hundred souls there now but it will grow, even without me. Kephas recruited lots of other angels. We may even know some of them."

I filed that thought away for later. "And you really think this is going to be better than what we've already got?"

"If we can make it that way, yes." He sounded sincere—almost stupidly sincere. "You know . . . you could be there too, Bobby. I know you've thought about the same things I have. I know you get tired of all the secrets and the other nasty shit we've had to do."

"Yeah, thanks." I straightened up. "But I'm not quite ready to drink that Kool-Aid. Not yet." I was bone-weary, and Clarence would be regaining consciousness soon. "Go on. Get out of here, Sam."

He stared. "Wait—you mean . . . ?"

"Yes, I mean. Get the hell out of here. Go join your crazy friends and build your little afterlife commune. Better you than me. I'll tell them you got away."

"They'll never believe you."

"That I screwed up again? They'll fall over themselves in their hurry to believe that." I winced a little at the thought of what General Karael was going to make of my newest dazzling failure. "Go on! I'm not going to beg you."

But instead of stepping through the misty portal, he turned and came toward me. For a moment I was terrified he was going to hug me. I'm not afraid of being hugged, mind you—not too much—but the idea of Sam doing the hugging was like the idea of your parents making love: it might actually happen occasionally, but you didn't want to be a witness. Luckily he stopped a little out of embracing range. "Hold on," he said. "I have to give you something before you go. Now, don't get your undies in a bunch, B, but I have to reach into your pocket."

"*My* pocket?" I began, but he had already slipped the glowing, God-Gloved hand into my jacket pocket: I could feel it against me like a hot stone. A moment later he straightened up again and transferred whatever he'd found to his other hand and held it out.

For several seconds I couldn't do anything but stare. It was an astonishing thing, as amazing in its own way as anything else he had shown me. It was a golden feather—*the* feather, obviously—but it was just as clearly not of this world. It glowed and sparkled, not like a window display of jewelry, but with an inner light that made it seem more real, more *present* than anything else around, most definitely including me, Sam, and the Door Into Thirdwaysville.

"What . . . ?" Okay, it wasn't my sharpest moment. "How did that get there?"

"It's been there all along—sort of." He laughed. "You remember that night with the lady who drove into the bay? Clarence's first night? When you got into a fight with Howlingfell?"

"Some fight," I said. "I stomped him like a grape."

"Well, when Grasswax was pulling Howlingfell off you, I saw him slip something into your pocket. I couldn't imagine what a prosecutor would be planting on you, and I knew Howlingfell worked for Eligor, the other party in—" he indicated the rustic view, "—*my* little project. I thought it might be some kind of frame-up or something. I only realized when I touched it what it was, so I decided to hide it. With this." He lifted the God Glove and displayed it like he was modeling a Lady Bulova on a shopping channel. "I made a little piece of Outside right there in your pocket while I was dusting you off, and I put the feather in it. It's been there all along, but nobody could reach it because it also *wasn't* there, if you know what I mean. Sorry if it got you into trouble, but it was a spur of the moment improvisation."

Which must have been why my weird friend Foxy could smell something that wasn't there. "So Grasswax was actually telling the truth," I said. "At least as he knew it. That's one for the books, huh?" I reached out and carefully took the smoldering golden thing from Sam. It lay in my palm with no weight at all, but it did not waver or move even as I swayed my hand from side to side. It was hard to look at anything else. "And do you know who this belongs to? Who made the deal with Eligor?"

"Kephas, as far as I know—whoever or whatever *that* is." He gestured for me to take it. "You can do whatever you want with it. Give it to our bosses, if it will keep you out of trouble."

"But if Eligor kept it to blackmail this Kephas, our bosses could probably trace it."

Sam shrugged. "It doesn't matter—our thing is too big now. It's already rolling. Me, Kephas, we could lose dozens more and the idea would still go on."

I thought about it. "Put it back in my pocket. With the God-Glove. I don't want to have to hide it somewhere ordinary."

"You sure?" He lifted it in his glowing hand. I felt the warmth through my coat as he put it back.

"Okay. Now go. Get out of here."

He turned toward the funhouse mirror, then paused, looking at me over his shoulder. I couldn't read his expression. "Stay in touch, Bobby."

"How?" I'd almost said *"Why?"* but although I still didn't quite know how I felt about him and what he'd done, I knew I'd miss him.

"We'll figure something out." And then he stepped into the mirror. The hole closed behind him, so I didn't get a chance to watch him go, but I'm guessing he walked up that long road like a man finally going home.

I started back toward the Kingsport Plunge. As I patted my pocket to make sure the feather was undetectable, I discovered something else nestled there already—Howlingfell's phone. It had got very wet, as I had too, but like me it was still functioning, so I rang the last number Howlingfell had called. Someone picked up but didn't speak. Still, I was pretty sure I knew who was listening on the other end.

"Guess what," I said. "That whole 'Mission Accomplished' thing? A bit premature, as it turned out." I looked up at the sky, which was beginning to cloud over, shrouding the moon. I was tired of being wet, so I walked a little faster. "But what I really wanted to tell you was that I *do* have the feather, and if you fuck with me or anyone I care about—*anyone* I care about, do you understand?—I'm going to use it as proof when I tell your Hell-buddies about the deals you've been making with Heaven. Is that clear? Oh, and tell the Countess that I'll see her again. That's a promise."

I didn't wait to see if Eligor would respond, I just threw the phone as far as I could, then listened until I heard it hit and shatter somewhere in the shadows. I knew that what I'd said was true: I was going to find Caz. I was going to find her even if I had to go to Hell and yank her out of Eligor's arms to do it. I was going to free her so that someday she could stand in front of me and at least tell me honestly how much of what we'd had was real. I wasn't going to rest until I knew the answer.

Clarence was sitting up when I got back to the pool, dabbing at his mouth with his sleeve. He'd obviously thrown up, but otherwise he didn't look too bad. "What happened?"

"To Sam? He got away when you went down, I'm afraid."

"No, what happened to me? What hit me?"

"The *ghallu* must have had a reflex twitch. Got you with its tail. Knocked you silly."

Clarence squinted at the monster's corpse, which was already beginning to turn into sludge, little rivers of gray and black trickling away into the cracks between the tiles. "That thing doesn't *have* a tail."

"Its leg, then. Doesn't matter. Come on, let's see if your ride is still waiting. I'm too tired to walk all the way back home."

He asked for his dart gun, but I didn't give it to him. He made a face at me like an angry third-grader. "You'd better start trusting me, Bobby. We're on the same side."

"Trust you?" I laughed. "Kid, you tried to arrest my best friend! And you hacked my phone."

"It was nothing personal," he protested. "I was doing my job." He gave me a significant look. "I don't have to tell them anything except what I learned about Sam and the Third Way. Everything else is your own business. Including your pal, the Countess."

It was friendly blackmail, but it was still blackmail. "Where did you come from, anyway, kid?" I asked him. "Where did they find a piece of work like you?"

"Took me right out of Records because they knew you and Sam'd be too suspicious of anyone with a background more like yours."

"A competent background, you mean? Yeah, well, they definitely fooled me, I'll admit it. But I'll decide for myself whether we're on the same side. You're still on probation with me."

Clarence was outraged. "Probation? You're the one who should have to prove yourself to me! You let Sam get away."

I tucked his needle gun into my pocket. "Yeah, kid, but you're the one who got your skinny ass kicked by something I'd already killed."

thirty-nine

the dirty streets of heaven

ONE MORE nasty surprise awaited me. As Clarence and I made our way (in my case, my staggering, exhausted, stinking way) off the footbridge on the mainland side a car waited for us in the Garcia Park lot. But it wasn't a Lincoln Continental or any other kind of old lady car, it was the ugliest, pimped-out red gangsta mobile imaginable.

I'd seen it before.

Garcia Windhover was wearing what I imagine was his idea of a stealth-mission suit—all black, including a do rag that made him look like L'il Wayne's severely anemic nephew. The stealth aspect was undercut a bit by the immense words "FUCK ALLA Y'ALL!" written across the front of his baggy XXXL t-shirt in screaming white letters.

"Mr. D!" He spread his arms exactly like he was welcoming me back from a tour of combat duty. Although in some ways it was true—in fact I felt like I'd been dropped out of an airplane without a parachute—G-Man was not exactly the person I would have hoped to find waiting for me when I got back on home soil. I ducked his enthusiastic bro-hug like a weary matador.

"What the hell are *you* doing here?" I turned to Clarence, who at least had the good grace to look sheepish. "Why is he here? How do you two even *know* each other?"

"I told you, I knew where you were, where you went," Clarence said. "Because I didn't know what you were doing—I didn't know whether you were in cahoots with Sam. And so . . . well, I was kind of checking up after you."

"Then he told me how he was your partner," said Garcia with all the relish of a teenager confirming an urban legend he had heard from someone who had heard it from the guy it happened to. "So here I am, dude!"

I glared at Clarence, who shrugged and couldn't quite meet my eye.

"I needed a ride," he admitted. "I could tell something big was going down when you guys left the hotel, then I heard what had happened to the hotel on the television news."

"You called *him* for a ride?" I said quietly as Garcia opened all four car doors, even though there were only three of us. "Shit, Clarence, you're the worst undercover agent ever."

"It takes about half an hour to get a cab up to Brittan Heights, Bobby. I was in a hurry, and he told me that he'd worked for you before."

"Totally," said Garcia, brushing some loose popcorn kernels out of the back seat. "I can be your wheel man."

"No fucking way," I said. "We are not 'partners.' I am not partners with you, Windhover, or you, Special Agent Treacherous Bastard." I glared at Clarence.

Garcia looked intrigued. "Can I have a code name too, Mr. D?"

"Yes. 'Idiot.' And you may not call me 'Mr. D.,' either."

"Then what should I call you?"

"Five minutes ago I would have said, 'an ambulance.'" I dragged my weary bones into the back seat, then stretched out, dripping all over Garcia's leather upholstery. My head was pressed uncomfortably against the door, but I didn't care. "Now I just want to take three or four showers and sleep until August. So let's go."

"We could be your 'associates,'" Garcia said cheerfully. "That sounds more bad-ass anyway."

I groaned and closed my eyes and let the dizzy darkness climb back over me. I dimly felt the thump of Garcia backing over a concrete parking stop, the hydraulics in his stupid car setting the whole thing wobbling like a waterbed, then I surrendered to oblivion.

I finally made it to The Compasses about eleven the next evening, limping and bruised and burned but finally clean and at least partially rested. I waved to Kool Filter who was puffing furiously and talking into his Bluetooth, then I trudged up the stairs.

The place looked pretty good considering that the end facing the street had been reduced to rubble only a short time earlier. The floor had been swept, the worst damage hauled away or covered with plastic tarps, and Chico had a makeshift bar going, a big slab of one-and-a-quarter-inch plywood on trestles with boxes of booze stacked behind it. He had also salvaged enough chairs and tables from the wreckage that, if you squinted, it didn't look all that different from an ordinary weekday night. Monica was sitting with Sweetheart, but she trotted over when she saw me and gave me a hug. The mere fact of her being kind and female was enough to make me mist up, but I didn't want to mist up, and I certainly didn't want to confuse Monica with all my weird emotions, so after just a few seconds I broke free. She let go only reluctantly.

"When we heard about the Ralston we thought you were dead or worse!" she said. "I was so worried about you, Bobby. Where's Sam? Is he okay?"

Obviously the real news had not got out yet—Clarence had actually kept his word. I wondered how hard my bosses were going to try to hush everything up. "He's okay, yeah. But I think he may be taking a long leave of absence."

While Monica and Sweetheart pondered this, I asked Chico for one of his pricier iced vodkas and some orange juice—in two separate glasses; discovering how out of shape I was had made me consider adopting a healthier lifestyle. Drinking the orange juice separately seemed like it might fit the bill.

For about an hour I chatted amiably (and in large part untruthfully) with the Whole Sick Choir in ones and twos, but Monica and the rest could see I mostly wanted to be on my own in a room full of people, and so they didn't stay long at my table. We've all been there, all had something go so bad that it clung to your mind for weeks. That's one of the best things about The Compasses—everybody gets it. Besides, I knew I'd have to go to Mecca the next morning and make my official report, and since I didn't know exactly what I was going to say, I didn't want to box myself in too much now—a lot of people were going to be looking over my version of what went down at the Ralston and afterward. And of course, my bosses must already have been wondering if I'd been contaminated by my friendship with Sam—which was, of course, quite true. I'd let him go, hadn't I?

While everybody else talked and laughed, I sat and rehearsed a few possibilities of how I could play it with my bosses. I was feeling flimsy and weightless, but not in an entirely bad way. Like a feather, maybe. Like the invisible feather I'd been carrying with me without even knowing it, and which I still carried. It was strange to think I was sitting here surrounded by the old familiar while I had something in my pocket that could blow everything familiar sky high. I had to hope that Heaven really *was* Heaven, or at least a good copy, because otherwise I knew way too much about too many things to be left walking around.

Thoughts like these kept swirling round and round until at last I gave up thinking for the evening. You can overthink until you get paralyzed. I'd decided I'd come up with some useful half-truth for the bosses, and then I'd hang onto those half-truths no matter what anyone said. At least I'd find out once and for all if anyone can lie to Heaven.

It wasn't that different from what I'd been doing for years, anyway, I told myself—just a more straightforward approach to deception. Another day at the office, really. The streets of Heaven might be paved with bullshit and paperwork, but I'd been walking those dirty streets for a good long time now. I felt pretty sure I knew what to say and what not to say. After that, it would all be in His hands.

Eventually Young Elvis started a stupid discussion about the hotel fire, yammering on and on about how he was certain it was one of the demon-lords trying to off a rival (which was partly true, but his list of suspects had no relationship to the real events). I stopped listening when Walter Sanders suggested that Young Elvis had blown up the building himself because they wouldn't let him into the conference.

Mostly I just watched. Mostly I just waited for Sam to walk in, even though I knew he wouldn't. And I thought about Caz, of course. I thought about Caz a lot. Thinking about someone you can't have is a special kind of Hell you can summon without drawing a single pentagram.

It was a bit after midnight when Clarence entered. No Garcia Windhover tagging along this time, all praises to the Highest. The kid said hello to Monica and the others, hesitated, then got himself a beer and slid into the chair across from me.

"How are you doing?" he asked.

"Why did you do it, Junior? Really?"

He looked surprised. "Because I had to, Bobby. They chose me, and it was my job. I'm . . . I'm sorry about Sam."

"Yeah. I am too. So now what? Back to Cloud Nine to get a medal pinned on your robe? Did you finally earn your wings?"

"Actually, I think I'd like to stay here. I mean, I like this job. The real job, not . . . not what they sent me here to do."

I wasn't sure I was ready to believe that. "Sam said you made up all that bullshit you kept asking him about. All that 'Why are we here, what's really going on?' Pretending to doubt the status quo."

A strange look flitted across his face. "Yeah. Made it all up to see if I could shake something loose. Why? Don't you ever ask those kind of questions anymore, Bobby?"

I tried to hate him, but I couldn't. He was just an eager young officer trying to do his job. Just another righteous angel of the Lord. "I told you once, kid, I only ask questions I can hope to get answered."

He nodded. "Sensible. Keep your sights set low. That way you won't get into trouble."

Now it was my turn to give him the strange look. Was the kid trying to get me to say something incriminating, or was he warning me not to? Or was something else going on with him—something more complicated?

No. Not biting. I pushed myself away from the table and stood up, which in my condition was harder than it sounds. I'd spent too much time already getting dragged around by questions like that, and I badly needed to sleep again. I needed other things, too, but sleep was the only one I was likely to get. Anyway, it had to beat sitting here listening to Jimmy the Table and Sweetheart laughing over the old story of the guy who fell through a skylight and died burglarizing a house and then tried to convince his heavenly advocate that he'd only been checking the neighborhood rooftops for endangered birds.

Not that it wasn't a good story.

I nodded to Clarence and then headed to the door. Monica was looking the other way, which saved me having to say goodbye.

My car was still in the parking lot at the Ralston Hotel, so I was walking, which suited my mood. It was a decent late-spring night, and a few folks were coming out of the bars on Main Street. I let myself drift with them, listening to the conversations, marveling at the bubble these mortals lived in, the things that went on all around them that they couldn't and wouldn't want to see. I could have walked back to my own apartment, but I hadn't slept there in a long time. It would be cold, and the bed would need making, which made the whole thing seem like work when all I wanted was to take a long shower and collapse. Instead, I headed back for one last night at the motel where I'd made Garcia and Clarence drop me off after Shoreline Park. After all, I was getting used to motels.

I limped up Jefferson as the clubbers and bar patrons gradually split off to find their cars or a bus stop, until I was the only person still walking. The apartment buildings on either side of the street had gone quiet, with lights on in less than half of the windows, the patterns of illumination as abstract as modernist paintings. I stopped in a corner bodega and bought myself a bottle of something to drink. The guy behind the counter barely looked up from the Punjabi soap opera on his little television.

When I finally reached my room at the Mission Rancho Motor Lodge, I found I wasn't that sleepy anymore. I dumped my coat, turned off my phone, turned on some music, and carried my drink out onto the balcony. Across the park the old mission was dark but for that single bulb over the door. Lights burned in some of the other motel rooms, but for once the guests were pretty quiet. A guy went by whistling on the street down below, walking an old dog who stopped every few steps to sniff something.

After a day like I'd had, I decided against using a glass. Instead I drank my orange juice straight out of the bottle as I watched the bugs circle the little light in front of God's first house in San Judas, and I kept company with all my ghosts, the old ones and the new.

Want more?

If you enjoyed this and would like to find out about similar books we publish, we'd love you to join our online Sci-Fi, Fantasy and Horror community **Hodderscape.**

Follow us on
Twitter @Hodderscape

and visit our Facebook page at
facebook.com/hodderscape

You'll find news, competitions, video content and general musings, so feel free to comment, contribute or just keep an eye on what we are up to. See you there!

HODDERSCAPE